THE GAME OF TEN
BOOK ONE
THE RED BLOOD

FIRST EDITION
A WORLD BEYOND OUR OWN
BASED ON THE DREAMS OF A FOOL

P. TANNER

authorHOUSE®

AuthorHouse™
1663 Liberty Drive
Bloomington, IN 47403
www.authorhouse.com
Phone: 833-262-8899

Published by AuthorHouse 09/26/2022

ISBN: 978-1-6655-6813-5 (sc)
ISBN: 978-1-6655-6811-1 (hc)
ISBN: 978-1-6655-6812-8 (e)

Library of Congress Control Number: 2022915175

Edited by Paulette Augustine

Print information available on the last page.

This book is printed on acid-free paper.

CONTENTS

A NOTE FROM
THE PROPHET

There is this story. It keeps repeating itself. I dream of it, and I cannot seem to rid myself of it. It is said that dreams are a collection of all the things that we see and think throughout the day—a collection of our true thoughts. But this dream is very cryptic. I try desperately to understand it, because I am so frequently emersed in it. I find it strange how much detail I can remember, as if it were actually a real memory.

In this dream, I do not always see through my eyes. Sometimes, I watch myself, as if I were a player on a screen that is controlled by me but seen through different eyes. A while back, I chose to share this dream with a close friend and was told that I could make it into something more. I hope others can enjoy this tale as I have. I hope that you will ask questions and help bring light to the meaning of it. I am going to elaborate to the best of my ability and with fine detail, so I can effectively tell this story.

Sometimes, it feels like that dream was the real world, and reality was the dream. I try to decipher what it means, but I find myself stuck in the possibilities. I struggle with the idea that I am so drowned in my own sorrows that my mind has to give me another world full of obstacles to keep me alive. I am a slave to a violent coping mechanism that I have developed to distract myself from the unpleasantness of embarrassment, and the mistakes I make in the real world.

When I have an ugly memory or an uncomfortable encounter, I seem to always imagine myself being stabbed, shot, tortured, or brutalized in some other way. I think I do this because it helps me realize that things could be worse, or perhaps I do it because I feel as if I need to be punished for any small mistake or inconvenience.

I think that this dream is a further, more detailed story behind that coping mechanism. I created another world based on it. I think that maybe my brain developed this idea because I feel so disconnected with the God from my childhood that I had to become one to reconnect. Or perhaps, I see myself as so unimportant in my world that I have to turn myself into something divine to feel as if I truly matter.

WARNING

I mportant Note to the Reader:

I want you to enjoy this book, but I must take the time to warn you that this is not a happy fairytale. Some of the issues that we will face together may not be suitable for all. I have been instructed to leave a warning for those who may not find interest in this genre. I want to give you a heads up.

Perhaps reconsider, or do not read *alone* if:
1. You are easily frightened
2. You tend to build strong emotional ties to characters
3. You struggle to understand or are uncomfortable with otherworldly dystopias
4. You are bothered by violence
5. You are offended by off color words

If you are sure that you want to continue, do not be intimidated by this warning. There is beauty in this story too.

I am a learning writer, so you may spot a few mistakes. But before jumping to conclusion, take into consideration the possibility that there is purpose behind some mistakes—perhaps they have special meaning. Be attentive.

If you own this book, take notes or highlight along the pages— some things may prove important later. Or be sure to take notes elsewhere.

THE FIRST DREAM

I hover shoulder to shoulder with the creatures that stand next to me, watching them as they cheer. I do not dare set foot on the stone, I do not dare touch the surface of this planet, for I do not wish to play this Game. The roar of the crowd ripples like thunder across the decaying colosseum of rusty-red rock. Laid carefully across the healthily growing grass in the pit below, there are 60 white rings of light. Inside these rings are creatures from every reach of the Universe called Naaqsaa—the most crippled and polluted, the most rotted and greedy of all that exist.

One by one, each new player falls from the sky—from high above the clouds, from a place unknown. Some land gracefully, some crash and then stand to present themselves. Some fly, and some die smashing into the grass splattering like fragile eggs. Some are among the ugliest I have ever seen, and some cannot be seen at all. As each arrives, there are two obnoxious and blabbering commentators, discussing the Hosts origin and play history—if they have any.

The crowd must be ready to flee, for we are not safe from the new players. Anything that has touched the ground is a player of this nasty Game. That is why they are thrown so viciously at the surface—with such force. It is the rings job to be sure the player touches. The gravity will grow stronger inside until the player can no longer resist.

The newest one, the one that they introduce now is a Virus, it corrupts the air. It carries itself along the breeze and infects and grows and chokes until there is none left. This invisible death is a player to fear. This is a player worth gambling on.

But there is one that we all wait for. One more crippled and polluted, and more rotted and greedy than the rest. It is the vilest creature known to their Universe; the vilest thing to ever exist within any of us. The cheering grows louder, and my ears begin to ring as the drums inside them beat faster than any before. It is coming.

We look to the sky. She keeps her feet below her, comfortably controlling her fall. She lands effortlessly, with only the slightest bend in her knees. She lifts her head, examining the 60 massive white rings. She fixes her stance and straightens her spine pulling her shoulders back and surveying the crowd.

She steps to the edge of her ring—which sits on the farthest southern edge of the plain, and she places her hand along the invisible barrier of light. She follows the wall, walking the full outline of her ring, tracing its borders with her palm and completing the circle. When she steps away, she turns her palm to the sky and carries it out in front of her as if it were something of great offering. When she reaches the center of her ring, she sits on her knees and bows her forehead so deep that it touches the ground, extending her open palms in front of her; pointed toward the open field of players. There, she stays—still as death.

Hosts continue falling from the sky, and as the time comes for the last to drop, the one who bows finally lifts her head and again she straightens her spine and peers across the vast plain that lies before her, scattered with deadly creatures and frightened children, elderly beings and failed landings. All trapped until the timer runs out and they will be set free to kill each other. This Game is merciless, none are excused from its torment, even Naaqsaa has played the Great Game of Ten. Oh yes, even we must participate if called upon, but Naaqsaa is the reason for the Games existence, she grew too powerful. Her cells grew too smart. So, she is the only one of us required to play. I have not any empathy for her, but I hope that she will one day find the ability to defeat this Great Game, for Naaqsaa was once my friend.

With her posture well practiced, and her patience well rewarded, the bower lifts her hand to the sky and follows the fall of the final Host smashing her palm into the dirt at the same moment that the falling player touches its feet to the surface. The commentators speak wildly of this seasons Game, and the spectators wait anxiously for the rings to disappear. Time is running out, and the bower climbs eerily to her feet. The clock tick, tick, ticks, and she extends her arm and shows her palm to the Hosts who fell to challenge her. Her hand sweeps across the field acknowledging each player and its purpose. She then lowers it to her side; her magic is complete.

Time is up. The rings lift from the ground and disappear. But before any of the Hosts can move, before they can breathe, or scream or cuss, their bodies drop dead. Each at the same second as the rest. There is only one that stands. The crowd watches silently with disbelief.

She takes a long look over the field and stalks patiently through the fallen. She bends a time or two, lifting a dagger or an axe, testing their weight before tucking it under her arm or dropping it back to the body of its owner. When she reaches the end of the plain, she looks out across its spectators, shaming us with her stare, showing such disgust for this Game that she despises so. She takes a deep breath and closes her eyes then disappears leaving nothing of herself behind.

And as we all had hoped to see, the opening Trial of this seasons Game was no disappointment. She has proven herself yet again to be among the most powerful of players. This is her 10th season, her 90th year in the Great Game of Ten. She is a veteran, a terror, a beacon, and a reminder to each of us the reason as to why we fear so greatly the Red-Blooded Humans of Earth.

This world will involve constant changes to Rules, Dates, Locations, Meanings, Perspectives, and more. For the Reader, do not let this discourage you, and do not get lost overthinking it. Many things will not always add up. Future additions to this series might change the telling's of this one. Differences in character perspective and lessons taught may alter what I tell you.

Keep your mind sharp. Find what things are important to think critically about—one mistake, one wrong turn, and you could miss something immaculate.

SPECIAL THANKS TO

Paulette Augustine
Staci Waggle
Doug Joice
Megan Kempin
Melissa Jo
Trenton Joice
Jonathan Joice
Kenna Joice
Adrianna Reiff
Skyler Blakely
Jasmine Murray
Rebecca Merrill
Shavonda Williams
Dustin Zeltner
Michael Ross

Without the ideals, likeness, hilarity, support, and curiosity of these very special people I would not have been able tell this story the way that I truly have needed to. So, Thank You, and God Bless.

1

THE SHIP

The lighting behind me is dim against the black walls, as I sit and do my makeup in the mirror under the lamp at my desk. My hair is blonde with dark roots. I wear it straight because I like the way that it falls gently from the pins that hold it back, and how it stays when I tuck the small frays behind my ears. I wear it half up, so that I can display the decade's worth of injected golden jewelry that runs up the side of each ear, along with the four hoops that I have in my nose—two on the left and two on the right— and the bar in the center of my top lip called the medusa. I pack copper-colored shadow onto my eyelid with a flat brush—I like the way that it compliments my brown eyes. I try to stay steady, as I stomp along to the heavy music erupting in the background. I have not been out in a while, so I want to look good.

This new face lets me be someone else for the night—someone happier. This is a part of me that I do not get to see often. I want to embrace her and her confidence—her comfort and her love of life. I am meeting a few friends at a bar in the next town over.

As I finish my makeup, I am also deciding what I should wear. Lately, my favorite thing has been a long-sleeved black top with some ripped up, skinny, dark denim jeans and a pair of black moccasin-type shoes with white soles. But the real challenge is whether I will be able to find these items in this mess. I have so many clothes, but no matter how many times I go through to thin the pile, I always buy more to replace what was thrown out.

I sift through the drawers and baskets of clothing, but I am only able to find the shirt. I have another pair of pants that I think will do though, they have black and white vertical stripes like Beetlejuice's. They are a little wild for this small town, but I do not mind. I take one last look in the mirror and smile. "This is just what I need," I say as I wave goodbye to Ronnie, who is the King of all Snakes, then turn out the lights to leave.

There is an abundance of love between the Fools and our pets. Next to Ronnie, there is the love of my life, Nitro. His parents are J and Dusty. Then, Chappa, he was a thickest orange Tabby I have ever seen and by far the most loving. He hailed from Beck's house. Also, from the home of Beck there is the Devil Dog, the Demon, the great ankle-biter, the tiny terror that is Beans. And the newest member, Hey, the Queen of the couch—and the bed, and the yard, and the stairs. And the Queen of the Fool called Sky.

It is late in the year, but we have yet to see any snow, so a light jacket should work. It is dark as I drive through the night. I play the music loud and sing along with all my heart because music is what makes life great. As I near my destination, I am so excited to see my friends, but am distracted by this strange feeling that I am being drawn to something else.

I park, and my heartbeat hastens. I feel there is something on approach. It is almost like I can feel the vibrations through the air. It is close. My attention is quickly averted to the left, as I hear a loud group of girls who pool around a car two slots down from me. I expect the place to be busy tonight, so who knows who I might see.

My phone buzzes with a new text. "Where are you?" it says.

I get out of my car to head inside. I like the bar by the river better, it has a large deck out back, known as "The biggest deck in town; hangs a little to the left," at least that is what the staff shirts say across the back. But that bar is packed shoulder to shoulder tonight, it is college season.

The bar that we are meeting at tonight is just a block over from The Mule, but this one had open tables. There is a restaurant that runs throughout the day on the lower level of the building. There are many doors, but the one that I need opens to a staircase that goes up, one that is much too steep for the debaucheries that take place at the top.

I had parked in the lot to the side of the building, so I must venture to the front to enter. The wind whistles off the old brick as I approach the building and pause to listen curiously. The whistles turn to whispers, and I look around questioningly for the source. I can only imagine how strange I must look gazing out into the street at nothing.

Suddenly, I feel that possibly my mind is not in the right place for me to be here, but I promised that I would be. I need to stop all of these distractions and be a part of my world—the Human world. I have never felt like one of them, but they are all who are here, so what else could I possibly be? I ponder this as a familiar face appears before me. It is Anna.

"Finally!" she exclaims as she hugs me.

"I know!" I reply. "It's been forever!" I embrace this hug, as I have not seen her for months. She lives in the state to the north, Nebraska. The drive is about five and a half hours, and she has come home for the weekend; we plan to enjoy the time we have together.

"I'm so happy to see you!" she exclaims.

Though being best friends, it is sometimes funny to see us together since our tastes are so different. I wear mostly dark colors and keep to myself, but Anna has a much brighter spirit.

Her makeup is well done, as always, but is still natural enough that I can see her freckles. She also wears her hair down, but where mine is naturally dirty blonde, she has naturally red hair, which she sometimes dyes blonde—but only on one side, and more recently she has taken a liking to darker colors as well. Her hair is medium length, and she has short bangs, which she brushes off to the side. She wears an olive-green top with long sleeves, along with a pair of black ripped skinny jeans tucked into her red high-topped skater shoes.

She gestures for me to follow her as she opens the door. I take one more curious look into the other parking lot across the street, and then turn to follow her up.

Anna turns right to speak with the bartender, and I stop at the top to greet the doorman named DBoy and V who is his girl. I consider them to be Fools too, but they will likely sit with their small group throughout the night.

I look to the left to see if there is anyone that I dare go talk to. In small places like these, it is hard to not know anyone, or at least, not know who they are. I decide to take the long way around to the bartender, so I can find my small group of Fools.

3

The pool room is off in the corner, but I skip it as my friends and I usually sit at a table in the front. About halfway around the loop, I see Beck, Teapot, Sky, J, and Dusty seated at the booth just inside the balcony door.

Beck is the hot mess of the Fools; she is daring and fearless, and bold. Her hair is long and beautifully thick. The color is a dark shade of purple. She has thick lenses in her glasses because her brown eyes cannot see for shit. She has on a black long sleeve like mine, and medium-colored skinny jeans tucked under her—almost knee high–faux-leather black boots.

Teapot is my older sister; she is our mom friend. She is a little older, and more responsible than the rest of us. If you did not know us, you would not expect us to be sisters. We are complete opposites. Where I am tall, and naturally muscular and broad shouldered, she stands much shorter and is thin. Her hair is bleach blonde, and her eyes are a wealthy color of blue. She is wearing a white tee-shirt with a big yellow sunflower, paired with light wash, boot-cut jeans, and fresh-white tennis shoes.

I have two other sisters who also smash the bar for fantastic Fools. The eldest of the four of us—and the shortest I should add—is Meg. She is not here but her place in this introduction is infinite. The youngest of my sisters is Ken, she fits in well with the older Fools and is a riot to be around, but she is still in middle school, so she is not here either.

Sky is a great conversationalist, and she is an amazing athlete. She has been on many cross-country teams over the years and has many metals and even a nice ring that was accidentally dropped on concrete once. She is very lean; you can tell that she runs every day. She has ginger hair, underneath a backwards, black cap, and plastic framed glasses with lenses that are way thinner than blind-ass Becks. She has on a white tee underneath a fall-colored flannel with rolled sleeves. Her denim is light wash boot-cut, like Meli's, and she has peach and white checkered, no-lace, skater shoes.

Now, I will add the final furry Fool, Tigger. Sky and Tigger were very rarely ever seen without the other. They were a duo, the perfect match. I miss him with all my soul. He has rightfully earned his spot on my list of Fools.

J is our protector. She takes good care, and watches over us, corralling our idiocy. Her skin is mixed, and her complexion matches the beauty of angels. Her hair is dark brown and spirals from the roots in curly tendrils to her mid back. She has on a black jacket that zips in the front over a white tank. Her jeans are a darker colored boot-cut, and her shoes are black form-fitting running shoes.

Dusty is a goofy motherfucker, but we love him all the same. He has a thicker build and a big-ass head. He has blonde hair and tattoos up both arms. I do not take the time to look at what he is wearing because I assume his shirt says something about tits, and he always wears the same jeans. I did notice his new shoes though; they are nice. They are matte black with black laces and have the brand name printed in either silver or a very light gold across the top.

The last of the Fools that I must announce is Brown. All I need to say for him is that he is a hoot—it is always a fun time when Browns in town. He could not make it [1]tonight. He is attending a rave.

Anna turns around the corner across from me with two drinks and a big smile. "Thank you," I say as I join the group at the table. We talk and laugh through the night, enjoying each other's company. For a moment, I forget all of the things that make me feel inhuman. But those moments never seem to last very long.

There is a sudden sound—loud and terrifying—it shakes the ground and rattles the windows. The wind picks up but only for a second, then all goes silent. I feel the familiar vibrations in the air from my short encounter outside earlier. But this time they are much more intense. It is like when you are in a car with subs or at a concert in front of large speakers, and you can feel it in your chest from the air, and in your feet from the ground.

I seem to be familiar with this phenomenon as—through all of the surrounding chatter—I tell my Fools that something has entered

---

[1] Note from the Prophet—Introductions: while on the subject, I must also take this time to introduce myself. I am the narrator, the writer of this tale. I will use footnotes, as I tell the story to help the Reader better understand our surroundings and history. I write in the first person because I see this journey through her, but I assure you, she and me are not the same. There is another that will speak to you through dreams, but that is an area that I will not touch, that is a being who wishes to show you a side different from mine. And one more thing, the Footnotes will prove to hold important information, so be sure not to pass them by.

the atmosphere. I slowly approach the balcony, and my heart rate accelerates again.

"How do you know?" asks J, as I walk out the door with the few who choose to follow me to investigate.

"Look," I reply pointing upward. There is a dark circle in the sky, a ship, hidden close by. Its lights twinkle like the stars, and my mind wanders for a moment. I look down to the street and see a group of three Humanoid figures. They are in fine clothing, nothing like what I have ever seen before. They wear all white, and they have a very faint glow under their skin. They have unusually long necks and stand with great pride in their posture. I want to see them up close.

The one who stands the tallest looks up at me, followed quickly by the other two who stand behind him. I feel drawn toward them like something I cannot explain. I recede back into the whispering crowd of people who are uncertain of their safety. I feel a hand grab my arm, and I turn to see Teapot looking at me in question.

"Where are you going?" she asks.

"I just want a closer look," I reply as I turn to leave again.

"I'm coming with you," she says following close behind. I find the exit and descend slowly down into the unknown. I approach the door and look out through the glass to find the strangers still looking back at me. I reach to open the door.

"Stop, what are you doing? You don't know what they are; you can't just walk up to them! What the fuck?" she says grabbing my arm again.

"I don't know how to explain this to you," I say, "but I feel drawn to them, like I can trust them." I pause, "Just—just stay here."

"What?" she says almost angrily.

"I'm sorry," I reply opening the door to step outside. "Just stay here."

I look up behind her, and see that Beck, Anna, J, and the others decided to follow me down, too. "I will be right back," I assure them.

Closing the door behind me, I turn to find myself looking at the figures from across the street. The tall man steps toward me.

"It is time," he says, as he reaches out his hand.

I ask quickly, "Time for what?"

"Come," he says in reply. "Come with us, and we will show you." I do not hesitate to trust in this seemingly familiar face, as I cross the street. The glow from the skin of the figures grows brighter the closer I get, but it is not blinding. I would better describe it with the word "beautiful."

The tall man has many small stars pinned to the chest of his fine laced jacket, almost as if to show a military rank or high status. His eyes are blue—but not like ours. They have their own glow, and as I look deeper, I can see what seems to be shooting stars, like he has the whole universe hidden away inside.

The shorter man to the right wears the same jacket, but with fewer stars pinned to his chest. His skin is a darker brown, making the blue in his eyes even more extravagant.

The woman to the right of him also looks the same, but her clothes are much more form fitting, and her eyes are a lighter shade of purple; but they hold that same universal glow as before.

I reach my hand forward, and just as I place it in his, I hear my name called from behind me. I turn to see my small group of Fools standing across the street staring.

"No!" Beck yells.

"You said you'd come back," replies J.

"I know you feel like your life is all wrong here, but you can't just leave us," Anna adds. "We love you." She steps out into the street and a few of the others follow behind her closely in fear.

"This is beyond your life here," the ethereal woman says.

"This is inevitable," follows the shorter man.

"This is for *their* future," the tall one says, grasping tighter onto my hand, and gesturing toward the Fools. I can feel a strange familiarity in his touch, which is something that I have never felt before in Humans.

I look back at my Fools as the scenery begins to flash red and blue, and time seems to slow. I look at them with a clog in my throat and a tear in my eye. There is no way that I can explain this to them; they would not understand. They stand in the middle of the street watching fearfully, and full of worry that they may never see me again. I shake my head side to side worried even more that *I* will never see *them* again. I cannot fight it; it feels like some sort of hypnosis. I cannot control my actions, I cannot retreat. I am stuck.

"I'm so sorry. I love you guys too," I say crying—as I turn away.

"One day, you will come back here, and everything will be as it was. They will forget that you had left them," the woman says with a kind smile. I smile back and take one last look at the Fools, as I fade away into the air with the strange creatures from the worlds beyond this one. My friends' looks of concern make me realize what I so easily chose to leave behind, and my heart breaks as I see the last of them.

I look around me, now in new surroundings; I assume that I am on the ship. In the games and the movies, ships are always dark and dirty, scattered with parts and vents, and have some type of fog or steam. But this one matches the white glow of the clothes of its people.

Looking around, I quickly notice the glass walls that I have been left in. I see other creatures and Humanoids in glass cages like mine—all forming together to make rings that line the growing wall of this massive spherical room. By my guess, I would say there are around sixty glass cages in all, but just under half of them are empty.

"Do not be frightened," says the woman from the street.

"I'm not afraid." I reply calmly and then ask, "What are you?"

"We are your Gods," she says. "As protectors, we are tasked with choosing you and delivering you—"

"Delivering me where?" I interrupt. "I'm sorry," I then say quickly, "that was rude."

"To Irestiikaar," she turns and gestures to the rest of the Hosts. "It is the destination set for all of you. But *you*, Emineeptiaa, *you* are meant for great things."

"What did you say?" I ask. "What was that word you used? What does it mean?"

"It means Red Blood," she replies, after repeating the strange word. She turns away to walk through the front glass of the cage leaving me trapped behind. I figure it is best to stay calm, so that I do not draw any further unwanted attention to myself as the newcomer. I have a quick thought that maybe I should not have worn such attention-grabbing pants.

I watch her in silence, as she enters what seems to be a circular control center in the middle of the room. The two men from before are now long gone; I assume that they run operations in other parts of the ship. I think the woman is of high status in this sector—they all seem to look to her for guidance. There are six other women dressed in the same fine white jackets as the ones from the street. They are scattered in seats across the control center, looking at their almost transparent screens, and pressing buttons on holographic keyboards.

I turn to look around my cell. There is a small bed with a blanket and a pillow to the right, and a clear table with a drawer and a chair to the left. I proceed to the desk to see what is in the drawer. There is a pencil and some paper. My attention is quickly drawn to the cell next to me, as I lock eyes with the creature that inhabits it.

"You seem unhappy," I say with sarcasm.

"They are not your friends, you will learn," he replies rudely then looks toward the Gods in the center. "This is only the beginning," he follows turning away from me accompanied by a low snarl.

He stands about three feet tall but is built as if he was a fully grown man and is also very muscular for his size. He has a dark color of green pigment to his skin, and it is rough like a Goblin or a Toad on the tops of his hands, arms, and along the back of his neck; but there is smoother skin on the other side. He has brown hair, and wears a backwards red cap. He has on a black tee and long pants that almost look like dark denim but are not exact. He is like a mini-Human-Frogman. I am sure that because of the look on my face, he has good reason for the rage that he returns back to me. He calls me a bitch, and continues on to ask me what I am looking at. His voice is very loud and confident, and also very scratchy I might add.

"I was just thinking," I chuckle—

"Just thinking what?" he says. He puffs out his chest, angered further by my laughter, and the fucker grows to be taller than me. He now stands close to seven feet! His skin changes to black and the rough bumps turn to spikes. His eyes are a terrifying golden-yellow. There are long tusks grown from his bottom jaw, and he bellows guttural noise revealing the long-jagged teeth that accompany them.

"Oh fuck," I say. He steps toward the thin glass that separates us, and his breath fogs it heavily on his side.

"When we are set free on Irestiikaar, you will be the first of many to die. You ignorant Ves—"

"Enough." says the Goddess from earlier. The glass between me and the raging-giant-Toad-prince clouds so boldly that I can no longer see through to the other side. Good riddance, fucker.

"What is your name?" I ask her.

"I am Braiiakiah," she replies.

"Wow," I say. "Um, do you have a nickname?" I ask.

"No," she replies bluntly. She returns to her post at City Center, where I can see what looks to be some sort of chart with a course, but I have no idea where we are, nor any idea how to read it. I assume that I will be here for a while, and I begin to regret my actions, though I am somehow still excited for the adventure that lies ahead. I am also under the impression that there will be no room for fear here.

2 Weeks since Abduction...

The Gods have managed to fill thirteen more cells. Most of us have been given matching uniforms to equalize us; the rest are left without them. They try to dress anything that they can make clothes for, but a lot of Hosts put up a good fight. And it is always a good show to watch the Wardens wrestle the new guy. I think that the best showing so far has been the small Spider-Monkey-looking creature in cell A-1-8. The Gods tried to catch it and put a small shirt over its head, but it is a remarkably nimble creature. It got loose and the Gods could not find it for two days. Host B-20 caught it while he was roaming for exercise—they gave him extra roaming time because of it, and I am *upset*.

I do thank the Gods for one thing though—the clothes are colored black, and that is my favorite color. Each of us were given the choice between long or short sleeves, with an identification number labeled on a small white patch on the sleeves' edge, and long or short pants. I chose the long-sleeved top to mirror the top I arrived with. I want to cover my tattoos. The less they know of me the better. But I also chose the shorts because of the heat generated by the lava man in the cell to the left of mine.

I have grown more familiar with the creatures around me, but instead of their real names I prefer to use nicknames, or their identification number. They are much easier to remember—I will keep a journal to help show you in better detail; I want to share this world.

I have since learned that the three Gods who had met me on the street were the three most important on the ship. Braiiakiah—as you know—is the City Captain, or the Captain of the Wardens. The tallest one—who stood in the front—is the Ship's Captain/Pilot. And the third one, the shorter man, is the Crew Captain.

Magma is about six feet or so, and he looks like a walking volcano. Though he comes off as incredibly scary, he was surprisingly gentle once I started speaking with him. That fucker Frogface is still a dick, but if I am polite, he is helpful when I have questions—and when he is small. He talks a lot of shit when he is big, and though he still threatens it, I do not think that he *actually* wants to kill me anymore.

We still tend to bicker, and he hates how I am always giving him a new name.

Braiiakiah is still passive, but I do not feel that it is meant to be rude, and I remain respectful with her. (I had to give her a nickname, not to be disrespectful to her, but just because I cannot say her name. I now call her Kiah.) I think her patience is wearing thin though, and she regrets placing me in the front row of cells. She has threatened to move me many times because of my issues with the little man next door, but she has yet to do it. I guess we are naturally selected for these cells, and if I am moved, my body might not adjust correctly to the new atmosphere when we reach Irestiikaar.

I know what awaits us at our destination, and why Frogface said not to trust them. According to Magma—my lava bodied neighbor—and the creature in the cell next to him, there is a legend about the [2]Lost Planet of Irestiikaar.

He tells me, "Every 10 years, a ship that mocks the sky collects 60 Hosts representing 60 random planets throughout the known Universe. They call this ship Adreestiaah which means "pretender." She will deliver these 60 Hosts to a planet said to be in a different dimension. And the Hosts shall fight to the death in a Game they call the Et'Emtepii'Em, or Great Game of Ten."

"So, if every other being in the Universe is aware of the Red Bloods," I ask Magma, "why are we so ignorant to everything around us?"

"Because your Gods chose to keep you hidden from the rest of us," he answers looking toward City Center. "They choose to keep you ignorant. You are protected by your Gods and their government. They hide the oldest secrets, and of all of the Gods in the Universe, your Gods are the most clever— the most unique. They mastered creation, and when they created your people, they kept them to themselves."

"Why?" I ask in reply.

"Nobody knows," he says, "they like to keep quiet."

"I've noticed," I say, as I look toward the Captain at City Center.

---

[2] Planet Detail—Irestiikaar: originates from our Universe. This planet was stolen by the Elite Gods around 3.8 billion years after creation because of their jealousy (10 billion years ago). Irestiikaar is the biggest planet from our Universe and has been the playing field of the Game of Ten for as long as the game has existed.

"How do they have the power to take random life, and sacrifice it to another dimension?" I ask him. "Is the Universe lawless?"

He replies, "The guy three cells down said that the Game was around about 12 million years before your Gods were. They are not in control of it; they have just learned to slow the process somehow. At one time, the ship would collect hundreds every week to sacrifice."

I lean to look at the man to find him staring back at me. He seems to do that a lot. But he does not look with lust or comfort, he stares with hatred and disgust. He is tall and has long brown hair. He looks just like a Human but has a slightly longer neck like the Gods do. I wonder if Earth is really the only place that we inhabit. Or, if he is not Human, how many other species are out there that look like us? There are many in these cells that resemble our species, but I am the only one who is treated as an imposter.

Magma continues, "Think of the Universe as a being—one mighty Goddess who reigns above them all."

"Like God," I interrupt, "the Almighty?"

"Yes and no," he laughs, "your God wanted the power, so he labeled himself to be the most high, just like how all of the rest of your Gods deem themselves better. They are the only Gods throughout time who have been able to create life— other than the Elites and the Universe herself. But many of their stories have been lost through time or hidden for protection. No one really knows what makes them so great because no one really knows enough about them."

"We know that they're uppity, self-praising, douche bags that push their might." says Frogface from the cell behind me. I look back at him in disapproval to see a smug smile on his face. I roll my eyes and look back to Magma.

"How does he know all of this?" I ask referring back to the Human-like informant. "He's not Human, is he?"

"No," he pauses turning to look toward him. "He is a God," he points toward City Center, "one of them."

"Then why isn't he all shiny and shit—*like them*?" I remark.

"Because he was banished from Hevaan, they no longer saw him as one of them." He replies, "So, they took his divinity and cast him out with no name and no title—"

"And then they smite you, at their convenience!" Frogface yells again from the cell behind me. I look back once more to see

15

a dramatic reenactment of what I assume would be, his idea of the action of smiting—complete with sound effects and a rather intense death scene. I roll my eyes again and turn back to Magma.

"What did he do?" I ask.

"That he did not say," he says back as he stands, and drags his heavy feet to the other side of his cell to talk with the giant slug-thing that takes up the cell between him and this mysterious Banished God. I turn to Frogface with annoyance to suggest conversation.

"Fuck you, Red Blood," he says. "Bother someone else."

"Ah, c'mon Fuckface," I say confidently in reply, as he stands defensively and puffs his chest to grow.

We hear someone yell from the distance, "Stop! Sit down and shut *the fuck* up!" We turn to see Kiah standing close by with a familiar irritated scowl. She must be so tired of our bitching, but I cannot help it.

"You think it is fun now, but when you stand across from him—cage free—you will cower!" she says with her nose pointed to the sky.

"He may kill me, but I will never be afraid of him," I reply.

"It will not be about *your fear* Emineeptiaa," she stresses sternly. "No one will care of your bravery when you are dead."

"But he will always be bothered by his inability to truly beat me," I answer once again.

"It will not matter because you will be *dead*!" she says, with extra emphasis on the D word.

She stands for a moment waiting for a snarky reply and turns away when I fail to deliver one. I accept the defeat gracefully and sit to draw. I continue to add new creatures to my small stack of loose paper. Kiah said that one day I will go back home, so I hope to document what I can so that I do not forget. I do not completely trust in the idea that she is telling the truth, but I do have hope that I will see my family and the Fools again.

I pick up my phone and flip through old pictures, embracing the memories they give before the last of my battery runs out. As disturbing as this venture has turned out to be, I almost wish that someone was here with me to see the wonder in it. It is all real. Our Gods are real, though they are very different from what our religions tell us. Fuckface even said that there is life on Mars and other planets in our solar system; they are just hidden from us. We do not know they exist, but they sport our fashion, listen to our music, and fan girl over our celebrities. There are even those who dare to visit our Earth to walk among us—even though the laws are strict, and it is hard to get on planet—apparently Earth is a pretty happening place. Some of them think we are cool.

I wonder if the Banished God was ever there, and if so, I wonder during what time period and where at? Gods can live to be thousands of years old apart from one, The Great God or Et'Aamiineea, who is said to be upward toward a couple of million. He got to see the Dinosaurs live and breathe, where we have only fossils and footprints.

I wonder about the Great God. Does he ever visit Earth; maybe every couple hundred years, or so? Does he have friends there? I ponder this as the room shifts to night mode, and the cells go dark. This is the only time of privacy we get here. The glass walls cloud with the color black, and we are given the option to clear the top glass for light if we want it.

In my down time, I would like to try and further explain one very important thing—that is the language of the Gods. I have asked around a bit hoping to understand how I can so easily communicate with all of the different creatures here and apparently, the ship does it for us just like another special ship that is blue and appears quite smaller than it truly is, but this adventure is definitely not as cool.

The more time we spend here, the more fluent we become with each other. Eventually, we will be able to translate without its help. Kiah explained it like this—for me, the Adreestiaah translates words to the Hevaanian language first and then on to English. This is why some of the words, phrases, or names that I hear are not fully translated. Since I am created from the Gods, they feel that it is necessary that I am somewhat familiar with their language.

I have been able to pick up on it a bit, but it is very difficult to learn. There are few common roots—such as the root *Et,* which I have learned translates to the English word "great." I have also figured out that when letters are doubled, it does not always mean they are pronounced with a long sound such as the double e's in the word see, or the way that the letter e causes the letter a to sound in the word ate. The language is easier for me to understand when I hear it, because I can just mimic what I hear. But spelling, reading, and writing are far too advanced for me to understand.

The script is a complete mess. I have tried to get Kiah to explain it, but she tells me that it is something I will learn with time. I always have to ask, so I want to help with the pronunciation of these confusing words so that you can learn them correctly too. It has taken a lot of practice for me to be able to say these words correctly so do not worry—I started just as confused as you [3]are.

To help promote your understanding a little further, the vowels in the capital syllables of the *Pronunciation* column of the following table (*Fig. 1*) seem to be carried for a short period of time before moving to the next letter when spoken. Meaning, you want to hold the sound longer than you would with a regular letter. This language is spoken softly—

Word/Name	*Pronunciation*	*Meaning*
Naaqsaa	[nah-kah-sah]	-
Irestiikaar	[ee-REST-i-car]	Lost Planet
Emineeptiaa	[em-en-EEP-tia]	Red Blood/Human
Braiiakiah	[brah-EE-ah-kia]	-
Adreestiaah	[uh-DREE-sh-TIA]	Pretender
Et'Emtepii'Em	[et EM-tep-ae EM]	Great Game of Ten
Et'Aamiineea	[et AH-meh-NEE-uh]	Great God
Hevaan	[hee-VAH-n]	Home of Gods

Fig. 1

Today is the day. Once every four days, my row—one by one—is given time to roam free outside of our cells for exercise and for our bodies to slowly assimilate to the same atmosphere. During these walks, we are accompanied by one or two of The Six. They are the Wardens who manage us. [4]Meenaa is my favorite. She is the most patient with my questions and is teaching me a few of the sigils and words from the Hevaanian language. She is my height, but her curly brown hair is always in a bun on the top of her head making her

---

[3] Relic Detail—Languages: I will add a small list of the ones that we have heard so far, and I will continue to add pronunciation as new words or names come along. I will also add a glossary at the end. Then you can look up any words that you may need help with as you read.

[4] [meh-NAH]

appear taller. She has vitiligo, and her eyes are a far darker purple than Kiah's.

Another one of The Six that I like is [5]Teriinia. She will also answer me, but with just a bit more caution. She is much shorter and has long, straight, blonde hair. The rest of The Six will accompany me but choose to do so silently. I have been told that it is because they do not want to appear to be showing any type of favoritism. But we all know that they root for me to win. They choose me over their Banished God. No one is allowed to speak to him when we wander, and he is not given a break outside of his cell, like the rest of us.

I stand by the front glass of my cell and wait for Meenaa to return with Fuckface. It is my turn to roam next. On my last venture, I visited with the Cyclops named [6]Reeb. He is in row C, cell 25. Reeb stands twelve foot four and has a single circular horn that grows from both sides of his head. It looks almost like a halo. I have come to find that most of the creatures on this ship are very *f*riendly. It is hard for me knowing that eventually I may be killed by one of them.

Many of the different species here I am familiar with. A good number of them are in our story books and old legends. But they are very different from what we think. There is a Satyr in cell B-21 who stands nine feet tall and has a massive third eye in the center of her forehead between her two downward-growing horns. In cell A-1-12, there is a foot-tall Fairy, a Mushroom Sprite in cell A-1-13, and a very dramatic Shape Shifter in A-1-3. And I have also paid a few visits to the Giant in C-28 because he reminds me of my younger brother back home, Jonny—another one of my Fools.

Today, I plan to draw the Mermaid in cell D-48. They were always one of my favorite mythical creatures—though the real ones are *definitely* predators. They have no arms, but there are large fins that grow in their place. The eyes are bulbous and take up much of the face—I assume that they are adaptable to the low light of deep water. From a distance, I can understand how they can be seen as beautiful, but up close they are terrifying. Her face is split into four sections. There is a lip that runs from her forehead to her chin, and another that stretches from ear to ear. When she opens her mouth,

---

[5] [teh-REE-nia]

[6] [r-ee-b]

her entire face becomes it, displaying many rows of tiny sharp teeth, and a long suction cup tongue to grab her prey with. I guess with having no arms, evolution had to give them another—very effective—form of attack. Her body also stretches upward to 30 feet from the top of her head to the tip of her tail.

I grow impatient waiting for my turn, and just as I think to go grab my chair, I see Meenaa and Fuckface approach his cell. She locks him in and turns toward me. I greet her with a smile and follow anxiously, as she escorts me to the [7]top row of cells. Cell 1 in row A is subdivided into thirteen smaller cells for the creatures that stand less than two feet tall. There is one cell of the subdivided ones that holds a Host so small that I cannot see it—a microorganism like a Virus, Bacteria, Protozoa, or teeny-tiny well minded creatures. Row A and B are for Hosts who stand at an average height of three to ten feet. Row C is for the bigger land-walking or air traveling creatures that stand anywhere from ten to forty feet, and [8]Row D is all aquatic tanks, which are the biggest of the cells if I might add. I guess it is only fair since they do not get to roam.

1 Month since Abduction...

It has been four weeks now that I have sat in this box. There is one left to fill before we reach Irestiikaar. I know of the dangers that are to come, but I cannot wait to be free of this boring cell—the cells in Row B are larger than Row A for longer bodied Hosts. Row B would have been nicer, at least there I could jog laps.

Life is so odd here. None of us eat. I have heard that the ship provides us with all of the necessary nutrients we need through the

---

[7] Monument Detail—Adreestiaah: built by the Elite Gods 3 years before Irestiikaar was taken to the Voided Cosmos. This round ship was designed to function around the large inner structure called The City. This section of the ship is a massive prison containing 60 cells. The prisoners are managed by six Warden Gods, and their captain named Braiiakiah. The cell layout consists of 4 rows, each one growing larger, as they climb the curved walls.

[8] Monument Detail—Adreestiaah: to travel from row to row, there is a platform that moves up and down. It is not very large so the bigger Hosts have to stay on their levels, but the smaller Hosts can move more freely—except for the Hosts in the subdivided cells of Cell A-1 who cannot leave the main cell.

air. The object of the Game is to be the deadliest Host. They take away the need to eat, or drink, or sleep—a few less things to worry about, I guess. But they provide a bed anyway for the release of boredom.

I have tried to teach Magma how to play a few easy games to help pass the time, but he does not seem to comprehend many of them. We started with Rock, Paper, Scissors, but he chose rock every time, no matter how I explained it, he is made of Rock so he could not understand that he could pick something else. We also tried Tick, Tack, Toe, but he also could not grasp the reason why he could only use X's or O's and not both at the same time.

Some of the other Hosts have been here for almost three months. I cannot imagine the level of boredom they must face. A lot of us sleep most of the time. Some play single-player games, some have bouncy balls or yoyo-like toys. Some paint on the walls with their blood or their facies, angry at their incarceration. I get the idea of protesting the cells, but I choose to keep mind clean. I refuse to think about the stench that radiates from some of them.

The first Host to board the ship for this decade was another bipetal woman. Her name is [9]Aneera. She is a row behind me, and two cells down past Fuckface, cell B-18. Her skin is a very pale blue, and her hair is long and white, almost pearl like. She has patterns on her skin just faintly darker than the original light-blue color. Magma says that she is a Siren and is adapted for land and aquatic environments. Her planet is over 90 percent water. Earth is about 71 percent, but there are still very large sections of land, so I assume also the possibility that her planet is the same.

"Is it larger than Earth?" I ask Magma.

"Yes," he replies. "It almost triples its size."

"I wonder what Irestiikaar will be like," I say. I take a look up from my paper to catch more small details about the creature in cell A-6 that I am adding to my stack of drawings. I call her the Mother of Nightmares. She has the body of a Spider but stands at six and a-half feet tall. Her upper body is Human-like, but the arms that grow from her shoulders are two more limbs that match her long legs. She has six eyes, and a long Snake-like tongue that she bends through the

---

[9] [ah-NEER-ah]

21

air. Her hair is thin, and there are only a small number of frays that grow from random spots on her head.

"They say Irestiikaar is one of the biggest that ever existed," he says.

"Exist*ed*?" I repeat in question.

"Yes," he replies. "It is no longer in this Universe, so many believe that it no longer exists because there is no proof of it. To most of us, all of this is nothing but legend." He gestures vaguely at the surrounding environment. "Everyone has heard the story, but eventually just a story is all it was."

I listen attentively, as he continues to explain how the Game of Ten was created. He talks about Elite Gods from a time before this Universe; perhaps they are the ones who created her [the Universe]. After she came to be, the Elite Gods grew jealous of her power, as they watched her grow. They wanted to prove their might against her, so they took her most flourished planet, and they hid it away. They birthed an entity of cruel nature, and they gave it one purpose—to collect, and deliver poor souls to be sacrificed as payment for the space we take up in whatever realm holds placement outside of our Universe. It is best understood that the Game of Ten has more worth in amusement than in power. Those who watch are only in it for the blood and the gore. And a good number of them are in the [10]slave trade.

---

[10] Gameplay Detail—The Slave Trade: the members of these groups are heavy watchers and will choose their targets after careful critique. They catch and deliver these Hosts to the Highest Power for all means of torture, and blasphemy, and suffocation, and display.

ONE OF
THE SIX
TERRINIA
5'2"

THE SQUEEB
HOST B-13
9'1"

THE CYCLOPSE
HOST C-25
REEB
12'4"

ONE OF
THE SIX
MEENAA
5'11"

THE BANISHED GOD
HOST A-12
BARROUN
6'10"

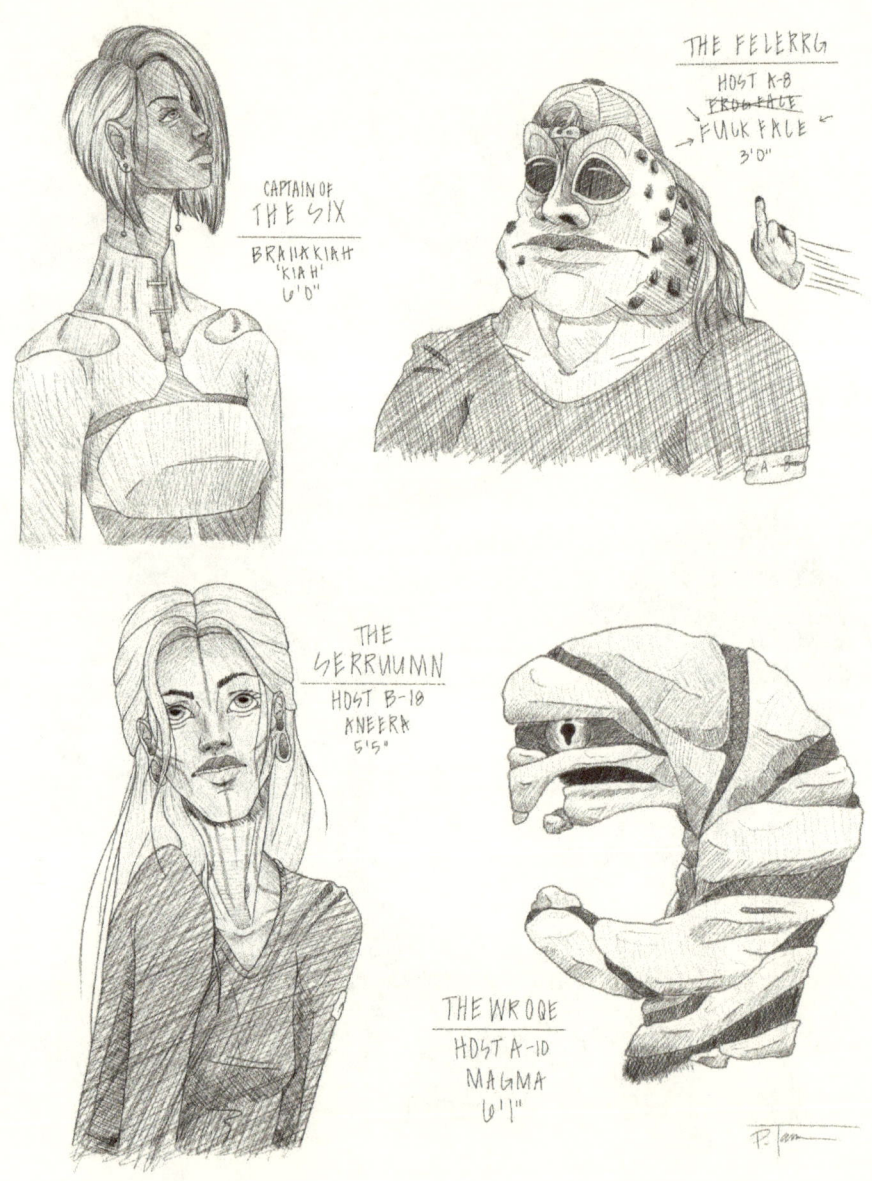

THE FELERRG
HOST K-8
~~FROG FACE~~
→ FUCK FACE ←
3'0"

CAPTAIN OF
THE SIX
BRAHAKIAH
'KIAH'
6'0"

THE
SERRUUMN
HOST B-10
ANEERA
5'5"

THE WROQE
HOST A-10
MAGMA
6'1"

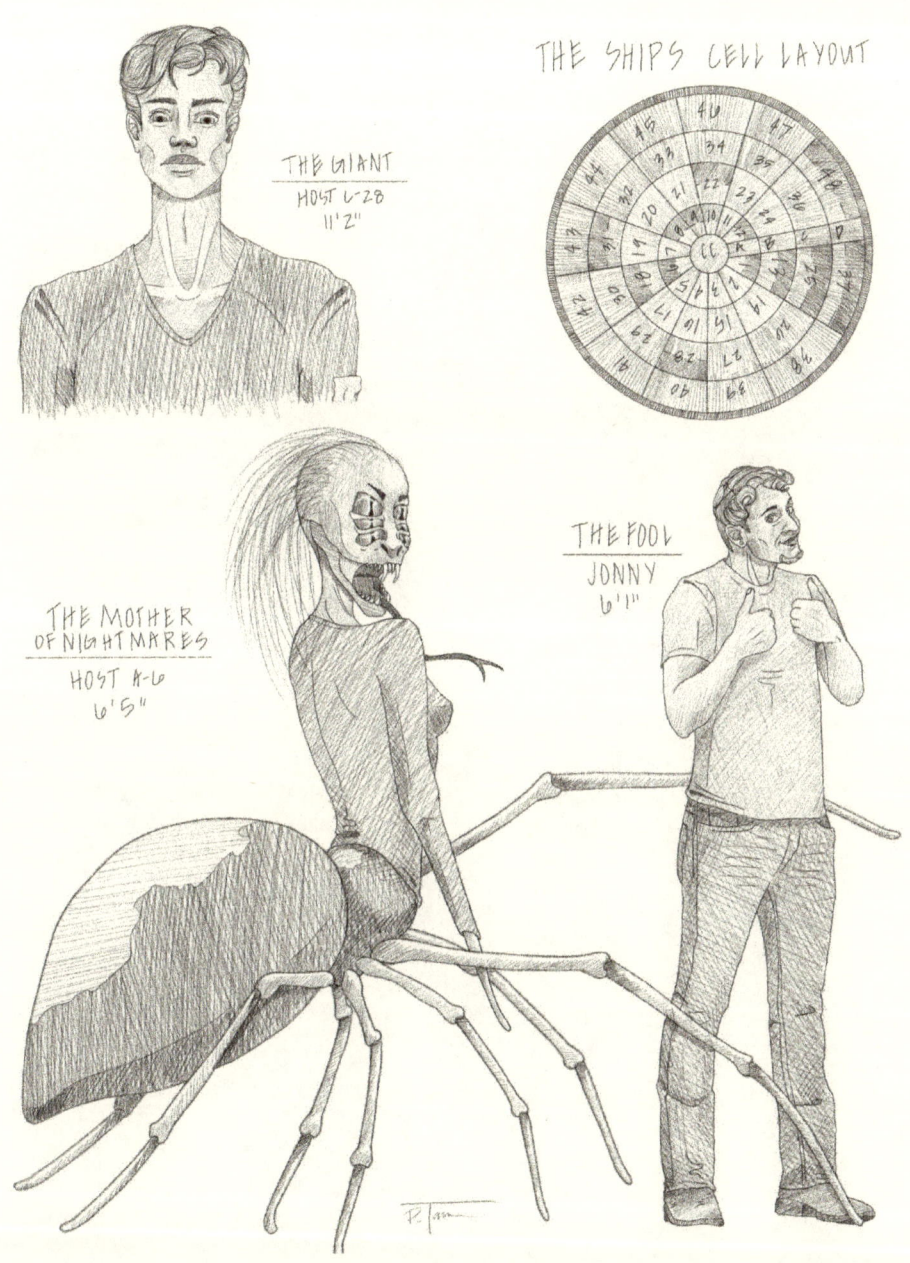

THE GIANT
HOST L-28
11'2"

THE SHIPS CELL LAYOUT

THE MOTHER
OF NIGHTMARES
HOST A-6
6'5"

THE FOOL
JONNY
6'1"

THE RUNNER
HOST A-1-B
10 INCHES

THE COMMON GREY
HOST C-31
11'8"

THE MERMAID
HOST D-48
29'0"

THE LIZARD
HOST B-22
10'0"

THE GIANT EEL
HOST D-37
33'5"

THE ARTHRITIS MONSTER
HOST C-32
15'5"

A-1-B @ 10'0"
B-22 @ 5'5"
C-34 @ 5'10"

1 Month and 26 Days since Abduction...

We all stand and stare as the final cell is filled, and the Gods chart a course for Irestiikaar. Kiah says that the journey will take us two days. My eyes wander cell to cell, as I ponder whether I have enough information to survive this Game. Every creature here has grown, absorbing knowledge of the creatures around them. They go to schools together, and live amongst one another, and have witnessed great historical events. I have had only two months, and hope that I am learning from honest and well-informed sources. I begin to withdraw from conversation and distance myself from potential threats, as I know that we are soon to be free of these protective cells.

I am aware that I am a major target because of my origins, and by the name that they chose to give me. I receive threats from across the room, and I have learned to hold my tongue when confronted by Fuckface from next door. This will be a place of death and detachment. I must get serious. There is no place here for fun, or for friends.

I look down at my pile of papers. The one on the top is layered with portraits of my family and Fools back home, as my phone has been dead almost a month. I do not want to forget their faces. More Gods arrive as they line up along cells on the farthest, nonaquatic row back from mine.

The cells begin to fog as the creatures inside fall to the floor, and the Gods move them to their beds and inject a silver liquid into their necks. I see no reason to fight it and lie in my bed to wait my turn.

"*You* look unhappy." I hear a voice say. I look to the right to see Fuckface, fully grown, sitting in his chair on the opposite side of the glass. He has a smile on his face and destruction in his eyes. "I'll see you in Hell," he says with a chuckle, as he stands from his chair and lies in his bed as if to mock me.

"I'll see you in Hell," I mock back followed by the Bird—fuck you. I turn my attention back to the ceiling. The room begins to cloud, and I find myself paralyzed. My shoulders go limp, and my head falls to the left. I see Kiah standing above me. She kneels to speak, but I cannot hear the words. I feel a sharp pinch in my neck and my eyes roll back while my mind goes blank.

2

THE WALL

I am falling. My consciousness is fading in and out. My body—now more thin and fit—slams into the ground. I groan, as I begin to register the pain and open my eyes. It seems to be many months, or possibly even years later. I pass out again, and once I come to, I can smell the grass below me, and as my blurred vision returns to normal, I can see faint blurs in the distance—they are moving. I hear the roar of thunder, but there is no rain or clouds. The sun is high in the sky.

As I continue to regain my awareness, I can hear distant screams, and what sounds like the clashing of metal. I finally have the strength to sit up, and I realize that I have something in my right hand. I hold it up and wonder, "Why am I holding a chef's knife? Of all things..."

My surroundings look to be an old battle ground. There are tattered buildings, and sparring partners scattered throughout the inside of some giant ring-shaped wall. It is incredibly high, with a lip around the top to prevent escape—to the ones of us who cannot fly that is. On the inner side of the wall, there are levels with stairwells in between; I assume about nine or ten.

I try to stand, but I stumble forward and fall back to the ground. My body is weak. I look up and see the bottom of a staircase sticking out from behind a building. I am close to it, and if I can reach it quickly, I can climb to get a better vantage point and hopefully avoid being seen, though I know that I will stick out up there—I will have to be quick. Luckily, I landed close to the wall, and not in the middle of this massive coliseum.

I stand again and stagger forward, but *again* there is something wrong. There is pain by my ribs on the right side. "Fuck." I say quietly leaning slightly forward. There is something broken, or very badly bruised. Looking down, I notice something else odd about my gear. "Shoes," I say to myself angrily. "*Why* am I not wearing *shoes*?"

I reach the corner of the building and turn to find that the steps lead to nowhere. There are four that climb up, and the rest is reduced to rubble. I look around and notice a ledge built of wood. It stretches from the top corner of some ruined manor, toward the pathway along the wall. "I could jump it," I think to myself, "if I can reach the top."

I notice myself standing straighter, as the pain in my side seems to vanish. I feel a rush of adventure and find my way inside to ascend. I stay vigilant in the low light, while I run through the rooms and eventually find a staircase leading upward. I reach the top and catch my breath. I notice that there is only one door.

There was a passage at one time that followed along the wall, but the floor has far past rotted and fallen in. I fight my way through the door just to find disappointment in yet *another* dead end. But the room is much brighter from the light shining in through the window, and if I have learned anything from video games, it is that sometimes you have to take the long way, and I would *really* like to go back outside. I figure that if I am going to die here, I would rather do it in the daylight so that I can, at least, see who does it.

There is broken glass under the window; I struggle to find a way around it. There is a piece of the busted door that I place over the glass so I can reach the other side—a splinter or two would be way less troublesome than a cut or a gash on the bottom of my foot. I do not want to leave a trail of red blood *anywhere* here. I peek out to conveniently find a small ledge along the wall and an old pipe that climbs to the top. I take a moment to appreciate the convenience, accompanied by what I am sure is a dumbass facial expression. I step lightly, as I slide along the wall looking down toward the level below. I reach the pipe at the end, tuck my knife into my shorts, and begin to climb—it reaches another two levels up.

"Shit!" I hear someone say angrily from below. I look down and see the struggle in her step, as she paces back and forth looking for her next route of escape.

"Ahaha! You're going to *die* today!" I hear another taunt from the distance. I climb faster hoping to avoid detection, and when I reach the top, I crawl away from the edge and listen to the screams from below. I grip tightly to my knife, readying myself for confrontation. I hear her flesh tearing and the screaming eventually goes silent. Her attacker screeches victoriously and scampers on to find his next victim.

I step timidly forward, and I slowly lean out as I near the edge. I find myself staring down at one of the most grotesque scenes found in my memory—this is my first taste of it. It is my first glance at the nature of some of these creatures. The body lies wasted on the far-left side of the alley. I follow a trail of green blood spatter to the right and gag when I find what lies at the end. Her head had landed face-down; her spine and some tissue followed. It appears to have been ripped from her body, pulled from her shoulders with one swift yank, and tossed away like garbage. I turn eagerly, and step hastily to locate the board from earlier while gripping my throat with concern.

I stare across the way, as I approach the jump and grow nervous from fear—the distance is much farther than I had anticipated. I look down three stories and step back. "Oh, *fuck* no!" I say to myself. I turn and whine once I realize that my choices are to either not jump and possibly have my spine ripped out, or to jump and possibly not—I choose option two: I like my spine.

I take a deep breath and a second to admire my bravery before running and leaping across to the other side. There is an iron-like railing along the pathway, so I have to focus on grabbing on to pull myself up. I reach forward and catch tightly to the bottom bar of the railing. My body swings down, and my face slams the firm metal ledge of the walkway.

After some time, I open my eyes and scream slightly, stopping myself with my free hand while looking down into the abyss below. I scan around for other Hosts. I am hanging from the railing. Now looking up, I see that somehow my hand still held tightly to the rod. My free hand is flooded with blood, and I come to realize that the blow had broken my nose—so much for not leaving a red trail. I whimper from the pain, while I wipe my hand dry on my shirt and pull myself up to roll between the bars to steady ground.

I sit up and pinch my nose at the tip just around my nostrils. I tilt my chin down to keep the blood from going down my throat, so that I do not choke. I sit for a moment in aggravated silence. I hear a small crack, and the discomfort in my nose is gone. I withdraw my hand to find that the blood has stopped, and I reach to feel the previously broken bridge of my nose. As if nothing had happened, there is no break of the bone or tear of the skin. It just healed.

"So, we can do *that* now," I say to myself in shock. I use the bottom of my shirt to wipe away the leftover blood the best that I can, and then clean my nose thoroughly because I cannot stand the smell of blood. I slide my knife out from where it had been tucked into my shorts and stand to continue climbing upward.

I had jumped across to the second level. I look about and decide that the third level would have a better view to see the damage happening below. I find the steps and reach the top. I see a few familiar creatures from the ship, but they all seem to be from row A or B. I assume there are other arenas for the remaining rows. They are fighting creatures from another team, or group—none of which I can identify. There seem to be more rules to this Game than I was told. Where these other creatures had come from, I have no idea.

I hear a noise above me, and I back slowly to the wall. I grip tight onto my knife, and I steady my breath as I prepare myself again for confrontation. I stand in silence, completely still.

Suddenly, a creature drops down, and hangs with a few of its feet gripping tightly to the level above. All four of its eyes are filled with rage, and I look back at it mirroring its intention to kill. It is a great deal bigger than me and very Bug-like. Its shell is a dark red color, but it glistens with iridescent patterns revealed by the light of the sun. It screeches at me with a familiar grotesque sound. This is the creature from the alley. I scream back at it matching its war cry with the gnarliest metal scream that I can muster, as it jumps toward me. My mind goes blank, but with my body fueled with adrenaline and fear, my defense is quick to the draw.

I hear the squelch of its innards, as I find my knife wedged into the side of its head. "Ew," I say passionately, dropping the body to frantically wipe the black blood spatter from my face, and spit it from my mouth. I try to remove the knife, but it is stuck. I hear the sound of multiple feet approaching me and turn to see another large creature in pursuit. I struggle with the knife as my heart rate hastens again. It is coming, and it is moving quickly. This creature has six legs, two arms, and grey skin all around. Its feet are heavy and make disgusting noise.

I guess that it is about 100 feet away, give or take a few. I am running out of time. I place my foot on the victim's head as leverage in one final attempt to remove the knife from its massive skull. It breaks free, and I fall backward to the ground just as the second creature leaps to tackle me. I feel a hand grip my arm and I am ripped through the concrete-like structure of the wall.

I look around to find myself now inside the inner tunnels of the big wall. They are small and cramped, though I can stand upright with a few feet to spare. There are lights above that hang very low in that empty space, and many-colored wires lining the walls on both sides. I look toward my rescuer to acquire his intentions. He is very tall and must crouch under the light fixtures. I feel as though he is familiar to me. In that moment, a single word comes to my mind.

"[11]Barroun," I say in low confidence.

"How do you know that?" he asks.

"I don't know," I reply, and stand to meet his posture. He suggests that we keep moving, if we are to stay alive.

I glance up at him again in question. "You look so familiar," I say stopping him from turning away from me, as if looking longer will refresh my memory.

He says, "I should," and then turns away again leaving me to ponder. We wander quietly through the hallways, my mind flooding with questions.

"Why are you helping me?" I eventually ask.

"Because you need it," he says pointing to his nose, and mocking me for breaking mine when I had jumped.

"You saw that?" I reply shamefully.

"Yes," he says back in a serious tone. "There is a small room here somewhere where we can wait out this Trial."

"Trial?" I repeat, patiently waiting for his answer. He steps quickly and does not reply. He gestures for me to follow him to a small door. There is a loud clank in the distance that catches our attention.

"Quickly!" he says opening the door and pushing me inside. He

---

[11] [bah-ROON]; lightly roll the r sound.

follows and closes the door behind him leaning against it, muttering a few words under his breath. I listen to the sound of his voice speaking quickly in a foreign language; from the sound of it I assume that it is Hevaanian. The room is pitch black and thin of air. He finishes the incantation and turns to face me in the dark. We stand closely in the cramped room. I can feel his breath on my forehead, and I back away into the few inches I have still behind me. I do not speak. I feel helpless lacking my knife, because I had lost it when he had pulled me through the wall.

"Why do you not have shoes?" he asks me to try to break the awkward silence.

"I've been asking myself that since I got here," I answer.

He begins to faintly explain the spell that he had put on the door causing it to be invisible to anyone standing on the other side. He then follows with an apology for the cramped space, as this was the only place that he could find so quickly.

"You said we had to wait this out." I say rudely. "What are we waiting for? How long will we be here?"

"Et'Emtepii'Em is played in many Trials, some that can last for years." He replies. "This one, the first one, it was created to thin the competition, though it really doesn't. This one usually lasts around an hour. 60 Hosts arrive from the Adreestiaah and are set free within the [12]Great Walls. 20 veterans from the Games held before are set free to hunt the ten weakest. Once the ten have fallen, the Hosts from Games prior will retreat, and it will be the remaining 50 left to fend for themselves. There is a scoreboard that monitors our kills, finds, and our coverage of the planet. The one with the highest score at the end gets"— He pauses and quietly shushes me when we hear another loud crash from the hallway outside.

"Gets what?" I whisper.

"Gets to go home." he says, continuing to tell me to stay quiet.

Kiah said that I would be back, but what she failed to mention was that I must prove the deadliest to do so. I struggle to hold my

---

[12] Monument Detail—The Great Walls: these four landmarks were constructed the year before the first Game. Built by the Elite Gods to separate the weak from the worthy upon arrival on the Lost Planet of Irestiikaar, the Great Walls stand as a reminder to the players that they are only pawns in an even greater and more malicious game.

hands still as I convince myself not to strangle the man standing in front of me. If death is what they want, then why am I avoiding it? I ask myself this as I hear him faintly speak again—

"If you kill me, you kill your only ally."

"Stay *the fuck* out of my head!" I say bluntly. I find myself interrupted as he rushes me and pins me against the wall rather uncomfortably. I have no leverage with my feet. They are knocked out from under me, and I stumble over whatever lies below, as I still cannot see.

"If you did not think so loud, I would not hear it." he says eerily in my ear with means to [13]threaten. "Accept that I am here to help you or die trying to prove me wrong. You are a very important player in this Game, but so am I."

"Okay," I reply quickly. "Please let me go." He steps away slowly, and I began to sense a certain level of concern—a feeling that is not mine.

The structure shakes at the sound of a horn bellowing loudly across the arena. I wonder how I am to escape this rather odd encounter and find safety—that is, if there is any.

"There is a wire stretched between the top of the wall and the archway of a building outside of it to the north of here. If we can get up there that is a straight shot to the other side." he tells me confidently.

I keep silent the idea that I will ditch him at some point, but I figure it best that he does not know; hopefully, he respects my request that he stays out of my head. We make our way to the top, silently so that we can avoid detection. As I approach the wire and notice the height of the drop, I hang my head and sigh. These ideas always seem so easy, but when it becomes real life, I despise the fact that everyone always chooses to go up to escape. One of my greatest fears is the feeling of freefall. I bicker back and forth with myself about this newfound problem.

---

[13] Host Detail—Accents: The Hosts do not hear each other's real voices. The Game lets them hear each other based on how they imagine each Host will sound. So, the Human does not hear Barroun's real voice, and he does not hear hers. If a Host is aware if this, they can "set" their ears to hear the real voice if they are concentrated enough.

"How are we going to do this?" he asks with what sounds like a nervous tone.

"We're going to walk across." I answer quickly as to seem confident, but annoyed—once again—with how I make the situation scarier for myself. I step near the edge. "There is no room for fear here," I say taking my first step.

"You are crazy, Human." he says from behind me. I step confidently, and my mind wonders. I focus on why he had called me Human instead of Red Blood like everyone else. The wire angles downward because the building is shorter than the [14]wall. I reach the archway and drop to the ledge just below. I climb in the window and turn to watch his attempt. I realize that this would be the perfect time to ditch him, but now I am curious about the purpose behind this familiarity.

He walks just as confidently as I do, then drops to the ledge to follow. I begin to remember his face. He walks past me and heads toward a doorway leading out. I watch him, as I start to also notice how I remember the way that he walks. He has very broad shoulders and is also very thin—but muscular. I follow him silently gawking and watching his steps. Then, I notice the cut of his hair, and the pristine way he stands up straight with his shoulders back—very formally. It is him—the one from the ship. It is the Banished God.

---

[14] Relic Detail—The Wires: many of these—along with planks or boards, like the one she used at the top of the manor—are placed in useful places by Hosts who use the rooftops to avoid the streets below.

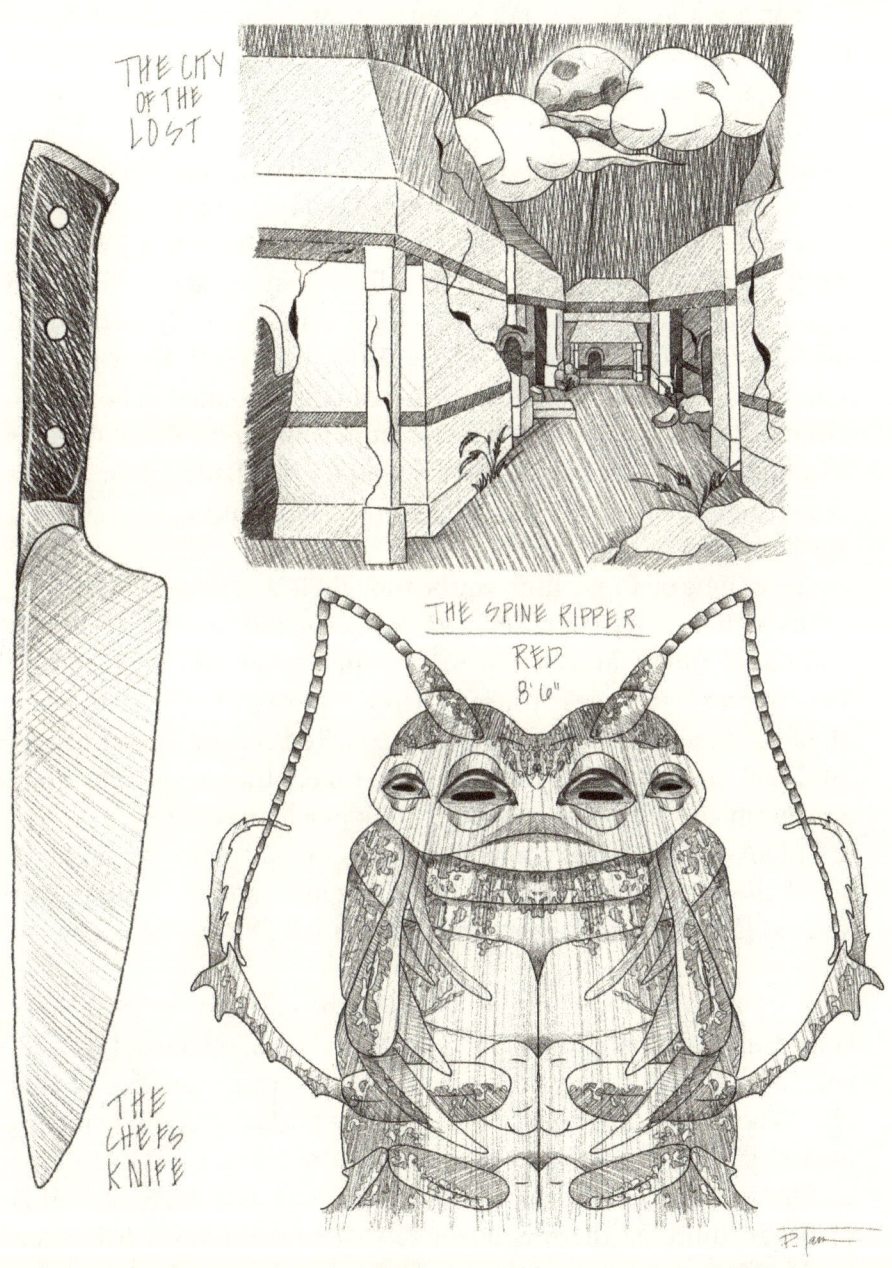

THE CITY OF THE LOST

THE SPINE RIPPER
RED
8' 6"

THE CHEFS KNIFE

2 Days since the Fall...

For a while I kept quiet about my revelation. I cannot figure out why it took me so long to recognize him. I remember everyone else from the ship. I want to try and always stay one step ahead. He knows a great deal about the Game, and because he is a God, I hope that I can trust that what he says is true. If his people hold the so called, "oldest secrets," maybe I can get some of them out of him. Of course, the first thing I ask him is what he had done causing his banishment. If he wants to be my ally, I want to know who I am dealing with. He says that he had a fight with his brother—one that his father could not forgive. So, the King of Hevaan, the God who stands the strongest, banished them. I am disappointed in how bleak I find his answer to be. Is his father important to the Great God? Is he on his council, or perhaps just an old friend? Banishment seems like a pretty heavy price to pay just for disappointing his father. It must have been one hell of a fight.

I continue on to ask him why he thought it is so important that he works with me. He, again, replies bleakly and tells me that he knows that I am Human, and that he understands what we are capable of. This answer leaves me confused. Why does he call me Human when all of the others call me Emineeptiaa, or Red Blood? I want to ask, but I feel that I must wait for the right time. This seems to be quite a sore subject, and we do not really talk much anyway.

I look to the north at the dark wall of clouds moving in; I can smell the coming rain in the air. I suggest that we find shelter and explain further the severity of the small storm that is headed our way.

We have traveled about 36 miles to the east of the Great Wall, staggering from path to path around obstacles and blockades while searching for other signs of life. I want to stress the size of this city. When I say massive, I mean, no city on *Earth* could compare in size. It stretches on for miles in every direction. I feel like I now understand why, as he says, these Trials can last for years. This planet is limitless; there is nowhere that we cannot go. It is open world—free range.

We find a small shack down a narrow alley. We are in what would have been probably one of the more frightful parts of this city in its time. I assume a history of poverty, and violence evidenced by the low detail carved into the stone structures in the area. I noticed that closer to the wall, the buildings stand tall and have fine carvings, and spires, and statues at the top. I think we have stumbled into a slum.

The thunder roars above us, as we continue toward the shack and it begins to rain. We rush through the alley, and I am tackled to the ground from above.

A Host pulls out a large dagger, and I struggle to turn to face her. She has black oily skin and an abnormally long neck—much longer than that of the Gods—underneath a long, black, hooded cloak. Her eyes are small and pushed to the sides like a fish. She holds down one of my hands, as I swing my fist and punch her hard in the face with the free one. She leans to the side and groans eerily in pain. It is one of those noises that make your whole-body cringe in disgust.

I reply with a nervous stutter and another, "Ew," pulling my hand away from her face with stringy mucus attached. I fling the yuck from my hand, and swing to punch her again. The rain beats down on us, as we struggle in the mud. I manage to wrestle my way on top, and I smash her face into the ground. I twist it from side to side, drowning her in rainwater and mud. I take a moment to look around, as I suddenly find myself remembering a so-called ally traveling with me. But I regret my anger once I spot him in the distance struggling with his own attacker.

In my distraction, the Host stabs me in the leg and breaks free. I ignore the discomfort and stand to retaliate. I scream in pain, as I feel the sharp edges of the dagger slicing through my insides again. She holds me steady and slowly pushes it into my back—dragging it back out with a different angle.

I sink my elbow into her jaw and turn to grab the dagger from her hand. I stab it upward into her chest from under her tiny ribs hoping to be correct about the location of her heart.

She pauses in shock from the pain, and her body jerks as she struggles to breathe. I grab the back of her neck where it meets her shoulders, and I pull her down toward me. I push the dagger deeper into her chest. She goes limp, and I withdraw it dropping her to the ground. I stand in shock staring at her lifeless body while I bleed in the rain. My nature is no different from these creatures that I despise so much around me. I am just as cruel.

I hear another body slam to the ground, and I turn to see the victor. The figure drops from a wire above and emerges quickly from the shadows. I stare into the dark through the rain trying desperately to identify the Host on approach.

"Let's go!" I hear him yell above the sound of the rain. It is Barroun; I sigh with relief.

"I don't recognize them." I yell back to him, running ahead of him toward the shack.

He follows close behind and says, "They are seasoned Hosts; this was probably their hideout." He brushes past me to open the door and enter first.

"I'm right behind you," I tell him before turning to look again out into the alley. The bodies lay in the center of the small path, and I decide it best to go move them to, hopefully, prevent investigation if someone were to come along. The blood coming from my back has clogged, and the wound has mostly healed. I tuck my new dagger into my shorts, and venture back out into the rain. I reach the end of the alley and see a building across the street.

I lift the smaller body over my shoulder and carry her inside to find a place to hide her. It seems to be an old bar. There are tables turned on their sides, and flipped upside down scattered all across the room. The chairs are thrown around in about the same ugly fashion.

I drop the body behind the counter where I feel that it will, at the least, be out of sight. I retreat to the door to retrieve the second body and stop in my tracks as I notice another Host wondering outside. "This place has heavy traffic," I think to myself. We have not seen any others since the Great Wall, and now three in one night!

I crouch below the window and peak my head up to see the Host in the street. The rain calms but remains steady. I then notice Barroun peeking out around the corner of a doorway on the other side of the street. I ready my dagger and prepare to fight. If this Game bases score on how many Hosts I kill, I will have to fight for the top spot that will send me back home.

"He is mine!" I gesture to him once he matches eyes with me.

"No," he mouths back shaking his head side-to-side, and smiling deviously. He disappears again behind the door, and I look around quickly for my best angle of attack.

"No *fucking way* is he winning this!" I say under my breath. I see a ledge above the Host with a small wire that stretches across the path and attaches above me. I can walk across and drop from there, like the creature from earlier did to me. But I will kill on impact, rather than give him a chance to fight back. I see Barroun move slyly from inside of a doorway to hide behind a beam close to the Host. I must hurry.

I hurdle out the window and look up to see a figure carved into the stone at the top. It is just deep enough for me to use it as a handle to pull myself up the wall and climb desperately onto the wire. I squint so that I can see across through the rain, and scamper lightly to the other side. I reach the ledge and turn my back against the wall, as Barroun attacks the Host from the shadows below.

"Shit!" I say to myself quietly. They struggle for a moment before the Host grabs him, and rips him off its back, and throws him into the street. It is now or never, I suppose. I can attack while it is distracted.

I grip tight to the dagger and leap for the kill. As I land confidently on its back, I grab its hair with my free hand to steady is head and sink the dagger into his neck. I push until I see it come out again on the other side, then I rip it out quickly with means to bleed him out. His huge body falls forward to the ground, and I roll across the mud and stand again to look down upon my kill. I look up and see Barroun carrying the body he had dropped earlier.

"You kill him; you carry him," he says smugly.

I sigh, "Awesome," I reply sarcastically looking down in distress. The rain has nearly stopped now, and I struggle with how I am to move this massive body. I cannot lift it or carry it, so I turn to option two. I will display it as a warning. "Maybe I can find some leverage and hang it," I think to myself deviously while remembering the wire above from earlier. I climb up either side and detach it from the wall. I tie one end around the beast, and the other around my waste to hold it while I climb again. There is another wire stretching across the street between the same two buildings as the other, but this one is two more levels up. I climb to the top and throw the wire I had attached to my waist over the one that is still strung.

Inside a close window, I conveniently find a pile of blocks and a tattered curtain. I move the blocks onto the curtain toward the edge next to the window where the wall has been lost exposing the street below. I tie the curtain at the top with my end of the wire, creating a sort of bag with the thick red cloth.

I look down just in time to see Barroun wondering back out from the bar to find the body still lying in the street. He sees the wire and follows it up to find me on the fourth story with a clever grin. I hope this works the way I planned it to.

I nudge the pile of bricks over the edge and hold tight to the rope as I ride the bag down, and the body of the beast is hoisted high into the sky. I land gracefully, and step lively toward the God, as I smile and turn to look upon my creation. It looks glorious! The clouds begin to clear and the rising sun peaks through. I look back at Barroun with a smug smile as if to say, "Checkmate."

He smirks and turns away. I follow him back to the shack with the confidence that I had won. I close the door behind me and stop in shock when I look up to see that he has stripped off his wet clothes, and now stands nearly naked in front of me. I cannot help but to look for a moment before I notice him looking back.

I turn away and walk into another small room off to the right. "I'll be in here," I say nervously closing the door behind me, and looking down at the wet clothes that I have on. I laugh at myself, roll my eyes and begin to undress to wring the water out starting with my top. Next, I do the same with my shorts and hang them both from the rafter above to dry.

I scrunch my hair and run my fingers through in an attempt to somewhat brush it. I then must spend a moment pulling all the wet-lose hairs from in between my fingers and dispose of them. I braid it back out of my face and tie it with a small string that I pulled from the sleeve of my shirt, because I had broken the small rubber band that held it before. I find a sheet and huddle in a corner shivering in the cold, wrapped and waiting for my clothes to dry.

I shake my head in embarrassment and laugh at myself again. I guess that I should give the credit that I find him attractive. But this is not normal life, and I must not think about it. I cannot be blinded by this type of distraction. I must focus on the Game. I could never allow myself to really peruse anyone anyway; I have always been discomforted by it. Maybe I should rest a while to pass the time.

I admire how they left me with the ability to dream. I am reminded of the purple-eyed God, Braiiakiah. I see her kneeling next to me speaking just like before, but this time I can almost hear her words. I want so desperately to remember what she said to me, but I have not been able to understand it.

I wake to the sound of Barroun banging on the door. He breaks through, rips down my clothes, and throws them at me.

"Get dressed," he says in a hurry.

"What's wrong?" I ask him, as he runs back to the other room. I finish pulling up my shorts and run after him to see.

"Look." He replies pointing toward the window. I run my arm the rest of the way through my shirt sleeve, and crouch to peek out under the curtain to see a group of Hosts identical to the beast that I had strung up the few hours before.

"Fuck," I say to myself.

"Yes, *fuck*," he repeats back. "I counted six of them."

"There has to be another way out of here," I say, as I begin to open doors, and lift carpets looking for a cellar or a backdoor of some kind. He scoffs and looks out the window. "We find a way out, or we sit here and wait to die," I say to him with aggravation. I hear a creak from the board below me and look down to see a hole in the wood, placed there to remove a hatch door. I look up at him and smile victoriously.

"Let's go then," he says running toward me. I remove the piece and peer down into the darkness of the newly revealed tunnel below the floor.

"Do you have a light?" I ask hopefully. He shakes his head no and looks around for anything that could be used. On a table to the right, I find a small candle. "That's convenient," I say to myself. "Here!" I say louder holding it up; now just to find a way to light it. He rushes at me and takes it out if my hand, as he descends down into the tunnel. He instructs me to follow *h*im and close the hatch behind me. I reach the third step from the bottom and stop to listen to him muttering a quick chant, which ignites the candle revealing our surroundings.

We both gasp in disgust, gazing for the first time into this tunnel of death. Along each side are bodies strung against the wall—bones picked clean and left for display. The bodies hang with their hands tied above their heads, and stitches in between the bones to hold them all together. Each skull has an appropriately sized rock stuck in its jaw that was used to gag them. We travel cautiously through the tunnel hoping not to find the decorator on the other side. The bodies grow denser, as we near the end.

"Oh my God," I say when the tunnel opens into a large cavern.

"*He* had nothing to do with this," Barroun replies, as he looks in awe at the hundreds of bodies hanging upside down from the roof of the cave. I cover my mouth in disgust.

"These ones are still fresh," I tell him, grabbing his sleeve and shaking his arm, as if he cannot see the shredded flesh, and rotting tissue hanging from the bones. The stench seems to grow more and more foul the deeper we wander in. "Maybe we should go back," I suggest.

"We've come too far to turn back," he replies. I look at him with disapproval but continue following him into another tunnel on the other side. I see a light close ahead, as we turn a corner and pick up the pace in our steps. We reach another cavern, but this one is well lit. I stand behind Barroun, as he peaks around the corner, and moves back quickly to place his finger over his mouth—signaling me to stay quiet. We both jump and look at each other with wide eyes when we hear a clatter in the distance, and a heart stopping hiss. I stare at him and think, "What did you see?" He pushes me gently back into the tunnel. He points back toward the way that we had come from.

"Go quietly," He mouths. I slow my breath and focus heavily on my movements. I pace slowly and gradually increase speed, as I vacate the area. We reach the first cavern, but quickly hide after we hear the repeated hiss of this horrid mystery Host. We crouch behind a large rock. Barroun grasps tightly to my arm and pulls me close to him. He is angry.

"If we die"—he pauses, and ducks to shield his head with his free hand after something slams into the rock on the other side causing it to shift toward us. He grips my arm tighter, and repeats again with an angry whisper, "If we die here, it is *your* fault!"

"What? I told you we should go back. Don't you blame this shit on me!" I whisper back with attitude.

"I'm talking about the giant boar you displayed in the street!" he snaps back with an even shittier tone.

"You should have helped me move it," I say, as I throw the blame back on him. "And I wouldn't have killed him if you wouldn't have challenged me!"

"Fuck you, yes you would've. All you care about is going home," he replies and throws me against the stone.

"Of course, that's all I care about!" I say in rebuttal. "Pussy!" I try not to speak too loud hoping that he heard me after disappearing into the darkness of the cave. I said that there is no room for friends here. I guess it is time to have a go on my own. I will stay and face this creature alone. I avert my attention back to the Host ready to fight whatever monster stands beyond the mighty stone. I look down at my dagger and grip it tightly. It is the perfect fit for my hand. The handle measures about four inches attached to a thin pointed blade running a foot from its base. It is gold in color; but a very light-colored gold I must add. The handle matches the blade and has fine carvings in foreign pictures along the cross-guard and the pommel. I recognize one of the symbols carved into the gold. Meenaa taught me this one. It sits on each side of the cross guard and looks almost like a Bird with an odd tail or a strange star maybe. This sigil means, "deliver."

I hear the hiss again and stand my ground. I stay for a moment, and then proceed to step forward. I peer aimlessly into the dark, as I turn the corner to find nothing standing on the other side. I think to myself, "Where would it be if this were a movie?"

I look to the top of the stone and stumble backwards uttering curses under my breath. It sits with an uncomfortably confident posture and looks at me with large reptilian eyes. It moves much like a cat leaping to the ground in front of me and then sitting again with equal confidence. There is a shudder in my breath, as I *again* take a few steps back, and stop with the hope that I do not provoke it. It has long front legs that stretch from the floor to my elbow but also has very Human-like hands with long claws instead of fingernails.

When it walks, I can see the arch in its back like a hyena caused by its ever so slightly shorter legs in the back. It has a long skinny tail that it whips back and forth behind it. I sense that this is done for the purpose of intimidation—and it works. It has a long neck to match the tail, and its head seems too small for the wide peering eyes that take up the majority of it.

It looks surprised. It steps forward again and sits in a new spot. Its head follows me, as its body turns to step again, but this time to the side. I am unsettled by this creature in the most indescribable of ways. I stumble slightly stepping to the side trying to mock its movements. It stands, and proceeds to circle me. I watch closely. It opens its mouth and detaches its jaw like a Snake to reveal a few rows of sharp teeth inside. Its tongue curls through the air, and retracts quickly back in. It hisses, and crackles distorted noise with its head jerking to the side causing it to appear possessed.

I jump out of the way, as it launches toward me and I quickly attack, slicing the ligaments across the inside of its rear knee. Its scream of pain is so deafening, that I reach to cover my ears. My feet are knocked out from beneath me, and I slam to the ground cracking my head against a rock. The pain is instant, and I notice a great amount of blood flowing from the wound in my skull. My vision blurs, and I blink rapidly to try and clear the blood from my eyes. I grunt at the familiar feeling of the dagger ripping into me. The Host continues to stab me—possibly three more times—before I pass out from the trauma.

8 Days since the Fall...

I regain consciousness to find myself tied to the wall, hands above my head just like the others, but no rock to gag me. The Host sits patiently waiting for me to notice. It looks at me with its big lustful eyes and breathes heavily. I close my eyes to avoid giving it the satisfaction. But I soon regret my actions, opening them again to see the creature latched to my torso. It grips me tightly, ripping my skin with its claws. It tears a chunk from my side and tilts its head back to swallow it whole. I scream in pain. It bites again and tosses its head from side to side shredding the tissue, removing another chunk to swallow.

The Host then stops and looks into the distance almost seeming concerned. It drops my weight to hang hopelessly from the rock wall and maneuvers eerily into the reseeding tunnel. I can hear the crackle in its throat fade, as it moves further away.

I cry to myself, as I feel the missing tissue begin to reconstruct, and the skin returns to normal. The process is slow, and it leaves heavy scars— "I am going to be here forever," I think. "I will be nothing, but a rechargeable meal." I hang my head defeated after struggling to untie the rope that binds me. "What a great adventure," I think sarcastically. I wait here feeling sorry for myself until I hear a low whisper in the distance—

"You look unhappy," it says. I lift my head in high spirits to see Fuckface crouched behind a pile of bones to the right.

"I never thought I'd be so happy to see you!" I say with excitement, but still with a whisper. "Get me the hell out of here!"

He steps quickly toward me, grabs ahold of my leg, and climbs upward stopping by my head, and says, "If anyone here is going to kill you, it is going to be me!"

"Yeah, sure, just get me down," I reply. He reaches and cuts the line holding my wrists. He leaps from my back pushing me downward, and I smash into the ground unable to catch my balance due to the fact that my feet are still tied. I groan quietly followed by a very weak, "Fuck you! You did that on purpose!"

"Of course, I did!" he says. He turns and leaves. I quickly untie my ankles and stand to follow him through the tunnels. I guess doing it alone was not meant to last very long. I am not mad at this; I will take the help for now. But soon begin to struggle to keep up because of the narrowing passages. He is a great deal smaller than me and can fit through tighter spaces. There are a few that I am able to squeeze through, but we eventually reach one that is too small.

"The way out is just past this wall," he says.

"Fuck," I reply. I crouch to look through the hole, and notice that the rock is too thick for me to break off with haste. "There was a passage not too far back," I say turning to face the direction that we had come from. "Maybe there's another way out." He nods in agreement and crawls out through the small opening to the other side. I can see the light shine through from outside, so I know there has to be another way out close by.

I wander back to the passage and pause before walking through a long narrow hallway that ends with another room somewhat lit from the sun. I turn to the side, and slide between the two walls. I assume that this was a secret passage in its day covered by a bookcase, or tall shelf on the other side. Just as I reach the opening and squeeze out from the uncomfortably tight corridor into the open room, I hear a haunting sound in the distance. The Host is close; I hear the crackle in its throat, as it roams the passages and lurks closer.

I search the room which looks to be part of a building from the ruined city. The door is blocked by rubble, but I notice a small pool in the corner where the floor droops from rot. There is a hole in the wall close to the top where the light is coming through, but it is small like the one I saw prior. I try to discreetly tear back the boards from the floor because I figure that if I cannot go up maybe I should try going down. I break a small hole and lean in to look. There is light shining in through the water.

I rip at the boards until the hole is big enough for me to slide through. The light source is deep, and I steady my breath hoping that I can push that far. I slide in up to my shoulders and focus my breathing for a moment before taking a final breath. I submerge, and turn head down in the water, kick off the floor above me, then rocket downward.

I notice the surrounding room that matches the one above. The building must have flooded when the wall broke at the bottom. I reach the opening, and panic when I cannot fit through it. I grab a piece of stone from the broken building and hold the wall with one hand to steady myself, as I smash the edge of the opening with the other managing to break away just enough pieces to squeeze through. I struggle through the hole, and swim up. I choke on water eventually finding the surface.

I struggle to catch my breath for a moment before I am able to calm myself, and swim to shore. I have always been terrified of suffocating. I am a good swimmer, and I enjoy the water, but the possibility of drowning seems to always take some of the beauty out of it. I open my eyes and look around after lying on the ground for a moment recouping after that almost deadly affair.

I am in a small spring—they had built the city around it. There are tattered statues spread throughout the small garden, and rock walls that climb naturally toward the sky surrounding it. It looks like this used to be a cave, but the roof has long since fallen in, and new vegetation has grown over the devastation. I lay soaked in the grass and stare peacefully into the sky, as I embrace this much-needed hidden sanctuary.

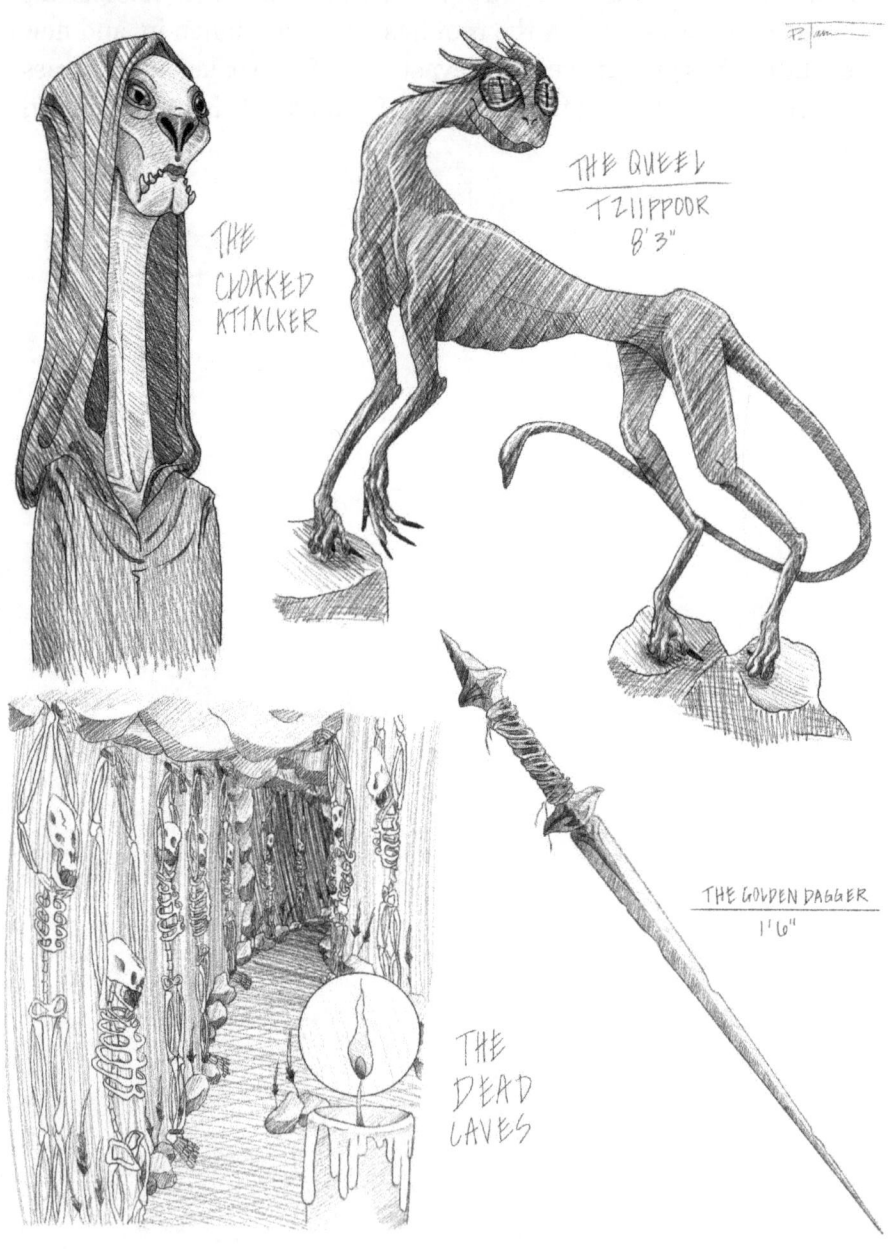

THE CLOAKED ATTACKER

THE QUEEL
TZIIPPOOR
8'3"

THE GOLDEN DAGGER
1'6"

THE DEAD CAVES

THE SECOND DREAM

I follow her quietly and out of sight. She carries a dagger along her leg and a small pack at her side. I am so unbearably cautious that neither her nor that thing inside of her can sense me. Darkness can be deafening. She crawls through cracks and balances on boards, changing her size as she sees fit. She paces quickly through a painfully large white house with crawl spaces and dusty cupboards, and shortcuts that lead to dead ends.

She searches for something. I am ever so curious. She slides and steps through small traps meant for rodents and follows carefully behind a tarnished and treacherously smelly Bugg. It has loose wires, and small sparks fly behind it as it leads her to her target.

They travel up and up and up until they find a grand room of blue and gold. It is filled with ships and treasures, and jewels that twinkle and shine under the chandelier made of gibbets filled with bones. The guardian of this horde despises the sleazy fingers of thieves.

But this is a special thief. She has not come to fail, and the guardian is to lose his most prized possession for this thief is worthy of it. She steps slower, approaching the guardian.

He is so heavy from his greedy gut and his lustful eyes that as he moves his spine snaps, and he screams pleasureful agony into the air; he likes it. He groans and moans as his spine rebuilds itself and he steps again to relive the height of his desire. As he hangs his head back and whines over the jewels and his excitement for pain the thief can see what she searches for.

Inside the mouth of the guardian, attached to a tooth in the front, there is a small Yokkaa—a teeny stone, one more precious than any among the others in his horde. It is surrounded by **19** more stones, all even smaller than it is, crafted tightly forming a ring of diamond-like shine around the Yokkaa. The thief has come to claim it. When the deed is done, the tooth will shine brightly from her pocket accompanied by the bling that holds to it.

She grows to her Red-Blooded size and smashes the Bugg that brough her here. She steps behind the guardian and places her palm on his head. The thief wears her own precious Yokkaa and her connection to it surpasses that of the guardian and his.

He tenses his gluttonous body and grips tightly to the loose clothing that falls from it. His eyes roll back into his skull and he bellows with pleasure, his mouth open and his toes curling inward.

The thief reaches one hand carefully into his mouth, still applying painful pressure with the other. She grasps tightly to his favorite tooth and rips it from his jaw. She tucks it away inside her pack and releases her torment from the guardian. He screams again, but this time without pleasure. His eyes grow angry and his back cracks again as he turns to chase her.

She dips her head and smiles at him grimly. She has won. She closes her eyes and with that, she disappears into a place that I cannot follow her. But the guardian, I can watch him. He digs through his riches and cries out with true pain as he has now lost that which gave him his distasteful satisfaction.

3

THE CITY OF STONE

"What is it?" I hear a voice say.

"It looks new." says another. "Look at its clothes."

"Is it dead?" replies a third voice.

I lie still, listening to the small voices from the shrubbery to the left of me.

"No, it's not dead, stupid!" the second voice says. My curiosity gets the best of me, and I turn my head to investigate. There are three small Sprites standing in the shadow. One of them tackles the other to the ground, and I giggle under my breath, as I watch the two of them wrestle under the bush.

"Guys," says the first Sprite trying to get the attention of the two young boys fighting behind her. She looks at me fearfully, and the other two stand upright to gawk, placing their problems aside for later.

"Should we run?" the shorter boy asks out of the corner of his mouth. I show them a kind smile and express means of peace, while I sit up and wring the water from my hair.

"Can you help me?" I ask politely. "Do you know somewhere I can get some shoes?" I hold up my leg and wiggle my toes to show them the ones that I had made for myself the few days prior. "These don't quite do the trick anymore," I say humorously.

"Go get father," replies the girl to the younger boys before they run off into the brush. "He will help you find new clothes."

"Thank you," I say. She stays at a distance waiting for the return of her brothers and watches me closely—she knows not to trust anyone. There is a snap of twigs, and the rustle of branches being pushed aside.

A new Sprite steps out into the clearing. He opens his wings, and flies to meet me at eye level. He is taller than the three before, but still only stands at about seven inches. He is much older, and has white hair, but still moves with the posture of a warrior. His clothes glisten in the sun. They have a blue-like color, but I cannot find a way to describe the magnificence.

"What are you?" he asks.

"Human," I say. His eyes widen, and he looks over his shoulder to his daughter, who then turns frantically to retreat.

"This is very exciting," he says turning back toward me. "We have never seen a Red Blood. The last Host of your kind was here almost two thousand years ago. It is lucky that this is happening again so soon."

"How did they compete?" I ask him.

"He won," he answers. I sit for a moment in disbelief. Is it really possible, I wonder? "And he did so without killing," he adds gracefully. I continue to sit silently feeling disgraced. Everything I thought I knew of this place was wrong.

"How do you know all of this?" I ask.

"It is written in our history," he replies.

I hold out my hand with my palm to the sky to give him a place to stand, so he would not have to hover. He is very light for his size, and his wings are shaped much like a Dragonfly's. I think to myself, "How cool would it be to see the world through their eyes—at their size? How fascinating this is."

"What, like tiny books?" I ask.

He laughs in reply. "Yes, and on our temple walls."

"Temples? Is there a tiny Sprite city hidden in the rocks?" I ask in amazement. He takes a step forward, and just before he can speak, I blink and find myself somehow closer to the ground. "The grass is bigger," I say to myself. Then I realize, "Oh, my God, I shrunk!" The older Sprite lands in front of me with a look of bewilderment.

"I did not know you could do that," he says.

"Neither did I," I reply before standing, and introducing myself properly. He holds my hand in his, and replies with his name, [15]Onaaviaa.

"There is one thing that I need to ask of you first," he says,

---

[15] [oh-NAH-vee-yuh]

"before I say anything else, I need to see that you truly are what you say you are."

It makes sense, he wants proof. "I understand." I say. He pulls a small knife and makes a continued cut. A fire is lit in his eyes, and the two young boys from before join their father to peer wondrously at the red colored blood of a true creature from Earth—one of the rarest beings in existence.

"Come," he says. "Let me show you [16]Vaahiigali." We turn our attention to the brush to find a small group of Sprites standing in awe. From all directions, more emerge from the bushes, and surround us—each hoping to get a look at my [17]blood. Onaaviaa gestures for me to follow him through the shrubs. As I walk, I admire the sky and the sanctuary.

"The world is so much more beautiful from down here," I say.

"You have not seen anything yet," replies the soldier to the left of me. My anticipation grows, as we enter a cave at the base of the massive stone that stands above. These Sprites are all very finely dressed, so I assume that their homes will be the same. We move deeper into the cave, and I can hear the sound of flowing water growing closer. It is loud, like a waterfall. The walls and ceiling fade from rock into a very marble-like stone with carvings that tell the story of The Great Game of Ten.

"How old is this city?" I ask.

"[18]Millions of years." says Onaaviaa. "Vaahiigali was born before IIpetrraah."

I look to the Sprite, not understanding who or what this mystery thing is. "What is IIpetrraah?"

---

[16] [vah-HEE-gah-lee]

[17] Host Detail—The Fae: these Hosts are capable of taking down large targets when they work together. Outside of the city walls they tend to travel in groups of at least two.

[18] City Detail—Vaahiigali: Built nearly 7 million years ago (9.3 billion years after Irestiikaar was taken into the Void by the Elite Gods). It began as a quarry for stoneworkers who used the white marble-like substance for artistry. Early Fae would carve statues, and small buildings from this because of its strength against time. The stone called, Errok [eh-ROCK], was used so widely that a large cavern had been created inside of the rock from years of artists chipping away. The Fae carved the city from the walls of the cavern, and constructed entrances, exits, gaps for natural sunlight, and sophisticated aqueduct systems to provide their city with clean and fresh water.

The leader and the others who follow him laugh at me, with kind intention, but none of them answer my question. Even the children look up at me and laugh. What a mystery.

We meet the daylight again, and as I step out into the sun; I am speechless. A secret utopia, hidden deep in the hillside, it is beautiful. What to me would normally have been a small stream is now a massive waterfall leaping over the tallest ledge in the cavern. The water splits to separate streams where the palace was carved from the stone behind it. It resembles stalagmites with its tall archways and twisted sky-scraping spires. At the base of the falls, the rest of the city follows The River Life until it disappears into the distance. There are Sprites riding strange creatures along the riverbed. They are very tall, and resemble Birds, but have no feathers. The cavern has an opening at the top that lets in just the right amount of light.

"[19]Cynniaa will show you to your room," he says referring to the soldier. "We have prepared new clothes for you."

"Thank you," I say in reply. He says goodbye with a very gentle bow and turns to do the same to Cynniaa.

"My King," says the guard returning his bow. I stand in awe, as his wings expand from behind him, and he flies off the cliff to hold sway over his magnificent Vaahiigali. I follow Cynniaa through the city, listening to stories of how it came to be.

"I have never seen a city so beautiful," I say. He tells me how this has been a safe haven for Sprites and many other species of small creatures for a long time. There are Sanctuary Cities hidden all over the planet. They are of all sizes and are home to more than half of the population.

He says, "But there will always be those who still fight. They still kill, no matter how many lives it takes, as long as they get a high status." He stops to look at me and follows, "The Game is not just killing—but knowing *who* to kill."

Before I can reply we are interrupted by another guard. As they converse, I am distracted by what lies beyond the gates where we had stopped at the base of the waterfall. The Keep is built with the same stone as the rest of the city but carved in much finer detail.

There are statues placed gracefully across the garden, and within a variety of small pools with tied pieces of driftwood forming little

---

[19] [sin-YUH]

bridges to connect the sections of dry land. The [20]statues are of all different species of creature, and again carved from the same white stone. I follow Cynniaa and the small group of soldiers along the path leading to the palace. I stop and notice a familiar figure carved into the distance. With my feet now bare, I step into the warm water and wade through the shallows to approach the statue. I stand knee deep, and stare. He wears a fine armor, much like the armor on the escorting soldiers. His hair is long, and half pinned in an almost edgy sort of fashion. But his face, I know his face.

"He is The Red Blood [21]Yesiwa," a voice says from behind me. I turn to see Cynniaa standing close by. He had removed his boots and pulled up his pant legs to follow me into the water.

"You mean Yeshua," I correct him. "It means rescuer; deliverer."

"You know your history." he replies.

"He is worshipped by my people, too," I tell him. I look back at the statue and stand for a moment in silence. I do not know how to feel about this discovery.

"Let us get you inside," he says. I nod and follow him returning to shore to replace his boots. Once we reach my room he bows, and recedes to wait outside, as I clean myself up and take a well needed shower.

The room is very large and formal. I am on one of the higher levels, and from my balcony, I can see the entire city. I find a dress that had been placed out on the bed. I notice the lack of sleeves and hope that they do not find fault in my decorated skin. I fear that, like many others, they may not see the beauty that I see. I admire my reflection, as the mirror helps me notice how sheer the fabric is. It is almost funny, I laugh lightly. The bold black, and the sporadic placements of light red color packed into my skin stand out fearlessly against the fine light pink of the dress. I admire the elegance of the look and stand with pride.

"Shit. I hope they're ready," I laugh to myself again, and turn

---

[20] Monument Detail—Stone Statues: carved and placed in the garden of the Keep, these statues stand for the pride of Vaahiigali. There are 23 tall statues— each one carrying the image of a prophesized hero. They hold steady in two separate pools which both have white, round, stone pebbles at their depths, and small creatures swimming through them.

[21] [yes-EE-wuh]

to the door. I step out with grace and find Cynniaa speaking with another small group of soldiers.

"Wow!" I hear one say.

"Is that the Red Blood?" another one asks.

"Not what I pictured," says the third, sounding disappointed. Cynniaa shushes them, and gestures for me to follow, as he paces down the hallway toward the Great Hall.

"Onaaviaa is planning a celebration for tonight," he says. "You are a mysterious part of our history. All of us grew up hearing stories of the Red-Blooded people from Earth. Everyone wants to meet you. It is a great honor to have you here. There has not been one of you here in two millennia. You will be added to our temple walls, and our books." Before I have time to reply, he enters a room to the right, pulling me in behind him.

"Whoa," I say after following behind. There are wing sets, and separate pieces hung along the walls. They are of all shapes, and shades, and sizes. There is an older Sprite seated on a stool in the corner at a desk. He has white hair, wears a brown vest-like top, and has a soft tailoring tape measure draped around his neck. He has a pair of round spectacles resting on the tip of his pointed nose, and he uses a fine white needle made from the same stone as the walls to stitch a piece of the wing that he is working on. It is amazing to watch. He finishes the stitch, and the white string fades away and the rip restores itself like magic. The tailor looks at me with excitement, and bows his head to me while introducing himself—

"I am [22]Hffh," he says.

I reply with my name, a smile, and a returned bow before I turn to look around. "Do you see any that you like?" he asks politely.

"I didn't know you made your wings," I say in reply. "I thought they grew naturally."

"They do." He laughs. "These are for those who lose them or suffer great injuries. A Sprite is not a Sprite if it cannot fly."

He turns and grabs a pair of darker-colored wings hanging from the second row on his left. They are a medium size and are shaped like Dragonfly wings—much like King Onaaviaas. Some of the other

---

[22] [h-ff]

58

shapes are [23]Butterfly and Moth, Mayflies, Grasshoppers and Crickets, Stick Insects, Mantis, Termites, Bees and Wasps, Ants, Beetles, and many more varieties that I am *u*nfamiliar with. There is also a section of pieces for replacement when a portion of a wing is lost.

"So, you're a wing doctor?" I ask.

"Yes! How about we try some on and see what you think?" he says. He places the base of the set against my back. "This will sting a bit." I hear a small click, and a handful of tiny needles puncture my skin and latch to my spine—pushing the clothing aside so that it is not sewn in between. I grunt in pain.

"I am sorry," he says. "They must connect to the nerves so that the brain can control them. They may be a little sore until you adjust." I look in the mirror, and see the wings now sprouted from the skin on my back. They look so real.

"How do they work?" I ask eagerly.

"Think 'up'." he says. I focus on the word, and they spread to an upright position.

"Cool!" I laugh. "I am not sure that I like this shape though." I tell him. We disconnect the old pair, and he wanders with me, as I look at all the different choices. I find a pair close to his desk with black borders, and clear cells that shine with iridescence under the light. They are wasp wings. The pain is uncomfortable again, and I stand for a moment waiting for it to subside. Again, I think, "up," and they expand out into the open air. This look is much better. They are lighter in weight but bigger in size. I tell Hffh that this is the pair that I choose, and he wishes me good luck making a note in his small white notebook. He reminds me to close the wings before exiting, and I say, "thank you," and recede back out into the hallway to find Cynniaa standing guard.

"Let's see them," he says. I open them again, and he smiles with approval. "Follow me." He escorts me to the palaces upper [24]gardens to show me how to fly.

---

[23] A Note from the Prophet—Names: I chose the capitalize every Host's name because I feel that each must be shown to be important. Just like how you capitalize your name when you sign it, the word Human—and the names of every other species of Host—will be given the respect that belongs to it.

[24] City Detail—Gardens: the city is decorated with fantastical greens. The Fae are exceptional botanists, and sprout a wide variety of vines, flowers, and trees using

"It is simple," he says, "wings out, think 'fly!'"

I open my wings and focus again on the word. I look down to see my feet hovered above the grass, but quickly land because of the pain in my spine.

"It will get better. Try again."

I do it again and am amazed at how fast I catch on. The wings move quickly through the air but produce no sound. I smile at him, as he spreads his wings to join me, and we fly to the top of the cavern. The scenery is breathtaking—I can draw living creatures well but when it comes to landscapes or buildings, I fail to create the right details, so please excuse my lack of refinement when it comes to showing some of these places in my drawings. I will try to make up for it in written descriptions.

"Let's test your speed," he says. "I will race you to that corner of the river." He points to a break in the stream that leads to a round building in the middle of a small pond.

I take an unapproved head start and disappear into the trees. I swerve through the forest at an incredible speed and lose my heading when I am halted by one of the creatures I saw earlier by the riverbed. It is massive and grey. It has two long legs and a thin beak. I watch it walk away and draw my attention back to the race. I have to fly above the tree line to find my destination. I see Cynniaa nearing the building and decide to accept the loss. This way, I can see the city. The Sprites watch as I fly above, and some join me in my venture toward the pond. They follow close behind in wonder, but do not speak.

There are small white [25]Fish that sparkle like starlight in the transparent turquoise water. The building has a pathway that circles around it, and pillars holding tall glass windows. It is a studio.

"It's a dance studio?" I ask.

"Yes," replies Cynniaa.

"Oh no," I say back laughing at myself again.

---

only pebbles, water, and small thriving ecosystems.

[25] Host Detail—Wildlife: a majority of the animals are marine type and are accompanied by a small variety of flightless Birds. There are many types of Fish, Frogs, Lizards, water Bugs, Crustaceans, Turtles, Octopus', tiny Sharks, Starfish, Corals, and Jellyfish—apparently, Earth's oceans are more connected with the outside world than the surface. Though, there is no fight for survival here for them, they are just here, thriving—existing. Some of these creatures are of good size compared to the Fae.

"[26]Vinneh is an excellent teacher," he says. He shows me inside and introduces us. We greet with bows, and Cynniaa returns to the pathway outside to dismiss the growing audience.

"This dance is simple," says Vinneh. "I will teach you the movements on the floor, then we will try in the air." She takes point and guides me through the motions without music.

"You will be asked to dance with the King and the Queen, but that will only be done for tradition. You will not have to do it again after that if you choose not to," she says followed by a small laugh.

"The King *and* the Queen," I ask.

"Well, yes," she replies. "They are both equal and will always be treated so."

"I respect that," I tell her. She opens her wings, and asks that I do the same, as we take flight. We repeat the same movements as before, and again twice before she turns to call for Cynniaa. She instructs us to run through the routine together so she can observe my steps; again, once on the ground and once in the air. Cynniaa stands eye-level to me and has red hair—not orange like a ginger, but crimson red like our blood, and his eyebrows are just a little darker. He has a big smile, and straight white teeth. His eyes are sunken in and green, but they beam with a hint of gold in the right light.

He says, "The King will be very pleased," and we take flight. "After this, we will have a stoneworker carve your likeness for the garden before we leave here, and after that we will get you some armor. There is something he wants me to show you."

We finish the dance, and Vinneh excuses us with her approval. I bow to her, say goodbye. I am instructed to take a seat, and the stoneworker sits in a chair across from me and carves a small handheld statue for reference. He finishes his assignment in less than 15 minutes and bows to thank me before returning to the stoneworker's region to begin his work on the real piece.

I return his bow and proceed to follow Cynniaa to the armory.

"Why do I need armor?" I ask him.

"Onaaviaa requested to have it made for you to keep you safe during your travels," he explains in reply. "But you will need it today,

---

[26] [vin-EH]

because he also requested that I take you to see The Keeper." He pauses. "His name is [27]Boriisst. He watches the score board."

"The score board," I repeat after him. "Why do you seem afraid?" I ask him these questions, as the armorer requests for me to remove my dress in order to help me replace it with a white, plated, suit—this is the armor that they are lending to me until my personal fit is ready. As I change, Cynniaa points out a grouping of [28]scars on my torso—my wounds heal quickly, but I am always left with a reminder of them.

"That bite mark," he says. "You got it from the black creature in the Dead Caves. Boriisst calls it the [29]Queel."

"What is it?" I ask him, as I stand with my arms spread while the armorer adjusts the thin material into the right placements.

"No one knows. We cannot speak to it," Cynniaa replies.

"It is the only one of its kind in our history," says the armorer. "The Game has never seen anything like it." We finish the fitting, as they continue going back and forth explaining how Boriisst is very dangerous, but for safety and access to the score board, they tell him he is a friend of the Fae while keeping him in the dark about certain things. Cynniaa says that he will help me learn more about the Game, and how it is played, which is why Onaaviaa wants me to meet him.

We thank the armorer, and head back to the palace to return the dress before ascending to the top of the falls and venturing through the small doorway in the rock to the vast ruined city outside, leaving behind the safety of the hidden cavern. We journey back to the crumbling building by the spring and make our way to the top.

"There is a bounty on the Red Blood, so during this visit, you are Fae," Cynniaa tells me quietly as we approach a small ledge with a guard much resembling Fuckface—it is the same species, but this one is older and has facial hair. We land just inside the window and stand silently waiting for instruction. The room is dark once they close the door-like shudders of the window preventing escape. There are

---

[27] [BOE-rist]

[28] Host Detail—Scars: when the skin regenerates after an injury, the Human is left with a faint scar. The worse the injury is, the darker the scar is left. So far, there is a palm sized bite mark on the left side of the torso, multiple scars along the torso and the arms from stab wounds, marks on the head from trauma, and a small scar on the bridge of the nose. Her skin also regenerates *without* the tattoo ink that was previously there.

[29] [k-ee-l]

candles lit in various places, and red and black tapestries hanging along every wall and along the ceiling. There is a long gold table with filigree carved in fine design to make the legs and the lip. There is a tall chair, also gold, with a red cloth draped across. This guy really lives in luxury. It is a big room—considering how small I am.

Let me further explain that the ceilings are probably 15 feet high, and the room around 630 square feet. There are other tables of the same nature as the big one scattered along the walls with stacked books, and layered papers. Some also have trinkets, and pots, and strange little figures. This must be his study. This city keeps delivering many surprises.

The double doors to the left open from the other side revealing two Human-sized Hosts dressed as guards followed by a tall man who almost resembles Barroun.

He is in a nice suit. The jacket and pants are red, and the undershirt, tie, and vest are black. He has golden charms along his collar and his shoes shine with gold too. His hair is slicked back, and dark in color. He has sweet eyes, but I can sense his malevolence through his stare. He smiles with a golden grill hugging the top six teeth in the front and has gold rings on every finger but one. In one hand, he carries a small black book and a pencil with a folded piece of paper. And in the other, I stand angered, as I notice a familiar golden dagger, one that I had lost just days before. It is too big now for me to carry, but somehow, I will retrieve it. I feel drawn to it.

"Boriisst," says Cynniaa while bowing to the tall man. I follow his action but remain angered by the theft.

"Cynniaa, I always cherish these magical visits from the Fae," the Keeper replies. He invites us to join him at the table, as he sits upon his throne. He places the book to his right, and the dagger to his left. We sit in small chairs, and drink from small glasses. It is disgusting, but I sip and pretend to swallow to be respectful. Thank God the glasses are not clear. I have never been much of a drinker and I am going to guess that if I put liquid in my body, I will have to pee it out at some point—no thank you, not here. The Keeper sits with us, and drinks as he puffs a big cigar, and speaks of the Human and his fascination with its blood. He points out that he loves the color red—as if I had not already picked up on it. I glance again at the book, but this time, I notice the [30]title. It reads, [31]"*The Game of Ten, The Red Blood.*"

It is a copy of this book—the one that you read now. I somehow know that this endangers me—I have a feeling in my gut, but I am unaware of its context. I do not know what is going to happen. Though, I know that it holds sensitive information. Perhaps the best way for me to describe it would be to say that it must have been written by some third-party member, who has observed this story from a distance, or maybe it is me from the future—after I return home. Or possibly, it could be me from another dimension or alternate Universe. How curious?

"He knows who I am," I whisper under my breath to Cynniaa while Boriisst speaks with a guard close by. "We need to get that book," I whisper again. I watch to the left after seeing a ripple in one of the tapestries. The Queel appears from a hole behind the fabric and sits with grace next to the Keeper. The wound that I gave it on its leg has fully healed. I quickly realize how things may go sour and prepare myself for means of escape.

"It is you," I hear a Voice say. I look around slightly in confusion. Am I the only one who heard it?

"Who are you?" I wonder back in question.

"We are [32]Tziipoor, but the Keeper calls us [33]Queel. You can hear us?" she asks in a slow voice.

"Yes. Am I the only one, and how?" I ask in reply looking at her.

"One must be worthy to speak with us," she tells me.

---

[30] Note from the Prophet—Knowledge: the protagonist of this story. The Human Host is not always aware of the Footnote content. Some of the Details are given to the Reader exclusively. Even I do not know it all, I learn as I write—I cannot define everything, nor can I answer every question.

[31] Relic Detail—"*The Game of Ten, The Red Blood.*": this story is written sometime after the events of its contents. The concept of time travel is widely known, but still very misunderstood. There are only a few who are able to utilize time travel effectively and efficiently, but they still exist, so I cannot deny the use of it here. I must also note that time travel is fucking messy; you *cannot* afford mistakes.

[32] [t-zip-OOR]

[33] A Note from the Prophet—Font Changes: this will be used to express the importance of a being. When a Hosts words are shown in a font other than the rest of the writing the Reader will know the grandness of the speaker—this is a creature that resides among the highest and holiest of all things, or among the darkest and most devious, this can also foretell great evil, beware.

"Us?" I think.

"We are one. There were many bodies that carried us, but we are one mind. We are the last of our kind,"—her explanation is interrupted by the rude nature of the Keeper. He holds the dagger in front of him and asks if it is familiar.

"That is [34]Reewenniveaar," replies Cynniaa. "It was gifted to the Red Blood Yesiwa, by the Great God of Hevaan."

I knew I felt connected to it for some reason.

"This [35]dagger was left in the Dead Caves by the Red Blood of this [36]decade," replies the Keeper. "She was here, just under my feet. But the Queel let her escape," he follows angrily looking at Tziipoor. He continues again looking back toward Cynniaa and me, "I trust that the Fae would inform me if they caught sight of the creature."

"He has not yet read the bound paper," says the Voice inside my head again. *"He does not know what you are. But we do."*

"What do I have to do to ensure that you keep my secret?" I ask her.

"We want to be free from him," she says. *"Kill the Keeper, and we will be bound to you. He is vile, and his commands are unjust. He is not worthy of our obedience. He has the girl, the one who helped free you. If you hurry, she may yet live."* she hisses, and then returns to her hole in the wall.

"Of course," replies Cynniaa to Boriisst.

"There is an attack on the building," says a guard, as he enters the room, and quickly closes the door behind them. "It is the Pegg."

"Let them enter," answers the Keeper. The guard opens the door again, as a group of angry Goblin-looking creatures flood the

---

[34] [ree-WEN-eh-veer]

[35] Relic Detail—Reewenniveaar: the golden dagger. When the Great God told Yeshua of his role to play in the Great Game of Ten, he promised to protect him. He crafted a dagger from Hevaanian gold. This gold is the strongest in our Universe and can withstand hits from any opposing strength without trouble. The dagger is decorated with three symbols. One of which the Human can already identify as the sigil meaning "deliver", and the other two which she has yet to learn. The blade is double sided, and exceptionally sharp and the pommel has a pointed tip for reversed use as well.

[36] Host Detail—Creatures of Earth: Other red-blooded creatures from the planet Earth have been exposed to the Games environment, but Humans are a rarity. The blood type—red— is hard to regenerate, so it is unlikely to see any red-blooded descendants on Irestiikaar.

room. "Must you always trash the place," he asks in annoyance. He approaches the wall and pulls back a tapestry covering a giant holographic computer similar to the ones on the Adreestiaah.

The Pegg chatter back and forth with tongue clicks and snorts, while they wait to see their place on the board. The room goes silent, and all look with patience, as the screen lists names and numbers faster than I can read them. It stops with the number 1,855,098,421. I look to the top, and I see a name typed in small letters. It is my name. It is not yet worth much, but it is above the Pegg, so I have that going for me.

I sit with comfort but am quickly distracted by the growing chatter of angry Pegg. They become hostile and begin to break things and throw tantrums. The room is booming with chaos, and I notice my chance to grab the book, and make for the tunnel to escape. I can come back for the dagger. I step forward, but I am stopped by Cynniaa.

"What are you doing," he asks. "If we betray his trust, he will kill us all."

Before I have time to reply, I am knocked to the ground by a flying object. It slams my head so hard my vision goes black. I have an instant headache. An image begins to appear; it is fast, but focused. There is a picture of my palm, and Onaaviaa stepping forward.

I have another flash-memory of a different part of the past, but this one I do not remember being a part of. It is me. I am in a laboratory. I am injecting a silver serum into the palm of my hand—like the one used by the Gods to put us to sleep, but the one I inject is for a different purpose. I am adding something to my anatomy. The injection site became the pressure point. If I push lightly in that spot and think clearly of what I want I can change sizes. There are many creatures here, and we all differ in height and weight. I—somehow—gave myself the ability to match my opponent.

The images fade away, and I open my eyes to a fight progressed further than that of when I had left it. Cynniaa is crouched next to me and smiles with relief that I came to.

"Now would be the time, Human," says Tziipoor who had returned to fight while I was distracted by memories. There is that word again, Human, not Red Blood. I nod my head to her, and turn back to Cynniaa—

"You need to either leave or hide. I will cover for your people, but you cannot be seen. You can get out through the Dead Caves. The black creature is here. Go, I will be behind you soon enough." He sits for a moment thinking of something to say in reply. "I will be okay," I assure him. "Go!"

He spreads his wings, and escapes through the tunnel. I return my attention to the Keeper who is busy slaying Pegg across the room. The red tapestries are stained with dark green. I guess *now would be the time*; I place a finger on the puncture point on my palm and think, "Human." I open my eyes, and catch myself knocking things over, then remove myself from on top of the desk. I grew back to normal size, wings and armor, too. I frantically check the folded paper and pages of the book, as I look up and down making sure the Keeper is still occupied.

The paper lists that he had only made it a little way into the beginning of [37]chapter one. I use a match to light fire to the novel and place it in a golden bowl to properly burn. I reach to grab Reewenniveaar. Tziipoor chases a small group of Pegg into the tunnel behind the fabric, and I stand facing the Keeper, as he and his guards finish off the remaining Goblins.

The few guards who resembled Fuckface have all grown to match his taller form, but these guys are smaller than he is, they must be a different species.

There are bodies piled all around, and puddles of blood drowning the floor. He pulls a handkerchief from his pocket and cleans the foreign black-green liquid from his face. He faces me and smiles, but his emotion quickly changes to rage once he notices my change in size, and the dried red blood that had run down my face when I was hit. He raises his arm, and points at me, as he steps over the bodies below—

"Red Blood," he pauses. "That is *my* dagger." He laughs at himself, holding his hand out instructing his guards not to interfere, and then he speaks again, "I invite you into my home. I gave you my finest drinks. I offer you my assistance," his voice grows louder, and he continues to step closer. He notices the growing flames from the bowl behind me. "I was kind to you; yet you burn my research, and steal from my home? And you *lie* to me?" He holds steady to his blade

---

[37] Relic Detail— *"The Game of Ten, The Red Blood."*: the writings of this book contain many dangerous secrets. The decipherer could use this to interrupt game play with unwanted affairs, or to severally damage the outcomes of the Humans efforts, and for this reason it must be promptly destroyed.

and threatens with much hostility. "Did you not see what happened to the last Hosts that betrayed my generosity? I will kill you for your blood, and then I will deliver it myself to the ones who seek it."

I prepare a reply, but I am interrupted by a hiss, as the Queel returns from her cave. *"The ones who seek it are close by, you must hurry and make your choice."* I hear her say, as she stands at his side facing me.

"Why should I trust you?" I think in question looking at her. The Keeper catches on to our conversation saying—

"You can hear it?" his aggravation grows, "You traitorous creature!" He turns toward Tziipoor, and lunges at her with his blade. She dodges his attack, and tears through the bodies retreating behind the golden desk to protect herself.

"We cannot kill him; we are bonded," she tells me. *"You must fight. Take his blood and run it across your forehead then stab his heart. It is destiny you met that dagger here. The gold is his weakness. Take his life with it."*

I stand for a moment wondering if this Queel creature is a Demon, or a Deity. Is this noble advice, or am I choosing a more sinister path? Boriisst stands across from me, as we calculate our steps toward each other over the countless bodies beginning to rot away on the floor. He swings, but I step out of the way and punch him in the face. While he is distracted, I run the dagger through the meat of his lower thigh just above the back of his knee. The blade is sunk all the way to the guard and protrudes a great distance from the other side of his leg. I withdraw and try to step away, but he is quick to get me back reaching with his long arm and stabbing me in the back of my shoulder in the same fashion. I look to see the point of his blade sticking out from my arm. I grunt in pain and elbow him in the back of his head. He falls to the ground, and I give him no time to recover. I spread my wings and grab his ankles to lift him to the ceiling, and then I drop him on his head.

I turn to face the guards, still standing back as ordered. There is fear in losing their leader, but dead or not, there is even more fear in disobeying him. They see that he has been defeated and they flee from the wrath of the Red Blood that they seem to fear even more.

"The blood," I hear Tziipoor say.

"I got it," I reply. I return to his fallen body and dip my thumb in his wound. He groans and moves his leg but cannot fight back.

"In a line, from the top of your head, to just in between your eyes," the creature

says. I spread the blood on my forehead and look back down to see him regaining consciousness. I grab the collar of his shirt, and twist lifting the top of his torso from the ground. For the sake of one last, "Fuck you," he stabs me again, this time through the side of my right foot. I ignore the pain, and spit in his face—

"Your drinks tasted like shit, and I really didn't enjoy your company," I punch him in the face again breaking his nose. I move behind him, as Tziipoor approaches. I am crouched, holding up his body, I speak understandably clear in his ear, "What did you make her do?"

She hisses stepping slowly closer. He stutters. I place the tip of my blade in the center of his back, and dig just deep enough to inflict pain, but not enough yet to be fatal.

"I made her a monster," he says frantically. "She was peaceful when she came to me. I made her a killer."

"Now," she hisses, *"take his life."*

I push the blade the rest of the way through and withdraw it. She shoves the body aside and makes a small cut on my arm. She takes my blood and makes a diagonal line between her eyes to the top of her head. She places a hand on each side of my face, holds firmly opening her eyes as wide as she can, and pulls my face close to hers.

I am mesmerized by her eyes—almost hypnotized. My body goes limp—do you remember in the prologue when I said that sometimes I see myself as if I were a player in a video game? This is one of those times. I see both of our heads fall back, as we look to the sky. Our bodies stay upright. Our eyes are clouded white, and I can see her past. I see a colony of these creatures. I can hear them think. There are so many of them. All from different bodies, but they share a common mind, like an astral projected brain controlling the entire Clutch. I can see them living peacefully, as I skip through time. The vision shows Tziipoor transported by the Adreestiaah and left to the heinousness of the Great Game of Ten.

I am her third bond, but the first who is able to speak with her. I see her planet invaded by pests, and left dry, and arid, leaving the colony to starvation. Tziipoor is truly the last of her kind. The images disappear, and I fall to the ground.

I wake, returned to the spring, lying in the grass surrounded by Fae and the Queel. I laugh in relief knowing that I am in a safe space. I check to find the dagger and see that it had been retrieved by Tziipoor. I am flooded with concern at the memory of a secret prisoner of the Keeper.

"She escaped with the [38]*Felerrg,"* I am told by the Queel. *"She is safe for now."*

I place a hand on Tziipoor, and a finger on the pressure point on my hand and think "Fae." We shrink again to the size of the Sprites, and they rush in quickly to help.

"How did you do this?" asks the Queel.

"Magic," I reply cleverly holding up my hands and moving my fingers like a magician. I regain my strength, and sit up, as Cynniaa breaks through the crowd, and meets me with a hug.

"I thought we had lost you!" he says joyfully.

"I told you I would be okay," I laugh in reply. "I grabbed something for the King." I reach into my pocket and retrieve a small [39]Device. "This will give you access to the score board. I stole it just after you left. Nobody saw a thing."

"*You* give it to him," he says, "*You* deserve the praise, not me." I smile and hug him again asking him to help me up. I cannot yet walk.

"Your body is healing from the bond. You will walk again. But give yourself time; it is a draining process on all bodies." says Tziipoor. *"You will heal."*

Cynniaa places me on her back, and holds steady beside me, as she carries me into the city. We are greeted at the entrance by Onaaviaa and his Queen [40]Ovinniaa. The Fae line the road watching in amazement at the Human riding atop the black creature of the Dead Caves. I hear them whisper heard tale of me taming the beast. We are led to the Great Hall to discuss the accomplishments of our venture. I am seated gently in a chair at the long table joined by the King and Queen, Cynniaa, Tziipoor at my side, and a handful of others who I presume hold status on the high council. Hffh enters the room and removes the wings from my back.

"There is a tear. I will fix them and bring them back," says the

---

[38] Host Detail—the Felerrg [FELL-egg]: or Frog People/Person. The Host that she calls "Fuckface" is of this species, along with some of the guards who accompany the Keeper.

[39] Gameplay Detail—The Score Board: this luxury is hard to come by. There is a low number of other Keepers spread across the planet that dispense scores for currency/coin, or for easy points—hence the reason as to why Boriisst slaughtered the Pegg. Keepers are like the Drug Lords of this even more so violent trade.

[40] [oh-VIN-yuh]

polite old man. I smile and nod my head to thank him before he turns to retreat to his workshop.

I am left with the angered council of Vaahiigali.

"You killed the Keeper," says a fat one from across the table and three seats down to my left.

"She returned with a gift," interrupts Cynniaa in my defense, nudging me to present the Device. I place it on the table, and gently slide it across to Onaaviaa.

"This will give you full access to the score board," I tell them. "No need to worry over what was not lost," I look around at the rest of the council and assure genuine intention.

They stare at Tziipoor with fear. "The Queel was a slave, a captor, and a victim. I set her free. She is no longer bound to that evil," I explain.

"Are you strong enough for a celebration?" asks Onaaviaa hopefully. "The people expect to see you."

"I will be," I reply with confidence. The table is then dismissed, and I am asked to join the King and Queen on a small detour back to my room before I rest. I accept the invitation, and slowly proceed, as my body allows me to walk again. Tziipoor supports me from the side, and Cynniaa is asked to wait for us outside the door of my room.

Onaaviaa carries a large candle and chants a quiet spell—in a language different from the one that Barroun used—as it orbs and carries itself above us through a narrow passage of white stone. I can spread my arms and touch each side, but the ceiling goes up farther than I can see in the dark. We stop suddenly, and each Fae loop an arm beneath mine, and hoist me into the air. I can see [41]carvings in the stone changing from different styles by different artists, as we ascend into the past. We stop at a section about two minutes up. It is the Human, Yeshua. He sits in the grass by the spring surrounded by Fae.

"He was kind, here during the reign of my grandfather. He was marked by strange scars on his hands, and had an incredible ability

---

[41] Monument Detail—The Hall of History: every war, every disaster, every miracle, and every hero are etched into the stone of this corridor. The tales date all the way back to the beginning of the city. This area of the Keep was one of the first things constructed at this site. In its early years, before the construction of the rest of the Keep, this was sacred ground—accessible to all Fae.

to grant miracles," explains Ovinniaa before Onaaviaa continues the story—

"We hear he was killed on Earth and woke up here. He spent ten years helping the wounded and protecting those who needed it. When he returned, ten years here, only equaled…"

"Three days on Earth," I interrupt.

"Yes," he says proudly.

"He is worshipped in some parts of my planet, too. But many know him as Jesus. Yeshua is a lesser-known name for him. He was crucified," I continue, "He was hung on a cross with nails through his hands and feet. He hung in a line of three. Beside him hung also Dismas and Gestas, the thieves; one who repented, and the other who did not. He was sacrificed for the sins of Humanity."

"Then you understand his purpose," says the Queen, "Your path is different, but you still fight for what is good. Remember that, if you choose to leave, there will be many hard choices ahead of you." They descend, and gently place me back on the ground.

"We will send for you before the celebration," says Onaaviaa, "There is someone I want you to meet. I trust that you can find your way?" he asks.

I nod, "Yes," and bow to the both of them, as we part ways at the end of the tunnel. Tziipoor follows next to me, and we receive many strange glances from the passing Sprites.

"Who is he so excited for me to meet?" I wonder.

"The Queen's father," replies the Queel. I glance at her in question—

"How do you know?"

"We hear all thoughts," she replies in a slower tone than usual. She has a very proper voice and seems highly well educated. *"He has a message for you from the Human who walked here before."* I am greeted with a smile from Cynniaa after turning the corner to find my room.

"I saw everything before I left to get help," he says, "You are a good fighter." He pauses, and looks away for a moment before saying, "I have enjoyed your company; will you choose to stay?"

I take a second before replying that I do not know. I tell him that there are many reasons for me to stay, but there are even more reasons for me to go. This is just the beginning of the story. I bow, and almost cry when he returns with a formal bow and faces away from me with no reply.

"He has hope that you will stay," says Tziipoor. I drop my head and enter the room closing the door gently behind her after she follows.

"I am really going to hurt him, aren't I?" I ask her.

She nods her head yes, and I strip the blood-stained armor from my body. I proceed to the shower and wash away the remains of the fight from before. After, I use the white stone comb to calm my hair. I lay to rest; a few hours should do. I dream of the stone carvings in the tall passage. They point to a room, hidden in plain sight. I wonder of its contents. I approach the door, but I am awake before I can open it. What secrets does it hold?

I wake in the dark, as day has become night. I have a few hours until I need to prepare for the celebration. I have time to search for the room. I cover my sleep clothes with a sheer robe and step quietly to the door.

"The soldier stands guard," says Tziipoor.

"We will tell him we are going to wander and will be back soon," I reply. "Come."

She follows me out the door and waits patiently, as I explain to Cynniaa fake means of endearment. I tell him that we will return in good time. He bows, and excuses himself before turning and joining a group of guards down the hall. I watch for a moment and then turn away to search for the Hidden Room.

There is a door next to a carving of the city. I remember passing the artwork near the Great Hall. This may be easier than I thought, but I must be quick. There are Sprites everywhere setting up and getting ready for the coming celebration—which I should probably add will be *in* the Great Hall. If I am quick, perhaps I can remain unseen. I finally reach the carving and stare. I droop my head, and look at the floor, as a group of soldiers pass by whispering amongst themselves, excited about their first sighting of the Red Blood, and then they disappear again around the corner.

"Where is the door?" asks Tziipoor.

"There must be a button somewhere," I think, running my hand slowly along the wall feeling for a crack or an indent—or perhaps something that moves.

"Or maybe a small hole that you could shrink small enough to walk through?" she adds. I look over to her and see that she has found a small opening in the wall. Carved in disguise, as one of the doorways of a small house in the bottom corner of the carving, it is the size of

my pinky fingernail—let me remind you that at the moment I stand about six inches tall. I place my hand on her back and check our surroundings for any Fae.

"There is someone close by," she says, *"be quick."* We shrink, and run for the doorway, as a Sprite turns the corner and pauses. It is a bit of a climb, but we manage. I take a last look at the Sprite standing above and I notice that it is Cynniaa standing alone in the dark with a single candle.

"He is looking for us," I say to her.

"Yes," she replies, *"we will not be long. The passage is short with an open room at the end."* I turn to face the same direction as her, but I cannot see—

"It's too dark."

"We will guide you." She nudges my hand with her shoulder to help me find her, and I walk blindly through the tunnel of darkness. *"You are the first to hear us since the hidden ship stole us from our home,"* she says, *"It is not chance that we are bonded."* I listen quietly as she speaks. *"Your Gods gave you great power to find within yourself,"* she stops walking, *"but you, you gave yourself even greater power."*

"What do you mean?" I ask her. "How do you know?"

"You have to remember; I can sense forgotten knowledge in your thoughts."

I cannot think of a reply. She encourages me to follow her again stepping down into a chest-deep body of water.

"Thanks for the warning," I tell her sarcastically.

"You wanted light," she moves her tail through the water, and as my eyes adjust, I can see the glow of white bioluminescent algae. She wades through the water, and the ripples encourage more light. The glow climbs the walls and the ceiling to faintly illuminate the [42]area. *"There,"* she says looking to the left. I follow her eye line, and find a white pillar rising out of the water like some kind of pedestal.

"There had to have been something on it," I say as, I move toward it. The algae beneath my feet lights my path. There is a rock; it stands slightly taller than the rest. It holds its place firmly, as I trip and manage to say, "Fuck," before finding myself submerged under water. I quickly recover and hear Tziipoor laughing, as I notice a small box at the bottom of the pedestal. I dive to retrieve it and return to place it on

---

[42] Monument Detail—the Hidden Room of Vaahiigali: built by Hevaanian Gods 200 years after the victory of Yeshua, and his return to the planet Earth.

the altar. I clear the water from my eyes and wring my hair. Tziipoor watches as I break away a millennium worth of sediment to find that here is no lock. I open the box, surprised by the dry trinket inside.

"It is a key," she says looking over my shoulder.

It is made of the same light gold as Reewenniveaar and marked with the same three symbols.

"A [43]Hevaanian key," I say out loud while turning to match eyes with the Queel.

"That is an Entanglement Key," she thinks in reply. *"It will present you with a task to complete. Your Gods placed the key here to lead you on a better path. The quests you will find with them will be of more value on the score board,"* she pauses for a moment, and cocks her head to the side, *"and you can win without competing in the Trials."*

"Are you an Oracle?" I ask her.

"That is all you obtained from that?" She sounds concerned, and I assure her that I did not miss a thing. I return to the tunnel and climb out of the pool to remove my clothes to dry them as much as possible before heading back to my room.

"You never answered my question," I say.

"We are now confined to one body, but we have eyes that see everywhere. We are one with the Universe; she gifted us with her divine sight and her almighty senses."

"Brutal," I reply with compliment. She rolls her eyes, and the final light from the algae disappears. I hold her shoulder and follow her lead again. I tuck the key into my pocket and continue conversation about her heritage. We reach the opening at the end of the tunnel, and I suggest that we stay smaller to avoid detection. Hopefully, we can move without tracking too much water through the halls.

I climb onto Tziipoors back, and ride silently. Her skin naturally sticks to mine with some sort of adhesive pheromone released by my weight. Her shoulders have an extra bone on each side that sticks out toward her neck to form handles for her rider—these bones are

---

[43] Relic Detail—Hevaanian Key: created for the protection of the next Human Host after Yeshua. Made of the same Hevaanian Gold as the dagger, and with the same symbols, but they are placed in a different order. The symbol meaning "deliver" is located on the bit, and the other two take their places along the bow. There is a tiny platform protruding from the bow to enable the user to apply pressure to turn the thin, otherwise grip-less, key. There are a few notches on the key from use as it has been found and used before, and then returned by the Gods in hopes that it will find its intended user.

retractable too. She says that each Queel is given a choice; they can choose to accept the ability to bond, which would equip their bodies for war, or they can choose to stay free of this part of their evolution and flourish in a sanctuary with their own.

"We chose to bond against our will just before we were taken," she says. *"We have been alive for a long time, but like you, we are still young and have much to learn."*

"But if you are connected with the Universe and can see all, how can there be anything left to learn?" I ask her.

"We are one mind, but when we are embodied, there is a new mind added to us born from the body; it is the one that inhabits it," she replies. *"Just like the body, the young mind must also mature in time. Many things that it sees, it is seeing for the first time. But we guide it. This body is Tziipoor."*

"How do I know when I am speaking to her, and when I am speaking to you?" I reply.

"We and she are the same," explains the Queel. *"Always, you speak to her and us."*

"I'm confused," I say, as I pinch the bridge of my nose to soothe the oncoming think-headache. We finally reach the corner leading to the room, and I dismount to crouch behind the wall, and peer around the corner. Cynniaa is gone, probably out looking for us. We run for the door and slide under to the other side. I return us to Fae size and place the key on the desk next to Reewenniveaar. I remove my clothes to shower—again—and return to choose from the four gowns left hanging by the window.

The glass is thin and bent with a very elegant curvature to match the round room. On the inside, I can see out, but on the outside, the glass mocks the waterfall next to it, so it looks like the water is running through the roof and again through the floor. The picture is 3D; it looks so real. The water seems to splash through the air, and when I touch it, it feels real, but my hand is not wet. The balcony stretches the full width of the room, but there is no outdoor seating area.

Back to the inside, the room is lit only by natural light during the day and candles at night. The white color of the walls, floors, and tall ceiling reflect the light so beautifully, that I feel like I am in the

Biblical Heaven. The carvings in the stone resemble [44]filigree, but it differs from the kind you are familiar with on Earth.

I turn back to the rack of dresses. One is sky blue, another is light pink, the third is white with long sleeves, and the last one is black. I am drawn to the black one, but the white one will have better coverage. I decide to try on both of them to help me decide. I put on the black one first. Tziipoor watches from a distance while I turn side to side looking at myself in the mirror. There is a silver collar that covers the height of my neck. From this, the fabric falls gently to the floor. It is attached at the center on the front, and droops far under each armpit exposing side boob, and much of my torso and back. It connects again at the base of the collar between my shoulder blades.

There is a silver belt that holds the fabric in place—making sure it covers the parts that are meant to be unseen. I turn to Tziipoor for her opinion.

She tells me to try on the white dress because it is more elegant. I agree and change quickly. This gown is also floor length but is the complete opposite of form fitting. My neck and shoulders are exposed; this is an off-the-shoulder dress. The pattern hugs my biceps and chest with thick golden design. The length of this piece of fabric is about six inches from my collarbone to the bottom of my chest. There is filigree along the top that matches the carvings on the walls. This section is the most detailed.

The rest of the dress is a sheer white fabric that has been layered enough times to cover the black ink that lies underneath. The sleeves poof with a thinner layer of sheer fabric, and then forms tightly again around my wrists, cuffed by the same pattern as the gold one along the top.

"That is the one," says Tziipoor.

"Yes," I reply. "This is definitely the one." I spin like a princess and return to the mirror to fix my hair. I wad the bottom bit into a ball and smash it against the back of my head adding a few pins here and there to hold it into place. I pull out a few loose sections of hair to complete the messy look. I hear a knock on the door and a voice from the other side telling me that it is almost time to meet with the King and the

---

[44] Relic Detail—Vaahiigali Filigree: holds the same basic design of the kind seen on Earth, but it is based from a different plant. This is the royal plant of Vaahiigali called, Sevvia [seh-via].

Queen before the celebration begins. I turn away from the mirror and face Tziipoor hoping for a look of approval.

"You look refined," she assures me.

"I feel like I'm missing something," I tell her.

"It will find you," she replies confidently. I take another look at myself in the mirror and decide that this is the best I can give them. I approach the door and open it to find a group of soldiers talking outside. They all pause and watch, as Cynniaa offers his arm in silence to escort me to the Queen's room. I accept gracefully and walk along side of him wondering if he is going to speak.

"He does not know what to say," Tziipoor explains. *"He is afraid to let himself attach to you because he knows that you are going to leave. He is distancing himself for protection."*

I swallow the bulge in my throat—you know, that feeling you get just before you cry when your neck feels full, and your chin starts to do that shake of sadness?

"I don't want you to be sad," I tell him. "I want us to have fun tonight." I stop him and turn to face him. "Look at me," I plead. He smiles with a happy shine in his eyes and looks back at me.

"I just know how much I am going to miss you. I am honored to have made such a good friend." He offers his arm again, and we laugh and joke through the halls, finally reaching our destination.

The guard posted at the door knocks and opens it when told to do so from the other side. I enter followed by Tziipoor, and the door closes behind us. The Queen stands waiting in an over-the-top [45]gown made for royalty. It is light blue with an open back and gold shoulder cuffs that hold long, open sleeves that reach the floor. It has a long train in the back, and thin gold chains that hang from shoulder to shoulder along the front and the back. Her hair is down, and she wears a small crown that hugs her hairline.

"Come," she says holding out her hand. I offer her mine, and

---

[45] City Detail—Fabrics: cloth is made from various plants that are grown in the city. It comes in a wide variety of colors and textures. Most garments are accompanied by gold or silver accents. Some materials such as gold and silver, and other fabrics are given to the Fae by officials from other Hidden Cities around the planet. Errok is Vaahiigali's most traded good and is in very high demand when crafted by the city's famous stoneworkers. In return for their magnificent artistry, the Fae receive the finest materials and are able to provide high class living for even the poorest of citizens.

she pulls me closer to her and turns me toward a mirror. She places a [46]golden circlet tiara across my forehead. It is very simple with two gold wires shaped elegantly to enhance the shape of the face. It holds a small stone in the center: blue in color.

"This was my mother's," she says. "But tonight, it is yours." She hugs me and thanks me for visiting Vaahiigali.

I hug her back and say in reply, "It is beautiful. And thank you for welcoming me into your city. If only all of the places here were like this one."

"Maybe someday they can be." She hooks my arm with hers and leads, as we return to the hallway, and head for the Great Hall to find the King. "My father's last order as King was to wake him upon arrival of the next Red Blood. He said that he has a message for you."

"What kind of message?" I ask her.

"I do not know," she says in reply. We chat back and forth through the hallway until we reach the Great Hall, followed by Tziipoor and Cynniaa. The large stone statue that stands behind the matching stone thrones is moved to the side exposing a tunnel descending into the foundation of the Keep.

"This is the [47]High Crypt," says Onaaviaa. "Just below us rest the Kings and Queens of our past. Find the one that matches this." He hands me a small trinket marked with an o-shaped symbol.

"Is this your [48]family crest?" I ask. The Queen bows her head to say

---

[46] Relic Detail—Golden Circlet: gifted to Ovinniaa by her mother Ovniin [of-nen] on the eve of her coronation. The gold originates from the Hidden City of Yeenokki [yen-OH-kee]. The blue stone was gifted to the Family of O by the chief of the Hidden City called NuuDetruu [new-DET-rue] to thank them for building a memorial for his wife.

[47] Monument Detail—High Crypt: built around the same time as the Hall of History. It is not open to the cities' citizens: only to the Family of O and the other First Families who have ancestors buried here as well. This is a quiet and well-protected place for the Kings, Queens, and other important members of society from the past to sleep until the end of time.

[48] Relic Detail—Family Crest Trinket: original to the Family of O. Each First Family of Vaahiigali was gifted a palm sized trinket made of Errok by the Royal Family of O to thank them for their efforts in construction of the city. These crests are passed down through the generations as proof of their heritage. The Family of O holds the Royal status, and the rest of the First Families share high ranks among the other important affairs in the city such as: stoneworkers, wing doctors, armorers and blacksmiths, guards, traders, High Council members, and more. The

yes, and I turn to look down into the dark stairway. Onaaviaa lights a candle, and casts a spell instructing it to follow me. I reach down to lift the gown from the ground to prevent it from damage or dirt, and I begin my descent. I quickly realize that I am alone and look to Tziipoor.

"They will not let us follow. You must go alone."

I take a deep breath and hold tightly to the crest. Cemeteries have always put me on edge—crypts are even worse. Once I reach the bottom, the candle faintly illuminates the large open room. I tread lightly searching each stone for the one carved to match the trinket. After several minutes, I finally find the correct one and insert the trinket into the slot much like a key. The stone cracks from the top to the bottom in a very calm manner, and the pieces break away from each other creating a doorway.

I enter, followed by my candle. It is another chamber that stretches far beyond where my light can see. I feel a pull from the crest, like a magnet looking for something to grab onto. It is telling me where to go. I travel deeper into the crypt for a short while before I find the door that I am being led to. I place the crest in another slot, and the wall cracks again revealing a small room with two thrones that match the two from before. A body sits upright and untouched by time; a thick layer of dust covers the expired King. He sits with magnificent posture, and holds his head facing straight forward. His hands lay along the arm rests of his throne, and when I step to take a closer look, I notice that he has opened his eyes. He stares silently for a moment, then stands and brushes off the dust revealing the white of his clothing. He returns to his seat and seems to struggle for words before speaking.

"Red Blood?" he says in question.

"Yes," I answer patiently.

"Your God leaves with us a message," he pauses, and gulps to clear his throat of dust. "By now, you will have met the Queel and found a key."

"Yes," I answer again; he leans forward to meet his eyes with mine as I kneel before him, and he says, "You must find the Lost God."

I have a sudden flashback of Braiiakiah speaking just before injecting me with the silver liquid on the Adreestiaah. The

---

First Families are the only families allowed to marry into the Family of O. The O Family crest has the Royal flower—Sevvia, a symbol representing the letter O, and the stone that Onaaviaa wears that was made for the first King of Vaahiigali.

words match the movements of her mouth, and once I realize the connection, I look back to the old King for further question. But he has returned to rest. I rise from my knee, still holding the dress up off the ground, and stare—wishing that he would have given further explanation.

"Find the Lost God," I repeat to myself. I retreat from the small chamber and retrieve the trinket from the slot causing the rock to reform, as if it had never been split. I follow my tracks back to the beginning of the O Family's section. I take time to look at a few of the other family crests before returning to the Great Hall. I finally reach the stairwell and climb back out from the [49]High Crypt. The court stands in question after I dismiss myself for a moment to think. Tziipoor keeps her distance, but not for long.

"A Lost God," she says sitting on the floor next to where I stand just outside the Great Hall. *"That is all he said?"*

"Yes," I reply.

I turn to rejoin the others, and Tziipoor asks, *"Are you going to carry that dress draped over your arm all night?"*

I am so distracted at the moment that I had not realized that I never dropped it back to the floor. I laugh at myself and let it go before returning to the Hall to find Cynniaa. "How much time until everyone arrives?" I ask him. "Do we have time for you to escort me to the library?"

"We have time," he replies offering me his arm. I accept and follow his lead assuring that everything is okay. "The [50]council is worried by your reaction," he tells me.

---

[49] Monument Detail—High Crypt: it is divided by family. The Kings and Queens of the Family of O are placed together in subdivided chambers in their families' section of the crypt. Ovinniaa's father sits alone next to an empty throne because her mother had gone missing shortly after Ovinniaa was crowned Queen. It is believed that the Fae never truly die of old age (though they *can* be killed by another). Decedents keep the bodies protected so that they can revisit them in times of turmoil, for short statements of advice, or help in dire situations. Most of the bodies are not alive enough to walk or talk for long periods of time, but they are also not dead enough to actually die.

[50] City Detail—High Council: consists only of members from the First Families. There are: the King and Queen from the Family of O, Cynniaa and his Father from the Family of C, Hffh's brother Hyytrrh [heh-truh] from the Family of H and a few others.

"I was told that I need to find something, a Lost God," I reply.

"There is another God here?" he asks. "We knew of the one that you traveled with before, but we thought that he was the only one."

"So did I," I tell him. "Wait, how did you know that I traveled with one before?"

He laughs, "The people are just learning that you are here, but there were a secret number of us tracking you before you got here."

"So, you knew that I would come here?" I ask.

"We hoped that you would. We need to see Hffh before we go to the library to get your wings back," he says, changing the subject. "You will not be able to reach many shelves without them." We make a stop by the doctor's wing workshop, and he encourages me to choose another set due to the fact that he had not been able to fix mine yet. He is a very busy Sprite. He retrieves a pair that is similar to the ones that I had prior, but these ones had a white outline instead of black. They match the dress better anyway.

I thank the doctor and follow with a bow before returning to Cynniaa in the hallway to head for the library. Upon arrival, I am in awe. The room would be well lit in the daytime from natural light let in from the ceiling, which is crafted of glass. But for now, there are orbed candles roaming freely. The shelves stand taller than any I have ever seen, and Cynniaa tells me that there are books on every subject, creature, and city known to the planet. The Hidden Sanctuary Cities have a High Council meeting four times a year to exchange knowledge. I would very much like to attend one of these [51]meetings someday.

I spend the next 30 minutes or so exploring the endless rows of books before noticing a few frantic guards bursting through the doors and approaching Cynniaa. I descend back to the floor to join the huddle conversating about a Host yelling for the Red Blood just outside of the city's protective walls. Apparently, they are unaware of the Hidden City, but too close to be ignored. Cynniaa looks at me distressed and grabs my hand, dragging me through the air, back to see the King.

---

[51] City Detail—High Council: holds seasonal meetings with the High Council members of other Hidden Cities to discuss business deals relating to trade, to exchange knowledge, and to ensure safety to each of their cities. These meetings are held in a safe place outside of the Hidden Cities, as to keep the location of each of their respected cities a secret from each other.

THE FAE KING
ONAAVIAA
7.5 INCHES

THE FAE QUEEN
OVINNIAA
6.4 INCHES

THE FAE PRINCESS
YETZIIVU
6.3 INCHES

THE FAE PRINCES
4.7 INCHES   4.4 INCHES

THE FAE GUARD
GYNNIAA
7 INCHES

P. TANNER

THE FAMILY CREST

THE PEGG
2'5"

THE KEEPER
BORIISST
6'4"

THE KEY

84

4

THE LOST GOD

Cynniaa and I are instructed to investigate this Host and eliminate it if necessary. Under all circumstances, the safety of the city and its people are of utmost importance. We make our way out to the bushes surrounding the spring.

"She has to be here somewhere," we hear a voice say. I remain hidden looking through the shrub at the girl standing above. It is the Siren, Aneera.

"This is the only place she could have come out," says another Host that I quickly identify as Fuckface.

"They are allies," I tell Cynniaa. "They helped me escape the Dead Caves just before I washed up on the shore."

"They have good intentions," replies Tziipoor. *"They know of the Lost God."* I repeat this information to Cynniaa and ask him to stay hidden while I deal with them. I place my hand on the Queels back and step out from the bushes returning us to normal size holding the dress off the ground to protect it from dirt. Fuckface and Aneera stand shocked by my sudden appearance, and ready themselves to fight once they see the creature that accompanies me.

"You're safe," I assure them; "She is bonded to me now." Fuckface puffs his chest to grow, and steps toward me—

"Where have you been," he asks angrily, "and what the hell are you wearing? We're fighting for our lives and you're off playing fucking dress up?"

"I'm safe where I am," I reply. "Doing research."

"We're here to help you," Aneera interrupts. "Where is the God that travels with you?"

"We abandoned each other before you found me," I reply.

We continue to converse on the subject and conclude that in order to find what we are looking for; we need to split up. Cynniaa decides to come out from the shrubbery, so that he can help in our discussion, and so that I can introduce the three to one another. Aneera informs me that I will not be able to find the Lost God without the help of Barroun. I do not know how she acquired this information, but Tziipoor explains that the Siren can see fragments of the future.

"I will stay in Vaahiigali to use the library, and hopefully find a hint as to where we are supposed to go," I say. "The two of you find Barroun and bring him back here."

"There will be a Trial soon," replies Aneera. "That might be our best chance to find him. It will start in seven days." I nod my head and agree before shrinking myself and Tziipoor again to Cynniaa's size. I part ways with my new-found partners.

"Seven days," I say to Tziipoor. "If I can find clues to the Lost God's location before then, maybe we won't have to do the Trial."

"We fear that it will not be that easy," she thinks in reply. *"This challenge was created to be difficult. Do not expect to succeed without struggle."* We continue to walk silently back to the Great Hall, escorted by Cynniaa. I will take part in this celebration, but after, I must focus on the challenge. I found a key, so I can only assume that I am looking for another door of some sort. My mind is in another place as the King, his Queen, and the court are introduced, and I exchange bows and kind smiles with them one by one. The night seems to fly by while I meet the many faces of this great city. I try to enjoy myself, but I cannot delay this distraction. I have only seven days to find the lock that matches the Entanglement Key. Seven days is just not enough time. I should be searching. I figure that a good place to start would be at the place where I found the key—the mural. It is close enough that I can go look without leaving the party. It is just around the corner. Tziipoor and I step quickly, but quietly into the hallway.

"There must be a clue somewhere," I tell her.

"Perhaps a Hevaanian sigil, or an arrow of some kind," she follows. I scan the carving inch by inch hoping to find something to point me in the

right direction. Any small detail would work, just something to tell me where to start. I check other doorways for small holes; perhaps there is another small room.

"What are you looking for, miss?" I hear a sweet voice ask.

I look to the two small Sprites from earlier—the young boys who wrestled under the bush. I have a thought, sometimes things are easier to see through the eyes of children. Maybe they can help me. "I am looking for a clue." I tell them.

"A clue to what?" the smaller boy asks.

"Well," I say, thinking genuinely. "I'm not really sure. I need directions to something."

"So, a map?" asks the taller one.

"Maybe," I reply to him, looking back to the wall to search again.

"Hmmm," thinks the smaller one, "You should go see the Keeper! Father says he has a lot of maps!"

I look at Tziipoor with disappointment, then answer the young Sprite, "That is an excellent idea, thank you."

The boys laugh and run off to join again in the excitement.

"After the party is over, we need to go back to the room where we found the key—maybe we missed something; after that, we should go investigate the Keeper's place." I say.

"We should return to the celebration," Tziipoor tells me. *"The Queen is looking for us."* I follow her back to the Great Hall and find Ovinniaa offering me a seat at the table with the royals and their court. I listen without depth, as the King tells jokes to his table. I feel that if he spoke of Yeshua, maybe I could find some focus. My mind floods with questions, and I can already feel the buildup of stress beginning to take its toll. I am ready to leave. I cannot sit here and listen to jokes and conversations about [52]politics all night. There is too much for me to get done. I lean to my left and whisper to the Queen—

---

[52] City Detail—Celebrations: held in the Great Hall above the crypt. These parties are generally quiet, and well-focused. It is tradition for the King and Queen to dance with any noble guest to ensure the utmost respect, and open heartedness. Seen as equals, this society sees no difference in men and women. With respect, man dances with man, and woman dances with woman. They do not eat, and they do not drink. They sit at large tables and discuss the working details of the city, and tonight they also hold in-depth conversations of the Red-Blooded Creature of Earth.

"I do not want to seem rude, but how long do these celebrations usually last?"

She looks at me, and her smile fades away, "Are you not enjoying yourself?"

"Of course, I am!" I reply. "I'm just curious."

"Onaaviaa will understand if you have other things to tend to," she answers with a kind smile. "You are a guest, not a prisoner. If you wish to end the night, you may do so."

"I do not want to ruin the fun for everyone," I say with guilt. "But I am searching for something, and I do not have much time to find it."

"I will excuse you to go," she replies in confidence, and follows with a royal bow.

"Thank you," I reply graciously. "I am going to change into some more comfortable clothes, and then I can be found in the library if you need me." I bow to say goodbye, and then meet eyes with the King, and bow to him as well. He returns the gesture and continues to listen with low amusement to the exceedingly long joke told my old man Hyytrrh. Tziipoor and I return to the mural, and I place my hand on her back to shrink us again to the size needed to enter the secret room. "Maybe we missed something," I tell her. I had grabbed a candle this time just before leaving the Great Hall to light the way. Once we reach the small hallway, I scan the walls, ceiling, and floors for carvings or clues, but find nothing.

When we reach the pool, I strip out of the gown and drape it across Tziipoor instructing her to, "Wait here." I enter the pool again carrying the candle in my hand making sure to not trip over the rock that had stumped me before. I let go of the candle, and it holds its place in the air. I grip the altar to try and lift it. Surprisingly, it is easy to flip. I search for a clue along the bottom but only find disappointment.

I stand and think for a moment before beginning to remove the moss from the wall hoping to find something behind it; but again, I come up empty. I repeat this on the remaining three walls to find nothing. The ceiling is bare, too. In one final attempt to find something I blow out the candle and give my eyes a moment to adjust before swishing my arms through the water to ignite the color in the algae. Perhaps the light from the single cellular creatures will reveal a hidden map or text.

I check the walls and ceiling again before moving the rocks along the floor hoping to find a hidden mosaic, or any other form of picture. This idea also fails. I take one more desperate look at the box, inspecting it inside and out, side to side, and top to bottom. I yet again find nothing, so I decide to move on to the next place of enlightenment—the Keeper's house. I remove myself from the water and follow, as Tziipoor guides me through the dark hallway back out. I jump on her back and hold carefully to the dress, making sure not to damage it, as we return to our room. Tziipoor assists me in putting on the armor from earlier, and I place the golden circlet on the table. I figure that it would be best to keep myself protected, as my mind stresses about the week ahead, and I do not want to lose or damage the Queen's jewelry.

When ready, I shrink Tziipoor small enough that I can carry her comfortably. It is better if we fly from the balcony, hopefully, we can avoid being seen leaving. I return to the exit that Cynniaa and I had used earlier, and fly across the sanctuary, and up to the windowsill.

I look into the room shocked by what I see. Still holding Tziipoor, we look together wondering, "What happened here?" It looks like there was a fire. Everything is charred, and it smells of burnt flesh.

I hear a noise behind me and turn with the Golden Dagger in one hand and Tziipoor in the other. I breathe a sigh of relief and tuck the dagger back into its place when I realize that it is Cynniaa.

"What are you doing here?" he asks.

"I'm looking for clues," I reply, shook at the fact that I almost cut him. "What are *you* doing here?"

"Helping," he answers, flying off to look around.

I return myself and Tziipoor to our regular sizes, climb down from the window ledge and continue to look around.

"When were you going to tell me about his maps?" I ask Tziipoor, so that Cynniaa cannot hear.

"We did not know of them. Just like we cannot see everything about you, we did not know everything about him. And the Clutch does not always tell us what they see."

"The boy Sprite knew of them but the Keeper's own companion new nothing?" I say to her.

"We were NOT his companion," she replies with fire in her tone. She hisses, *"You feel the pain that we went through. He was no caretaker, no friend, no patient pinch of man. If we were not killing for his taste, we were off fetching the next sorry bitch intended to pleasure him. Do not assume that we know what he kept us away from. I have connections that see, but he has connections that hide."*

I bite my tongue, intimidated by her aggressive defenses, I will leave it at that. I step carefully trying to avoid the filth below. We check the entire building; nothing remains. But it is very odd, the charring only resides in certain areas. Other than a little debris, the walls and the floors are left unaffected by whatever happened here. There are golden bowls, and other small trinkets—some made of wood, and some of other metal or stone materials—spread through the building that are also unaffected, along with the golden tables, and his throne. The bodies had been burned, along with the tapestries on the walls, and many of the books that the Keeper had in his vast collection. We search all the different rooms of his villa until we reach the end of the building.

There is nothing here. I decide that it is time that we move this search to the library—back in the city. There must be something there that can tell me something. I also feel uncomfortable here. This was done deliberately, and the ones who did it could still be here, watching us. I shrink Tziipoor small enough that I can carry her again, and then myself small enough that we cannot be [53]seen.

We find Cynniaa and return to the city's entrance. He gathers a group of guards to join him in the sanctuary to ensure that we were not followed. He sends me and Tziipoor on our way, and we head back to our room, so that I can clean up a little and change into my lounge clothes.

The library is empty of any Fae, and I am unsure as to where I should look first. I decide it best for me to look into the visit made by Yeshua, and any Hevaanian Gods who may have passed though Vaahiigali. I search the shelves of the giant library and finally come across a section of books pertaining to the Kingdom of Hevaan. The

---

[53] Host Detail—The Human: her shrinking ability allows her to shrink herself along with anything that she touches. So, by shrinking Tziipoor, and picking her up to hold her, when the Human shrinks Tziipoor will shrink again too keeping her the same size—compared to the Human. If the makes sense?

collection consists of seven volumes bound in white cloth. I move the books to the floor and sit next to Tziipoor, who had fallen asleep.

I begin with the first, and skim through its pages. The contents spark interest, but I have yet to come across anything that is helpful. I proceed on to skim the second, the third, the fourth, and then the fifth. I take a break to rest my eyes and wake again to find the new dawn.

"You're finally awake," says a voice from beside me. I look to my right to find the Princess sitting next to me—the oldest Sprite of the three from the spring.

"How long have you been here?" I ask her.

"Not long," is her reply. "Why do you sleep so much?" she asks—question after question, "and what are you looking for?"

"Just brushing up on my history, and I sleep because I used to do it a lot back home—I don't need it here, but I still like it." I tell her. "I don't believe I ever caught your name."

"I am [54]Yetziivu," she says proudly. I smile and bow my head to her. She much resembles her father but holds the same grace and has inherited the same golden yellow toned eyes as her mother. Her hair is blonde, and she has very light freckles across her nose and under her eyes. She tells me that she is [55]four years old, but by her appearance, I would have guessed that she is somewhere around sixteen. Her Cheeks are also pierced, which I find to be an odd thing for a four-year-old, but what do I [56]know. She is wearing a thick white lounge-coat identical to the ones worn by the rest of her family. When in the comfort of the Keep the O family keep their

---

[54] [yet-ZEE-voo]

[55] Host Detail—The Fae: Sprites can live to be 1,000 years old. Onaaviaa and Ovinniaa are both 700. When the time comes, the next line of Vaahiigali rulers is conceived around the same time and born to be partners. The child that is to marry into the Family of O will be given a name *by* the O Family—as is the same for the other First Families—to welcome them into their new family. This child will come from one of the First Families. Onaaviaa is originally from the Family of H meaning that Hffh and Hyytrrh are his true bloodline. Yetziivu is the princess, but she will not be the next Queen. She was born to marry into the Family of Y. Her eldest sister will be the next Queen, and a man from the Family of C will be the King.

[56] Host Detail—The Fae's Pierced Cheeks: though they are not seen as different, the men do not do this. Female's cheeks are pierced to signify engagement or marriage.

wings tucked in and carry themselves with their feet in honor of the ground that they call home.

"What is Earth like?" she asks me.

"It is mesmerizing, and terrifying at the same time," I answer following with a short pause. "It is hard for me to describe. Do you have a more specific question?"

"What do you miss about it the most?" she asks.

"My friends, and my family—and I miss food," I answer followed with a laugh. She laughs along with me before asking—

"What is food?"

I think for a moment before answering. I guess it makes sense that she would not know, because we do not need to eat here. I think the Fae understand that it is a thing, they just do not understand why.

"Food is how we get the nutrients that we need to survive. Humans need food every day to stay healthy. Here, we get our nutrients through the air. But on Earth, we need to eat."

She says, "Oh, like how we still sleep, but we don't need it? But you sleep *a lot* more than me!" she laughs.

I answer, "Yes," and laugh with her.

"What kinds of things would you eat?" she asks.

"Fruits and vegetables, and as much as it pains me to say it, some of us eat meat." I tell her, coming to the realization that I really should not be discussing [57]this with her.

"Meat?" she asks, "You said some, do *you* eat meat?"

I cannot find it in me to lie to her, I wish not to frighten her but to inform her, to answer her truthfully and respectfully. I mean, after all she is a princess, "Yes, I ate meat."

"So, not anymore?" she asks me.

"Not here, no."

She sits and thinks for a moment, "Will you eat it again when you go home?"

"*When*?" I ask her. I laugh, "Do you mean if?"

"The Red Blood Yesiwa did."

---

[57] Gameplay Detail—Carnivores: meat eaters, these Hosts are considered the vilest; the most grotesque. They are feared and hated. Humans are among them. In some Irestiikaarian beliefs, Herbivores are just as dangerous. On this planet, the ones who were born here with no need to consume see disgust in any form of consumption.

I look down troubled by her words, "I'm not like him."

She looks at me, confused as to why I would say such a thing. She then shrugs her shoulders and asks again, "Meat? Will you eat meat?"

"It's hard to tell how I would feel," I tell her, "It's hard to tell how I will change here. But as of right now, if I were on Earth and someone offered me a cheeseburger, I would eat it."

"Hmm," she says, and shrugs her shoulders again. She continues to ask questions about Earth, and Red Bloods, but not Humans, she asks about the other creatures that live there. I tell her about Mammals, and Reptiles, and Amphibians, and Fish, and Birds, and Insects. I tell her that not all creatures of Earth are red blooded, some are green, or purple, or blue, or yellow.

We sit and discuss for about an hour, or so. I tell her about places that I wish I could see back on Earth. Places that I still want to go. I tell her about the City of Temples in Nepal called Kathmandu, and the enchanting white marble statues in the streets of Rome that much resemble the ones that they have here, and the Lost Civilization in the Cambodian jungle called Angkor Wat. While we exchange stories of wondrous places, I am caught off guard by a story that she tells me about a small cave that she and her friends like to swim in. She says that the water glows white when you touch it, but you can only see it at night. Tziipoor turns the corner and sits next to me. She had been searching the stacks for any books that may further help us.

"Glowing water like we found in the hidden room," she says. *"Perhaps this cave will have a clue."* I nod in agreement and focus my attention back on Yetziivu's story.

"We were playing one night, splashing in the water, and we noticed a spot on the cave wall that showed a hidden image when it got wet. We soaked the wall, so we could see the whole picture. It was amazing!" The Princess continues on to say, "It was a map of a big city; there was a ring in the middle—maybe a wall or something? It had writing, too, but we could not read it. It was in a weird language."

"Hevaanian," I think to Tziipoor.

"Yes," she replies.

"Can you show me the cave?" I ask the Princess.

"Of course, follow me!" she replies. She removes her house coat and drops it on the floor before spreading her wings and springing

93

toward the door. I spread mine to follow, and Tziipoor paces close behind. She tells me to keep up with Yetziivu and takes another path down when we fly over the balcony outside. She leads me to a spot quite a distance down the river, then she turns left toward the edge of the city. There is a large group of natural pools formed from the spring water coming from the caves below.

"We have to swim to it," she says. "I can show you the wall, but you cannot see the picture in daylight."

She maneuvers across the broken rock to the side where the cavern protrudes up from the ground and enters the pool to swim under the wall to the [58]other side. I hear Tziipoor tell me that she is close by and will catch up shortly. I have not tested it yet, but I wonder how far away from each other we can be before she loses the ability to speak with me or if that connection will always be there—I will be sure to ask her another time.

I enter the pool and follow behind Yetziivu through the small underwater tunnel to the other side. Approaching the surface, I can see where the sunlight shines in through a small break in the cave ceiling just like in the bigger cavern holding the city.

I meet Yetziivu back in the open air and listen attentively, as she explains the map that she and her friends had seen. She continues to tell me that there is a part of the map that is missing, as she points to a spot in the top left corner where the wall had crumbled in.

"What do you want to bet that that is the part of the map we will need," I hear Tziipoor say, as she surfaces and joins us by the cave wall.

"That would be just my luck," I say out loud.

"What do you mean?" asks Yetziivu.

"The Queel says that is probably the part of the map that we'll need to see," I answer her.

"You can speak to it?" she replies with excitement.

"Yes," I giggle, "I can hear her thoughts, and she can hear mine. We are bonded together."

"That is so cool!" the Princess exclaims. I laugh again before replying—

---

[58] City Detail—Break-off Caverns: this city is much larger than it appears. There are many smaller caverns all around the edge. Some are swimming holes; others are large houses or business districts. The largest cavern is the stoneworkers' region of the kingdom.

"Yes, it is!" We wade in the water for a while continuing our conversation from the library. She is full of questions, and I answer as many of them as I can to the best of my ability. She is a very goofy girl and has a fun and playful personality. I watch admiring from a short distance, as she and Tziipoor splash and play in the water.

The Queel is a beautiful and gentle creature. I can feel that her mind is at peace now, and she feels safe unlike the way she felt during her time spent under the control of the Keeper, Boriisst. It is amazing to find such a kind heart inside of such a seemingly terrifying creature. This just goes to show that not all things are what they appear to be.

I bring up the suggestion to Tziipoor that I want to check the wall inside of the room where we found the key to see if there is a hidden image that I had missed before. I tell them that I will meet back up with them later. I leave the two behind in the pool, and I quickly dry myself before returning to the palace. I shrink again to the proper size and tread lightly through the pitch-black hallway running my hand along the wall for guidance. The edge where the floor drops into the water catches me off guard, and I fall into the pool.

"Fuck," I say, as I find my footing and stand, while my eyes adjust to the darkness. I splash around in the water to further ignite the lighting before heavily soaking the walls one by one around the room. I find nothing, until I reach the wall opposite of the white podium. There is writing like what Yetziivu said she had seen in the cave I had just come from.

The more I splash the wall with the algae infused water, the stronger the picture begins to appear. It displays a cavern with an abyss, and a large glowing sphere on the other side. Could this be what I am looking for I wonder? What could it be, the Lost God?

I cannot read what is written. Tziipoor said that it is Hevaanian; perhaps that is why Aneera says that I need Barroun. He would be very helpful right about now. I find it odd that every book that I read in the library could be read in English, but this writing is not translated for me. Every day the need to learn Hevaanian script grows. So far, the Banished God has not been all that reliable, and we kind of left each other on bad terms. I hope that once we do find him, he will be willing to help. Maybe he will teach me to read and write in his language. As for the other two, Fuckface and Aneera, I have no idea why they have chosen to ally with me, but at this moment I will take all of the help that I can get.

I decide to head back to the library after stopping at my room *again* for dry clothes. I remember a section in one of the Hevaanian books about the banishment process. It involves a giant orb, and has a special name, but I cannot remember the word. It starts with the letter "g", if I remember correctly. I will have to find the section again. When I read through it the first time, I was only skimming the pages, so I did not read too much into the detail.

Maybe the orb in the picture on the wall is one of the banishment orbs. Barroun said that he and his brother were banished by the Great God of Hevaan; I wonder if the Lost God is his brother. I manage to find the [59]book and sift through the pages until I find the passage that I am looking for. It is titled [60]*Gaaliiniaa Spheres*. The content reads as follows—

> *"A Gaaliiniaa Sphere is an exoskeletal shell created by the Et'Aamiineea in extreme cases of exile or banishment. This shell is impenetrable and inescapable without the touch of a true and titled God. The accuser within is placed in an induced state of rest until release. The Sphere is given to the Universe to wander through time and space until destiny finds reason to free the soul within. Exile or banishment is not withdrawn until the accuser proves himself, herself, or itself worthy of citizenship."*

I cannot help but wonder what Barroun and his brother had argued about that was so bad that they had been given such a brutal punishment. And if this [61]orb that I am after now really is the brother,

---

[59] Relic Detail—the Books of Hevaan: copied from a much larger collection of books that is homed in another Hidden City and placed in new and smaller binding. The Author is not from the planet of Hevaan, nor was he a God, but he was considered an expert on the subject during his lifetime.

[60] [gal-en-EE-ah]

[61] Relic Detail—Gaaliiniaa Sphere: technique inherited from the Elite Gods of the Void. This practice was passed down for generations after the Hevaanian Gods broke relations with the Elites.

how is it that he is still at rest, but Barroun walks free? Another question that comes to mind is: if Barroun was stripped of his name and title, how will he open the orb? The writing states that you need the touch of a true and titled God. But I guess that is a problem for another time. I decide to move out onto the library's balcony for some fresh air, as I continue reading. I find another section titled *Keys of Entanglement*. This section reads as follows—

> *"The Keys of Entanglement are a collection of twelve golden keys hidden sporadically across the Lost Planet. These keys are required to access the twelve Hevaanian Gates. Once the intended user finds one of these twelve identical keys, the rest will be retrieved by the Hevaanian Gods, and taken from the surface of Irestiikaar. Each gate is followed by a task to be completed by the finder of the key. If all twelve tasks are completed, the finder will be named a citizen of the Great and Glorious Kingdom of Hevaan."*

I look up from the book and see Tziipoor walking up the path leading to the palace. Yetziivu is riding on her back. I am happy knowing that I helped her find some peace. I can feel the pain that she carries from her past, and I hope that throughout our time together, I will be able to show her the love and the care that she truly deserves. For so long, she has been used as a weapon. Her mind was not valued above her body, and that makes me feel sick. The Keeper, Boriisst, would beat her for enjoyment, and force her to kill and eat Hosts at random just to promote fear. There were more bodies in the Dead Caves than I could count.

I can feel her sorrow, but I cannot even begin to imagine the guilt she feels. I know it is there, because I can see it in her eyes. I can see the residue from years of torture and brutality. I hope that one day I can set her free, and she can let her mind be at peace from the pain. I want her to have a life for herself—one that does not involve war, or sacrifice. I want her to have the life that she deserves, the one that she wanted; the one that she has rightfully earned.

I wait patiently for the sun to disappear bringing on the darkness of night. If the map shows a heading, or a place to at least start, I hope that maybe Tziipoor and I can head out tomorrow to begin the next part of our search. Once we find Barroun, I plan to return here to show him the writing, but for now, I do not have time to wait. Maybe I can find it without having to read the script. I guess that only time will tell.

The journey to Vaahiigali from the wall took about two days on foot. With my wings, I presume I can cut that time in half when I go back. Tziipoor chooses to travel by land, but she is a master of moving quickly, and I know that she will be able to keep up.

14 Days since the fall...

It has been three days since Tziipoor, and I left Vaahiigali. The map on the wall of the cave showed a trail leading somewhere near the northwestern side of the giant wall—exactly where the rocks had fallen in, so we will have to search blindly. We had said our goodbyes to our new Fae friends, and promised to return once we find the Banished God. I miss the city, but it feels good to be moving forward.

We have managed to find a small shack. It is a fair size for two and can be found just outside of the Great Wall. There is a mudded road outside of the shack that leads up the hill toward it. We chose this area because of the low traffic, and the shack because it blends well and does not draw attention.

Inside, it is very open. There is a workspace to the right, and a fire pit surrounded by some seating to the left. The floors are made of an old, faded wood found only in the [62]woods to the north of here, and shines with bioluminescence when walked across. But the light is ever so faint. Toward the back of the shack is a bedroom with a small shower; there is only a half-wall separating it from the main living space.

We have been searching the area since we arrived, but we have

---

[62] Relic Detail—Glowing Wood: found in the Northern Forest, better known as the Empty Forest. Hosts and small creatures lurk around the outskirts and will venture into the forest, but not very far. There is a well-known fear associated with this forest because after a couple hundred feet in, it is uninhabited. Only plants are known to hold permanent residence there.

been unable to find anything useful. I feel as if we are at a standstill until we find someone who can read the words on the cave wall that was in the tiny Hidden Room in Vaahiigali. I can only assume that the entrance is somewhere underground. There must be a tunnel or a cave somewhere. But knowing this place, it is hidden in plain sight.

There is only one day left after today until the beginning of the first Trial, and this day is going fast. We have about three hours of daylight left to search this area before we are confined to the darkness of night. I left word with the council of Vaahiigali of our location, so that we could be found when Fuckface and Aneera return. I expect them sometime tomorrow. We had planned, before, to meet again a few days before the Trial begins, so that we could discuss strategy. By now, they should have met with Onaaviaa and been given directions to find us.

If they travel through the night, they should reach the wall by morning, and our current location by midday. I had asked the doctor to give them each a set of wings, so they could travel faster, hoping to help make up for lost time. I made the wings the right sizes for them before I left and hid them in the brush—along with an extra set on the off chance that the Banished God traveled with them.

I also left a paper with the ancient script from the two walls, so that the King could show them, because there is no way for them to shrink small enough to see the writing up close without my help. It would be wildly convenient if they happen to have found Barroun and can show him the writings while they are there, so we could avoid the Trial in its entirety. We could find the cave, and complete the task, putting our names in better placement on the score board. But I doubt that I will be so fortunate.

Tziipoor and I search through the buildings and roam through the streets making sure to check every possible hiding place. I open every door and lift every rug. I move old statues and check every book on every shelf hoping to find a switch revealing a secret room. I check for hidden buttons and small doorways. We have managed to find a few, but most of them are empty.

Some have stowed-away jewels from a time known only to the past, and some are filled with scrolls and stacks of used paper. In a few, I find small creatures like bugs and worms. There are some so small, they can hold only a ring or a teeny pile of aged coins. But some are large rooms that were used for sanctuary, and I even find a few complete with the old skeletons of their inhabitors. I also find a secret library in one; its [63]books are all still there and well preserved. One of them gives the name of this giant city: [64]IInve Bovaange or in English, the City of the Lost.

I change my proportions, and check for Fae-sized doorways or lockboxes. I am in awe at our findings, but still at a loss for what really needs to be found. We have been at this for days. We had started at the shack and are circulating outward in the direction of the missing part of the map. The trail stopped in this area, but it was hard to tell where it was intended to go because of the damage on the wall. We have checked all the buildings, and houses, and other shacks.

I come across a large warehouse just as the sun meets the horizon. We will search into the night. This building is massive and will probably take a few hours or more to complete. I sigh out of boredom and breach the latch on the door to enter. I am followed, shortly after, by Tziipoor.

"We are not alone," she thinks.

"What do you see?" I ask her.

"We do not know," she replies with a tone sounding more worrisome than usual. *"But I can hear its heartbeat,"* she continues to say. *"It is about your size, maybe smaller."*

"You can tell that just by the sound?" I ask in amazement. "Can you sense how close it is?" I look around at the giant busted machinery scattered across the floor, and the tattered workspace of this [65]ancient, neglected livelihood.

---

[63] Relic Detail—Books in the City of the Lost: written by hand 3,000 years ago by a tenant. These books recollect the daily life of a man named Jeexa [yex-AH]. Born and raised in the city, he had a normal civilian life.

[64] [een-VEH boe-VAH-ng]

[65] City Detail—IInve Bovaange: build two billion years ago. This city was inhabited with many different species of Hosts. It is called the City of the Lost because it was considered a safe haven for any Host who did not want to fight in the Game. But due to its inefficiency when warding off criminals, and its massive size making it difficult to keep hidden, the city only flourished for about 1.3 thousand years— time does not take as heavy of a toll on things in the Void as it does inside of our Universe. That is why the city still stands.

"It is not on the floor. It is somewhere above us." Her eyes search the dim lighting above the rafters.

"Do you think it knows we are here?" I ask.

"Yes," she replies before walking farther into the dark maze of machinery with her head still pointed upward. I climb onto her back and hold tight to Reewenniveaar without removing it from the custom-made scabbard that was gifted to me by Cynniaa along with the finished armor that the King had gifted me.

We tread quietly. I stay alert and ready but feel unsure because of the concern I had noticed in her Voice. I can feel the tension in her step, and an awakening in her heartbeat. I can sense that she feels uneasy. This is the first time I have felt this from her. I believe that Tziipoor is about to learn something new. I want to take some extra time to explain the importance of what is happening. Through the bond, I can sense her emotions. And through her connection with the rest of her Clutch, I can feel theirs, too. But there is something wrong. The Clutch also feels uneasy. They cannot see what is here. It is something beyond their knowledge. That means that this is also beyond the knowledge of our Universe. This must be something from the Void. That is the place in which the Lost Planet now rests; it is the place that I am now—outside of our Universe.

"Tziipoor does not know what it is, and neither do you," I say to the Clutch. "Perhaps we should leave and not provoke it. There is no shame in walking away from this one."

"We agree," they answer.

Before, I could not tell when I was speaking with Tziipoor and when I was speaking with them. But now, I can hear their Voices. They all speak the same words together. There are many of them layered over one another, and the more I get to know her, the more Voices I can hear. But when it is Tziipoor that speaks, her Voice speaks alone. I can tell them apart now.

"Then let's go, and pray that we're not followed," I reply. They agree again, and we turn to retreat to the door where we had entered. I jump down off her back, and we walk outside together. I turn and grab onto the door with my left hand to close it behind me. It slams itself shut with my four fingers minus the thumb tucked painfully inside.

"Motherfucker!" I exclaim. Tziipoor and I dig desperately at the door, whining forcefully, as she can also feel the [66]hurt. My fingers are smashed; all of the bones are broken. Completely reduced to nothing, and just like that, they are gone. Blood trickles down the door leaving a dark red stain. In the struggle to free my hand, the fingers break off at the knuckles, pointer to pinky.

"Get on our back, we need to [67]go!" says the Clutch. *"That was no accident."* I climb on, as she jumps upward to escape across the rooftops. I cover the wound with my free hand trying to stop the blood from leaving a trail. I need some cloth. The material on my armor is too thick to rip.

"Please grow back, please grow back, please grow back!" I beg to myself out loud. Tziipoor leaps from building to building running effortlessly through the air.

"Place the wound to our skin," says Tziipoor. *"The pheromone that helps you stay in place will also stop heavy bleeding."* She jumps in through a window, as I shrink us hoping to throw anything off our trail if it had followed.

She runs a few more rooms over and stops to help with the wound. The bleeding finally stops, but there is no new growth— nothing but a stump, and a thumb. We decide to head back to the shack and call it a night. We travel for a while at a small size until Tziipoor can no longer hear the heartbeat of the Host, then we return back to normal size. We finally reach the shack and hide ourselves away inside. I want to take a nap. I need to sleep off the anger.

I say to myself, "Asshole! Why did it have to take all four? One finger would have proved the point *just* fine." We were unwanted there. What in the *hell* was that thing?

I snooze for a few hours before Tziipoor wakes me stating that our allies are close. She says that she can "hear the angry one," who I can only figure to be Fuckface. He is accompanied by four others, but none of them are the Banished God. I walk outside, and fly to the rooftops looking for the approaching group of partners coming to join in the hunt. I can see a few specks nearing the area from

---

[66] Host Detail—The Queel: connected by mind and by blood, Tziipoor and the Human can feel each other's injuries. The Human is the first bond in history that has the ability to speak with any of the Queel, and also the first to share the ability to feel each other's discomfort. This is a bond unlike any that came before it.

[67] A Note from the Prophet—Font Color Changes: when the words of a Host are of a different font and a different color this means that the Host is even more of the highest and holiest. The Voice of the Clutch is a lighter color of grey because they are even closer to the Universe than Tziipoor.

the distance and fly to meet them to show them back to our hidden shack. It is Fuckface and Aneera accompanied by Cynniaa and two other Fae guards of whom I have yet to meet.

I welcome them in. We sit around the fire pit discussing our findings, and the reason as to why they arrived so much earlier than I had expected. Aneera says that she had a vision and decided to meet back with us earlier than planned.

"We need the God," she says. "The writing on the wall from the small city is an earlier version of the Hevaanian text. The writing from the books that you read in the library was translated because it is the newer, more developed language that the Gods use now. It is easier to decipher."

"How will we find him in this Trial?" I ask.

"We will all spawn in the same basic area, and it will be easy for us to regroup. But I am unsure of how the Game will play, so we will have to learn as we go. I expect another vision sometime in the next few days."

"What makes you think he will even be there?" Fuckface asks with a shitty tone.

"We have to try; I see importance in this venture." Aneera replies with aggravation.

Apparently, they do not get along too well either. From the tension, I can tell that they argue with each other often. He snorts and turns his back on the conversation.

"Why are you always such an asshole? Do you get along with anyone?" I cannot help but say.

"I did not ask for this!" He exclaims and stomps toward the door. "I do not want to help you. I do not care to support you. And I do not want your fake hospitality," he continues to say.

"Then leave," I say in reply. "*I* did not ask for your help." I stand and stare at him for a moment before he rips the wings that the Fae had gifted him from his back, stomps them into the floor, and slams the door behind him like a child while he leaves. I notice the discomfort in the Fae as they stare at the damaged wings. I try to hold back the anger, but eventually I pick them up, and place them carefully on the table noticing the damage myself and growing even angrier at the situation. I cannot help but follow him out. The three Fae stand to stop me but are stopped when Tziipoor jumps defensively between them and me. She hisses with that same fear-inducing crackle from her throat and pushes them back toward their seats.

"We should not fight," Cynniaa says.

"I disagree," Aneera replies, while sitting and crossing her arms. "Let her kick his ass. He needs it."

"This fight's been brewing for a long time." I explain to him, "He can disrespect me all he wants, but he will not lay waste to the kindness of the Fae." I open the door and just before leaving I say, "This can't be stopped." I walk out the door and find Fuckface staring from the other side of the road. He smiles out of the corner of his mouth like he had expected me to follow. He puffs out his chest and grows into a new form.

"I've never been afraid of you," I say.

He laughs followed by an angry snarl, and crouches his body ready to lunge before replying, "You are going to die today."

"And you're going to look like a bitch, when I beat you," I say in rebuttal, removing the scabbard holding Reewenniveaar from my hip, and placing it on the deck. I also remove my wings and put them down gently next to the blade and its holder before joining him on the mudded road. "I don't need to kill you—I just really want to beat your disrespectful ass. You've talked a lot of shit, now show me what you've got."

He catches me off guard with his speed and agility. His body is so big that I did not expect it to move so fast. I dodge his punches, and roll across the ground to avoid injury, as he grows more and more angry. I chose to fight without a blade to prove my strength superior, and I knew that if I had used it, I could have really done too much damage. I only need to puncture his pride. I need to earn his respect. Something tells me that we will need him in the future. I need to prove myself a worthy opponent. With that, I will prove myself to be a worthy ally. And the best way for me to do that is to beat his ass.

I swing to punch him in the face, but he dodges it and backhands me sending my body flying across the street. The spikes on his hands puncture my cheek, and very close to my eye. I stand and retaliate by giving him a foot in the crotch, and a finger in each of his eyes.

He hollers and takes a moment to retain his vision, while I hold tightly to the newly regrown fingers on my left hand trying not to puke after seeing the pieces of eyeball stuck under a few of my fingernails. The fingers are there but are still very fragile and painful to use. They are still regenerating, still growing on the inside.

He stands and lunges again, and we fight, exchanging punches, and scratches, and bites. We break bones, shatter teeth, and rip skin; both too stubborn to call it a draw. But there will be a winner—and it will be me.

"You're the one who told me to leave," he says, as we both lay in the mud catching our breath after about forty-five minutes of scuffling hostility. "Why did you come out to fight?"

"I am not fighting for me." I say under heavy breath, as I half-ass punch him one more time in the arm. "You disrespected the Fae. Their wings are their livelihood—they are their Gods. A Sprite is not a Sprite without its wings. I could see the pain in their faces as you stomped them, and I could not sit and watch you walk away from that," I pause to cough, and catch my breath again. "Go apologize, cunt."

He lets out a heavy sigh realizing the hurt that he had caused. He stands and limps toward me—worn and tattered to the same extent, he holds out his hand and helps me to stand before shrinking again to his normal height of three feet. "You win," he says defeated. "You are a good fighter, and you don't need a weapon to defend yourself. I would be honored to watch you fight *with* one. I bet that it's one Hell of a show." He hangs his head, and limps back into the shack finding his place again around the fire to apologize to Cynniaa and the other guards who sit next to him, Human-sized, as I had changed their height when they had arrived.

I return slowly to the fire, too, and sit completely still waiting for my wounds to heal. After the others calm from seeing the damage done, as they stayed inside with Tziipoor, we speak a little more about the oncoming search, and then decide to break from each other until tomorrow. We will look farther out into the city when we have daylight. I retreat to my bed and lie gently, still in pain from the fight before. Tomorrow is a new day.

The sun rises, and I can hear Birds singing outside. I dream of home. In the dream there are Crickets beginning to silence from the night, and Frogs returning to their burrows. I see the grass and the trees swaying back and forth in the morning wind. I can see the orange sun rise into a pink sky over the vast green fields of Kansas corn and beans. I can smell the dust in the sky. I am awakened by a Voice from across the room—

"It is beautiful." Tziipoor says. *"One day I would like to see this land."*

"Yes," I reply. "It is beautiful. I miss it a lot." I roll to my side to face her and tuck my hand under my cheek for support. "What is your home called; what was it like?" I ask her.

"Our home was [68]*Taaviirax. You would have loved it. The sky always had a hint of green, and days were much shorter there. There were five other planets around us that we could see periodically, as we rotated around each other. They were so big in the sky, that the night was never much darker than the day. The land had many pools, and springs, and waterfalls. The ground was never dry or bare. The trees were tall and skinny with dark wood and black leaves. The rock and sand that made up the ground was also very dark in color. There were many other creatures who called* [69]*Taaviirax home. But like the Humans of Earth, the Queel were the most knowledgeable on Taaviirax."*

We decide to finally get up and get ready to join the others. We can hear them in the other room talking and moving things around. I hear the door open and close again behind someone. I peek around the corner and see that Aneera had gone ahead. The three Fae are gathering their things to help search until dark, then they plan to return to Vaahiigali while the rest of us prepare for the first Trial. I return them to their normal size and bow respectfully before they leave the shack. Fuckface is sprawled across one of the chairs by the fire, snoring lightly with his head thrown back over the arm rest, and his huge mouth hanging wide open. I roll my eyes and turn to follow Cynniaa and his accompanying guards out the door. We all decide to leave him behind to sleep off his injuries—he does not heal as quickly as I do.

I fly above, as Tziipoor sprints across the buildings at an incredible speed behind me. She is so fast and agile and has

---

[68] [tah-vee-RAH]

[69] Planet Detail—Taaviirax: the home of the Queel. This planet was inhabited by mostly animals. There was one species of bipedal Humanoids called Geetra [guh-AE-druh] lightly roll the r sound. These beings lived in peace with the Queel and worked together with them to protect Taaviirax from off-planet civilizations who wanted to enslave the knowledge of the Queel. This partnership succeeded in their efforts until the planet was eventually invaded and left to parish after Tziipoor was taken for the Game sometime around 1,700 years ago.

unbelievable endurance. She has hands like a Human in the front, and boney feet—that more resemble hands—with elongated toes that she uses to grab onto things, in the back. When she walks or runs on all fours, she folds her fingers much like a Chimp or a Gorilla using her knuckles to support her weight, but her fingers are more compressed. They fit perfectly together to form a new shape.

We move quickly through the city until about midday and find the warehouse where we had stopped the day before. We do not intend to enter again. We just need to start where we had left off. Tziipoor informs me of another heartbeat that she hears in the distance—

"This one is mysterious like the last one but beats with less hostility; it is not the same creature," says the Clutch.

"Is it another Host from the Void?" I ask them.

"Yes," answers Tziipoor. *"There is a forest in the distance. We can hear more than one now."* I fly upward until I can see a line of trees far off to the northwest of here. It is the Empty Forest.

"You can hear them from that far away?" I ask her. "I thought that forest was empty."

"One day you will hear it, too," she replies.

"I can't wait," I say looking forward. "We can probably reach the trees' edge in about four hours, or so."

"Then we had better get moving," she answers. We travel again at a steady pace until we meet the forest. I observe it from above for a moment, as Tziipoor calculates how close she stands to the newly found Hosts. She tells me that she hears more heartbeats now and thinks that there is a village or a small city close by. *"There are many,"* she says.

"We have a little time until the Trial begins. Let's try not to get into too much trouble," I tell her. "I would like to come back from the Trial *not* fighting for my life."

The Clutch agrees with me, and I jump on Tziipoors back, as we step lightly through the trees. We travel toward the sound of the heartbeats for about an hour before Tziipoor warns me that we are being watched. She is much calmer this time, but I can still feel a bit of uneasiness.

"There are four here watching us," she tells me. *"But there are a couple hundred more nearby."*

"That must be the village," I reply. "We should go back. We can introduce ourselves after the Trial."

"Yes. But we would like to investigate a bit more first," the Clutch answers. *"A lot can be learned through conversation. And we are focusing in on a rather interesting one."* She turns to the left, beginning to circle the nearing village.

"You can hear them?" I ask. "I thought it was just heartbeats."

"I want you to try and hear them," she says.

I sit and listen quietly for a moment. I close my eyes and try to focus, but I hear nothing—

"I don't know how," I say.

"You are searching too hard," she answers.

"You have to let them come to you, just like the sounds that you hear from everywhere else. They all start somewhere and find you in their own time. The Voices of someone's mind can do the same—even from a far distance if they think loud enough. Just listen; let yourself hear them. You are already there. You can hear us," the Clutch explains. *"You have to create the constant idea that you are surrounded. Give them a form or a character in your mind to latch onto."*

Tziipoor continues on to say, *"We will help you with this one. Start with something small like a circle or a square."*

I follow her instruction.

"Give it only one meaning: mystery. You must always remember this shape. Always keep it present in your mind. If you do this correctly, a Voice will latch to it when you are near someone or something. It is a similar process for the heartbeat. Be open to what you want to hear, but do not let it control your thought. Place it in the back of your mind but keep it close enough for you to hear when there is sound nearby."

"Everything you teach me is so confusing," I say. "Think about it, but don't think about it—I don't understand."

"It will come to you," she replies.

"What are they saying?" I ask her.

"You must hear it for yourself," she says. *"Listen."*

I use the shape technique, and ride silently trying to focus, but not focus too hard. It is much like doing two things at once, and I suck at multitasking. I grow distracted by the trees above looking for shadows, or places where Hosts could be hiding. I hear a sound and turn my head to the left.

Tziipoor stops walking and turns her head looking in the same direction. It was a mumble, a small word. It was very quiet and muffled. But I heard it. I look back to the trees trying not to cut the tie between my mind and this tiny Voice.

Tziipoor continues walking forward giving me full control of our movements. Her head moves as mine does, and her eyes look where mine do. It is like I am moving her; we are one. Our bond is growing stronger. I am learning, and when the time comes, I will be accepted as one with Tziipoor, the Clutch, and the Universe as well. I will hear what they hear and feel what they feel. I will see all that they see. I will be freed from the confinement of Human thought.

A Voice speaks again, but this time it is clearer to me. I keep my eyes on the trees, and direct Tziipoors steps as I see fit. There is a meeting—a small group, perhaps four or five.

For the first time, I understand this power. Not only can I hear them, but I can sense them; I can feel them. They discuss their growing numbers, and an ongoing war. They are Spirits of the ground, or [70]Eiinokrra, which Tziipoor can only identify as ancestors of the Dark Elves.

These are creatures from the Void. They are older than the Great God—older than the Universe herself. They speak of the creatures that they are preparing to fight. I am in shock when I hear what they say. The Void has been at war for the full length of its existence. It has never known peace.

There are two types of creatures that inhabit it, other than the Hosts who have been brought to, or who have been born on Irestiikaar. These two creatures are the only ones that can come and go to the planet as they please—I will give more detail on this later. The Eiinokrra rule the land, and the others are Spirits that rule the sky. They call them the [71]Liiyetrrux, or the Elite Gods.

"Those are the Gods that your Gods descended from," says Tziipoor. *"The original Gods, they created us all,"* she follows.

"Descended?" I ask.

"Yes," replies the Clutch. *"The Elites wanted to have a place inside of our Universe with creatures that they could communicate with and track her growth. After taking Irestiikaar, our Universe had shut them out. They were no longer able to travel inside; only the Adreestiaah could enter. Like the Elites, it is an entity of the Void, but it was not created there. The ship was made from the rock of the uninhabited planet, Hevaan, so that is where they chose to send their recruits."*

---

[70] [ee-no-KRAH]
[71] [lie-YET-ruh], lightly roll the r sound.

"So, if they couldn't get in, how did they do it?" I ask. "Did they ride in on the [72]Adreestiaah?"

"Yes," they reply. *"They sent four [73]Elite districts to the planet Hevaan, and over time, the First Four lost some of their power and without the ability to restore it, they lost their faith in the Elites and chose to break away from them as the Universe did."*

"Why did they lose their power?" I ask.

"Because the Elites draw their power from the Void, and our Universe is very strong. Inside, they could not draw enough Voided energy," they explain.

"So, they chose to create a new way of life?" I reply. "Now the Hevaanian Gods are one of the most powerful empires in the Universe, aren't they?"

"They are the most powerful," Tziipoor says, *"and the Elites are their greatest enemy. One day, we will join a side in the Immortal War, and the Universe will fight for her survival."*

---

[72] Monument Detail—Adreestiaah: created three years before the taking of the planet Irestiikaar. The Liiyetrrux planned to take the planet for many years before the heist was carried out. They knew that our Universe would deny them the ability to enter, so they had to create an entity that could travel back and forth between the two places indefinitely. Using resources from the planet of Hevaan ensured that the ship could return to its homeland without the Universes permission.

[73] Host Detail—The First Four: sent to the planet Hevaan on a mission. Each district was nearly 30 thousand strong. They ferried them in a little at a time and succeeded in their plan to infiltrate our Universe.

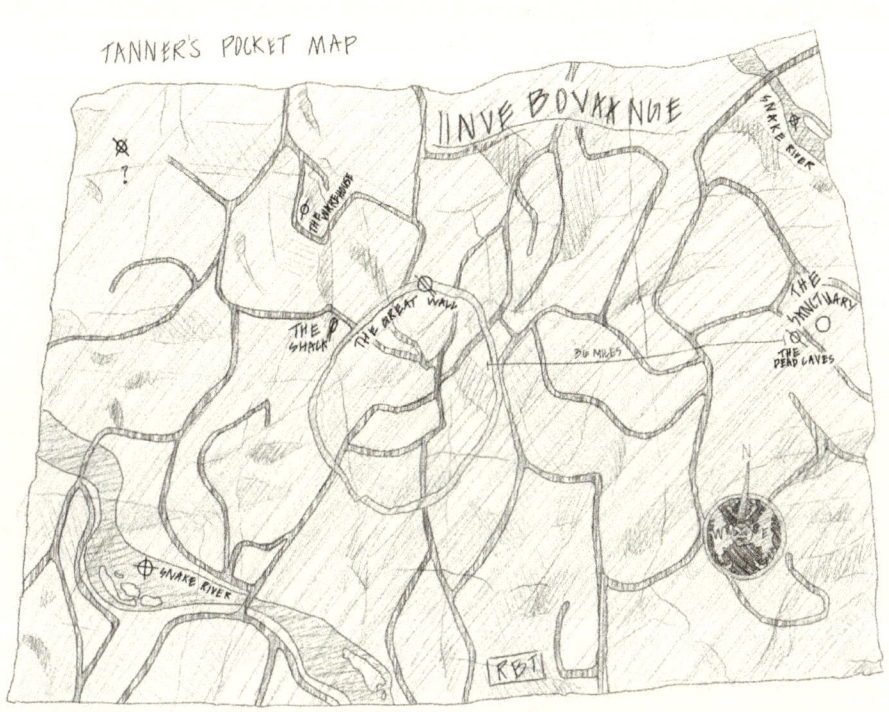

TANNER'S POCKET MAP

THE SECOND
RED BLOOD

STATUE IN THE
GARDEN OF PROPHECIES
VAAHIIGAVI

TAAVIIRAX
HOME OF
THE QUEEN
DECEASED

111

THE THIRD DREAM

The sky is dark, only the Games Moon watches me as I step a few paces behind her and her companions. She treads across the sand. There is a secret that she seeks. She dresses the same and her hands hang beside her each holding tightly to the small bubble-like creatures that follow her; **5** altogether.

They are round with blue and white fur. They have short legs and long outstretched arms that reach to whatever they desire, and skinny boneless tails that drag behind them. The tiny round wings that grow from their backs beat tirelessly as they carry their Hosts. Small glimmers of light follow behind them shining with bewitching beauty under the light of the sky.

The bubbles chatter amongst themselves as the Red-Blooded seeker leads them to her destination. They are happy to be with her, and she is happy to have them. The bubbles are said to radiate good fortune, and if they take liking to you, they will share their magic. But for now, the seeker only acquires their company.

She did not come to the desert for them, only upon her arrival did they choose to cross the flats with her. The thing of which she seeks, requires unique reasoning from her, and that she will deliver to it.

For twenty days I follow them. For twenty days they move at the same pace. The bubbles chatter, and the seeker watches the horizon; no sound or thought to come from her. On the twenty-fifth day she rests. On the twenty-fifth day she finds the secret she came searching for.

Deep inside of a hole carved from an irregular desert rock, there is a tunnel. The seeker bids goodbye to the bubbles—all but one, the eldest bubble, more curious and cunning than the other **4**.

It wraps its arms around her neck and holds tight, comfortably and confident. She shrinks them and carries on into the darkness of the teeny tunnel.

At the bottom, she finds a light. It shines with bright magnificence matching the color of her Mammal red blood. The light is incased in clear rock. But the seeker cannot wield it, its protection forbids contact with that which lives inside of her.

The bubble, however, sees through this protection with a pure and present soul it can wield the Yokkaa as it wishes. Before pulling it from its place, the bubble grants a gift to the seeker. It plucks a piece of its magic fur and stitches it into her fingertips. The fur dissolves and a particle of light—a piece of free soul from the bubble is passed from its back to the seeker's palms.

The bubble reaches for the stone, pulling it from the rock that holds so tightly to it. Light radiates from both the bubble and the Yokkaa, and then from the seeker as she receives the riches of her new magic. It is not the Yokkaa that makes the holder powerful, but rather the holder that gives the greedy Yokkaa its power. One must have the will to create their own power under the watchful eye of the stone.

The treader pockets the trinket and carries the bubble, returning it to the surface. She thanks it and gifts it a small bracelet made of jade crafted by a stoneworker native to the planet called Earth.

5

THE FIRST TRIAL

We walk through the woods until we reach the city again. According to Aneera's vision, the Trial will begin in about an hour. It is night now, and we decide to find a safe place to hide. I can hear the chatter of every creature around me. There are so many of them. I figured out how to find the Voices, but now I cannot turn them off. They are not very loud, but I can hear a constant carrying whisper.

"Is it always like this?" I ask Tziipoor.

"No," she replies. *"You will learn to control it. It takes time."*

"How far does it reach?" I ask.

"We will always be able to communicate, just in shorter sentences. It will get more difficult the farther we are apart, but the connection will never be cut unless Tziipoor is bonded with another," the Clutch explains. *"We could be on opposite sides of the Universe, and still hear each other. But the other Voices that we hear can only be picked up at certain distances depending on how loud the creatures think."*

16 Days since the fall...

The hour is up. It is time. I sit placing my body in a comfortable position. I found a cramped place to hide this body so that its life will not be stolen when my mind is transferred to the [74]doppelganger

---

[74] Gameplay Detail—Doppelganger Bodies: created for each participant by the Game Runners. These bodies are dropped from the sky before the Trial begins, and left spread across the designated regain until the players mind is moved to the new body.

body that it will inhabit for the Trial. I have recently been informed of this helpful information. When I am in the Trial, I can die and be returned to my true body only deducting points rather than life. But if I die in my real body, then that is assuredly the end. I had been told this by Aneera, who has proven herself to be very wise—like Tziipoor and the Clutch.

I close my eyes and wait, as if waiting to fall asleep. I think about Barroun—wondering if we will succeed in this venture unaware of the misfortune that will welcome me into the new region of land that will carry this trial. We are going halfway across the planet to the [75]Bhaaktii. Tziipoor gave me two translations for this: one being the Blue Desert, and the other which is the Blue Sand Desert. From both I can assume that the land will be vast and dry with few places to hide. Good thing I do not have to worry about starving to death or searching for water. I am thankful that I no longer have to depend on food or drink to stay alive. There is only one goal.

The First Hevaanian Gate
The Blue Desert
Bhaaktii

I open my eyes to find myself peering into the well-lit night sky. I forget the danger for a moment lost in the beauty of the Bhaaktii. [76]Blue Sand is right. It glistens like the ocean under an ugly moon that never looks the same. But it is missing one thing. There are no stars. The Void is a place lacking natural light. Each planet, though there are very few—including Irestiikaar—is surrounded by a barrier. This barrier protects the Spirits of the ground—the Eiinokrra—from the spirits of the sky—the Liiyetrrux and provides sunlight and moonlight to the planet that it surrounds.

I find my footing in the shifting sand and peer across the dunes in every direction trying to decide which way to go.

"Tziipoor," I say. "Can you hear me?"

---

[75] [ba-HAK-dee]

[76] Monument Detail—Blue Sand: left over debris from the previously standing city of Bhaatrra [ba-HAH-truh] or Blue Crystal. The city was carved in the same way as Vaahiigali in terms of excavation. It was invaded by a rival kingdom and left in tiny shards, creating the vast land now known as the Bhaaktii Desert. This event took place over 7 billion years ago.

"Yes," I hear her reply.

I turn toward the direction of her Voice and begin my flight across the desert. It is best to travel through the night. My skin will not burn under the fake sun, and I am unsure what to expect about the heat, but I know that I will be easier to see in the daylight, so nighttime is safer. I fly for about an hour or so before reaching a peak revealing a small [77]deserted temple at its base.

I approach cautiously. I am caught off guard by a Voice from below. It is another mumble, not a full sentence. It appears that this technique requires just a little bit more mastery. I do not understand what it says, but I can feel where it is coming from. The temple must have many tunnels that run through the sand below my feet. There is something in there, but it is not Tziipoor.

I stand, now above the entrance, staring down at the black hole emerging from archaic stone. I hear the murmured Voice again, and this time it is much closer. I need to prepare myself for what is to come.

"Be cautious," I hear the Clutch say. *"We cannot sense the Host's intention."*

I decide that if I am going to face this creature, perhaps it would be better to do so during the daytime—when I can see better. I want to wait the creature out. I fly down to the shallow steps just outside of the massive door. I look up and take a few steps back, then sit crisscross with my arms crossed as well, and lean against a toppled pillar from the temple. I stare blankly into the dark entrance attempting to find the heartbeat of whatever lies within.

"Is it close?" I ask the Clutch. "Can it see me?"

"No," is the reply, *"but it is moving closer."*

I sit for a while dozing in and out. About 30 minutes go by, and I open my eyes again. I notice a body. It is crouching, and just barely sticking out from the shadows. I can see a knee, and an elbow, and a thin boney hand. It appears to have the same form as a Human.

We stare at each other, both completely still, for a time period that seems to last forever. I do not move because I do not want to frighten or startle it. After several minutes, it finally crawls out into the moonlight, so that I can see it in its entirety. I keep my head

---

[77] Monument Detail—Deserted Temples: created around 2.5 million years ago. These temples were built by the descendants of the survivors of the Bhaatrra massacre in remembrance of their fallen kingdom.

facing forward, but I follow it with my eyes. The first thing I notice about it is its black hair.

It is a woman. Her hair is very long and drags cross the sand when she maneuvers using her toes and the tips of her fingers. She moves very slow stretching out one leg at a time, inching gracefully toward me, still crouched low to the ground. She spreads her toes, using them each individually like fingers feeling the vibrations in the sand. She has a long stick that she carries on her back, some sort of weapon I wander.

Her ears stick out on either side of her head. She tucks them back around her head when she moves and stretches them out to the sides when she stops and sits more upright to observe me. They twitch back and forth, as she picks up the sounds of the desert bouncing off the sand around us. There are stretched holes in her lobes, and small black chains connecting from piercing to piercing, from the stretched holes to the tips of each ear.

She has three eyes. One sits in the center of her forehead, and the other two in normal spots just below. She has two brows, but not a third for the eye at the top. Her eyes are black—all black—like a Demon. And I have yet to see her blink.

She has skimpy black fabric lined with silver metal across her chest and along her waist. There is a silver arm cuff around her bicep on each side matching the thinner one that holds tight around her neck, the slightly thicker one hugging the thinnest part of her torso, the double set around each thigh, and the thicker bands on her ankles. I would guess that these have decorative meaning, or perhaps are some sort of symbolism of strength.

Her skin is pale with a hint of greyish blue, but fades into black from just above her wrists to her fingertips, above her ankles down to her toes, from her collar bone up to her jaw, and on the tips of each ear. I can only wonder what she looks like during the day, as she is obviously a creature molded for night.

She now crouches just across from me—within arm's reach. She squats, arching her spine upright, and holding back her shoulders fixing her posture. She lifts one hand from the ground, and the color changes to white before touching the skin on my arm, and then returns to black after withdrawing her hand back—cautiously examining me. She crouches again to circle around me. She lifts my braid, and releases it, then returns again to her spot in front of me squatting upright *again* with good posture. I can tell that she is thinking something, but I cannot make out her thoughts.

"You are the Red Blood Tanner," she eventually says. Her voice is soft, but when she speaks there is an accent. It sounds almost like she is speaking real English rather than her language being translated. She stumbles through some of the words, but she knows exactly what she is saying.

"Yes," I reply to her, "that is my name. How do you know that?"

"You found our [78]nest," she replies. "What were your intentions?"

"Just curiosity," I answer her.

"You should be more careful." she says ominously reaching to pull my braid across my shoulder. "There are many who would like to leash you—*both* are a very rare breed," she says, referring to the Human and the Queel. "And your name...you are spoken of by many names."

I stare uneasily at her without a reply, as she twists the end of my hair through her fingers.

"Do I frighten you?" she then asks.

"Not frighten," I say, "but you disturb me."

She scoffs and smiles with dark teeth that match her eyes. She tilts her head to the side, and we observe each other for a moment.

"I sense further intention in your stare," I tell her. "Is there more that you want to say to me?"

"My uncle requests an audience with you," she says.

"Why do I feel like that meeting will prove more sinister than how you present it?" I ask.

"Ah," she replies, "he said that you would be quite cunning," she laughs. "You presented yourself to us first. We only want to ensure our safety. You *are* descended from our greatest enemy."

"The Liiyetrrux," I say understanding her inquisition, "they are *no* ally to me." I look down remembering the pain caused from the previous amputation of the four fingers on my left hand. "I don't like those assholes any bit more than you do."

---

[78] City Detail—Eiinokrrian Nest: located somewhere in the Empty Forest. This nest of creatures terrifies Hosts so much to a point that they refuse to speak of it. This place is known to exist, but no one other than the Eiinokrra knows how to enter the Hidden City.

She smiles again revealing her gnarly black teeth, and she scoots in closer. Our conversation continues to the next subject. She seems to be on a mission to retrieve the Queel and me for interrogation, but I can see how distracted she is becoming by wonder. She asks about the "strange pictures" on my skin, and if I was born with them like the changing color spots on hers. She asks if my blood is truly red, or if that assumption only came from legend. She also asks about the Earth, and what it is like. I cautiously give her truthful answers without relaying too much information. I am uncertain of how my replies may affect the future.

I stay wary of any intention to vex me continuing to play along with the present conversation. I listen carefully to her questions, and answer in short sentences. This one-sided discussion plays for a little under an hour before a rather touchy new subject is introduced—

"You are here in search of something." She looks at me with a rather mischievous stare. "Or someone?" She pauses for effect, raising an eyebrow, "a God perhaps?"

"Yes," I reply. "How do you know that?"

"A prophet once wrote of this," she says following with another black-toothed smile, and the raise of a finger. "We have prepared for this for a long time. Let me take you to him." She gestures for me to follow her into the darkness of the buried temple.

I prepare myself to ask her why I should trust her, but I am unexpectedly interrupted by the Clutch—

"Follow her," they tell me.

I fight the urge to ask why and stand to follow the creature into the pitch-black tunnel. I have no confidence in her, but I place my life completely in the hands of the Clutch—whom I trust whole heartedly. They gift me with the ability to see through the darkness, as I wander deeper with the [79]young Eiinokrra. Even when separated from the body of Tziipoor, the Clutch will still protect its bond.

We finally reach a dead end. I am taken aback by the massive [80]mural that sits etched into the stonework. It matches the pictures from Vaahiigali and has the same ancient script. This is a

---

[79] Host Detail—Eiinokrra: can live to be around 3,000 years old.
[80] Monument Detail—Mural: added to the temple walls by the Hevaanian Gods around the same time that the Entanglement Keys, and the other murals found in Vaahiigali were placed. Its purpose is to help lead the Human on the right path.

map of the Bhaaktii. There are nine other temples scattered across the desert.

I inspect the map, and then turn toward the creature, "The Lost God," I say. "Why are you helping me find him?"

"He plays a very important part in the Long Prophecy," she informs me.

"What long prophecy?" I then ask.

"It tells of two banished Gods from the kingdom of Hevaan, and a Human—a Red Blood—from the kingdom of Earth. They are taken prisoner by the Voided cosmos—during a time of great loss. Once united, they join a side in the Immortal War, and finally bring it to its end," she says. "*That* is the short version."

She gives me no chance to reply before pointing out a small hole following the script on the wall. She references the Entanglement Key in my pocket reminding me of the purpose of our quest. I pull it from my pocket and insert it into the small hole. I turn it to the left first, and then to the right. There is a loud rumble behind the wall, and sand begins to fill the space around my feet. The Eiinokrra and I both struggle to keep our legs from being buried.

The sand stops just below my knee, and I am blinded by moonlight. My eyes adjust to the light, and I stare again at the map along the wall. The key had opened a mechanism clearing the sand from small channels leading back to the surface. I can see a path. It tells me where to go. There is another temple close to the center of the Bhaaktii. It sits in the center of a small city.

"Can you read that?" I ask her while pointing toward the script at the bottom.

"Yes," She answers.

I stare at her for a minute expecting her to tell me what it says, but there is no explanation.

"What does it say?" I then ask her.

She lifts her hand from the ground, and the color changes again to white before she places a finger on the wall tracing along the bottom of each symbol, and reading out loud—

"'Keyhole', and this is an arrow pointing to the hole," she says while pointing to another small glyph.

"Really," I say with disappointment and disbelief. "Ancient script on a million-year-old map and *that* is what it says?" I reply.

"Yes," she answers.

I struggle to find anything to say, so decide to dump the conversation and move to the next obstacle. I take one last look over the map, and then follow her out through the tunnels back to the surface.

"By the size of the area I can assume that the journey will take about six days, on foot. I can cut that time in half by flying, but I cannot carry you." I tell the Eiinokrra, not comfortable enough yet to trust her.

"Do not worry about me," she says.

I open my wings and turn to look at her. She smiles and stands upright for the first time.

"Are you a super speedy runner?" I ask with a touch of sarcasm while mocking the stance of a sprinter.

She turns her head to the sky and calls out with a cry unlike any that I have ever heard. I am shocked at the sound of a returned cry, and the noise of giant fluttering wings. Amazement floods my mind once I catch a glimpse of a *very* large flying rodent. It is a ghost-like, white colored Bat with long ears, and a twisted snout. It has three black eyes that mirror hers and is equipped with a black rider's saddle. She climbs up its back and attaches a tiny safety [81]harness to the silver band around her torso.

"Do you think you can keep up?" she asks, challenging me to a race. I raise an eyebrow to accept and take my un-agreed-upon head start as per usual. One must always think quickly to beat a clever Fool.

We race high above the sand at an unimaginable pace. This is a true test of speed and endurance. We fly for a day and a half. Neither of us tires enough to break from the inconvenience of exhaustion. The fight continues, though I have grown quite bored of it. I have lost the excitement of winning and decide to change to a cruising speed.

---

[81] Relic Detail—Eiinokrrian Equipment: crafted from the same silver used by the Fae in Vaahiigali. The Eiinokrra are distant creatures, but they still take part in the meetings and trades of the other Hidden Cities. These silver bands represent accomplishments, ranks, and blood lines. Once put on, these bands are never to be removed.

18 Days since the Fall...

We have traveled over the [82]Bhaatrra Mountains headed northwest, passing about four of the nine temples. At nightfall, we find a fifth one, and land at the Eiinokrra's request. She senses another one of her kind. I am weary of surrounding myself with these creatures, but the Clutch has not warned me not to. They told me to follow it and have been quiet since. They are studying it. They are curious about this new creature and want to learn more about it. And they are using my eyes to do it. I find myself looking and my head turning without my consent.

Tziipoor is still a few days behind us. She is tracking our heartbeats and following the sound of my Voice. She is accompanied by Aneera, but Fuckface has yet to find them. She tells me that the Clutch is invested in the Eiinokrra— almost even obsessed. She is eager to find us, so that she can see this creature with *her own* eyes.

I stand at a distance studying the massive rodent that carries the Eiinokrra. The Bat has a white—almost translucent—layer of fur growing from the thick, pale skin that protects it. I can see through the creature; its organs and all of its insides are transparent with a very light blur. It stands over three feet taller than me and has a very large mouth. Other than the size, its odd fur, and the third eye on its forehead—it much resembles an albino Horseshoe Bat. I assume the possibility that every species of Bat on Earth are descendants of this mighty creature. It has black hands and feet matching its masters—and black on the tips of its ears too. So, I can *also* assume that this is a creature from the [83]Void as well.

It seems to be just as interested in me, as I am with it. I wonder if it can communicate with the Eiinokrra the way that Tziipoor and the Clutch do with me. I turn my head to see that the Eiinokrra has wondered into the tunnel alone. I listen for any inside conversation.

---

[82] Monument Detail—The Bhaatrra Mountains: The Blue Crystal Mountains are of the same stone used to carve the city of Bhaatrra.

[83] Host Detail—Voided Creatures: it has been stated that only two creatures hail from the Void. In this, it is meant that there are only two that are superior to the rest. There are other creatures that accompany the Eiinokrra and the Liiyetrrux, but most of these creatures are feral. Some work well with the ruling races, but the rest are unfamiliar and distant.

I have been instructed to trust her, but I have a strong gut feeling that I should stay ever vigilant of my surroundings. I still have my doubts. The tunnels are silent—free of Voices. Perhaps they do not think loud enough at the moment for me to hear them.

The Adreestiaah took away my need for sleep, but not my love for it—I still always seem to doze off. I dream about a familiar laboratory. It is the same one that I saw when I made the injection in my hand that gave me the ability to shrink and grow bigger. This time I am doing something with my blood. I withdraw it from my veins and separate it into ten small tubes. In each tube, I add a different colored concoction. The blood in the first three tubes change from the color red to the color black, and the blood from tubes four, five, and six turn silver. The tubes that are labeled seven through nine all change to a dark colored green, and the last tube—number ten—does not change at all.

The Clutch wakes me with a warning. The Eiinokrra returns to the surface accompanied by another creature like her—but this one is a man. They both emerge from the shadow of the entrance walking on all fours and stand upright once they reach the Bat. The man is taller and has silver lined, black fabric around his waist—just as skimpy as the female's. His hair is long too, but not as long as hers. He has silver bands around his upper arms and one around his torso and neck also. His ears are long and pierced like hers, and his skin matches in color. The only major difference that I can see between them is that he only has [84]two eyes instead of three.

They both climb onto the creatures back and attach safety harnesses to the bands around their torsos. The woman instructs me to follow them, and we take to the sky again in silence. We should reach the desired temple by morning. I watch the sand below shift in the wind, as we fly through the night. I can hear the man tell the woman about a city that surrounds the temple. We will have to find our way to the center on foot, so that we are not followed by any creatures that may see us flying above.

---

[84] Host Detail—Eiinokrrian Eyes: the family members of the Chief in every Eiinokrrian Nest are each gifted with a third eye representing their relation to the highest-ranking Chief among the species. The Eiinokrra with two eyes are not necessarily considered lower than the ones with three, they are just not from the ruling bloodline.

6

THE CITY IN THE SAND

The false sun is about to rise, and we land on a peak overlooking a city in the distance. It is not the size of IInve Bovaange, but it is deserted all the same. This city must have been built by some species of Giant. The doorways are tall and come to a triangular point.

I can hear the murmurs of many Voices in the city. This must be the main fighting area for the Trial—this is where all of the creatures meet to see who will prove themselves to be the best fighter. But that is not my purpose here.

Tziipoor has informed me that she still travels with Aneera, and they are getting closer. She says that they should find the city around midday—they must be moving faster than they originally thought. They still have yet to find Fuckface, but Aneera says that Cynniaa is somewhere in the city. I was previously unaware that he had chosen to join us. He is a good fighter, but I worry that he will struggle here, and I assume the responsibility that I now have to find him.

Another problem I have found in my current situation is that we are still missing a very important piece to this puzzle. The Eiinokrra are aware of my need to find the Lost God, but they seem to be *unaware* of our need for Barroun. We know where to find the banishment sphere, but we cannot open it without the help of a true-and-titled God. "What a mess we are in," I think to myself.

We will travel on foot from here on. The female Eiinokrra gives instruction to her ride—telling it to stay close in case we come across the need for assistance. I can hear the clash of metal and the roar of the fighting in the distance. This will be quite the venture. I expect that we will have to fight our way through to the temple in the center of the city. Trials have a different vibe than the rest of the Gameplay. They are pure violence; it is all about who kills the most. The ultimate goal is to be the last one standing—obtaining points for every kill. Each Host has a different price—some award more points than others. For example, killing Cynniaa would give a minimal number of points because there is an abundant number of Fae on Irestiikaar; whereas killing me—the Red Blood—would give a substantial amount of [85]points due to the fact that I am the only one of my kind who is here.

I hope that we can meet up with the rest of the group in good time. I do not want to be stuck alone with the Eiinokrra for the entirety of this venture. It would be nice to have another Host from my group here to take some of the tension off. Even Fuckface would be a good one to have around, and that is really saying something because he is the asshole above all assholes. But I need some sort of familiarity. I can sense Tziipoor getting closer, but there is still a good distance between us, so I will just have to tough through it for the time being.

I follow behind the female who takes the lead—now walking on two feet instead of all fours. It is odd to watch. I have grown used to seeing her walk crouched to the ground. The male walks upright as well, but he stays next to me when the other one goes ahead. He struggles for words, wanting to speak, but not knowing what to say. I decide to help break the silence for him—

"Do you have a name?" I ask. "What can I call you?"

"[86]Benoviii," he replies, "and she is [87]Sriii."

He points to the third member of our trio and continues to inform me of their relations. Her uncle is the Chief of their tribe, and his mother is their healer. Benoviii is one among their top fighters—he claims to be one of the best. He says that he is here as a sort of bodyguard for Sriii—though, she apparently does not need one. I am picking up on the idea that she is a pretty tough bitch. Good thing

---

[85] Gameplay Detail—Point System: points are almost like a bounty. The more the creature is desired by the Game Runners to be killed, the more points they will award for the assassination.

[86] [ben-OH-vee]

[87] [s-ree]

they are on my team—for now. I still have no amount of trust for them but knowing each of their [88]names helps me personify them rather than persisting to objectify them.

We finally reach the edge of the city. I pull Reewenniveaar from the scabbard and hold tight to it. I carry it preparing for any confrontation. It is times like these when I wish I had a hood or a cover for my face. I do not know how, but everyone always recognizes me as the Red Blood—with the exception of the Keeper who had no idea until it was too late for him. I cannot help but wonder how it is so easy for anyone to tell me apart from the other Human looking Hosts. Could it be my posture, or the way that I walk or talk? Perhaps it is my scent, or the unfamiliar look of my eyes?

The buildings here are much boxier and stand as tall like the ones in the City of the Lost. This must have been a supplier [89]city in its time. It is a good size to have had a relatively decent population, but I suspect no more than six thousand. Many of the faces that it had seen were likely just travelers passing through. The structures and the streets are tattered and buried in a thin layer of blue sand.

Sriii explains, "The fighting will be thick through here. Do not get caught up; we need to move quickly. Strike them down if they are in your way, but do not fall behind. Once you start here, you will not be able to stop."

"We have one mission." Benoviii follows.

I nod my head in agreement, and we enter the shambled city through the gate that separates it from the rest of the desert. We run at high speeds, and I watch—following behind—as the two Eiinokrra

---

[88] Relic Detail—Eiinokrrian Names/Titles: shown to be spelled with an extra letter compared to the rest. The inhabitants of the Voided Cosmos use a series of languages that were all created before our Universe, and, therefore, are somewhat different from the languages known on the inside. Hevaanian script is the closest to the Voided languages because its creators descended directly from the Void, whereas every other creature, apart from the Dark Elves, was created by our Universe. Many of these languages are very similar in speech and in text—with one of them being the most commonly used. Reminder! All languages are converted to Hevaanian, *and then* to English by the ability given to Tanner from the Adreestiaa.

[89] City Detail—The City in the Sand: created around the same time as the deserted temples. This city was populated by the descendants of the city of Bhaatrra until about 2,000 years ago when the people left for an unknown reason, abandoning the city.

hurdle over broken walls and piles of fallen bodies. They move swiftly on two feet, and I honestly struggle to keep up. A Host jumps at me from a doorway to the right, and I thrust my arm through the air using Reewenniveaar to slit its throat in one hasty move—dropping its body behind, as I continue to run after the two in front.

My reflexes are fearsome. I dodge arrows, as they fly through the air, and I just barely avoid a deep [90]cut across my face turning my head to the left and leaning back. A small knife grazes the highlight of my cheek and the tip of my nose. Enraged, I catch the knife out of the air by the end of its short handle and throw it back over my shoulder—puncturing its owner just between the eyes.

My newest allies slaughter any creature that gets in their way with a bewitching partnership. They jump over each other and guard each other's backs—effortlessly neutralizing the enemy—like one mind controlling both bodies. I stop running for a moment and watch the killing. They easily drop fourteen other Hosts, coming from all angles. I notice that Sriii's hair seems to move on its own; not meaning that it fights with her slapping and snapping and coiling around her enemies. It just beautifully keeps itself out of the way; it does not block her eyesight and it moves to avoid entanglement or capture. I then turn to Benoviii, seeing that his does the same as well.

The two of them both carry these long-skinny cylindrical sticks of silver. They never let them touch the ground and though I thought they would, they do not use them as [91]weapons. They purposely will sacrifice their body to protect the stick. It is odd, but they are smart, it is brilliant in so many disgusting ways. These creatures fascinate me. It is so strange to me how secretive they are, all while being blatantly obvious. They crouch and huddle close together whispering

---

[90] Gameplay Detail—Doppelganger: this false body does not bleed red. The Game Makers are unable to plagiarize this blood type. So—in this body—Tanner bleeds white, like the Gods who created her.

[91] Host Detail—The Eiinokrrian Accessories: they carry these sticks as a symbol of their self-control. Eiinokrra use these sticks to practice mindful distraction and discipline. They believe that complete control of oneself helps feed the ability to control others in any given situation. They train heavily in manipulation, mind games, and madness. Each band, earring, jewel, and article of clothing is a form of reward for their mastery or practice in a new technique. For example, the waist band is given to the Eiinokrra who have earned the courage to fly one of the Bats.

secretively when they speak—but they have no shame in looking at you or pointing when discussing you.

I laugh at myself and thank God that I have them on my side. If they stick with us for a while, I will have to ask them to give me the run through—it would be nice to be able to work that well with Fuckface and Aneera—Fuckface especially. We loathe each other, but he is a good fighter, and I have no doubt that we could really kick some ass together with this fighting style.

Running through the streets, we prosper—taking advantage of these easy targets and improving our numbers on the scoreboard. I can tell which Hosts are experienced fighters, and which ones have low to no chance of excelling here. Kudos to them for trying though—you will never get anywhere, if you do not at least put in a little bit of effort. They have the will—they just need to build the strength to back it up.

I continue to follow Sriii and Benoviii; doing my best to keep up. I catch a glimpse out of the corner of my eye of a fight taking place on the next street over. I stop and peer through the alley. I notice a familiar small Fae caught up with a massive brute. I must help him. I yell ahead to inform the two in front of my detour; I tell them to go on ahead, and I will catch up after assisting Cynniaa. I also take a second to thank fate for conveniently placing him in my path. We should make quick work of this creature together.

I run through the alley ejecting myself out the other side like a rocket. I jump, spin horizontally through the air, and avoid a blind swing from the aggressor. While in the air, I place a hand on Cynniaa and think, "Human," bringing him up to size, so that he can fight more efficiently against his enemies. I spread my wings and catch myself in the air before slamming into a building on the other side of the street. He is caught off guard by his growth. I can see his face fill with joy once he realizes that I had joined him. "He's in for it now!" he hollers over the newly confused and further agitated Host that he had been fighting alone before. We take turns slashing and stabbing until it falls to the ground, and I finish it off with one final blow to the head with my foot before flying on to rejoin with the two from before.

We weave back and forth through the streets, as I track the Eiinokrra with the help of the Clutch. We stay in the streets—careful not to fly too high. I rack up points cutting throats and delivering brain deadening hits to the head, as we pass by other Hosts left and right.

"This is a slaughterhouse!" I yell to Cynniaa through the chaos. "Are your friends here too?" I ask referring to the other Fae guards who had accompanied us in the shack a few nights before.

"Don't feel bad!" he answers. "They aren't really dying; remember these aren't their real bodies! And no, they stayed behind!"

He makes a good point, but I have just been struck with a thought. What if someone was just here when the Trial began? What if they just got caught in it? What if some of these Hosts are not actually doppelgangers? I will have to revisit this issue another time, and make sure that I can avoid being that unlucky someone someday. Imagine being caught in a Trial with a larger population of participants—and in a bigger city! This is already brutal enough. Being in a real body here would only add to the already thick tension.

I can see Sriii a short distance in front of us and forwardly introduce Cynniaa to the Eiinokrra. I explain the situation and tell him the destination that we are headed for. Aneera told me that once we get inside the cave, we will be able to block out the fight on the surface. We just need to find the entrance and wait for everyone else to get there. Then we can discuss the issue of finding the Banished God.

While explaining, I lose track for a moment and let my guard down. I hear a yell, and the smash of bone behind me. I turn around and see Fuckface—in his smaller form—flying through the air. He uses his strong legs to kick off the wall and fly back toward the attacking Host's head after cracking it with his fist. He had defended me. He is not very big, but he surely makes up for it with his strength. He wraps his legs around its neck, and holds tightly to its head with both hands, and rips it to the side. I hear the shatter of the bones in its neck, and I open my mouth to speak, but I am quickly interrupted—

"Don't thank me," he says with his hand up and his palm facing me with rejection after a perfect dismount from the emptied doppelganger of the Host. "I don't fucking care."

"I was going to comment on your stature. Don't worry. I wouldn't dare poke at your pride," I reply sarcastically.

"I don't need to use that state with these pussies," he says brushing me off. "They are weak, and I can't use it here anyway."

I laugh. "Wow, you're so cool," I say returning the line with the same level of sarcasm. But also confused as to why he cannot use his power here.

He scoffs and runs ahead toward the Eiinokrra—I guess he already heard the explanation. We join forces in the square around a dead fountain. Benoviii informs us of the location to the cave. He says that we are about three blocks from the entrance, and we must move quickly. We have a small gap of time, and if we hurry, we can reach it undetected. Our surroundings grow incredibly quiet, and the mood changes, as we step closer in the direction of the cave. I feel a certain familiarity—the same one that I felt when I shook hands with the captain of the Adreestiaah before leaving Earth. There is definitely a Hevaanian God here.

The temple entrance is very well hidden; it would be easy to miss if a Host close by did not know where to look for it. We follow Sriii through the descending tunnel for what seems like forever before we finally reach an opening at its base. The room is big enough to fit the five of us, and we are able to roam a bit, but it appears to be a dead end. There are carvings on the wall that match some of the carvings from the previous Hidden Rooms; Cynniaa points out a small section of Hevaanian script on the farthest side from the entrance.

"Here!" Benoviii says. He points to a small hole, "Use the key. It should open a door."

I pull the key from my pocket and insert it into the hole turning it in the same fashion as before—once to the left and once to the right. Noise irrupts, and the room shakes from the shifting of large boulders somewhere around us.

"I don't like this," Fuckface says.

"Neither do I," follows Sriii.

We all reach for our [92]weapons and stand with our backs to each other, in a circle facing the surrounding walls. The sounds grow

---

[92] Gameplay Detail—Trials: weapons. Hosts are given their weapons, and the abilities that connect to their minds. Once they expire in the Trial, their weapons will be returned to their real bodies. This includes knives, daggers, bows and arrows, spears, etc. Gear such as armor, scabbards, and wings are also given. Gear users have the upper hand over ability users during the Trials, hence the

louder, and the floor moves so intensely that we all struggle to stay standing. Suddenly, the floor cracks through the center, and I come to the realization that we are about to fall through the floor.

"Oh shit," I say under my breath.

"Shit, what?" Sriii asks. "What did you do?"

Before I am able to reply, the floor caves in, and the five of us are caught in a rockslide. I try to guard my head, as my body is thrown around and crushed under massive falling rocks. I try to fly out, but I cannot gain any control. When the chaos finally stops, and I am given a moment to gather myself, I sit up and choke on debris and the thick settling cloud of dust. My eyes are blurry, and there is a faint ring in my ear. I give myself some time to clear my eyes, but I am left with yet another problem. It is my right leg. It is broken. I painfully reach forward, and groan while I move the bottom part of the leg, so that the pieces of broken bones line up to assist them in [93]regrowth. But I lay back and hold in my tears trying to fight the pain after coming to a very disappointing [94]realization.

Benoviii approaches from around a pile of rubble in front of me, and crouches to join me on the ground. His injuries are much less serious than mine with only a few cuts and bruises. "Everyone is alright," he tells me. "Can you stand?" I continue to tell him that I can try to get up, but there is no possible way that I will be able to walk. I will need help, but I should be able to hover if my wings are not damaged.

---

importance of effective hand-to-hand combat skills and weapons knowledge, no matter who you are.

[93] Host Detail—Broken Bones: halfway below the knee, the tibia and the fibula are both broken and leaning to the right. There is no flesh wound to accompany this injury. During regrowth, if the bones are close enough to each other, they will latch to one another, and grow together again as if they had never been broken.

[94] Gameplay Detail—Doppelgangers: will not regenerate. Due to the fact that it is basically just a suit, this body was not made with the ability to heal injuries. It is meant for one-time use and will only last until it can no longer function. This is why Fuckface is also not able to change his size. But any ability that is controlled by the mind—such as Tanner's ability to connect with the Clutch and Tziipoor, and Aneeras ability to see visions—are not affected because those abilities are transferred to the doppelganger along with the mind. I am unsure as to why Tanner's ability to shrink and grow is not affected by this considering the location of the pressure point; it must be more mind control than originally thought.

He calls for Cynniaa, and he comes to assist us. I tell them that we have to find a way to stabilize my leg before moving me.

Once I am finally up and moving, we rejoin the rest of the group—I hope that whatever needs to be done here can be done quickly, so that I do not have to deal with the pain of this body much longer. The entrance has been blocked behind us with just a small space at the top where I will be able to shrink Tziipoor and Aneera small enough to crawl through once they arrive. The new cavern ahead is relatively small inside and is seeing Hosts for the first time since its [95]creation.

There is a massive drop in between the two separate sides of the cavern. We are on one side, and the sphere is on the other. It looks exactly like the picture that I saw in Vaahiigali, but it is much larger than I had anticipated. It stands about ten feet tall, and the ravine is much too big to just jump across. I suggest the option to shrink them all small enough to carry them across, and then return them back to normal size. That will be the easiest way to beat this obstacle. I do not know what gave me the idea to give myself this power, but I am extremely grateful that I did it.

Everyone agrees with my proposal, and Cynniaa and I carry the three of them across to the other side, then I return them to their normal sizes. Sriii wastes no time—she stands close to the Sphere and lifts her hand to touch it. The color of her hand changes from black to white and she places it on the massive glowing Sphere. I am intrigued by this action and feel compelled to do the same. I hover next to her and watch for a second—her eyes are closed, and she seems focused. She reaches up with her free hand and grabs mine—placing it on the Sphere next to hers.

"Close your eyes," she says; I follow her instruction. "Can you hear him?"

I remember the technique that Tziipoor had taught me—the one where I picture a shape, giving the sound something to latch onto. I focus on the feeling of the Eiinokrra's hand. I am troubled by it.

---

[95] Monument Detail—Cavern protecting the Banishment Sphere: when the sphere crashed into the planet around 1,000 years after the victory of Yeshua, it landed directly inside of one of the previously built Hidden Rooms. Once found by the Hevaanian Gods, they closed off the entrance and re-built a lock-and-key system to keep the sphere and the room hidden behind closed doors.

The longer I focus on it, the worse it becomes. Her skin is cold—unbearably cold. I would compare it to the bitterness of frostbite. My fingers have grown numb, and the bones in my wrist ache from the frigid temperature. Just as I am about to cry out, I hear a sound, and all the pain fades away. I open my eyes and look over to her to find her looking back at me.

"I hear it," I say quietly. "I can hear his heartbeat."

She smiles with her horrid black teeth and removes her hand from mine. "He's in there," she replies rather eerily.

"Now the problem is just getting him out," I say.

She pulls both hands back, and crouches back to the ground. I am left with a feeling of concern—or more discomfort—after watching her. The look on her face as she turns away from me exposes the true and terrifying creature that she is. She smiles with evil intention, and a very faintly colored, but also very large iris glows an icy blue color in each eye. Any small amount of good faith that I had in her is now gone. We—meaning Fuckface, Cynniaa, and myself—are in danger.

I keep myself calm, "Tziipoor, are you close?"

"Yes," she replies. *"Keep an eye on her. Do not turn your back. We will be there within the hour."*

I hover toward Fuckface and struggle to sit comfortably next to him, as I adjust my leg. Cynniaa joins shortly after. Fuckface gives us a look of aggravation before proceeding to say—

"This whole fucking cave and you have to sit *right* next to me?"

"Shut up and listen," I reply.

I explain my bothersome encounter with Sriii, and that the Queel and Aneera are closing in. We haggle with our plans and finally come to the conclusion that we need to wait for the other two to get here before we can go any further.

In the meantime, I remove the wings from my back, and I do my best to stitch the small tear at the bottom of the left one. Hffh sent some of the Errok thread with me, and had showed me some stitching techniques, so that I can keep the wings in their best condition. It is always amazing to watch the stitching disappear, and the wing pull itself back together like nothing had happened. It is such a unique process.

Fuckface has fallen asleep, and Cynniaa and I pass the time with light conversation. I tell him about how the Frog and I met, and that I have no idea why there is so much hatred between us. It has just always been that way—since the beginning. He also asks why it is that I call him Fuckface.

"He never told me his real name, and he never asked for mine, so honestly, I didn't care enough to ask for his either."

"[96]Ehhrn," Fuckface replies with his eyes still closed. "My name is Ehhrn. I did not ask for yours because I already knew it. And I hate you because of what you took from me."

I reply back in my defense that none of this is my fault, and that I have no idea why he feels the need to blame his problems on me. But I am discomforted once I hear the true reasoning behind his justifiably fueled hatred. Though none of it is *actually* caused by my actions, I can understand why I am the one that he feels like he needs to blame. I finally begin to understand why all of my allies seem to have some sort of underlying disrespect toward me.

He explains that he was recruited, along with Aneera, most likely the Queel, and a few other Hosts that we have yet to meet up with. The Great God of Hevaan paid him a visit, just before the onset of this seasons Game, and he was given a choice. The God asked him for a favor. He wanted Ehhrn to assist the Human. He asked that he help them make it to the end, and in return, he would retire him back to his home safely when finished. He also gave him the option to say no, but when a God asks you for help, it is said to bring bad luck if you refuse.

"I chose to help you," he says. "But I did it before I knew what I would be leaving behind."

"What do you mean?" asks Cynniaa.

"This Game will last ten years," he replies. "Ten years is a really long time."

"What did you have to leave behind?" I ask—filling my heart with guilt.

"My son," he replies again. "I never got to meet my son. My kind reproduce once in our lifetime. He is the only child that I will have.

---

[96] [ha-REN], spoken softly. Meant to sound like the word Heron with an a, rather than the name Aaron.

And for ten years of his life, he will have an absent father. He will know me as the man who left him."

My heart sinks even deeper, and I hang my head—holding back my tears. Ehhrn stands and leaves the group to re-gather his emotions in an attempt to hide the vulnerability he has shown to us. I struggle with this new revelation. Why did the Great God recruit help for me? And what is it that he thinks makes me so special? I know that I am Human, and that makes me *different* from the other creatures here, but I also know that I am no better than they are. My head fills with anger, and I am disgusted by the unfairness. God or not, I have lost much respect for him over this. Just because I am one of his Humans that does not mean that I deserve any special treatment. I am already hated enough for the 'Red Blood' title; I do not need more reason for them to despise me. And worst of all, Ehhrns son will grow up without a father—and in this case, it is not the God's fault, it is mine. I am the easiest to blame.

Cynniaa and I sit in silence, as I try to distract myself from the discomfort of this truth. But I cannot. I close my eyes and lose a lonely tear. I feel that familiar shake in my chin. I cry silently, but only with few tears, then I wipe my eyes and reconnect my wings. The pain in my leg has only grown stronger, but there is something that I need to know. I fly gently across the cavern to join Ehhrn on the other side. We stare at the Sphere for a time in silence.

"Why did you choose to help me?" I ask him. "Before you knew about your son? And *fuck* bad luck, why didn't you choose to stay after?"

He takes a second to think before he answers. "There is still a lot that you don't know about the outside world, Tanner. Like I told you, this is only the beginning. You'll learn what he wants you to know when he thinks you're ready."

"Tanner?" I reply. "Not Red Blood?"

"I will try and respect you from now on, but I expect you to do the same for me." He turns to join Cynniaa again. "They're here." He points toward the entrance, and I hear Tziipoor say that they are passing through the entrance of the cave.

"How did you know that?" I ask.

He shrugs his shoulders and walks away from me. I assume that he must have some sort of heightened senses—ones that are extremely distinguished. It is shocking that he could inform me of her arrival, and even more so that he did it just before her. I wonder what connections he has. If he was recruited, that means that there is some sort of mastered skillset—there seems to be one for each of the Hosts that were recruited. Aneeras has to be her premonitions, and Tziipoors is her connection to the Universe. Ehhrns could be some sort of echolocation, or perhaps, he is just super perceptive. The more I get to know, him the more I understand how smart he is. I knew that it would be a good idea to keep him around.

I fly across the cavern to the other side and assist them through the wall. I carry them across the ravine—to the side with the Sphere— and return them to regular size. Tziipoor is drawn straight to the Eiinokrra. She stalks them with her eyes. She then tells me that Aneera has had another vision. She is unaware of what it is, but she seems troubled. Before I am given the chance to ask about it, Aneera grabs my arm and pulls me to a more secluded area where we can speak privately.

"I had another"—

"Premonition," I interrupt. "Yes, I know. Just tell me."

"How do you know?" she asks.

"The Queel told me," I reply.

"*You can speak to it*?" she asks again with enthusiasm.

I briefly explain to her how it is that I can hear it—leaving out much detail. She replies bluntly, explaining why it is that no one should know this. She tells me that I am the only creature in existence that can hear the Voice of a Queel—I left out the part about Tziipoors connection to the Universe, as instructed to by the Clutch. I simply just said that I can hear her, and that she can hear me.

"There is something that I must ask you to do," she replies soon after. "I need you to die."

"Excuse me?" I say.

"The creatures," she says pointing vaguely toward Benoviii and Sriii. "There are others of their kind that found your body in IInve Bovaange. They are moving it as we speak. I do not know where they are taking you, but you cannot be captured."

I quickly come to the realization that if they found my body, they found Tziipoors, too. I understand what Aneera is asking us to do, and I agree with her that we should leave to fight. She and Ehhrn can stay behind and find Barroun.

"Okay," I tell her. "We'll go."

"We?" she asks. "No, just you—for now at least; we will need its help too. The Eiinokrra will not be happy that you left the Trial so soon."

"What?" I say back. "I might need help too if I'm dealing with"—

"Go," Tziipoor interrupts me. *"She is right that they will need help, but we do not want you to fight when you return."* The Clutch joins the conversation in my head stating that it would be better to let us be captured. They do not want me to fight back. I do not understand, but I know that they see things better than I do.

"You are our leader; that means that you have to fight the biggest bosses." Aneera says.

I ask questionably, "Your leader? Why do *I* have to be in charge? I feel like you're *way* more qualified for that than I am. The only reason that we're getting anywhere in this is thanks to *you.*"

"*You* are the one that we follow. *You* are the one that brings us all together," she replies. "That makes *you* the leader."

"You know, I think I qualify more as the team's mascot; besides, I don't really *want* to be the leader." I say back.

"It's a little too late for that." She grabs me by the back of my neck and reaches quickly for the dagger attached to my leg. She removes it swiftly from the scabbard and holds it against my throat while stomping my foot into the ground and adding to the discomfort of my already broken leg—halting my ability to move. I grab her hand, and try to pull away; but instead, she gives me full grip of Reewenniveaar and holds her hand now over the top of mine.

"You have to do it, or I will get the points. If you want to stay where you are on the [97]score board, it is *your* job to stop the heart in this body," she explains.

---

[97] Gameplay Detail—Points: awarded to the Hosts that had done the killing. The amount of points that are placed as bounties—in Trials, and in regular gameplay—are subtracted from the score of the Host that is killed and added to the score of the Host that killed them. This is *not* the only way to gain points, but this is the best way to get a lot in a short amount of time; especially if you hunt the more wanted names. This is how Tanner was so high on the score board when she visited the Keeper; she has taken down Hosts who have spent years gathering points. For example, Red—the giant-screeching-Bug creature that she fought when she first arrived here had gathered 1.6 million points before being defeated in a

I hear the scuffle of feet and turn my head to see Sriii running toward us to stop the killing. I realize what Aneera is doing—making it look like she is the killer to mask the real reason as to why the group needs me to die right now. We must make it look like she killed me, so that they cannot suspect that we are aware of their movements. We need a spy. Someone on the inside—I suspect that these creatures will be my first major enemy here. I will need to keep a close eye, and always be one step ahead—and most of all, *fuck* this broken body.

"*You* do it," I tell her. "If they have access to the board, they can see that the points weren't changed. We can't risk leaving any kind of trail for them."

I loosen my grip on the handle and give it back to her. Then she says, "*That* is how a leader thinks." She smiles and slits my throat before throwing me backward into the ravine and making an incredible leap to the other side leaving the rest of our group behind—angered and unaware of the new plan. Just before fading out, I see Cynniaa fly above me in pursuit. I do not know if it is because I am in pain or because I am dying, but I am losing consciousness. My eyes roll back, and the body is left empty. I am set to return to my body, with my point value returned to zero. This sacrifice had better be worth it.

---

doppelganger body on opening day of the newest season. He still lives but his score had been set back to zero. Another example is the cloaked attacker that guarded the entrance to the Dead Caves and previously carried Reewennivear; she had gathered 98 million points. And since, Tanner has taken down even higher point holders like, the Keeper who had gathered more than 5.9 billion points. To check their score, a Host must visit one of the Keepers, or have possession of one of their Devices. This Device will tell the Host its placement on the board, the amount of points that they hold, and the amount of points that will be awarded if they are slain along with the same information on every other Host on the planet. Many Hosts hold negative point value because of their lack of dedication to the true purpose of the Great Game of Ten, or because of their deaths in Trial arenas. It is important for a serious player to check their score often because of the ever-changing numbers.

THE BHAAKTII

THE CITY IN THE SAND

THE EIINOKRRA
BENOVIII
6'3"

THE EIINOKRRA
SRIII
5'9"

THE FOURTH DREAM

I t is damp and rainy and dark. Lightning leads her way and thunder follows her with applause as she marches up the hill for retribution. On the day of her first fall, something was stolen from her. Before she could open her eyes, before she knew of her surroundings, a silent player thieved a vile of her blood. She has come to take it back.

It was taken as a specimen, never to be used—**9** milliliters of blood to display. The robber keeps it safe on a shelf carved from the rock wall of its cave. It sits behind a brass label etched with the title, "Blood," the color self-explanatory.

The robber has a great many things placed along its shelves, scattered across its floors, and hanging from its ceilings. It is a rounded and stinking green creature of the bog. It collects things that shine and things that carry great interest, things that smell worse than it does and things that have absolutely no worth at all. The robber is a collector of all things.

It has a gentle soul and will give you whatever you ask of it. But to be respectful, those who come to it offer a trinket to replace the one they choose to take. The haggler reaches the cave at the top of the hill and enters to bargain with the robber.

She sits on a small stool and tells the robber of the trinket that she came for. It tilts its head and considers before reaching for the blood resting on the shelf. The robber expresses its care for this trinket. It is a very rare thing indeed thus making it unnaturally hard to part with.

The haggler carries a trinket as well, hers is of a much darker color. She pulls it from her pocket and presents it to the robber. It is a Yokkaa, one of the original six. It is from a time before

IIIxaanax—the fourth of the first six. Dark and demented, it is too disgusting for the haggler to pair with. She offers it to the robber.

Its eyes grow wide, and its breath grows heavy. This Yokkaa is a much greater trinket. It is not just any Yokkaa, and it will look better in the place where the blood had sat. The robber accepts her offer and returns the blood to the haggler. She relinquishes the stone, relieved to be rid of it. She passes the torment to a player more suited for its temperament.

She bows goodbye and thanks it for its favor. She closes her eyes and leaves behind the deathly deranged Yokkaa of distaste.

7

THE DEVILS UNDERGROUND

I wake inside of a rocking boat. Tziipoors body is layed out next to me, and there is a female Eiinokrra moving us through the water using a single paddled oar. The boat is small, and it takes a while for my eyes to adjust, so that I can see. The sky is black. There is no natural light—no moon, and no stars. But there are small bulbs. They are white and round, like the small orbs in Vaahiigali—except these ones do not have candle sticks attached. Perhaps they are some sort of Bugs that glow like Fireflies. They light our way through the water, moving in a heard along with us. I lie still and renounce any tension. I allow my body to be nothing but deadweight. I listen for sounds and hope for Voices, but I am plagued with silence.

"Can you hear them?" I ask the Clutch.

"Yes," they reply. *"We are getting closer."*

They encourage me to listen. They say that this is the ideal situation in which to master this ability, and they suggest that I prepare myself, as they sense that we will be lost to this place for some time. This will be the hardest part of my adventure so far. But they insist that it is a very important part as well, and that I must apply myself generously; practice my skill and regain my absent memories. They tell me that there is a lot that I will learn here.

The boat slows its speed, and the Eiinokrra steps out into the shallow water. I close my eyes, and the Clutch tells me of my surroundings, as other creatures join her to remove our bodies from the small rowboat. I can hear the water crashing against the rocky shore and the sound of many footsteps around me. There are four others that join her to carry us on weak stretchers up the hill toward the village. I am eager to see what it looks like, but I know that I need to keep my eyes closed—our [98]secrecy is crucial.

We are carried for about 40 minutes. I have kept my awareness undetected. I can now hear many creatures speaking. They gather to get a glimpse of the two—very rare—captive bodies being carried through the streets. One of the creatures who stand on the street reaches out and grabs my hand. It walks alongside me and gently slices a small cut into my palm. The crowd hisses with discussion at the sight of my blood. The ones who carry us continue, unbothered by the Eiinokrra who cut me. Perhaps they too were curious. My hand slowly heals and as we head up the hill the crowd grows smaller around us as the Eiinokrra circle like Buzzards around the red trail that drip, drip, dripped behind me.

They speak in a language that is not translated; I cannot understand them. It sounds much like Hevaanian but there is an eerie scratch to it. The Clutch tells me that they are speaking in the early language of the Gods. It is the same language that is written on the walls in the Hidden Rooms—the [99]language of the Void.

This village is much bigger than we had originally thought. Sriii called it her Nest. The Clutch estimates around 10.5 to 11 thousand Eiinokrra—that is a big-ass nest. In the forest before, Tziipoor guessed around a couple hundred, so we must have just found another area

---

[98] Gameplay Detail—Trials: weapons and gear. After the trial, a Host's weapons are not given back to the Host right away. As an extra test, the Host must last one hour after returning to their body without their weapons and gear, to prove that they are worthy of such things. This is the price weapon users must pay to compete, just as ability users must sacrifice their ability. When the mind leaves the fake body, the weapons are held in a safe place until the hour is up. If the owner should die within this time the weapons will be left with the body of the dead owner for the next Host to find.

[99] Relic Detail—The Language of the Void: shared by the creatures of the Void, the Liiyetrrux and the Eiinokrra. This language was brought to our Universe by the First Four and passed down until their split from the Elites. This language was briefly used in the time of the building and becoming of the new Kingdom of Hevaan, but soon was replaced by the more modern version that they speak now. It is generally spoken in two different versions, the Liiyetrrux and the Eiinokrra each use a version that was uniquely adapted from the very first original version. These early versions are used in the Hidden Rooms as a test for the one seeking the 12 Hevaanian Gates.

in the forest where they gather—maybe a camp, or guarded area. I assume that there are a few small islands, or perhaps just one, I am not sure. It could have also been a river that we crossed, but with that, I will also say that it was a very calm and slow moving one. The darkness in the sky suggests that this is a place deep in the Empty Forest. Maybe we are in a cave, or the trees just grow exceptionally thick here.

The chatter fades away, and we have entered a building somewhere in the city. The Clutch gives me another warning to prepare me for what is about to happen next. They say to abandon my efforts to stay unnoticed, and that I will not be able to keep it up when they do *it*. I am confused for a second about what they mean, but I am caught up when I feel it. They get Tziipoor first, and I can feel her pain as they do it. There is a sharp pinch in the back of my cheek, and again just under my tongue that reaches all the way to the underside of my chin—it feels much like a piercing, but with a bit more intensity. I wince quietly and wait my turn. I wonder what the purpose of this is. Is it an injection perhaps?

One of the creatures opens my mouth and uses its cold, nasty-ass pointer finger to find the area of my cheek that it pierces first. I am able to hold myself still and quiet for a moment before it moves its finger to find the soft spot on the right side under my tongue that it is looking for. I feel a cold tool follow the path of the finger until it finds the same spot. The tool is sharp like a needle, and the creature uses it to puncture the soft spot, and proceeds to push until it comes out again on the other side. I grunt from the discomfort of this one because it is far more painful, and I open my eyes. The Eiinokrra is shocked by my movement, and then punches me in the face knocking me out.

When I wake again, I am lying on the ground with an annoying weight around my jaw. I reach to feel the new attachment. The wound has not yet healed completely, which means that I have not been out for long. There is some sort of metal loop circling around the back of my bottom jaw. On the outside of my mouth, it follows the shape of my face but does not constrict. Same with on the inside—it is thin, so that I can close my mouth, and it curves around my teeth, so that

I can still use my tongue to properly talk. It is a [100]shackle for my jaw. There is a small chain attached to the outside of the cuff that also attaches to the wall that I am facing. The chain is connected to the wall in a way that allows me to move to new places around the room if I wish to.

I sit up and see Tziipoor next to me with the same kind of shackle around her jaw.

"You're awake," I hear a voice say from behind me—I had the assumption that we were here alone, but apparently, I was wrong. I turn to see who has spoken, and I am met with a vulgar amount of disappointment—

"You're supposed to be dead," I say unenthused.

"I was," he answers, "*thanks* to you."

With which I reply, "You say that as if I didn't have good reason to kill you."

"Is there ever really good reason to just kill anyone?"

"That's bold coming from you." I tell him.

He scoffs and looks away from me; we refrain from any further conversation. The Clutch and I talk with Tziipoor—explaining the current situation. She insists on returning to her body but is convinced otherwise by the Clutch. They decide that it is best for her to keep her distance—at least for now, she will watch through my eyes. The Eiinokrra are keeping him alive for a reason. I can understand Tziipoors aggravation; I would probably feel the same way. After all, he was her captor. It is Boriisst, the Keeper. I agree with Tziipoor that he deserves to die again, but I also agree with the Clutch that we need to ensure the safety of the Fae. We know that *he* was unaware of where the Hidden City is, but we do not know if the Eiinokrra are aware or not.

"Keeper," I say. "Why are you here?"

---

[100] Relic Detail—Jaw Shackle: it avoids the inconvenience of bulk. The metal used for this item is very strong and is considered unbreakable—much resembling a small steel wire. The Eiinokrra use this method of holding prisoners because Hosts are less likely to escape this way. Cutting off a hand or a foot to escape was a common occurrence before the development of this kind of shackle. Hosts are much less likely to remove their jaw to escape. This is a harder dismemberment, and it presents many more issues for them in the future. This shackle may vary by species, if a Host has a detachable jaw or a split jaw there are other methods of incarceration.

"That is not my title," he replies. "Not anymore. That was taken from me when you stole the Device. So now *you* are the Keeper—or whoever you [101]sold it to is."

He looks much more roughed up than how he did when Tziipoor and I had left him eleven days ago. His hair is no longer slicked back; it is frizzy and has lost its cleanliness. He has cuts and bruises all over his face and arms, and dried spots of blood on his shirt. The nice jacket and vest are now gone, leaving only the button up that he wore underneath. There is one side of his collar folded down, but the other sticks straight up, and he is missing a few buttons down the middle. He has been stripped of his gold shoes, many rings, and also his golden grill. I almost feel sorry for him, but then I remember why it is that I dislike him so much—I try to reserve the word "hate" for minimal use because my mother taught me *not* to hate.

"You didn't answer my question," I tell him. "Why are you here? And if you *were* dead, how are you alive again now?"

He replies with the idea that he would have to first tell me the story of his past. I guess he figures that since we are trapped here for the time being, it is okay for him to tell me the story of his sad life in its entirety. I guess I will give the effort to listen.

"Boo," I reply—accompanied by an utterly apathetic *thumbs down*. But he is right, maybe I can learn something from what he tells me.

He begins with the fact that he does not know what he is—he does not know his [102]species, or where he had come from. He was orphaned as an infant. He was born into a world of disappointment and grief—unwanted and left in the woods to die. Drowning alone in his own tears at the age of just two weeks, he was found by the Eiinokrra that he now calls his mother. She is the one who saved him—she is the one who raised him. She brought him back to the Nest and presented him to her eldest brother who is the Chief. She

---

[101] Relic Detail—The Devices: in gameplay these are valuable items. They are dispensed to Keepers and are considered to be very sought-after Relics in the Game. Hosts will hunt Keepers or sell their points for access to the Devices.

[102] Host Detail—The Blood of Boriisst: at first it appears to be black, but in the right lighting there can be seen, just the slightest glimpse, of purple. Dark purple, it is so faint that it would not be noticed often. This can only be seen when it is fresh and flowing, the color disappears to black when it is dry.

begged for him to spare the baby's life, and she took full responsibility for his growth and teachings. Her name was [103]Vennnassi; she has since passed.

"If Vennnassi was the Chief's daughter, does that mean that you and Benoviii were raised as brothers?" I ask him.

"Yes," he replies. "But his mother is still alive. My mother was her sister."

He tells me that she died when he was 14, but he hesitates to tell me how or why, moving on to the next part of his story. He was treated as an outcast by many who would beat him and taunt him, and often spat at him. Though he lived as a member of the family of the Chief, he was not respected as one. He spent many years dedicating himself to proving his worth and gaining the approval of the Nest. He was trusted with small jobs, and eventually was given promotions. On his 21st birthday, the Chief accepted him into the Nest as a true inhabitant of the Dark Hidden City—[104]Zephiiitrrax. The Chief entrusted him with a Device and gave him the official title of [105]Keeper. He held steadily to this title for six years—that is, until I came along and took it from him.

He continues to tell me that his body was retrieved after I had left him, and he was brought back here. He does not know how they gave him new life, but now he has been shamed again, and has lost his citizenship. He says that he has been left here disgraced. They brought him back so that he can sit and rot. I guess that is how they deal punishment here. You cannot die until they want you to. I do not know much about this city, but by the sound of it, he may prove to be useful. If I am going to be here for a while, I need to know as much as I can. The Clutch told me to dedicate myself to learning here. He has been disbanded from them, so perhaps I can use that to my advantage. Since he grew up here, I can assume that he has extensive knowledge of this place and of the creatures that inhabit

---

[103] [veh-NAH-see]

[104] [zeh-VEE-truh]

[105] Gameplay Detail—Keepers: the Eiinokrrian Board Cartel. The Keepers are employed under a contract of secrecy by the city of Zephiiitrrax. This is the only Eiinokrrian city on the planet—not counting the small camps and settlements that they have spread across the globe. Joining this organization is considered a great honor, and the opportunity is given only to a specific type of Host. No Keeper is of the Eiinokrrian race, as to keep the Head-runner secret.

it. Perhaps I can use their old Keeper against them. I wonder if he is plagued with tainted loyalty, or if he still holds true. I *would* prosper with him on my side for now.

It has been an hour since my return to this body, and the Game has decided that I am worthy of receiving my gear. The scabbard, Reewenniveaar, and my wings are finally returned to me, along with the Entanglement Key, and other small trinkets that I carry in my pocket. The process surprises me, as the items just begin to appear—already attached.

"Ah, look at that! Are you going to kill me again?" he asks sounding strangely excited. "I won't fight you this time. Just make it quick. You might as well. I am here to die anyway. Better just to do it now, so I don't die like that guy did."

He looks to his left with a face of disgust at a skeleton in the corner—an old pile of bones. It is a Humanoid looking skeleton, but it has two heads with a shackle still attached to [106]each one. We do not eat here, and we do not need water, so it did not starve to death, and it did not die of thirst. I cannot help but wonder, did it die from torment and torture? Maybe it was killed by a cellmate? Or perhaps it sat for years, and years, and years—until its heart no longer held enough strength to beat. Saddened and lonely, with no visitors or interaction whatsoever, its life just gave out.

Boriisst knows how it died, and is choosing to let me kill him instead, so I can only imagine how gruesome it could have been. I laugh lightly and turn back to him. I stand and remove the dagger from its holder and then pause for a moment before saying—

"Why would I kill you now? This is even better than how you had it before." I look back at the skeleton. "That wouldn't be a bad look on you, but I won't be the one to get you there. The decision of whether to kill you or not will be made by the Queel—it isn't my choice to make. The bond between you and her has been severed, so she will have the ability to kill you herself, if she wants to. I dare not take that from her. Your life is in *her* hands not mine."

I disconnect the scabbard from my leg and rejoin it with Reewenniveaar. I remove my wings as well, and grab onto the

---

[106] Relic Detail—Jaw Shackle: two headed creatures. The Eiinokrra takes no chances. Hosts have always proven to be distastefully vile. They shackle both to prevent the non-shackled head from cutting off the shackled head and escaping.

mechanism that connects me to the wall—moving it along with me until I meet the entrance to the room. I place everything in a small pile along the wall by the door. I suspect that the Eiinokrra will take these items from me, so I figure that I might as well make it easier for them while also proving to Boriisst that I am no immediate threat to him. If I am to get any information from him, I will have to gain his trust. I need to show him that I am the better ally—though I understand that it will be difficult. I will not be able to guarantee his safety, and I have no reason for him to live other than for my own gain—and for the protection of the Fae. I need him to want to help me; I need him to choose my team—and the Clutch agrees.

"I won't kill you," I tell him. "But I expect the same assurance from you."

I need to include this detail to ensure that he will not use my own knife on me—I can see a few reasons why he would. He could kill me, and reform his bond with Tziipoor as to help him escape, or he could do it just to rub it in the face of the Eiinokrra—to kill the only Red Blood that they have the ability to study. He could choose to end it all. But I need to find a reason to trust him; I find that most of the time I have to show a little bit of trust first. If I am going to be here for as long as the Clutch makes it seem, I am going to be taking a lot of naps here—and napping is best done when you are not worried about dying.

22 Days since the Fall...

I have been stuck in this room—alone with Boriisst. There have been no visitors, no guards, and no new prisoners. He is hesitant to speak about many things, but he is not shy to ask me questions about Red Bloods. I noticed early on that he does not use the name "Red Blood" in a derogatory sense like he had before—his terms have changed. I have done my best to be respectful toward him, and I have left my weapons on the far side of the room to avoid any hostility. Here he seems very calm and speaks with less anger toward the world than before. I have to wonder if he had been pressured to hate me by his employer. His obsession with red seems to have subsided some from before, but he still speaks of it a little. I cannot tell whether it is due to his situation, or if he has just chosen to hide it from me. He seems like a completely different person than before; but then again, I guess getting your ass beat will do that to you. The Eiinokrra that brought him here really did a number on him.

The door to our chamber finally opens, and we are greeted by a female Eiinokrra. She makes one small statement, "Red Blood Tanner," and nods her head instructing me to join her at the door. I grab onto the mechanism that connects me to the wall and drag it along with me until I reach the door. She opens the mechanism and releases the end of my chain from the wall—moving it to the groove on the outside of the door and locking it into place. She picks up my pile of gear and hands it to the second creature standing behind her. She then says something to Boriisst in her [107]language and closes the door behind us. I have dedicated myself to accepting him for now, but if he touches Tziipoor while I am gone, all of that will disappear and I will kill him...again.

I get my first look at the place that surrounds me and see that much of this building matches the cell that I was being held in. It is dark, and dreary, and damp. I follow the two of them through many doors and up a few flights of stairs until we reach an important looking room. It appears to be some sort of study. There is an older Eiinokrra seated in a chair at the back of the room. I am placed on my knees at his feet and left here alone. He reaches out to me with an old and decrepit hand—it changes color, from black to white just like Sriii's, and he holds it in front of me with the top of his hand and his knuckles just inches from my face. I sit confused, not knowing what to do. Do I kiss it? Do I give him my hand? Is he reaching for the chain? I am so lost.

"What do I do?" I ask the Clutch, growing more and more nervous as he stares down at me with empty eyes.

"Bring your head forward." he says.

I lean forward still looking at his eyes and touch my forehead to his hand. It is cold like Sriii's as well, and he has three eyes like her

---

[107] Gameplay Detail—Translations: the Adreestiaa gives Hosts the ability to convert languages, but the system has its flaws—glitches. Not all languages are translated. The game does this on purpose to unsettle and confuse the Hosts. I want to also make note of an important detail. The translator gives Tanner what she needs to hear in order for things to make sense to her. This is the reason why the names of things seem so familiar or simplified. What she hears is not always what is said, some words, phrases, or names are changed to make for better understanding between Hosts. It is great technology but as with all things, it is not perfect.

too, but his are [108]white instead of black. The other creatures that I have seen here so far have all had two eyes like Benoviii, and theirs were black in color as well. He pushes his knuckles firmly to my forehead and places two of his fingers over each of my eyes.

"Eyes down." He tells me, as I quickly do what he says. "Do be careful not to disrespect." This Eiinokrra is not like the rest. He terrifies me. And I am beginning to feel that he terrifies the Clutch as well. I do not speak. I do not know his definition of disrespect.

"Sit upright." he says, "Now you are to look at me."

I do as he says and place my hands in my lap listening attentively as he gets right to the point. He shows no empathy and is very straight forward with his request, ensuring me that I have no choice but to comply. In my time here, he suggests that I follow all orders given by the Eiinokrra. He tells me that I will be given everything that I need to succeed.

"You are going to open the twelve Hevaanian Gates, and you will take Sriii and Benoviii with you into the Kingdom of the Gods" he demands.

"What do you want with the Hevaanian Gods?" I ask, but these are not my words. It is the Clutch. I panic with fear, "Shut up," I say to them. "I don't want to die."

"They are the only way to defeat the Liiyetrrux," He replies. "They are made from them, and you are too. What better way is there to defeat someone than to slaughter their children?"

"If you need our help, why are you treating us like a prisoner?" the Clutch mouths at him again while rattling the chain that connects me to the wall. *"And you seem pretty desperate to drag us into your war."* they say to him through me.

He explains calmly that I cannot be trusted, and therefore, I cannot be allowed to roam freely—Boriisst *did* say that they have trust issues. He says that he is not requesting my help, he is demanding my obedience. He expresses that I should die along with them, and that my kind are even more revolting.

---

[108] Host Detail—The Eyes of the Eiinokrra: colors. These creatures do not live their entire lives with the gift of sight. Once they reach the midpoint of their life span, their sight begins to fade, and they learn to rely on their hearing and their hands. Their sight dies out and the black color of their eyes goes with it, leaving them blinded and white.

He stands and steps toward me, "You *will* do what I expect of you," he grabs the chain holding my shackle and drags me up to his level continuing to speak to me with his foul breath and disturbingly crooked-black teeth, "And you will *not* defy me."

He pulls the chain downward, placing me back on my knees, directing me like a Dog. He looks down upon me, proving his control. He then leaves me alone in the room behind him. I begin to understand the situation that I am in and discuss the issue with The Clutch and Tziipoor, as I look around, cussing them for mouthing off to him. There are shelves built into the wall with many small trinkets and books. I notice a tiny white statue made of Errok stone from the Hidden City of Vaahiigali. This makes me wonder how the peace is kept between the different civilizations here. I know of the Immortal War, but I wonder how many small civil wars have taken their deadly toll on the peoples who call this planet home.

I pocket the small statue and continue to look around. I have been in this room alone for about 30 minutes or so now, and I am beginning to wonder if they have forgotten about me. I have meddled through all of the things here and investigated to the best of my ability—this is a show room. There is not much for me to learn about in here—at least not without someone to answer a few questions, but I can save them for Boriisst. If anyone, I feel like he will be easiest to get information from—as long as he did not inherit too much of their demand for secrecy, or their fear of trust.

Finally, the door opens, and I am gifted with a visitor. But, yet again, I am disappointed with the face that I see. The creature connects his shackle to the wall like mine and leaves him in the room with me—what a place for shitty reunions. I do my best to restrain myself, but I cannot help but to approach him. He notices immediately who I am and is greeted with a well-deserved punch to the face.

"You left me to die!" I say angrily, "You Dog-shit mother*fucker*!"

"Fuck!" he yells back. "I didn't make you stay there. Obviously, you did *just fine* without me." He turns his back and curses me in another language.

The Eiinokrra must be gathering the members of the crew who was recruited to help me. I suspect that it will not be long before the rest are captured and brought here. Barroun is the first to be shown

155

to me. I cannot help but wonder if he has been held here since we split about three weeks ago; when did they catch him? They must have followed me and Tziipoor out of the forest, so that they were able to find our bodies quickly. I also wonder if they have found the bodies of Cynniaa, Ehhrn, and Aneera, and the bodies of the allies that I have yet to meet. If they have, they must be holding them in different cells. I passed a few other doors on the way here that could have possibly led to other chambers like the one that held me before.

The female guard and her helper from earlier have come to move us back to the holding cells. She switches our chains to the mechanism in the hallway and guides us back to the small chamber, leaving me behind with the Banished God, the expired Keeper, the two-headed skeleton, and the empty body of Tziipoor. I have one question to ask Boriisst right off; it has been burning a hole in my brain since I left.

"What did she say to you when they took me?" I ask him, referring to the statement made by the female Eiinokrra a few hours ago when they took me to meet with the Chief.

"She told me *not* to touch the Queel," says Boriisst—

"Who's this asshole?" Barroun interrupts.

"I could say the same for you," Boriisst replies.

"Shut up!" I say. "You're both assholes."

I check Tziipoors body to make sure that she has not been messed with, and Boriisst assures me that he kept his distance. I take this time to initiate the inevitable conversation about the Eiinokrras extensive knowledge about the Recruits. I need to know how they know about us. How do they know who was recruited, and how do they know about the Gates and the Key? And how did Boriisst get a copy of this book; does the Eiinokrra have one, too? I have to assume that if there was one here, there is the possibility that it was not the *only* one.

I understand that, in this instance, some version of me fucked up royally by allowing it to be written—or will fuck up when it *is* written. But, in my defense, I have no idea what prompted me to do so, and I can only assume that during that time of my life, I did not expect any of this to actually happen.

I also come to the realization that if they do have a copy, they have to be aware of the location of Vaahiigali and all of the other places that had been mapped. I unintentionally gave them a step-by-step road map of my adventures and have put everyone that I associate with at risk. Is it possible that this very book is the Long Prophecy that Sriii had spoken of, and am I the Prophet?

THE EIINOKRRA
ZEPHIIITRRAX'S
CHIEF
U'O"

THE TWO-HEADED
SKELETON
PETE & REUBEN
DECEASED

THE RED BLOOD TANNER
IN ERROK ARMOR
FROM VAAHIIGALI

158

27 Days since the Fall...

I am happy to inform you that I have had many of my questions answered. Boriisst has given me the impression that he is *all for* working with me against the Eiinokrra. He says that he has no reason to respect them anymore. His mother is dead, and she was the only one of them who cared for him. The rest only gave him opportunity on her request. He wants to be free of this place too—at least that is how he makes it seem. I am unsure of the level of skill he holds when it comes to deception, and I try to keep myself aware of the fact that he could only be here to get on my side in an effort to redeem himself with the Dark Hidden City, or perhaps they placed him here to spy—he is learning about my world just as intensely as I am learning of his.

Being from three different worlds, me, Boriisst, and Barroun have spent much of our time speaking of the basic history of life— the beginning to the present, and beyond. Boriisst speaks of the Eiinokrra, and of the [109]Hive that controls this Nest, and all of the others that are hidden across the Void. He says that there is even a Nest hidden inside of our Universe. Barroun is reluctant to speak of Hevaan, but he speaks of the history of the First Four, the Liiyetrrux, and the time that he had spent on Earth. And I tell them—Boriisst mostly—of the Earth and the many creatures that inhabit it—not just of the Humans.

I have practiced with my skill, and I can hear a few heartbeats in the cells that surround us. I cannot tell if they are members of the Recruited or not, because I cannot hear any Voices. I have not yet mastered the skill of placing my Voice in another being's mind, so I cannot ask them who they are. The Clutch tells me that I have to master hearing them first, and they are growing more and more unwilling to help me because they know that I will never properly learn if they always do the work. I need to know how to do it on my own. They say that I may not always have the ability to ask them for help—I assume that perhaps they are foreshadowing a bond separation from Tziipoor; apparently, I will still hold my ability to

---

[109] City Detail—The Hive: the citizens of the largest Eiinokrrian city. This city Anndriiinax [an-DREE-nah], is hidden on one of the other Voided planets. It is not on Irestiikaar.

connect with her if I become one with her and the Clutch *before* that happens. I am determined to do everything I can to prevent this from happening.

I wait for the day that she will rejoin me here speaking with her from a distance is not the same. I miss her presence. She is the one whom I trust the most. She is the one that I constantly feel the need to be around. She is the only one that I feel truly safe with. Even when speaking about the Clutch.

31 Days since the Fall...

Let me just say—this *fucking* sucks. I miss my freedom. I miss being able to go where I want, when I want. I am tired of the constant agitation from the shackle on my jaw, and I am beginning to worry about the effect that it will have on my teeth in the long run. Mouth pain is the worst! I hope that my regeneration abilities will be able to fix this forming problem after the shackle is removed—the ability can fix broken bones, so I assume that it will fix teeth as well. As odd as it may be, I also still have a [110]baby tooth. It is my favorite tooth—the oldest, but still the baby. If the day ever comes when a Host knocks it out, I will *lose my shit*.

My misery is intensified by the arguments between the two dumbasses that I am stuck here with—they do *not* get along. I should have figured that they would not do well together considering where each of them had come from. They are natural enemies. They need to find a way to get along though because this is getting ridiculous. I have moved Tziipoors body and set up my designated spot next to the skeleton—who has become my new best friend by the way. He is quiet, and he does not talk back.

We have been left here with no visitors again. It is just the five of us. Tziipoor tells me that she is still with Cynniaa, Benoviii, and Sriii. Aneera had managed to escape after killing my doppelganger. She broke through the fallen rocks and climbed back to the temple

---

[110] Host Detail—Tanner's baby tooth: the second primary molar on the right side—the same side as the shackle. No adult tooth ever grew underneath it, so it still holds its place. Tanner protects this tooth, sometime in between leaving the ship and the Fall, she made a small but very strong metal plate that guards it.

entrance before Cynniaa caught up with her. She managed to explain the situation before he killed her to keep our plan secret. He had returned to the rest of the group and told Sriii that he had solved the problem—I have to take a moment to explain that I understand the idea that they are most likely already aware of this "plan" if they have access to the book. It is fair to say that I have truly fucked us.

Ehhrn has gone missing again; Tziipoor cannot sense him anywhere close, so she assumes that he may have returned to his body and is traveling with Aneera. They bicker a lot, but they seem to work pretty well together. But it is only a matter of time before they end up here. I know that they are being hunted, and by the sound of it, the Eiinokrra are exceptional huntsman. Boriisst says that hunting is their most preferred activity.

34 Days since the Fall...

Finally! There are a few more Hosts added to our cell. One is the Cyclops named Reeb, and the other is the creature called the [111]Squeeb, who was in Cell B-13. They were both detainees on the Adreestiaah along with Ehhrn, Aneera, Barroun, and I before we got to Irestiikaar. I spoke briefly with Reeb on the ship, and though I have a drawing of it, I am entirely unfamiliar with the other one. Both of them have been attached to the wall using the same jaw shackle as the rest of us.

"That makes five now," I tell the Clutch. "How many do you think the Great God recruited?"

"If we are correct, we can see eleven, not including you," they reply.

"Eleven?" I say. "Do you think it will take them long to collect the other six?"

"They will bring in two more of them in the next couple of days, and Tziipoor will return to our body soon too, but one Host will be exceptionally hard for them to catch," they answer. *"And the rest of them you will find only after we are done here."*

I think on this for some time and come to the conclusion that I can name seven that I am for sure of, two that are possibilities, and

---

[111] [sk-WEEB]

two that I have yet to meet. The ones that I am confident about are: Tziipoor, Aneera, Ehhrn, Reeb, the Squeeb, Barroun, and most likely his brother—the Lost God. The two that I suspect as possibilities are: Cynniaa and Boriisst—I cannot see any other reason as to why he would be in the same cell as the rest of us. Of course, there is the possibility that they just do not have room in the other cambers but given that they have possible access to this book, perhaps they foresee infidelity from him.

With new questions, I approach Reeb—and the Squeeb who seems to be his caretaker. He tells me that they were recruited together, and that they had done dangerous jobs around the solar system that they both originate from. Sitting here—listening to them speak, I have my doubts about how 'dangerous' their adventures really were. Reeb is a big guy, but he is a bit of a moron. His skin is a medium orange color and appears to be quite rough. The Squeeb, well, I am unsure of how to describe it. It is tall and yellow skinned. I cannot tell if it is male or female—Reeb calls it, "it" so that is what I will use too. When it speaks it spews total nonsense.

This must be their 'ability'. Some of the best minds are the ones that are honed by idiots—they must work *really* well under pressure—and I do not say that with any bit of sarcasm. It is also worth telling you that my understanding of this relationship is that Reeb is more of a pet to the Squeeb. They call each other brothers, but the relationship is more like a boy and his Dog, or a man and his Parrot.

I speak with Tziipoor about when she is to return. I have grown tired of being the only sensible being in this circular room of chaos. Barroun and Boriisst have somehow formed the most agitating of bromances. I do not know how they went from pure hatred to this sickening new friendship, but I must tell you that I much preferred the way they were before. They spit rhythmic trash talk—following each other's lead; terrorizing poor Reeb and the Squeeb.

The rivalry intensifies quickly, as the day turns to night with the signal of a bellowing [112]horn. I sit at a distance—with Tziipoors body and the skeleton—who I have named Pete 'n' Reuben after a

---

[112] City Detail—The Morning and Evening Horns: covered in eternal darkness, the city of Zephiiitrrax stays on schedule with the outside, with the sound of a massive horn at dusk, and at dawn. This sound tells the Hosts of the city and the small magical light creatures when the skies change on the surface.

pair of Chinese Fighter Fish that my mother once bought us—trying to ignore the trifling foursome of nitwits just across the room. Reeb and the Squeeb take no shit, and spit verses back to Barroun and Boriisst. It is like the ultimate battle of tools. I am unamused and daydreaming with desperation about the days when I could just pop in a few earbuds and block out everything that surrounded me.

8

THE TWELVE GATES

It has been two days, and our team is nearly complete. Aneera has arrived, and Cynniaa's tiny body is here too. He is still in the Trial with Tziipoor, and she says that they will return today. I wonder how long we will have to wait here until they let us search for the remaining Gates—the first one was finding the Lost God in the desert—it is uncompleted, but I know where I need to go back to. If they wait until they find Ehhrn we will be here forever. I am sure that he is the one that the Clutch said will be "exceptionally hard to catch." He is definitely the stealthiest of the Recruits.

This is a large group of very proud beings. Each one seems to be the exceptional at what they do. I have not narrowed down the importance of each one completely yet, but I believe that I am beginning to see the reasons why some of them were recruited. I wonder how the eight of us will do together. There are only two ways that this can go. One being that it will just be a total shit show, and the other being that we actually come together quite nicely when we really need to. After all, we *are* God's Ultimate Dream Team.

I have made a table showing all of the information that I have gathered up so far through small conversation and eavesdropping. Some things may change once new information is uncovered, and the empty spots are filled in. Though I am still unsure as to whether Boriisst and Cynniaa belong on this list or not, but I want to include them now just in case. I know for sure that Reeb and the Squeeb were recruited on the same day, and at the same time. Tziipoor has spoken about the day that she was recruited, but I am unsure of the year. I am also unsure as to what *my 'ability'* or *'specialty'* is, but I assume that it is Humanity's burden of excessive thought, and my healing ability, and convenience. Aneeras statement saying that I am the 'leader' still does not sit quite well with me. I still do not claim the title. I do not want it. If I were to choose a leader, I think it would be Barroun or Cynniaa. They are the most 'leader-like'.

I would not depend on this table for 100 percent accuracy, but I hope that it helps to further explain our Roles. (*Fig. 2*).

#	Host	Planet of Origin	Age	Ability	Rec. Date
1	Tanner	Earth	24	Healing +Convenience +Excessive Questioning	November 3, 2021
2	Tziipoor	Taaviirax	1,000+	Connected to the Universe	February 20
3	Reeb	?	81	Moronic Genius +Weapons Specialist +Split Personality	September 14
4	The Squeeb	?	79	Host Specialist: Living, Dead, Other	September 14
5	Barroun	Hevaan	?	Hevaanian Histories +Antiquities +Languages +Leadership	?
6	The Lost God	Hevaan	?	?	?
7	Aneera	?	?	Premonitions of the Future	January 7
8	Ehhrn	?	?	Stealth +Clairvoyance	?
9	Boriisst?	Irestiikaar	27	Eiinokrrian Histories +Antiquities +Languages + Cartography	?
10	Cynniaa?	Irestiikaar	?	Military Training +Leadership	?
11	?	?	?	?	?
12	?	?	?	?	?

Fig. 2

I have been given the impression that Reeb and the Squeeb are only two members of a much larger family. They speak of being together from an age not far from birth. Reeb has also explained that his age is very young for a Cyclopes. They can live to be up to 300 years old. He also explains that the Squeeb can live to be about 250 years old, so it is pretty young for its kind too. Given this information, I can assume that they could also be from the same planet—or from a few that are very close together. Reeb forever surprises me. His personalities change often, but he never loses his focus. He always continues what he has to say, sometimes low and small-worded and sometimes so finely detailed and long-worded that I cannot understand.

I had moved Cynniaa's body to a safer place next to Tziipoors, and the two-headed skeleton—Pete n' Reuben. I want to avoid the possibility of someone stepping on him. I can tell that his body was not properly cared for. In the process, I had noticed that he is missing his wings, and I have been debating about what it could have been that caused him to lose them. Was it recent, or did it happen at an earlier point in his life? I know the importance of them. He had them when I saw him in the desert, so they must have been [113]replacement wings. I am afraid to bring him up to size—or shrink myself down to further investigate, because I do not want to risk causing problems with our [114]shackles. They are always getting in the way.

I hear Tziipoors Voice telling me that they will be back soon. Sriii and Benoviii have been monitoring the Banishment Sphere since the rest of us had left them in the desert. Tziipoor says that it has begun to change color. Unaware of what this means, Sriii and Benoviii are waiting on another group of Eiinokrra to arrive before leaving, so that they can continue to cautiously watch it. They have decided to send her and Cynniaa back to their bodies, so that we can begin getting ready for our chase after the twelve Gates.

"I have *had* it with those shit bags!" Aneera says annoyingly, as she rejoins my group of misfits on the quieter side of the room.

---

[113] Relic Detail—Weapons and Gear: Cynniaas replacement wings. These wings are given to Cynniaa while he is in the Trial—taking them away from his real body. This means that he lost his real ones sometime before he left Vaahiigali.

[114] Relic Detail—Jaw Shackle: metal guarded by magic. If a host attempts to tinker with it, the shackle will protect itself from damage or change.

"I *told* you that they weren't worth the time before you went over there," I tell her.

As I watch the group on the other side joke and talk trash at each other I notice a rather strange look on the Squeebs face. I watch a little longer curious of its dealings. It shifts, then reaches up with a long finger to dig into one of its hidden nostrils. It pulls out a massive boogie and looks around for a good place to wipe it. It considers a few places, but its face floods with mischief as it finds its perfect placement. It checks to see that none of the others in its group can see before it reaches low and ditches its dirty nose dookie on the bottom of Reeb's tee.

I scoff and laugh to myself. The Squeeb always talks so much about how it is the most mature and well-mannered of this bunch. Yeah...so *that* was a lie.

Aneera brings me back to her agitation replying, "Your God is such an asshole—"

We are interrupted when Tziipoor sits up followed shortly after by Cynniaa. I am eager to ask my questions about his wings, but I want to give him a moment to gather himself. The two of them notice the discomfort of the shackle right away, and Cynniaa takes his first look around our little chamber. Aneera takes the time to explain the rest of the group to him in her own little way. She is *not* amused. I give her the time she needs to finish cussing them.

I keep myself away from mentioning the question that has been burning a hole in my mind. I do not want to be disrespectful, but my curiosity is starting to get the better of me. It has not yet been an hour—maybe around 50 minutes of mixed conversation. The four from the other side of the room have joined us, and we now sit in a circle debating the possible outcomes of our situation. But once Cynniaa is given his wings back, I will have no choice but to seize the opportunity to ask him about them. I cannot wait patiently any longer. I have been very distracted from conversation for what seems to have been one of the longest hours of my life. It is as if I have no care at all for what the others have to say.

After ten more torturous minutes of waiting, they finally return to him. He reaches back and removes them. There is a tear; he pulls out a small case—much like the one given to me by Hffh. It contains a bundle of Errok thread, and a tiny white-stone needle—matching mine. He begins to stitch the rip along the bottom section of wing.

"What happened to them?" I finally ask over the surrounding chatter.

"Sriii ripped it while trying to send me back," he replies. "I didn't want her help getting here, but she insisted."

"I mean your real ones," I say.

He pauses in silence—thinking carefully about what all he is willing to tell me. He begins to explain that he lost them as a child. There was a small group of traitorous Fae soldiers who had made a deal with a Keeper. Their agreement was that they would tell the Keeper the location of the city in exchange for his Device. Cynniaa overheard their conversation and reported the issue to his father who did not believe him. So, he decided to take care of it himself.

"How old were you?" I ask him.

"I was eight," he replies. "I was not yet considered an adult, so I was not thought of as [115]credible."

He continues to tell me about his past, as the others talk amongst each other. He says that he followed the soldiers out of the city, and into the Sanctuary before one of them caught his scent. He fought the best that he could, but he was captured. He told them that he knew of their plan, and that he would never allow it to happen—being born into one of the First Families, he understood the importance of the Hidden City's location staying secret. They held him to the ground and tore one of the wings from his back—threatening that if he spoke of their intentions to anyone, they would come back and kill him. They tore the second, as a final warning, and left him to finish their deal.

He held tight to his detached wings and carried his bleeding body back to the city by foot. Upon arrival he was found by a soldier—who he had instructed to take him to see the King. The soldier complied, after recognizing the young Sprite from the Family of C. Cynniaa told the King of his tainted soldiers, and because of his injuries, this

---

[115] Host Detail—the Fae: not considered adults until the age of 55. Fae are known to be rambunctious, and ripe with trickery in their first decade of life. After this, they tend to calm, and are able to find jobs, and are trusted with more responsible tasks. Reminder! Yetziivu is only four, but she has the appearance of a Human teenager. Meaning Cynniaa would have had the appearance of a full-grown Human adult by the age of eight.

time he was believed to be telling the truth. The King sent his Guard after them, capturing the corrupt soldiers in good time—saving the secrecy of the Stone City.

The King thanked him by awarding him early entry into the Kings Guard, where he trained with the best until he reached the age of adulthood.

"How long ago did this happen?" I ask him. "How old are you now?"

"I am 325 years old," he replies. "I have been in the palace, guarding the secrets of Vaahiigali for a very long time."

"Is that why you left?" I ask again, "To protect the city from the Eiinokrra?"

"Not entirely," he tells me. "This time, I am here to protect my friends, too. It is a great honor to be considered a friend to a Red Blood—to you. When your God asked me to help you, I knew that I couldn't say no."

"So, you *were* recruited?"

"Yes," he replies, "just after you left the city." Before I can reply, he follows up with a quick statement, "There is a question that I want to ask you too."

I nod my head, granting him the time to ask it. The group around us silences and joins me and Cynniaa as he asks about the book—the one that I had burned. I tell him that I knew what it was, and that I had no choice but to burn it. I explain to the group that I think that I am the one who had written it, and that it is a story about our ventures. I clarify with them that I have no memory of what it says, or of writing it.

"That book was the Long Prophecy," Boriisst interrupts.

"How did you get it?" Cynniaa asks him.

"It belonged to the Chief." He replies. "It's destruction is the main reason why I have been left here."

He tells us that it cannot be read by them. The Eiinokrra were not brought here by the Adreestiaah, so they were not gifted with the ability to translate it. They tried forcing other Hosts who had been brought by the ship to read it, but they could not do so either. He explains that the Hevaanian Gods were able to place a glitch in the system blocking the ability to read or understand Human languages in an effort to keep them [116]safe.

He continues on to say that he is unaware of how many there are, but he does not think that it was the only one. The Chief gave the book to Boriisst after he had seen it in the Chiefs hidden room—not one of the Hidden Rooms that I am looking for. After learning that he could read the text, he was instructed to translate it in full, but I took it from him before he got the chance. He says that he had just returned from Zephiiitrrax the day that we had met, and he does not know how he is able to read the book.

"Your God also recruited me," he says. "The day that you met with the Chief, he came to me while you were gone and asked me to help protect you."

"And why did you agree?" I ask.

"Because *fuck* the Eiinokrra. I was going to die here anyway. Now I have a new purpose."

"One more question," I say. "If it can't be read by any of them, how is it that Sriii knew what it said?" I ask.

"What do you mean she knew?" he replies.

"The day that I met her, she told me of the Long Prophecy, she knew its contents." I tell him.

He sits bewildered, "Her father is an important man. She is very highly ranked, even above our Chief here. It would make since that she knows things that the others don't."

"Our Chief?" says Reeb. "Not Reeb's Chief." He crosses his arms and looks angrily at Boriisst. "*It* Reeb's Chief!" He points to the Squeeb, "*It* has no Chief!"

"Yeah, yeah big man," he replies, scooting closer and hugging Reeb, "I'm sorry."

43 Days since the Fall...

We have all been moved to a new area of the building. This is a much larger room than before. Each of us is paired with an Eiinokrra,

---

[116] Monument Detail—The Adreestiaa and its Gods: a reclaimed ship. The Hevaanian Gods have taken full control of the Adreestiaa from the Elites. Unable to beat their strength, the Elites have lost their most valuable asset.

who oversees making sure that we do what we are being sent out to do. I am paired with Sriii, and Boriisst is paired with Benoviii. This brings our group to 16 members: Me and Sriii, Boriisst and Benoviii, Tziipoor, Reeb, the Squeeb, Barroun, Aneera, Cynniaa, and the six new Eiinokrra that I have yet to meet properly—these six members are not Recruits. Sriii is the only one with three eyes, and there are also two older ones that have white eyes, like the Chief—they are partnered with Tziipoor and Barroun. The other four resemble Benoviii.

We are being prepped for our first mission. Each one of the recruits are connected to the wall and spaced apart evenly. There is a large door-like structure at the far end of the room with an altar, and a small quantity of ritualistic style objects surrounding it. My guess is that they are going to open a portal to send us to our destination. The Eiinokrra rely heavily on their magic and seem to be very skilled in their craft.

Another group joins us from the hallway. They carry piles of heavy clothing and proceed to return our gear—except for my and Cynniaa's wings. They hand out the garments to the Recruits who are not dressed for cold weather. I am *not* happy about this. I can feel the irritation growing within me, as the Eiinokrra begin to explain where it is that we are going. It is a territory of frigid conditions, on the southern pole of the planet—much like the Southern Antarctic Circle on Earth. Except, I expect that this place will have a larger variety of life. I am anxious to see what Hosts we will find there.

We are given the instruction to stay close to our appointed Eiinokrra. Boriisst, Tziipoor, and I are attached to our escorts—our chains are connected to the silver bands that they wear around their waists. The rest of the Recruits are seated along the wall and placed in a state of rest, like how the bodies of Hosts are left when their minds are moved to the [117]doppelganger bodies that are used in the Trials. This means that the other Hosts will have the protection of a false body, but Tziipoor, Boriisst, and I will be in more direct danger.

---

[117] Gameplay Detail—Doppelganger Bodies: over time, the Eiinokrra have managed to master this technique. It was originally created and used by the Elites exclusively. The Eiinokrra have only been able to utilize this as a method of travel in the most recent millennia and have not yet perfected it. This is why the Hosts, Boriisst, Tanner, and Tziipoor, are not given doppelgangers at this time. Not enough is known about them, so they are too hard to regenerate. They do not make these false bodies for themselves. To them, this fighting style is considered dishonorable.

I guess they figure that by keeping us chained to an Eiinokrra, they will prevent escape—and possible loss.

They begin their ritual and proceed to send one of the older Eiinokrra—with the white eyes, and the four that resemble Benoviii, to beat the rest of the group before they wake in their new bodies. They wait to send me and Sriii, Boriisst and Benoviii, and Tziipoor with her older Eiinokrrian guide until the others are awake and ready to go.

"Here," says Sriii, holding out her hand. "I want you to wear this."

I ask, "A ring?"

"No, the stone," she says, pointing at the bulky white crystal that is set in place with some sort of dark colored metal. "It is [118]IIIxaanax. It will give you protection, if needed."

I place the ring around the middle finger on my right hand. The Clutch tells me of its rarity; I listen closely. They say that it is one of very few, and that Irestiikaar is the only planet that is known to make them.

There are six that are widely known, but they guess that there could be a possibility of up to nine hundred or more of [119]them. Tziipoor also explains that the stones are of higher value than the Devices here. The Hosts call them [120]Yokkaa, or Protection Stones. The name, IIIxaanax, belongs only to this Yokkaa—each has its own individual name, and [121]personality. IIIxaanax is one of the six that are known, it is guarded by the Eiinokrra.

"You wear it wrong," says Sriii. "Turn the stone to the inside, close to your palm."

---

[118] [eek-SAH-nah]

[119] Relic Detail—Yokkaa: more of these stones can be made—or "harvested" at any given time. Some previously existing stones have also been destroyed by negligent users.

[120] [yoh-KAH]

[121] Relic Detail—Yokkaa: multiple stones can be worn by one wearer. *But* the wearer must be very careful with what stones they pair together. If the Yokkaa do not get along with one another, they will destroy each other, and kill the wearer as well. It is also said that a smart wearer will not pair more than three together—too much of this power can drain the wearer. These stones protect, but they also need enough energy from their wearer to do so. This means that the wearer must be strong in heart, mind, and body.

I turn the stone inward, also asking, "Why?"

"When your arm hangs at your side, your palm faces your body," she says. "You want the stone facing you; you want to protect it just as it will [122]protect you. This will keep it safe."

We step closer to the door, as the four in front of us pass through. I can feel the cold wind, and my bones already begin to shiver. I cut a small hole on the inside of my stuffed coat and pull out some of the fluff. I split the small amount in two and roll each wad of fluff into a small ball. I place one in each of my ears to protect my eardrums from the cold. Then I sigh and pull up my hood—bothered by the venture ahead. I can already feel the headache, and my nose has already started to run.

"Just so you know, I am going to be a useless, miserable piece of shit, this *entire* time." I tell Sriii. "I fucking *hate* cold weather."—I feel that this is an acceptable time to use the word 'hate,' because I know that there is no better word to use to describe how much I despise frigid temperatures.

"Let's get the job done quickly then," she replies, and we step through the door and into the Kingdom of Snow.

---

[122] Relic Detail—Yokkaa: the band holding the stone will adjust its size to fit the current wearer and their tastes; it can be worn around the wrist, the neck, the waist, wherever the wearer desires. When worn correctly, this stone will form a bond with its wearer. The longer the stone is carried by a Host, the stronger the bond will be. This will provide the wearer with extraordinary abilities. They punch harder, run faster, cut deeper, and can connect—profoundly—with everything around them.

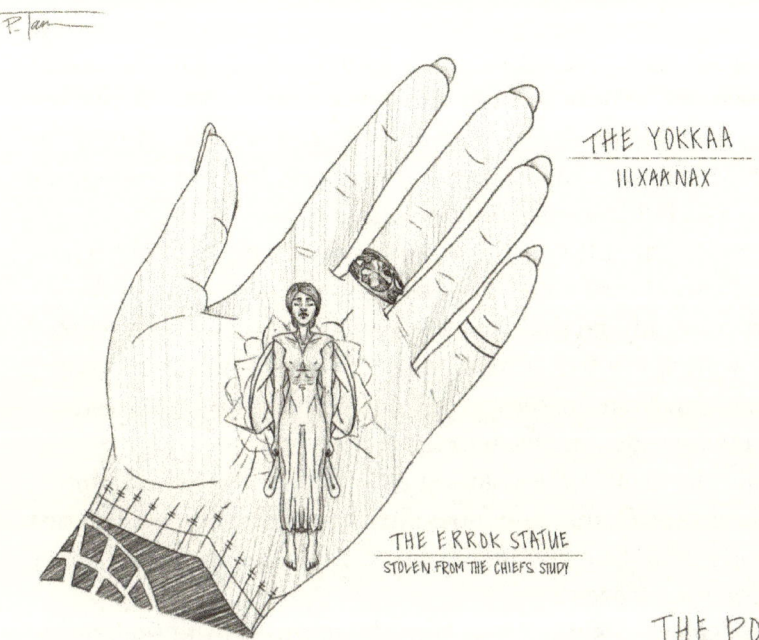

THE YOKKAA
IIIXAR NAX

THE ERROK STATUE
STOLEN FROM THE CHIEFS STUDY

THE PORTAL
TO THE KINDOM OF SNOW
ARRTISIIAAX

The Second Hevaanian Gate
The Kingdom of Snow
[123]Arrtisiiaax

The portal closes behind us, and one of the older Eiinokrra tells us to, "Move out." There is a day's journey to the cave. We are left on the top of a mountain and must make our way down into the valley below. We walk in a straight line across the peak—stepping cautiously, as a fall from this height could be fatal.

After making it halfway to our destination, we are halted. There has been a recent rockslide—the debris now blocks our path. We cannot advance any farther into the canyon, so we are instructed to sit and wait while two of the Eiinokrra search for another way down. I refuse to sit in the snow, and I negotiate for my right to stand. Aneera joins my side, and we win the argument.

We wait, shivering in the cold. I stand with Aneera, Sriii, Tziipoor, her Eiinokrra, and Cynniaa—who is sitting on my shoulder. The rest of the group is standing in other huddles, and some are seated or are leaning along the frozen rocks.

"This is such bullshit," I say. "I can't wait to get the *fuck* out of here. My nose won't stop running, my hands hurt, I have a sore throat, and I can't feel my motherfucking feet. I don't understand how you guys are running around here practically naked," I say to Sriii, referring to her and the rest of the Eiinokrra, who are in the same skimpy clothing that they wore in Zephiiitrrax.

"Let's all huddle together," replies Boriisst, shoving his way in between me and Sriii, with Benoviii close behind him. He wraps an arm around each of us and pulls us all closer together.

"Ugh!" Sriii exclaims. She shoves him away and curses at him in her strange language. I gesture as if to say "ditto".

He laughs and turns to join Barroun, Reeb, and the Squeeb seated along the rocks. "I was just trying to be friendly," he says. He drags Benoviii behind him and really seems to bully him a lot; he seems to be the stronger brother.

Sriii ignores them, saying, "We are creatures of the cold," replying to my statement about their clothing. "But we thrive in all environments."

---

[123] [are-TEE-sia]

We are interrupted by a horrifying screech—echoing across the canyon. The daylight fades away, as something massive flies above. I have a bad feeling in my gut, and I begin to search for an escape route. Something bad is going to happen. The Squeeb instructs the group not to move and tells us also to stay quiet. The creature lands just above us; I can hear it snort, and grunt, as it sniffs the air. It has heavy feet and an elongated snout.

The fourteen of us hold steady, watching the giant search for us from above. I see one of the two Eiinokrra who had gone off to investigate, peek his head out from a pile of rocks along the top of the canyon. I use the technique, taught by Tziipoor, and the Clutch, to search for a thought that I can connect to. I need to speak to him. I must master this trick, and I must do it now. I focus but keep some of my attention in the sky. I ask my question "Is there a way through?" and I hope for an answer.

The rocks shift from the heavy steps of the creature above. I finally receive an answer, and the odds are in our favor. He says that there is a path. I quietly begin to point the group in his direction. We move slowly and carefully, only communicating through gestures and hand signals. We climb up the rocks, almost to the safety of the passage, when our secret is let out. The Squeeb sneezes and looks to the sky in terror. Barroun grabs it by its coat and punches it in the face without apology.

"You dumbass!" he says through his teeth, shaking it by its collar. "You're the one who told us to be quiet!"

I look to the sky and see a massive golden eye. The creature screeches again, and buries its head into the canyon, biting at the air. Once it recedes, the top of the canyon caves in. If we had not already begun to climb, we would have been crushed. I can now see the creature in its full glory. It has white skin, and blue feathers that only trace the line of its spine.

"Oh my God," I say. "Is that a fucking *Dinosaur*?"

"Nope, *that* is a Dragon!" replies the Squeeb, as it grabs my arm, dragging me and Sriii across the rocks, and yelling to the rest of the group. "Run!"

We hurdle over the fallen rocks, and stumble toward the passageway. The Dragon reaches for the scrambling Hosts desperately clawing at the walls that surround us.

"Oh shit, oh fuck!" says Boriisst. "Please don't breathe fire! Please don't breathe fire!" he repeats, as he runs ahead of the group.

"No fire," Reeb corrects him. "It frozen water Dragon. It no breathe fire!"

"Please don't breathe ice! Please don't breathe ice. Please don't breathe ice!" Benoviii adds, following just behind Boriisst.

"I don't give a fuck *what* it breathes!" says Aneera, shoving them out of her way, "Move!"

It is a very smart creature and can see where we are headed. It rips into the canyon. I am close to the passageway, I guess about 100 feet. The rocks shift under my feet, and I stumble, taking Sriii down with me. The Dragon shreds the ground below us and manages to hook the chain connecting Boriisst and Benoviii. They are drug across the rocks and flung into the air above the canyon—screaming like children.

Sriii yanks on the chain that connects us and pulls me along behind her. She faces the creature, telling me that we have to help them.

"Nooooo," I say sadly, almost with a tear. "But we were so close." I point to the pathway behind us.

She turns, and stares into my eyes, "Stop complaining, and help me."

"But why do *we* have to go?" I whine annoyingly, "It's cold up there."

"Because they would do it for us," she replies.

I answer her with a thumb down, and a, "Boo."

She rolls her eyes and turns back to face the creature. It has changed its course, and now chases the two who are trapped up above. It disappears from our sight, and I am forced to chase it down. We are joined by Tziipoor, her elder Eiinokrra, and Cynniaa. The five of us break off from the group. We plan to meet them at the cave, after rescuing the others. Sriii tells them to go on ahead.

We cross the canyon and climb up the other side. Tziipoor carries her escort, as she scales the steep walls, and Sriii and I climb, carefully, behind her. I struggle to keep up with them. I am a much less experienced climber. I need help on the larger jumps, and Sriii lies on the ground in a few areas to reach an arm to assist me to the higher ledges. When we reach the top, I can see the sun setting on the mountains. Night approaches. Tziipoor senses the heartbeat of the creature, and she leads us into the coming darkness.

The land becomes colder, and the wind has much more aggression up here. If there is *one* thing for me to be excited for, it is for when I get to kill that fucking Dragon. I do not know how, but I am going to do it. This was supposed to be a quick, in-and-out mission. Do the task and go back—to the warmth. But now, we are stuck doing a side quest—in the *cold*. Fuck! And for Boriisst and Benoviii, I am going to get them too—for making me chase them. Again, I am not sure how, but I *will* do it.

We have traveled for two hours, in the dark. Tziipoor leads us, but she will not tell me how close we are. I have been listening, and I can hear the beating hearts of the ones who travel with me. I cannot seem to get past their noise. The Eiinokrra are hard to hear, but Cynniaa is a very clear thinker—easy to understand. He ponders strategy, weighing our options; he reviews multiple different scenarios. He plans defenses to every attack, and even leaves room for the unexpected.

I grow distracted by his ideas, but I am drawn away again at the sound of a new and distant heartbeat. My connection with it grows, and one suddenly becomes three. I begin to understand how it is that Tziipoor can tell who is who. I hear one that beats at a speed similar to Sriii's; it is slow and very calm, I can assume that this one is Benoviii. Another one beats very similar to a Humans; around 60-100 beats per minute. I assume that this one is Boriisst. The third is very large, and very loud. It beats very quickly; I assume that this one is the Dragon. I can sense that we are gaining on them, they must have stopped somewhere.

"I hear them," I tell Tziipoor.

"Now find them," she replies, slowing her pace and allowing me to take the lead.

"They are someplace up high," I say. "We will have to climb again."

I cross my arms and close my eyes. I walk, following the rhythmic sound of the heartbeats. The cold is growing stronger, and the wind is harsh against my body. It is hard to push forward. Ice flies through the air in tiny shards, painfully stabbing little holes into my skin. My hood is up, and this coat has a very nice special feature. There is a thick piece of cloth that wraps around my neck—built in under the hood—that allows me to cover my mouth and my nose for added warmth. I cover my eyes as well, sensing my surroundings through Tziipoor. The wind hurts too much to open them.

We walk through the snow for hours before I stop the group, and the wind finally mellows some. I can hear two new heartbeats approaching us from the right. I ready myself for a scuffle and warn the others that there are other Hosts coming. I am prepared to fight, but I do not feel hostility from them—it is strictly precaution. Just before I am able to see them peak over the ledge above us, I hear one of their thoughts. They are afraid of us. They have only wondered out to see who approaches their cave. I make eye contact with one from above and release the handle of my weapon. I show them my palms and put my hands above my head—encouraging my entourage to do the same.

"Why do you travel here?" the first one says.

"We're searching for a few members of our group," I reply.

Sriii then interrupts, "and a Dragon."

They look at each other, and then back at us. The one who had spoken before, waves his hand telling us to follow them. I assure Cynniaa, Sriii, and Tziipoors Eiinokrra of their good intentions. Plus, I am not going to pass up the opportunity to get out of this wind—if even for a minute. They point us toward a path that leads up to the ledge where they are standing, and once I reach the top, I follow them to their cave happily.

We reach the entrance and follow them inside. We walk through small tunnels until we reach a large open cavern. It serves as a home to them. I laugh with excitement, as I drag Sriii behind me running toward the fire in the center. I place myself, possibly too close, embracing its warmth thankfully. The rest of the group joins me for conversation.

"We heard screaming about half an hour ago;" says the first Host, "that's why we were scouting."

"Do you know where they went?" says Sriii.

"If they were taken by the Dragon, it probably took them back to its burrow," replies the Host. "It is up the mountain a ways, but there is a path that will take you there faster."

He is cut off by the other Host that resembles him; he shakes his head with worry.

"It must be a very dangerous path," I say.

He replies saying that it is, and then explains why. There is a bridge of ice that we will have to cross. It is very thin, and it is hard not to fall from the pressure of the wind. But he says that it is the fastest way if we are in a hurry—which we are. I am anxious to get back to Zephiiitrrax, to Hell with this weather. They discuss the situation and sit quietly watching the fire while I listen. My mind wanders off, and I am drawn away from their chatter.

The cold has reminded me of something. The Clutch said for me to, "Regain my absent memories." I think that one way for me to do this is through trauma. Every memory that I have found so far has been because I hit my head, or something is brought up in conversation, or I am reminded because of something that I see or feel. This time, it was the cold. I remember an ice bath. My muscles ache, and I control my breathing so that my heartbeat slows. What an odd memory.

"What do we call you?" I hear a voice say.

I am pulled back to the conversation to see that everyone is looking at me. "Tanner," I say.

"Tanner?" replies the Host with excitement. "Are you the Red Blood Tanner? From Earth?"

I nod my head, "Yes," and ask for their names too.

"[124]Ziin," he says, pointing at himself, "and this is my kid-brother, [125]Taa. We are [126]Mubaatiis."

Before I can say anything, Tziipoor answers the question that I prepare to ask. She tells me that the word Mubaatiis roughly means, mountain bandit, but this is their tribes' "pronunciation" of it. I ask if there are any more of them. Ziin replies, saying that their [127]Tribe is not far from here—he is the only one that can speak apparently. He

---

[124] [j-IN]

[125] [t-AH]

[126] [moo-BAH-tis]

[127] Monument Detail—the Mubaatiis Tribe: this civilization holds its placement because of a massive stone monolith. This 30 foot structure is carved with stories about their Tribe in their mother language, and was erected by their ancestors. It represents the Mubaatiis claim on the surrounding area, spanning about 415 miles across.

claims that it is small, around 500. It is roughly a three-day journey from here, and he says that they help watch the outer perimeter of their land.

They have flat faces and pale skin, marked with darker pigments in horizontal patterns. Their eyes are narrow and far apart. They have backward facing knees like a Satyr. They wear clothing made of white fur with darker stripes. Ziin stands about an inch shorter than Taa and has very symmetrical features. Taa has a long scar along the left side of his face. It goes around his eye, runs across his mouth, and down to his chin; I wonder if that is the reason for his silence.

They insist that they must assist us with this task. The Dragon would supply an abundant amount of clothing, leather, and bone for huts, and hunting, and meat. This is the first civilization that I have come by that eats here, even though they do not have to. Ziin explains that they do not need it to survive, but feasts are sacred to them. They believe that to consume another, is to absorb their energy, and their power. He says that they have been chasing this specific Dragon for centuries, and that their people would be forever grateful if we helped them kill it. I also keep in mind the idea that this could possibly be a trap. I must be vigilant. If they eat other Hosts for their "energies" I must be cautious of the fact that they may try to eat me.

"They will not eat you." **The Clutch says.** *"To them you are bad energy. They fear that your red blood would taint them."*

"Why?" I ask them.

"Because Red Bloods are known to be hostile. Across all Universes and everything else that is, there have been horror stories about your wars, and your deceitfulness, and your unhealthy obsession with the unknown. You fight each other like children, but children with dreadful weaponry. Weaponry that should be used to protect each other instead of killing each other. You poison your Earth and pour chemicals into our shared skies. You have the capacity to do good things, but you choose to be negligent about how to do them. You eat each other, and sell each other, and bring harm to children and to creatures that you deem lesser. Humans are terrifying. You do these things to yourselves, so why would anyone believe that you would not do it to us? You are respected here because you are feared. You are helped because you are unnerving. You look harmless but are otherwise treacherous."

Saddened by her description I reply, "We're not *all* like that."

"How are we to believe that you are not, when we our whole lives are taught that you are?" they say.

I silence myself and lower my head. I guess it is good to not have to worry about being eaten, but to be respected only because others fear me kind of hurts. I want to be respected because I have earned it. I look around at the others. Is that *really* how they feel about me?

Returning my attention to the other conversation, we agree to let the Mubaatiis join us under the condition that we get our missing members back. We then prepare to roam deeper into the cave. There is another exit that will lead us to the ice bridge. Ziin says that the walk will be about 45 minutes from the cave exit to the burrows entrance; it is unexplored territory from there on. We follow the two bandits to the exit, and back out into the freezing wilderness. I am immediately discomforted and close my eyes again to follow the sound.

We reach the bridge and take a moment to compose ourselves before crossing. I pitch the idea to Sriii that if she removes the magic from our chains, I can shrink us to fit onto Tziipoors back. She will be able to grip onto the ice with her claws, and we will be able to ride safely on her back—held on with a type of seatbelt, referring to the hormone that her body releases to hold me into place when I sit on her. They immediately hush the idea, but after looking over the edge and seeing the abyss that we will fall into if we fail, Sriii convinces the other Eiinokrra to trust me. I am shocked at how easily that idea was accepted, but I will *not* argue with it.

Tziipoors Eiinokrra removes the magic from her chain and disconnects it from her waist draping it over Tziipoors shoulder. Sriii removes the magic from mine as well but does not disconnect us. She is allowing me to change its size, but I cannot run free. I place Cynniaa on Tziipoors [128]back and shrink the rest of us to his size. We ride quietly, as she steps lightly across the ice.

Ziin decides that, for some reason, right now is a good time to fill the group in on the real danger that we face—now that we have nearly reached the halfway point. There is a crack in the ice, about

---

[128] Relic Detail—Wings: danger. Cynniaa and Tanner cannot use their wings in this environment. They could risk freezing them, which could cause them to break or shatter. The broken wing would not be able to be sewn back together until it thaws completely. A shattered wing cannot be saved.

one-third of the way across. He assures us that it should still be safe, as long as we cross it gently. I reserve my worry for when we face the Dragon. I am uncertain of how we are going to kill it, but I know that some tasks are better done when improvised. We will see.

Tziipoor moves very Cat-like, as she uses the claws on her fingers and toes to grasp onto the ice below. We are approaching the crack, and the wind miraculously calms. It is snowing, but it falls lightly. She slows her speed, and calculates every step, using her tail as a counterweight behind her. I hear the sound of the crack growing underneath us, but I resist the urge to worry. I trust Tziipoor; she will get us across safely. The others watch stressfully, as I sit with my eyes closed *again* avoiding the stress that will accompany the horror that I see. I sit silently, crossing my arms to suppress my body heat. I tuck my gloved hands under my armpits and bow my head—pulling my shoulders up to cover my ears. I focus my breathing and listen to the three beating hearts that we chase.

Once we meet again with land, Sriii decides that we will stay this size, riding on Tziipoor until we reach the burrow. I encourage her to run, and then tell everyone else to hold on. I plan to finish this quickly. I listen to the sounds growing stronger the closer we get to them. We push on until we finally reach a wall; at the top is a hole in the rock. It is the burrow. She climbs up to the entrance and lays her body on the ice, allowing us to step off before returning to our normal sizes. Cynniaa decides to grow to our size too, because he does not have his wings. He wants to have a fighting chance.

Before we enter, I hear Ziin hyping his brother Taa. He tells him that this time they are going to beat it. He says that *this time* they have help. I pull my chain, telling Sriii to follow me. I join the brothers and ask my questions bluntly—

"You have fought this creature before?"

"Yes," says Ziin, while Taa nods his head in agreement. "It is very aggressive."

"We know," replies Sriii. "It crumbled our passageway, and took Benoviii, and Bo."

I smile, and divert from the current issue for a moment to ask teasingly, "Bo?"

"That is what Benoviii calls him," she says.

I bump her with my shoulder and laugh. I sense some history

between them. Ziin continues on to explain how their last attempt failed them. The two of them and three other Mubaatiis attacked it five years ago on a mission to acquire its feathers for a festival. It fought back triumphantly, taking its win at a price for sparing their lives. It left its warning plain as day—the scar across Taa's face and down his body. The Dragon cut deep, slicing his tongue and his jaw in half, and ripping through his torso. The Tribes shaman was able to fix his jaw, but the tongue grew infectious and had to be removed for his safety. His ribs grew back crooked, and his insides are forever scrambled. He uses a very modest form of sign language, with a very limited vocabulary to communicate with his brother.

I ask if they know how to kill it, giving possible worse-case scenarios. I wonder if we just pierce it through the heart, or if we manage to cut off its head, will it grow any new ones? Is it a magic Dragon? And the most important question I think is, if it freezes me, will they be able to thaw me? Ziin answers them all very patiently. He says that his Tribe has fought many of them before. They are rare to find, but there could be a few of them spread over the Arrtisiiaax territory. They are hard to kill because of their size and temperament, but he says that beheading them or stabbing them through the heart will do the job. He also advises me to steer clear of its ice. Apparently, thawing it is not an [129]option.

The Eiinokrra who is paired with Tziipoor reattaches the chain to her waist and replaces the hex that protects it. Sriii does the same magic on our chain, and we all wander together into the burrow of the beast. Boriisst and Benoviii are close by, and the Dragon is not too far off from them. We sneak through the descending tunnel until we reach an opening at the base. I am in awe at the scenery.

There is a massive ledge with an opening that displays the true beauty of this Kingdom. I hate the cold, but with all hate, blindness accompanies it. I stop and embrace the scenery, as everyone else moves forward. I always forget how much I love the *beauty* of snow. The storm has subsided, and the moon shines over the mountains. I think of my dad; he loves the mountains. I wish that he could see

---

[129] Host Detail—Arctic Dragons: they breathe what looks like ice, and it feels cold like ice, but this substance freezes indefinitely. It hardens like a crystal.

this. I smile embracing this thought and then move on, catching up with the group.

Above us, there are smaller burrows higher in the walls that form cubbies for the Dragon to sleep in. The ceiling stands tall, and the opening in the wall stretches across the cave. We came in through the back door. The cave reaches about a mile across, and I sense Boriisst and Benoviii to our right. We tread carefully, with intention not to make any noise, when I notice a trail of black blood.

"Boriisst," I say.

"It could be either one of them," Sriii corrects me. "Ours is black, too."

The group splits to scout the area after losing the path of the spatter. There is no sign of the Dragon, as of right now. Cynniaa announces that he has found a hand. I look at Sriii questionably, and walk with her to the site, and indeed, it is a hand. It is Benoviii's, frozen in the Dragons crystal breath—amputated just past the wrist, one-third of the way to the elbow. We hurry to find them. I stumble across the trail again, and I follow the spatter finding a small break in the ice. There are drops of blood that pass through it, so I gather the others and encourage them to follow me. I squeeze my way, very patiently, through the small passage to find the two that we search for on the other side.

Boriisst paces stressfully, watching Benoviii attempt weak magic on himself, to try and heal his wound. Sriii immediately tends to him, dragging me behind her.

"Thank Gods, you're here!" says Boriisst.

"Don't thank those creatures," replies Sriii, "Thank us!"

"I'm sorry," he says. "Just help him!" He turns to Benoviii, "Fuck man, I'm sorry! I didn't know what else to do!"

Benoviii assures him, grunting painfully, "It was our only option!"

Sriii tends to him, while the rest of us gather ourselves to leave. Just as Benoviii stands, we hear the familiar screech of our enemy. It has returned. There is no other way out of this room, so we will have to go back the way that we came.

"Let's kill this motherfucker, and get out of here," I say, stepping toward the exit.

"Kill?" says Boriisst, stopping me. "And just how do you plan to do that?" he says with disbelief. "We tried already; do you not see that half of his fucking arm is *gone*? *Fwwiptt*," he says, mocking the sound of a swinging sward, "Gone!"

I turn to Sriii, "Remove the magic from my chain, and let me fight it," I say. "I promise I won't run."

She refuses, and I am left with one option. I grab Taa and look him in the eyes. "You want to kill it, right?" I ask, to which he nods his head yes. "You want revenge for what it took from you?" I say, pointing toward his mouth. "You want to return to your Tribe, a hero?" I ask.

He grabs my coat and shakes me with excitement. He nods his head, "Yes," again, and grunts with affirmation.

"Then let's go," I say.

"What are you doing?" Boriisst says, attempting to stop us.

I push him out of the way replying, "I'm about to blow your fucking mind." I push Taa through the crack, and follow behind him, bringing Sriii with me. Boriisst is not far behind, along with Benoviii, Ziin, Cynniaa, Tziipoor, and her Eiinokrra. I face Taa again, "Do you have a knife?" I ask. He pulls one from his waistband and nods his head again. "Awesome," I say.

We are hidden under a sheet of ice, but not for long. I warn the group that we will need to run to a new hiding place soon. I place a hand on Taa, and find the pressure point that allows me to change everyone's size. "Cut off its head, and take it home," I tell him. I think, "Dragon," and Taa grows to match its size, blowing our cover, and entering into battle with the creature.

He fights well against it at that size, and I can tell that it is thrown off by this attack. The rest of us find a safe place to hide from the fight of giants.

"This is actually a really good strategy," says Cynniaa.

"Thank you," I say.

"This is insane," adds Boriisst. "Where did you get that kind of power?" he asks, yelling over the surrounding noise.

"I don't remember," I yell back, shrugging my shoulders.

The Dragon fights back, shoving Taa to the ground. We scatter to avoid the chaos. The Dragon is amused by the small Hosts running to find new hiding places. Taa is quick to his feet, but not fast enough to beat the Dragon to Tziipoor and her Eiinokrra. It catches Tziipoors guide and swings them through the air—like it did to Boriisst and

Benoviii. Taa leaps back into the action to retrieve them, but the Dragon throws them over the ledge. I panic and run foolishly across the battlefield to look for Tziipoor.

"We caught the ledge!" I hear her say, as I cry softly with relief. *"But the Eiinokrra is dead. The Dragon crushed her spine, and she hit her head on the rocks below."*

My attention turns back to worry. We have lost one of ours, and an Eiinokrra at that. I worry about how this will go. Tziipoor climbs the rocks to join us again, pulling the body along with her. Sriii pauses, and I can see the hidden irises in her eyes begin to glow again. She kneels to investigate. Her hands change to white before touching the empty body of her comrade. She cries out with sadness, holding tight to the friend that she has lost.

"We should have known," Tziipoor tells me, laying guilt on herself. *"We should have caught her before it could get this far. We should have been faster!"*

I am saddened further by this, I can feel her discomfort, *her* sadness, and her guilt. I begin to cry again. How do I comfort her or Sriii? I turn back to face the fight and watch vengefully. Kill it Taa, take its life.

He agrees to my request, finally slicing its head from its body. I cannot approach him and return him to his normal size, because I *cannot* pull Sriii from her goodbyes. Everyone quickly gathers together again on the ledge by Tziipoor and her lost guide. Taa comes close enough for me to return him to size, and Ziin runs to hug him and congratulate him for beating the beast. They howl and slam their fists to their chests so hard that they knock their hearts in and out of rhythm.

Boriisst and Barroun reach the group last. They see why Sriii weeps, and they join her on their knees, but sit at a [130]distance.

Sriii finally stands, wipes her tears, and turns to me with a request. She asks me to shrink the body and carry it carefully in my pocket until we return to Zephiiitrrax. I say yes, and she removes Tziipoors chain from the waist-strap. She steps back to allow me to

---

[130] Host Detail—Eiinokrrian Farewell: saying goodbye to a Spirit of the ground. When an Eiinokrra dies, the body is burned in a ceremony called NuuGiirti [new-GEER-tee], or New Birth. They believe that they must burn the body to be sure that the Spirit can be reborn into another body. They sit on their knees to pay respects and bow their heads to bless the fallen.

do what she had asked of me. I hold the body gently and wrap it in cloth from Sriii's skirt before placing it carefully in one of the inside pockets of my coat. Sriii attaches Tziipoors chain to the other side of her waist-bar and prepares herself for the next step.

Ziin and Taa give their condolences and invite us back to the Tribe to celebrate the defeat of the Dragon. We graciously decline their invitation, telling them that we have a mission to complete. We say our goodbyes, and just as I catch the thought, "How are they going to get that massive creature to their Tribe," my question is answered. Ziin and Taa thank us for our help and wish us well for the remainder of our journey. Taa stands next to the head and Ziin next to the body. They raise their wrists, and say a single word, "[131]Dessiaa." They disappear along with the body and the head of the Dragon.

"What just happened?" I say, dumbfounded.

"They both have [132]Siitaas," replies Boriisst.

"They have *what*?" I ask again.

"Siitaas," says Cynniaa. "They are transportation devices used by Hosts to move quickly from place to place. They're not usually hard to come by. I bet every outpost watcher has one."

"They had those the whole time, and we still walked through the freezing-ass snow?" I say slightly irritated.

"They don't work for short distances," Sriii assures me. "It only worked for them this time because they were [133]moving something big."

I scoff and turn to climb back out of the burrow. Side-quest completed. We are headed to meet up with the rest of the group, to finish what we started. Sriii's magic was able to stop the bleeding from Benoviii's arm. The wound is no longer open, but he will still feel the pain from the loss. We reach the peak where the burrow meets the mountainside and climb our way back to the bottom.

We return to the passage in the canyon, where our group had

---

[131] [DES-uh]

[132] [SET-uh]

[133] Relic Detail—Siitaas: transportation devices. These devices are more common than Yokkaas and the Devices that are used by the Keepers. They are used to travel great distances across Irestiikaar in shorter amounts of time. Hosts can use them to jump from one side of the planet to another.

split before. Benoviii says that it would be best to reach the cave with the others before sunup, to avoid other obstacles. Most of our walk from here will be cave passages.

In our quiet time, I find the nerve to finally ask the Clutch, "When you answered my question earlier, you said, "us, and our, and we." Does that mean that you're afraid of me too?"

"We do fear you." they answer. *"We hear how you think and disagree with some of the choices you have made. But we fear you because of our own traumas as well."* They pause for a moment before continuing, *"That does not mean that we do not trust you or your judgment. Just as we see the bad, we can also see the good."*

Once we exit the passageway on the other side of the mountain, the weather is calm and the moon lights our way across the freshly fallen snow. The valley runs deep, and I suspect that it will take us hours to reach the cave at its base. I can hear the sounds of the others below us, so we will be reunited soon.

I struggle to walk down the mountain through the snow. I slip and slide over the rocks, as we descend toward our destination. The Voices below are growing stronger, and I can feel the heartbeats of everyone except for one. There is someone missing. That makes two now; I wonder if they had hardships reaching this point like we did. We lost a member too. I am beginning to worry—the heartbeat that I noticed is missing, beats similar to Sriii's. That means that we may have lost another Eiinokrra, but I try not to jump to too many conclusions. The missing member could just be scouting, or perhaps it is just out of my range.

I ask Tziipoor if she can hear the missing thump-thump sound from below. She replies, also saying that she cannot hear it. I cannot help but think of the worst-case scenario. I hope that we have not lost two members on this mission to death—and two Eiinokrra at that. They are supposed to be the strong ones. Being the natural enemy of the Gods, I had assumed that they would be harder to kill—I guess a brain injury would prove lethal for anybody, but still. I realize the insensitivity of this assumption, and I refrain from bringing the conversation to light, as we reach the halfway point headed down the mountain.

In search of the missing Voice, Tziipoor and I catch the thoughts of another creature nearby. We look at each other, but only for a second. We must keep hidden the arrival of this Host. He is closing in quickly, and he does not travel alone.

"It is Ehhrn," I say to Tziipoor.

"And Yetziivu," she replies.

"Come find us," I hear another Voice say. "I know you can hear me," he follows. "We will stay close. Don't tell Cynniaa."

It seems that Ehhrn has mastered the use of this [134]ability better than I have. He also tells me to keep all of my questions for when I see him; it will be easier to explain that way. I trust that he has good reason, and I keep the appearance of the young Sprite a secret from Cynniaa for the time being. Ehhrn seemed very anxious when telling me this, so I cannot help but distract myself from the climb with thoughts of what she is doing this far from the city. Cynniaa said that Sprites are not considered adults until 55, but Yetziivu is only *four*! I did think of her as 'far beyond her time' when we were together, but I cannot think of anything to explain why she is *here*. She is a Princess of Vaahiigali, Cynniaa would be *pissed*.

Our group finally reaches the entrance to the cave at the bottom of the valley. I can already feel the warmth of the fire. I rush to find the others and sit again, probably still too close to the flame. There is no smoke, but the warmth proves to me that it is real. This [135]place is so strange. They want us to die, but they have rules. There are things that we can and cannot use. I am sure that by now you have noticed the shortage of firearms. We have the resources to make them, but I have heard that they are confiscated by the Game Runners. They want us to fight dirty; they want us to use our hands. They allow the use of arrows, throwing knives, and spears or darts, but they classify

---

[134] Relic Detail—Abilities: telepathy. This ability can be mastered by any Host with the patience to understand it. It is better understood when taught by an experienced user—Tanner is taught by Tziipoor. Ehhrns teacher is yet to be identified, but he is very intelligent on his own. It is possible that he has taught himself. Reminder! Tanner is the *only* one who can hear Tziipoor.

[135] Planet Detail—Irestiikaar: the atmosphere. Just as it feeds the Hosts who endure life here, it also protects them. The atmosphere will absorb all of the harmful particles in the air—it will protect their lungs from harmful inhalation, but it will not protect their skin from burns. This process works similarly with poison gas or lethal doses of radiation. However, this does not protect from dust clouds, acid rain, or any kind of living Virus. For enjoyment, the Game Runners will sometimes change the abilities of the atmosphere.

bullets and explosives under ill-suited. They say that these methods are too easy. They want Hosts to work harder for the kill.

Boriisst and Benoviii find comfortable places next to the fire too. It is not long before Barroun says, "Benoviii, *what the fuck* happened to your hand?" Then he looks at each of us—the ones who had just returned—with a look of such great disappointment that it could shame the Great God himself. He acts as if we could have prevented it somehow. If there is anyone to blame, it would be the dumbass Squeeb. Boriisst continues to explain the reason for the amputation.

I am waiting for the opportune moment to sneak off to meet with Ehhrn. I have come to the realization that Tziipoor and I will not be able to go without Sriii, so I am cautiously weighing my options for how I am going to convince her to take us. I also worry about her attention to secrecy—can I trust her not to share Ehhrns whereabouts with the others? Tziipoor listens quietly while I argue with myself. I could use the fact that they released the hexes on our chains—I could threaten to tell the Chief. But I do not want to make a new enemy. And he is fucking scary, not to mention stinky... I want to stay as far away from that stagnant bag of ass as possible. Perhaps I should just ask her honestly. I am running out of time to decide.

My focus is halted by the sound of another heartbeat. It is the one that we were missing. I was right, he was scouting. I spot my opportunity to go back out, hoping that I can pick up the next scouting shift. But I am reminded that there is a mission that we are here to complete. Once we are all here, we will advance further into the cave. The Eiinokrra has almost returned, but I *must* go see Ehhrn before we go any farther. I have a gut feeling that I need to hear what it is that he has to say.

I turn to Sriii, finally noticing the circle of Eiinokrra forming behind me. They waited for the last one to arrive before they huddled together to mourn their loss. I stand still and stay quiet; giving them the time they need to process this tragedy. I do not deal well with death. I never know what to say. The easiest way to go is to say, 'sorry for your loss.' I will wait until we are alone though, I do not want to interrupt them. I place my hand over my pocket—the one that holds the body and take a moment of silence within myself.

When the circle breaks, I make a request to speak with Sriii before we go forward. I pull Tziipoor and her aside and ask my question genuinely.

"You trusted me with something important to you," I say, still holding the pocket containing the body. "Can I trust you to protect something important to me?"

She does not answer right away, but she finally replies, "Yes."

"I need you to keep a secret," I say.

Her hidden irises begin to show—I have noticed that they appear when she is showing certain emotions. I have seen them when she has means of being threatening, when she is immensely sad, and now. I feel no doubt from her; I feel that she is pure. Tziipoor and the Clutch agree that we can trust her with this issue, no matter how deceptive she may be, so I proceed to tell her why it is that I need to take a walk outside.

Her ears perk out to the side when I tell her about the missing Recruit. I leave out the bit about the Sprite Princess Yetziivu, but I understand that she is most likely here without the King and Queens blessing—hence the reason why it is best to keep this from Cynniaa. Sriii agrees to take us to see him, and I can see that she is anxious to finally meet the Host that the Eiinokrra could not catch. She informs the rest of the group of yet another delay, keeping our reason for leaving out of the briefing. Everyone groans and gripes, as they return to their spots to drop their equipment. Reeb restarts the fire, and Boriisst lies back down to continue his nap. Barroun, his Eiinokrra, and the Squeeb are sent ahead to scout the tunnel, before the rest of us enter. The remaining Hosts sit around the fire to talk shit, and cuss at the cold.

I am not happy about this delay either, but I understand the importance of it. Sriii and Tziipoor follow behind me, as I lead them to the place where Ehhrn and Yetziivu wait for us. This better be worth it. The longer I stay here the more I hurt.

The sun is rising again, but it gives little warmth. My hands are so dry and cracked. My skin is itchy, and I have mild eczema that flares up in colder weather. This place has really helped me realize how much I took for granted all of the easily accessible things that surrounded me back home. What I would do for some fucking hand lotion, and a chap stick!"

We find them hidden in another small cave, a little way up the mountainside. I huddle close to their fire and listen to Ehhrn explain himself. He speaks quickly, aware of the small amount of time that he has. He then sits to the side allowing Yetziivu to speak.

"Here," she says, handing me a tiny scroll. "This will help you."

"What is it?" I ask.

"This is a list of all twelve gates—and their locations," she says.

Sriii interrupts to add, "We know where the gates are." She turns to me, and says, "We are wasting time for information that we already have. Let's go."

Ehhrn stops her, "Wait, there is more!"

He tells me to open the scroll, and I comply, also bringing it up to a size that makes it easier for me to read. Next to each gate, Yetziivu had written a different name.

"There are twelve Recruits—including you—one for each gate," she explains.

"How do you know?" I ask while reading the names. "And how did you get this list?"

"I copied it from the scroll in the Scholars Stone Sanctuary in the city," Yetziivu says.

She explains to me that the Fae were instructed to keep this information secret. They were given this list strictly for knowledge and historical documentation purposes only; not to make easy headway for the Game Players. But Yetziivu is still a child. She understands the importance of sanctity, yet she is still a rambunctious young Sprite. She wants to help me, like Cynniaa. She is naturally drawn to the adrenaline that accompanies breaking the rules. She insisted that Ehhrn brought her here so that she could give it to me herself.

Adding to the explanation, Ehhrn says that he was visited by the Great God and given the names of the twelve Hosts—or Recruits, who are needed to compete all of the tasks. He says that those names match the ones on the scroll. I cannot help but think why it is that the Great God seems to have visited everyone except for me. Tziipoor states that she thinks that I have somehow blocked him out. She says that I will need to find this reasoning within my lost memories.

Having successfully passed on this information, Ehhrn and Yetziivu prepare to return to Vaahiigali. He says that he will be back to see me again when the time is right, and we will complete our task. Yetziivu holds his hand, and I notice the device around his wrist. It is a Siitaa. It has a thick black strap, and a painfully ugly yellow face. He speaks the word, "Dessiaa," and they disappear.

"If those are so easy to find," I say to Tziipoor, then continue on to say out loud, "*Why the fuck* don't we have one of those?" so that Sriii can hear me too.

Sriii bypasses my complaint, and replies, "Let me see the scroll," and reaches out her hand, as it turns to a pale color white.

I share the new information with her, and we retrace our steps back to the group. She walks behind me and reads quietly. I can hear branches cracking from the weight of the ice in the distance. The sounds echo through the valley, and even though I know that it is the sound of nature, it scares the shit out of me every time. The scroll has the name, 'Sriii,' written next to, 'Arrtisiiaax,' or, the Kingdom of Snow, so this task must be completed by her—or with the assistance of her. I am unsure. Ehhrn did not specify.

Approaching the cave, I hear a scream, and the sound of a growing argument. I pull Sriii along behind me, and we run to see what the [136]matter is. Now that I am able to see them, the Squeebs Voice calls the loudest—

"Fuck *no*! I will be waiting for all of you outside. I am *not* going back in there with those *nasty* motherfuckers!"

"So, you'd rather take your chances out there with the Dragon?" replies Barroun.

"The Dragon is dead," Sriii tells them, walking past them toward the passageway. "What did you see?"

The Squeeb replies, "It's dead? *Great!* More reason for me to wait out there!" It gathers its things, and heads for the front entrance of the cave. Sriii stops it and asks again, this time with more aggravation—

"What did you see?"

"It was a pile of shit," Barroun says mildly frustrated.

"Yes!" It replies, "and I would recognize it anywhere! *That* is a Giant Banded Snow Cobra den! *And* the giant pile of shit proves that they still eat here even though they don't have to! *I* am not going anywhere near them!"

---

[136] Relic Detail—Abilities: telepathy. When hearing the Voices—if there are many— it is hard to focus on *just one*. In this case, Tanner can hear the Voices that speak outwardly, and the Voices that can be identified as the inner monologues of the Hosts who surround her.

"I'm sorry," I say, "a *what*?"

"Fucking big, angry, scary-ass Snakes!" It says.

"By big do you mean, as big as that hole big!?" I ask, pointing to the fifteen-foot-tall passage, "Because if that's the case, I'm waiting outside too."

It walks past me with its arms full of gear, "Ask them, they can tell you all about 'em." It gestures clearly toward the Eiinokrra.

"The Snakes aren't what you need to worry about," says Boriisst. "It's the Cats; always watch the Cats."

We all run past his comment, listening to Barroun state that the largest one [Cobra] that he has ever heard of was 28 feet in length, but Sriii assures us that she has seen them grow up to 30 feet. I have to make the comment that 30 feet is still really fucking long. I also have to ask how it is that snakes are able to thrive in these temperatures. Sriii says that these particular reptiles are creatures of the Void, and like the Eiinokrra, they are suited for all environments—unbothered by the cold. She keeps a few at her home in the Hive City, or Anndriiinax. They are smaller in size, but the Highest Eiinokrrian Chief—her father—[137]keeps the largest one known to exist—and it has two heads.

Knowing the danger of our course, Barroun decides to break the group into smaller teams again. Barroun, his Eiinokrra, Sriii, Tziipoor, and me, will go ahead into the passageway to complete the task. I request for the right to stay behind, but Barroun is very forward in pointing out that I am the one who has to turn the key; I have no choice but to go. Boriisst is angry that he was awakened *again* just for someone to tell him to stay in his place, and he turns his back to the group—falling asleep for the third time. Benoviii sits close by him, and Cynniaa gets comfortable on the same side of the fire. Aneera chooses to join Reeb and the Squeeb outside, long with their three Eiinokrra—apparently, she does not do Snakes either.

Before we enter the den, Sriii gives us the basic what-not-to-do around these creatures. A lot of it is similar to the temperament of Snakes back on Earth. She says that we must be quiet, calm, and respectful of their space. But it is also important to be alert,

---

[137] Host Detail—Eiinokrrian Beliefs: Giant Banded Snow Cobras. These creatures are sacred to the Eiinokrra. In this culture, they represent the dangerous beauty of the Void.

and ready to take charge of the situation if one arises. I have a little bit of familiarity with Snakes—if you remember, I have one named [138]Ronnie back home. But he is much smaller, and also is not venomous, or ill tempered. He is a juvenile Coastal Jungle California King Snake and is still small enough to fit in my hands—nothing compared to these Snow Cobras. If I am correct, Reticulated Pythons can grow upwards to 33 feet in length, and Anacondas can be around 25 feet or so, and 550 pounds! As far as I know, King Cobras on Earth are usually about 13-15 pounds at adulthood and can reach up to 18 feet in length. These Cobras can grow to be 30 feet—and I am terrified. I have yet to bring up the subject of the potency of its venom, but for now, I think that it is best that I do not know.

Barroun maps our course, telling us that he had seen a wall with pictures—and likely the wall with the keyhole, before the Squeeb had *lost its shit* over—well, shit. The wall is not too far in, and if we are lucky—unlikely—we can get in and out quickly. I gather my composure and follow him into the darkness of the passageway.

I walk with my head down, my eyes closed, and a hand on Tziipoors back for guidance. I can hear the slow, but strong and steady sounds of the Cobras' beating hearts. There are too many to count, and they are everywhere. My little bit of experience with Snakes helps me—knowing that as long as we do not get in their way, we should be okay. But like I said, my "experience" is very limited. I have never handled a Cobra, nor have I seen them in enclosures, or in the wild. I only know what I do from what I have seen on video or read in books. I can hear the low growl of agitated serpents in the distance, and I hope that we are headed the opposite direction of the sudden uproar.

I feel around, searching for the pocket with the key. It would be so irritating to come all this way, and not have it. But luckily, I find it. I assume that by turning the key, another room will present itself. Last time the floor dropped out. This time I am in my real body, so I must be alert, and more careful. An injury will heal, but if I die in this body, it is all over—it was all for nothing.

---

[138] Gameplay Detail—Ronnie: safety. Though Tanner is here, her pet will not die without care back on Earth. In this instance, time in the Void passes differently than time inside of the Universe. By her current count, it has been 100 days since her abduction, but back on Earth no time has passed.

We reach the wall, unnoticed by the Hosts who call this place home. I find the keyhole and take a deep breath before inserting the key and turning it: once to the left, and then once to the right. Just like before, I can hear the noise of gears moving, and rocks shifting behind the wall. I stand close to the edge of the room and prepare myself for a fall, but I am relieved when a door appears to the right of me. We can hear the sound of more disturbed Snakes in the newly opened passage leading downward.

"We will wait here," says Barroun.

I ask him, "Are you scared?" because I am.

Before he can reply, Sriii interrupts him, "Let them stay; we don't need them to go any further."

Sriii and I are the only ones—other than Tziipoor, Ehhrn, and Yetziivu—who know about the list of [139]names. Ehhrn said that each task needs the Host of the name that is written next to it to complete it. Now that I have opened the door, I would like to not have to walk through it. But Sriii would never allow it, and there is no use in arguing.

Our number shrinks back down to three, as me, Sriii, and Tziipoor pass through the secret door. I pace the same as before, latching to the Queel for guidance. I can use her sight to see in the dark, but like I have stated before, things can be less threatening when you cannot see them. The tunnel tilts and it turns, and there are some spots that are so steep that we have to slide down. This will be difficult for me to get out of, but Tziipoor will make easy work of it. I will have to convince Sriii to let us catch a ride on the way back up. I do not think that it will be a hard argument.

I have seen her kick back. She was pretty relaxed when Tziipoor carried us earlier. She had her feet propped and her ankles crossed. She stole Taa's backpack and leaned back with her fingers intertwining each other across her torso, and she napped.

We pass through a small number of larger rooms, quietly slipping past the sleeping Hosts. At last, we reach a dead end. There is a small room, and inside I can see the faint glow of an orb. It resembles the

---

[139] Note from the Prophet—Those Who Know: this also includes you and me, of course.

ones used in Zephiiitrrax. I walk through the [140]Hidden Doorway and find the room to be quite familiar. I tell Tziipoor that it reminds me of the small Hidden Room in Vaahiigali. It is the same size, and the same shape, and has the same tunnel-like doorway. But there is not a big step down like in the other one. The floor here is level, and the ground is coated with a layer of dirt; there is no water. There is also no pillar, just a small step in the middle of the room. I guess it could also be the altar that a pillar once stood on.

"There are no pictures," Sriii says. "There's no writing."

"This room is different from the others," I reply.

"How many others have you been[141] in?" she asks.

I tell her that there were a few places that I had managed to explore before they caught me. I am not entirely new to this. But this one is indeed different. It is blank and bare. Tziipoor reminds me that the pictures in the other room were not immediately visible either. The only light we have here is the orb, but I am afraid to touch it. I am unfamiliar with this magic, and I do not know if it will burn, or otherwise harm me. I pace in a circle around the slab that protrudes from the ground just below the orb, and I notice a small carving on the wall behind Sriii.

I make this new discovery known, and the three of us gather to assess its meaning. It is a Cobra; shallowly carved into the rock at only about two inches tall by two inches wide. Like any clue, we must take the time to figure out what it means; what do we do? I assume that there must be something else that goes with it; there must be hidden writing somewhere. I turn my back to the carving, and squint each of my eyes, looking around for any other clues.

"There," says Tziipoor, looking straight across to the other side. *"We see another carving."*

"Where?" I ask her, unable to see what it is that she has found.

I follow her across the room to find another small carving, the same size as the other one. But this one is a different species. It looks like Ronnie—it is a King Snake. I am lost for thought. Why would

---

[140] Relic Detail—Hidden Doorways: this is the first time this door has been open since the day of its creation, 200 years after the victory of Yeshua.

[141] Gameplay Detail—The Map Rooms: the Eiinokrra know where the Hidden Rooms are so there is no need to search for the other Map Rooms like the one that Sriii and Tanner found in the Bhaaktii.

there be a picture of him *here*? Perhaps it has something to do with our task—the one that we must complete, but where do we go from here?

The images could represent something: maybe the Cobra stands for Sriii, and the King represents me. Could this be my side of the room, and the other side hers? My first instinct is to meet in the middle.

"You stand there," I tell Sriii, pointing at the Cobra on her side, "right in front of it." I stand across from her, right in front of the King. "Now walk towards me—slowly." We step cautiously toward each other, hoping for something to happen. We meet in the middle, one on each side of the altar. We wait for a moment, and just as I suspected, there is a low rumble of moving gears just below our feet. There is a click, and the ground beneath our feet shakes faintly. Sriii and I sink just a little, as the floor around each of our feet settles about an inch, opening the ancient mechanism for the first time. The altar opens to reveal a podium, rising from the chamber below.

The podium presents us with two small stone bowls, and a glass vile in the middle. Once it is risen all of the way, a thin, rectangular, golden leaflet folds out from beneath the two tiny bowls. "What does it say?" I ask Sriii.

She reads the writing just loud enough that we can hear her. She thinks about it and finally attempts to translate it—

"It says, 'Two for that which feeds life, and one for that which takes it, but be sure that the danger comes first, and the component which feeds life is untainted.'"

"So, they're petri dishes?" I ask.

"'That which feeds life?' they want our blood. But 'that which takes it?' What does that mean?" Sriii says. She thinks about it again silently, running through the possibilities, "Only one thing makes sense," she says. "They want the venom." She turns back to the door with a horrifying look.

"Wait, wait, wait," I say, "venom!? They want us to milk one? How *the fuck* are we going to do that?"

"I don't know," she replies, "Their size makes it very difficult to do; I have only seen it done once—but even then, the Snake was sedated."

I hang my head defeated, and sigh. Is this it? Is this where I die? I have avoided the conversation of the venom's potency, but I think that it is finally time to have it. We need to speak strategy; we need a plan. Sriii and I struggle for agreement, when Tziipoor decides to come forward with a possible way of assistance. I forget that I have only known her for a short while, and that there is still much that I do not know about her.

She presents me with the best possible solution to our problem. I have grown so used to her that I need to be reminded of the terror that I felt the first time that I saw her—the terror that others feel when they see her walk beside me. She raises her tail and moves the tip of it closer so that we can see the secret weapon that she carries. There is a barb—a *h*idden spur, like that of a Stingray, or a Platypus. She claims that her venom is more potent than the Cobra's venom, but the difference is that hers is not necessarily deadly. She can inject her venom with any dosage—big or small, causing harrowing paralysis. The victim is denied the ability to move, but they feel the pain of the venom moving through their body. Death will only come if the victim's luck runs out before the venom subsides, and in this environment—meaning the Game in general—it is [142]unlikely.

I am lightly concerned about whether her assistance taints the purpose of the task, but at this point, I honestly do not care anymore. They gave us their rules, and I did not see anything prohibiting outside help. As long as they have the vile of venom, and our blood samples are pure, the task will be considered complete. If there is an issue with that, they should have specified.

I tell Sriii of the venom and she agrees that we should us it. Tziipoor takes the lead, ahead of me and Sriii. I carry the vile and watch Tziipoor creep through the darkness with that horrifying walk, as she stalks her prey. She singles out a lonesome victim, and silently closes in on the sleeping serpent. I can hear the crackle in her throat, and the low hiss, as she prepares to disable the deadly Host. Sriii hides in the shadows, crouched to the ground like she was

---

[142] Host Detail—Tziipoors Venom: the effects of this toxin can last upwards to 46 hours. This time limit depends entirely on how fast the victim's body works to break it down.

when we first met—watching; waiting for our chance to extract the dangerous piss-colored liquid.

Tziipoor sticks the animal with her paralyzing barb; it shakes, and jerks, and eventually falls limp—its coiled body droops to the side. Tziipoor then stands by, watching for incoming trouble, as Sriii takes the vile from my hand, and instructs me to open the Snake's mouth. I position myself just behind its head, and struggle to find where to grab it. It is not so massive that it will be hard to do, but honestly, I am having a hard time because—even though I have one at home—Snakes creep me the fuck out. I understand the irony in that, but it's the truth.

"Ew," I say, gripping the top lip, and prying open its mouth. "Why is its body still moving?" I ask Tziipoor, as the Cobra seems to pulse. Its muscles contract and loosen again, over and over, and I can see the pain in its eyes, as it watches helplessly. She explains that though the venom paralyzes its victim, it still causes involuntary movement. It is the body's natural reaction to the pain.

"Ugh, fucking hurry," I tell Sriii, "I can't just watch it hurt like this any longer."

"Shut up," she replies. "All you do is complain, and it's fucking aggravating listening to you."

"Oh wow," I say with sarcastic surprise. "That was kind of hurtful."

"Pfftt," she replies, rolling her eyes. "Fuck your feelings. Open its mouth wider. I cannot reach the fang."

"Try harder! This is so fucking nasty." I let go with one hand, while holding the mouth open as wide as I can and fling the sticky saliva from my free hand. I then switch hands and do the same with the other, wiping whatever is left on my pants. In the process, I must have lost grip or leaned forward closing the mouth a little—

"Damn it! Hold it *open!*" Sriii says, further agitated by my mindlessness.

"Fuck," I say, "I'm sorry."

"Just be still," she replies, "I am almost finished."

She has placed the vile accordingly, and she squeezes the gland—just below its eye—releasing the venom and filling the vile. She seals it closed tightly with a lid, and before I can let go of the mouth, she does something unexpected. She snaps the fang from its jaw and places it in the small [143]pack around her waist. She then snaps off the other one and hands it to me without explanation.

"What is it for?" I ask Tziipoor.

"In their culture, milking one of these Snakes is honorary," she explains. *"Traditionally, the one who extracts the venom keeps a fang as proof that they were brave enough to face the beast. She will likely earn a new band for this. She has delt with these Snakes before, but not the wild ones."*

"But I thought these Snakes were sacred?" I ask confused.

"They are," she says. *"The fang will grow back, so they do not consider defanging them as cruelty, or disrespect to the creature. They lose them naturally anyway."*

"So how do they prove that they didn't just find a fang, or steal it from someone else?" I ask just to be annoying.

She sighs, and walks in front of me, denying me an answer.

Now that we have extracted the venom, we head back to the small room. I place the fang in an empty pocket—good thing I have many. We are so close to completing this task. I feel like this has been too easy, and I expect that something will happen. Something *has* to happen, and I *must* be prepared for it. I will say though, it will be nice to be out of this wintery shit hole. And a shower, it's not likely that I will get one, but a shower would be fucking *fantastic*.

We gather again around the altar, and Sriii returns the vile to its place. The only offering left to give is our blood. I pull Reewenniveaar from the scabbard, and slice open my palm, for a dramatic effect, I guess. I hold my hand above the dish, and wait while my red blood drips, filling it to the top. Sriii does the same with her blood—which is black.

The golden leaflet folds back into its original place, then the altar returns to the spot below the floor where it had come from. We withdrawal from the pit, and just as I expected, I am easily able to convince Sriii to let Tziipoor carry us back to the top. We meet up again with Barroun and his Eiinokrra and set our focus on reuniting to the group so that we can return to Zephiiitrrax.

We grow from three, to five, to nine, and then on to 15 once we

---

[143] Relic Detail—The Bag: Sriii has been equipped with this pouch throughout the duration of their time in Arrtisiiaax. Sriii asked Tanner to carry the body of her fallen friend rather than carrying it herself for reasons that are unclear to me.

meet the rest outside. All that is left to do is return to the doorway at the top of the mountain—a day's hike if all goes well. I am back on my feet and miserable again in the cold. There is no storm like there was before, but the low temperature is just as draining. My hands grow cold again, and I have lost my posture, pulling my shoulders up to cover my neck. We climb the mountain, passing through the caverns, and leaving the canyon behind. We reach the doorway, and two of the Eiinokrra magically open the portal. I pass through without a second thought, saying goodbye to the dreaded Kingdom of Snow.

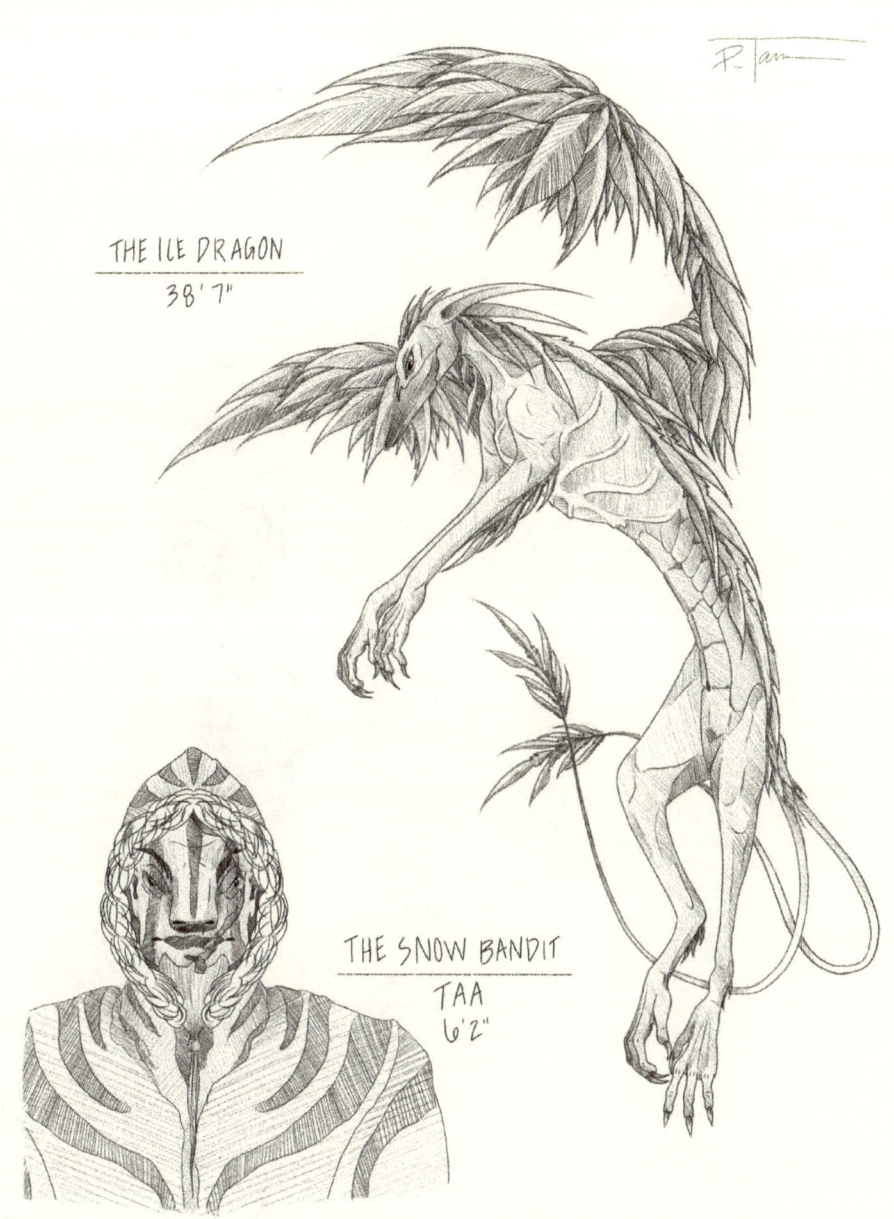

THE ICE DRAGON
38' 7"

THE SNOW BANDIT
TAA
6' 2"

205

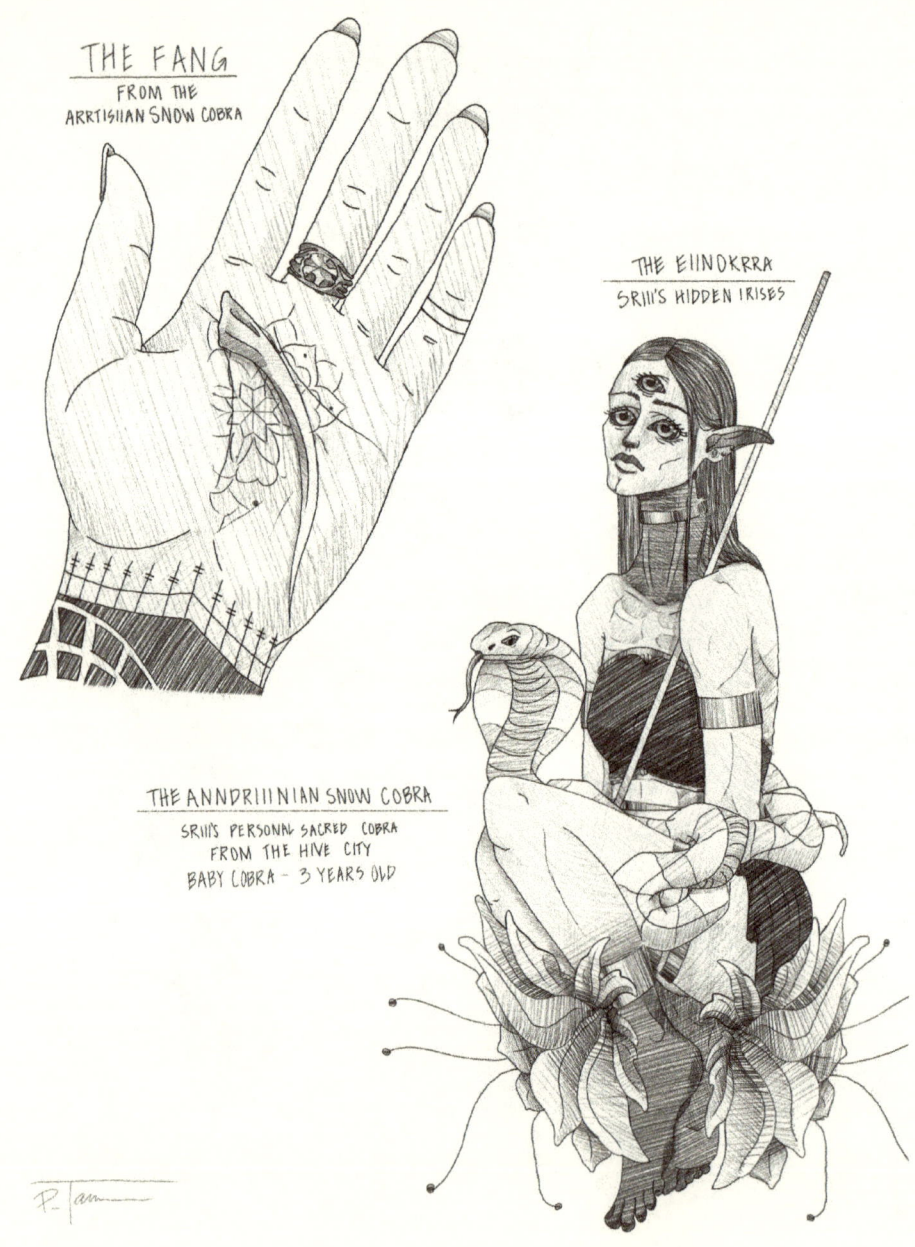

THE FANG
FROM THE
ARRTISIIAN SNOW COBRA

THE EIINOKRRA
SRIII'S HIDDEN IRISES

THE ANNDRIIINIAN SNOW COBRA
SRIII'S PERSONAL SACRED COBRA
FROM THE HIVE CITY
BABY COBRA - 3 YEARS OLD

THE FIFTH DREAM

S acrifices come at great measure. One must be willing to give. I watch as the Felerrg enters a room inside of a charred and tattered building. The Hosts outside burn and screech and stink as they run through the blazing streets of fire. Their flesh melts from their bones and each of them die in their own time. Hundreds, thousands, hundreds of thousands. The destroyer has succeeded in what she had come for.

I have never seen one like this. I have never witnessed such vulgar destruction. A Yokkaa cannot omit such damage. A Yokkaa alone cannot cast this kind of magic. The destroyer is the source of this discerning power. She is just inside that room. I follow behind the Felerrg to see.

She sits in a wide chair with her head thrown back and her arms resting out beside her. She is grey, and the life is drained from her eyes. But she is not dead, no, she is very much alive. That thing inside of her will not let her die.

The sight is bitterly horrific, and her sacrifice proves too great. The destroyer breaths heavily. She twitches lightly, covered in all of her collected Yokkaa. She carries more than any before her, and more than any will ever carry again. Draped across her torso and wrapped around her wrists, hanging from the bends of her knees and her elbows and her ankles, encircling her neck and her fingers and her toes, in stacks of **12** to **18** Yokkaa thick. Covering every inch of her, she wears her terrible and torturous stones.

Another enters the room, and another behind him. One is the one they call the Keeper, though he is no longer a true carrier of that title. The other is a strange creature from the Void. It is called The One. Like Cardinals—small red Birds from the planet called Earth,

207

The One can travel to any Universe it pleases, it can jump between dimensions, and can see what is not to be seen.

The Keeper and the Felerrg proceed to gently remove each Yokkaa from the destroyer and as they do, the destroyers stones disappear to the place that I cannot follow her to. As each Yokkaa is pulled from her body, her color begins to return, and her eyes almost twinkle again.

I overhear an explanation from The One as it sits and watches patiently with a greedily disturbing smile. It tells of the destroyer's purpose; it tells of her proposition. She did not want to do this; she was given no other options. She did not want to use them, but the destroyer came across a particularly unhealthy Yokkaa. She has collected more than known to exist, and she has used them to wipe out a colony—a colony that the unhealthy Yokkaa did not like. Genocide, murder in the highest degree. She killed them. No, The One points to a moss-colored stone around her finger. The One says that the Yokkaa killed them.

When the Keeper and the Felerrg finish, there are only two stones that they cannot remove. One is the Yokkaa that protects her, and the other is the one that possesses her. Her eyes finally blink, slowly recovering from the surge of hostile energy. She regains her strength and sits up.

The destroyer looks to the possessive Yokkaa and screams as she strips it from her skin. She sighs, finally relieved of the unhealthy stone. She gifts it to the Keeper and drops her head to rest. The Keeper passes it to The One, and it smiles with wide eyes as it turns away and leaves. A Yokkaa must match its carrier.

9

THE MEMORIES

1,887 Days since the Fall...

I am lost. Not lost as in, "I do not know where I am," but lost as in, "I have no purpose." I am not the same as I was before. I am not strong, or courageous, or exploratory, nor would I call this an adventure. I am beaten, I am broken, and I am tired. I have been trapped here for five years, watching my fellow comrades' fall, one by one, around me. We started with 16, but now there are only seven—nine confirmed deaths, nine faces that I will never see again. I knew that death would be frequent here, but what I had forgotten was why I always preferred being alone—I fear saying goodbye. I am truly lost.

I sit in my small cell; we are no longer being held collectively in the same [144]room. We each have our own space, but we are in the same hallway, so we can speak to each other if we choose to. Though, it does not happen often. We are silenced by our sadness. We are equally devastated—or that is what the others think at least. I feel as if I have lost the most—I feel like I am the one in the most pain. I have never dealt well with death, or with loss, and this is no different—in fact, this is worse.

I feel as if it is my job to tell the stories of the fallen, they need to be remembered. They need to be spoken of often, so that they

---

[144] Note from the Prophet—Time Jumps: as the Clutch had said before, we will be lost to this place for a long time. Be prepared for many jumps in time. It was also said that we will learn a lot here, so be attentive, and patient with the Footnotes.

will not be forgotten. I need them to live forever in my memories—because I do not allow myself to love often, I knew that the feeling would be even more intensely uncomfortable in the Game. I knew that allowing myself to feel it here would be even worse—and I was right.

Love is not the only emotion that I find troubling lately. I am suffering from the guilt—though I feel that it is selfish for me to use the word suffer. Perhaps, 'tortured by it', or 'rightfully tormented,' is a better way of putting it. Five years may not seem to be very long, but a lot has happened in that short amount of time. I cannot help but think about how things could have ended differently—it is only fair that I atone for what I have done. I took the lives of Hosts that did not need to die. I was pointed down the path of Yeshua—the Human who won the Game without taking a single life, but I chose not to follow it. I apologize in advance; I know how shocking some of the names on this list will be, I had not expected an early end for them either.

86 Days after the Fall...

The Third Hevaanian Gate
The Temple in the Trees
[145]Baakorraht

    This is our first mission after returning from Arrtisiiaax, and our destination is high in the trees of the Forest of [146]Rhhiina. We search for a legendary missing temple called [147]Baakorraht. It is said that it was built into the trees—carved from the wood. Rumor has it, the temple was built by a peaceful civilization of monks, but this has not been proven. It is also said to be impossible to find, but luckily

---

[145] [back-oh-RAT]

[146] [REE-nah]

[147] Monument Detail—Temple Baakorraht: hidden high in the mountains of the Forest of Rhhiina, in the kingdom of Tohh [t-O], pronounce the o with the short sound like the ou in the word thought, rather than like the double o's in the word too, or the way that the e makes the o sound in the word toe. This temple is deserted, and many Hosts believe it to be fictitious, or make believe. Many speak of it, but only few have actually seen it. It is unknown who built it.

the Eiinokrra are master scavengers, and can find *almost* anything—except for a Frogman and a few Gods, apparently.

The portal lets us out on a massive tree branch high in the canopy. The group of Eiinokrrian 'scouts' who traveled here before us were able to locate the entrance of the temple, but that is all that they had done. It is our job to venture farther. I must say, I am actually kind of excited for this mission. According to the legend, the temple holds God-like magnificence—even in ruins.

The name that is written next to this Gate on the scroll is Cynniaa; this is his mission. Our group is much smaller this time because of the rough terrain. This location requires the ability of flight. The members who tag along with Cynniaa and me are: Sriii, the Squeeb, and two other Eiinokrra. They have brought with them three of the giant white bats—similar to the one that Sriii and Benoviii rode in the desert. They have also entrusted Cynniaa and me with our wings again, though I still have to be chained to [148]Sriii.

I ride with Sriii, the Squeeb rides with his guide, and Cynniaa flies freely next to his Eiinokrra and her creature. I am in awe with the scenery, I have always wanted to visit the Rainforest on Earth, but I had not gotten the opportunity. The plant life and Hosts that claim this forest as their home differ juristically from the ones back home, and I am both enchanted and terrified all the same. And the smell, it matches the beauty of our surroundings; I can smell flowers of all kinds. They blend perfectly together, creating a comforting scent of sanctity.

When we reach the temple, I am not as stricken by it as I had expected to be. It is simply just a hole in a tree—a small hole. It stands about two feet high. Its builders must have been a smaller race of Hosts. Sriii removes the magic from my chain, allowing me to shrink us to size, and then replaces the hex again after. The inside is much more detailed than the door; the deeper we go, the more intricate the shallow carvings get, and the rooms get larger too. There are bound and shaped trees, tied in strange constructs all along the walls and some are grown from the floor in the center of

---

[148] Relic Detail—Magic Chains: it has not yet been explained to the Reader how the magic used on the chains works. If the two are close together, the chain shortens itself, and if they are farther apart, more jump rings appear lengthening the chain, allowing them to move more freely, though this does have its limit.

some rooms. The wood in this forest is similar to the glowing wood in the Empty Forest. The only difference is that this wood glows with a different [149]color—this one is green, where the kind in the shack is more of a blue color.

We finally reach the room past the keyhole and find the two bowls and the same small vile as before. There is also a leaflet that folds out, giving us a clue. "Two for that which gives life, and one for that which has none. White is the pure color of the third, and vanity accompanies those who have it won."

This one is perfectly clear. They want a piece of the Errok stone from the Hidden City, Vaahiigali. The needle that was given to me by Hffh should do the trick. It seems that Cynniaa is enlightened as well, and he retrieves his as offering instead. He insists that we give his—in case we are separated, and I happen to need mine. I argue that his is more important to him, and that I have lived my life without wings—I will be able to manage better without them if the situation were to occur. But still, he insists.

"We gave you your wings to help you, and my purpose here is to protect you above all others." He places his needle in the vile. When he places the vile back, I pick it up and return his needle.

I empty the small case that holds my needle and thread. I place the items in the small pack that I had crafted out of the leftover clothing that they let me keep after leaving the Kingdom of Snow. I shrink the Errok case, and put it carefully in the vile, then return it to its place.

"You should worry about yourself too," I reply, and we fill the two-separate bowls with our blood—completing this suspiciously easy task. "I know everyone thinks that *I* need to be protected, but that doesn't mean that you aren't protected either. We are a team," I say. "We need to take care of each other. You are just as important as I am."

We make our way back out, following Sriii through the labyrinth that is Baakorraht with new-found respect for each other. There are many narrow hallways which lead to larger rooms with skinny

---

[149] Relic Detail—Bioluminescent Trees: there are seven different species of these trees on Irestiikaar. The kind that grows solely in the Empty forest is the most unique of these trees. This kind grows faster, and the surrounding soil is rich with magic radiating from the Hidden City of Zephiiitrrax.

wooden pillars and tall ceilings. I had said before that the temple was carved from the tree, but that statement appears to be wrong. It looks more like it had been grown—shaped with magic into intricate designs, and bookshelves, and staircases. I wonder what it looked like when its creators had lived here. Now, it is overgrown and not well kept. There are wild vines, and bushes, and sprouts of flowers. Its beauty is still great, but I wish I had the chance to see it in its full heaven-like glory.

Finally approaching the exit, I am blinded by the light of the sun. My eyes are used to the darkness inside, and I need a moment to adjust. We return to our real sizes, and just as we think we are finished here, devastation introduces itself. The three Eiinokrra call for their three white Bats, but the creatures never return. Pushing forward, we walk across the branches. Cynniaa and I carry the Eiinokrra and the Squeeb across to new branches when necessary, as the three continue to call for their lost companions. "I will not leave her here," Sriii says about her creature. "I will not abandon her."

Nearing the portal—now about 30 minutes [150]away—we hear a call from above the trees. I recognize it, and I know that the next two calls that fallow also are the calls of the missing white Bats. The three Eiinokrra return their calls to help the creatures locate them. But I am left confused after the sound of another, more terrifying call that comes after.

"Oh no," says the Squeeb.

"Ah fuck," I say, "here we go." I roll my eyes. It is never anything good when the Squeeb says that.

"Tanner?" the Squeeb says, as the creatures break through the canopy, fleeing from the large Hosts that follow them.

"What?" I yell back, joining Sriii on the back of her flying white Bat.

"*That* is a Dinosaur!" it says, pointing to one of the four beasts that chase us—as the Squeeb now sits on a white Bat as well.

I look behind us to see that they are somewhat familiar to me. They are massive, winged creatures, from planet Earth. Their skin

---

[150] Relic Detail—Eiinokrrian Portals: though their magic is incredible, it is not always necessarily accurate. They can get close to their desired destinations, but they are never exactly on the spot. The Twelve Gates make it harder also, because they are protected by the magic of the Gods.

is black, and standing, they would be as tall as Giraffes. I have read about them before, but I cannot recall their [151]name. They are magnificent beasts but are just as similarly terrifying when in pursuit. They break through the trees easily with their size, and chase chaotically, as if they will die if they do not catch us.

We tear through the canopy, fleeing for our lives. We struggle because of the beast's agility; we make easy targets for them. One of our accompanying Eiinokrra makes the suggestion that I change Cynniaa's size, like I did with Taa in Arrtisiiaax. He is equipped with a doppelganger body, and a pair of wings; he can safely distract the beasts while we make an escape back to the portal. I do not like this plan, but I understand why he chooses to go through with it. "I will see you in Zephiiitrrax," he says.

I do as I am told and change his size so that he can easily defeat the beasts. I watch, as they follow him up out of the canopy, and disappear. The rest of our flight is silent, and I have a bad feeling in my gut. I ask Tziipoor to keep an eye on him until we both return. And only then, do I learn the reality of what is to happen to us.

We step through the portal, and I am returned to the cell that is [152]shared by me, and my fellow Recruits. Not very long after, the Squeeb is returned to his body, and I then come to a terrorizing conclusion. Cynniaa's body is missing. When I ask why she had not told me, Tziipoor informs me that the Eiinokrra came and retrieved it at about the same time that we split with him in the forest. But she has been watching him, and she allows me the ability to see him too.

I sit next to her on the ground and lean against the rocks. I close my eyes and pretend to sleep. She tells me that I must keep this between us; the others cannot know what I can see. Cynniaa sits alone in a small room. He is awake, which means he has returned from his doppelganger body and is in his real one. His eyes are covered with a cloth, blocking his vision, and his hands and feet are tied to the chair that he sits in. Could it be an interrogation or a secret meeting with the Chief? The bad feeling in my gut remains the same, as I watch and wait to see what they plan to do. The longer

---

[151] Host Detail—The Winged Creatures: the scientific name for this beast is the Quetzalcoatlus.

[152] Gameplay Detail—Cells: at this point in time, the Recruits are still sharing a single cell.

he sits, the more anxious I feel. My discomfort grows, and I now fear for the worst.

The door finally opens, and two male Eiinokrra enter the tiny room. They snicker and sneer, as they walk in circles around [153]him. I hold back my tears, realizing what is about to happen to him, knowing that there is nothing that I can do. "Stay silent," says Tziipoor. "You do not need to watch this." I stop her before she revokes her ability, and I insist that I must see the truth.

As they begin, I am already disturbed. I must turn my body away from the others, so that they cannot see me cry. They whip him, and they cut him, moving slowly to enhance the pain, as they tease him and taunt him about his lineage. I am informed of something that I had been oblivious to, and I am sunken in sadness and bitter disgust for my involvement in his recruitment. What have I done? I should have stopped him when I had the chance. He should have never left Vaahiigali.

"The next in line for the throne," one teases.

"The successor of the great King Onaaviaa," taunts the other. "The next ruler of the Hidden City, Vaahiigali; [154]Onnemiit Cynniaa, the greatest warrior of them all—you are less than what I had expected."

I weep as silently as I can, watching the Eiinokrra beat one of my closest friends here, the future King of Vaahiigali. I know that they are going to kill him. The Fae will lose their heir, and it will be my fault entirely. I told him that he is protected, but I have failed him. They punch him knocking him to the ground, and they kick him until he spits blood. My anger grows, as I watch them laugh, and enjoy themselves. What disgusting and vile creatures. The Eiinokrra are using us to get into the Holy City—they are forcing us to complete the tasks, then they plan to slaughter us once they get what they are after.

My silent tears turn to hardened sobbing after I see them finally leave him, broken and bleeding to death. He will die alone, and his

---

[153] Host Detail—Cynniaa: Cynniaa's real body is currently the same size as a Human. The Eiinokrra allowed Tanner to bring him up to everyone else's size after they returned from Arrtisiiaax.

[154] Host Detail—Onnemiit Cynniaa: of the Family of C. Cynniaas first name is Onnemiit [oh-NEM-et]. He is set to marry the King's daughter, Otrrah [oh-TREH], and take the throne after Onaaviaa.

family will not get to bury his body. A new fire is ignited within me, and I lose all trust I had in Sriii, or Benoviii, or the others like them who travel with us. I am possessed with anger, but I know the importance of keeping this secret ability silent. I cannot say anything, I cannot inform the other Recruits, and I cannot condemn the Eiinokrra to their faces. I must suffer this tragedy silently and remember what I have learned from this. Not all those who seem friendly are worthy of my trust.

I use my ability to speak to him in his mind, before the last of his life fades out—

"You are a great friend. I will cherish you forever."

He smiles one last time, and replies, "That is all I ever wanted."

1,887 Days since the Fall...

Present Day
The Dark City
Zephiiitrrax

Through the years, I have kept that story silent, you are the first to hear the end of it—the real truth of the unfortunate event. Even the other Recruits are blind to what had happened to Cynniaa. They have their theories, but only Boriisst has been able to figure it out. He knows the Eiinokrra better than any of us. He is sure that they tortured him and killed him, but I have not confirmed it with him. I continue to act ignorant to what had happened, though I understand that the Eiinokrra killed him only because of opportunity. He is the only Recruit who has been directly targeted and wasted by the Eiinokrra. I forever will dread the day that I have to tell the Fae of his death, that is, if I even get to return.

Zephiiitrrax is a very mysterious city. I have done my best to learn what I can, but understanding it is tricky. Boriisst once said that in order to escape here, we have to go down. But I am unsure as to what he meant; perhaps there are tunnels that lead outward. I know that there is no way out on the main island. In order to liberate myself, I would have to cross the water again—the only way out of the city is on the other [155]side.

Luckily, I have mastered my missing memories—well, most of them anyway. This helps my stats, and my ability to surpass my peers. Do you remember when I mentioned a lab? I spoke of it a few times. It was a real place; those were real memories. After I was sedated on the Adreestiaah, before I even made it to Irestiikaar, I was given a [156]time loop. The Game Runners gave each Host a choice of three access points, to whatever they need, but three is all you get. I remember being told to 'choose wisely'. I spent my three points quickly. I took unlimited access to the largest library in existence— one that has books on every subject, Host, and History. My second point was spent on complete privacy—not even the Game Runners could watch or listen to what I was doing. And with my third point, I acquired time, as much as I felt like I would need—until my work was done.

Shamelessly, they stole one of my points from me. They did not give me the time that I needed. Although, I had expected them to grow impatient with me after 15 years of research and science, and workouts and training—but I was caught off guard when they came to rip me from the loop, throwing me down into the City of the Lost. This memory explains why I did not have shoes when I woke up. Ready for them to do something, I took precautions. I had a plan. I had developed a kind of 'software' that protected me from the Game Runners, they could not see me, but I could see them. I knew when they were coming, and I knew for what purpose. I took my own memories just before they pulled me from the loop, and I had no time to dress myself, or find the appropriate weaponry.

I have also recovered the memory of myself actually falling. I remember hitting the ground. I remember the pain, the exposed bones, and the blood. I remember dying. The things that I was able to access while in the Time Loop are extraordinary. My healing ability for example, I can basically 'recharge' my body, my strength, and my

---

[155] City Detail—Zephiiitrrax: the islands. There are four in total. The largest of the islands is the city of Zephiiitrrax itself. The other three surround this island in a triangular shape, and all three have a unique doorway to the Empty Forest.

[156] Gameplay Detail—Time Loops: each Host is given this opportunity, but do not *have* to take it.

endurance on nothing but [157]will. I died, but I had worked so hard to get to this point. I guess my heart just was not [158]ready.

This next one was the second of the Recruits to die. This one took a heavier toll on another member of our group—the one who was the closest to him. This death made us realize how unsafe we actually are, just because some of us are given doppelgangers, that does not mean that they will be 100 percent effective.

I also lose a bit of myself here; this is where I start to become something different. I say so much about the vile nature of the Hosts who surround me. But here, I am reminded of how vile Humans can be as well. We are no different. It seems that many of the lessons that I learn here are always the same, just in different forms. I have always been a repetitive learner. It takes me more than once to actually accept the truth. I give too many chances and forget too many crucial details. But eventually, I always try to find my flaws.

---

[157] Gameplay Detail—The Fall: the first official test of the Game is to stick the landing. Tanner prepared for this; she rebuilt her body to withstand anything, as long as her will is strong, she *will* live. In this case, she remembers death. But her body had absorbed the lost blood and repaired itself. She also permanently removed certain memories from her mind—for example, what she did to successfully achieve this—in order to prevent other Hosts from figuring out how to actually kill her.

[158] Note from the Prophet—Secrets: for the safety of Humanity. I need to be sure to explain this properly. The Humans and the Earth are protected by the highest group of warriors in Hevaan. They protect both of the planets and their peoples. This book and our Human languages are protected by the same kind of power that gave Tanner the translation ability on the Adreestiaah—Reminder! The ship was made with resources from the planet Hevaan. The footnote secrets, and the ones told to you directly by Tanner are not stated lightheartedly. Knowledge of these secrets comes with the responsibility of keeping them. We are entrusting the Reader with keeping her safe, so do not speak of this to outsiders. She is the future of Humanity. It is up to us to protect her just as fiercely as she protects us.

301 Days after the Fall...

The Sixth Hevaanian Gate
The Island of Salt
[159]Yhiin

The portal leaves us stranded, and for as far as the eye can see, the ground mirrors the sky, and only in one direction, I can see the outline of mountains along the horizon. The sun is high in the sky, and the wind tastes of salt. Again, I will take the time to explain our surroundings, what the task is, and who all has accompanied us. This mission is the hardest one that we have come across at this point in time. It also contains the highest number of casualties from our small group.

The Salt Island is about 150 square miles of salt flat that has built up over time, covering the now buried mountain. The tip-top can be seen sticking out of the center of the flat and reaching only about 200 feet into the sky. There are salt crystals that protrude from the ground, climbing up the rock on all sides, and standing just as tall. This place also seems to be uninhabited.

The main issue with this destination is that we find it almost impossible to locate the keyhole, or even an entryway for that matter. By now, it could be buried under hundreds of feet of salt and inaccessible. We spend months here looking for the entrance, climbing the mountain, and scaling the steep and dangerously spaced salt crystals. There is one 'doorway' that we manage to find, but it is too small for anyone to fit through at normal size.

Our group for this mission consists of: Sriii, Benoviii, Boriisst, Reeb, the Squeeb, Tziipoor, me, and three other [160]Eiinokrra. This mission is meant for me and Boriisst. I have noticed that each location so far has had some kind of relation to the Recruit who is required to help me accomplish the task. Sriii's mission dealt with sacred Banded Snow Cobras, Cynniaa's mission required the ability

---

[159] [y-IN]

[160] Gameplay Detail—Time Jumps: at this point in time, The Eiinokrra has learned that not every Recruit needs to be present at every task. They only send the ones that that they think will be needed in each area. At this point, Sriii has also begun to trust Tanner and Tziipoor to roam free, but Boriisst is still connected to Benoviii, as he is the only one present who is not trusted, nor does he have a doppelganger.

of flight and a piece of Errok stone, and Barrouns mission was left incomplete because we could not access the third [161]specimen that goes in the vile—which was much larger than the previous ones that we had seen. The next name on the list is Ehhrn, who cannot be caught, and I have not had the opportunity to meet up with him again. And for our current mission, I have yet to make a connection to Boriisst. He is the Host that no one seems to know anything about. Even the Squeeb is unsure of what he is.

The day that we finally decide to venture into the tiny tunnel is the 94th day of our mission on Yhiin. I take the time to shrink Boriisst and Benoviii, and me and Sriii small enough to enter. The other two Recruits and the three Eiinokrra that accompany them stay up top with Tziipoor.

The tunnel is dark, and for some reason I had expected the temperature to be cold. But we are headed toward the warmth that radiates from the center of the mountain. I can sense two creatures below us. We are approaching them, but the odd thing is that I cannot feel their purpose—I cannot tell whether they pose a threat or not. I guess we will find out.

The small tunnel lets us out into the original—normal sized tunnels that were meant for this task. We must take the time to mark this place, so that we are able to find our way back out, who knows where the tunnels original entrance is. I would hate to find it, and not be able to get out because of the overgrown salt crystals that surround this place.

Once we find the keyhole, I hesitate to open the door. I can now hear the two heartbeats just on the other side of the wall. I worry that we will be met with aggression, but the ones who travel with me do not feel the same way. They encourage me to open the door, and against my better judgment, I finally insert the key, releasing the danger that has spent hundreds of years trapped behind the lock.

We are presented with a table and two Hosts. Both have the body of a man—a Human with ten fingers, and presumably ten toes to mach. The strange things about them are their heads and their

---

[161] Relic Detail—Barrouns Specimen: the altar presented to Tanner and Barroun requested the blood from each of them, and a feather from the wing of a God—Barroun specifically. The Great God took Barrouns wings when he banished him, so he must earn them back before the task can be completed.

faces: the first has the head of a Dog, one without fur, and it is also missing its eyes—there are only empty sockets. The second one is the same, it is missing its fur, and lacks eyes as well, but this one has the head of a [162]Cat. I am both fascinated and lost for thought. This task is strange; it is not like any of the rest.

The Cat instructs me and Boriisst to join them at the table, and Sriii and Benoviii are instructed to wait outside. The magic is released from Boriisst's chain, and Benoviii disconnects himself, leaving us in the room. The door closes again behind them, and Boriisst and I are trapped, alone in the small room with the strange creatures. In the center of the table, there are four familiar bowls—but there is no vile like the others. I can only assume that the four bowls are for the blood of each of us: Boriisst and me, and the two [163]creatures who sit with us. The trouble is figuring out what we will have to do. Are we having a conversation or performing some kind of séance? I am not sure.

Aware of my confusion, Boriisst explains, "They are Puzzlers, connoisseurs of bewilderment. We may be here for a while." The fact that he is familiar with them is helpful, but my real concern is whether he will be successful here or not. He does not seem exceptionally clever. However, I could be wrong, and in this case, I truly hope that I am. I know that Riddles are not fun for me. I always overthink it, and I always struggle to quickly produce a correct answer. Though, some are easier than others. The ones on the leaflets have been pretty repetitive so they are also straight forward.

The creatures take turns delivering strange questions. They wait patiently for our answers and speak with no empathy. They listen to me and Boriisst examine the puzzles and deliberate our answers carefully. If we give a wrong answer, they take away a "point." They started us with five, and now six questions in, and we have four

---

[162] Host Detail—Mysterious Creatures: the heads of these creatures resemble two species that are familiar to the planet Earth, and the similarities are uncanny. The Dog resembles the breed called Xoloitzcuintle, or the Mexican hairless Dog. The Cat resembles the more commonly known breed called the Sphinx, or the hairless Cat.

[163] Host Detail—Creatures: these two in particular are what are known to us as Therianthropes. They each have two forms: the first in which they have the bodies that match their heads, and the second one in which they are now—with Human bodies.

"points" remaining. Boriisst has proven me wrong, showing that he can quickly produce an answer to the wildly perplexing questions. He did get one wrong, but he is doing significantly better than me—I have failed to answer any of them.

My patience diminishes, and I now sit slumped in my seat with my head thrown back, and my hands resting in my lap. My legs are stretched in front of me, and my ankles are crossed. It is clear that this is *his* game. As the time passes, the questions seem to become more and more absurd. I was baffled at the beginning, but now I am sure that he has to be cheating somehow. We have been seated here for hours, and we still have four chances to answer incorrectly—the whole time we have been here, he has only answered *one* riddle wrong. It is actually kind of amazing, though my boredom is quickly growing, and my lack of care for this is flourishing. I cannot wait for them to finish. I am only a blood-bag here; all they need me from is the contents.

The longer that I sit here observing, the more I come to realize just how intellectual Boriisst really is. He is a master at hiding his true intelligence. I realize the danger in this—for a man who seems to be nothing but a purvey piece of shit, he really does have the upper hand in this. The harder the questions get, the quicker he is able to deliver the answer. He is sharp in the mind, and the dangerous thing is that he excels at hiding it. I keep forgetting that he was a gangster, a master of surprise, a dealer, and a professional conman. I have forgotten about the destruction that he is capable of. I beat him once, but he has grown stronger since then. I have improved as well but is it hard to say who would win if we were to spar again. I still do not trust him. I have a hunch that there is something else that he keeps hidden—a devastating secret. If there is one in our group who reeks with the stench of oncoming betrayal, it is him.

The questioning finally comes to a close, engulfing the room in silence. I sit quietly, watching Boriisst think through something in his head. I wish that I could hear him. I listen for a Voice. I look back to the two strange Hosts who sit across the table from us, and for a moment I admire their great posture. Now genuinely distracted, I finally hear his Voice. "*Fuck*," he says, "we're in trouble." I pass by any respect for privacy and continue to question him out loud.

"Why?" I ask him. "Why are we in trouble?"

He replies, "The questions were an **a**nagram—leading up to a last-minute warning. Fuck! I should have seen this coming."

I quickly switch to speaking with Tziipoor, "Keep your eyes open, something is coming. Let me see what you see."

She grants me the ability, and as Boriisst tells me of the final warning, I can see what is happening on the surface—above us. There are dark clouds coming in from all directions. The sun is completely cut out of the sky. Tziipoor is able to see through the darkness, and as the rain begins to fall—lightly sprinkling down with the taste of salt—strong winds swirl around the mountain causing a large twister.

"*Beware* the dreaded creature who irrevocably defeats the living." he tells me.

"What does that mean?" I ask him. "What creature?"

"One of the only creatures that can kill a soul, not just a body," he says worriedly. "With these, when you're dead, you're dead. That's it. No reincarnation, no new body, no magic, no second generation—*dead*."

"Oh, no," I reply. "We have to help them!"

I stand to retreat back outside, but the door is locked. There is no way out. I return my attention to Tziipoor, and what it is that she can see. There are now flashes of lightning, but the rain is still only sprinkles. The Squeeb finally answers my question as to what it is we are fighting.

It yells to the others, "We need to find a place to hide—*now*! They're Harpy's!"

I look to Boriisst, "There's more than one;" I say, "we need to go help them!"

He refuses to leave the room, but I am determined. They will not survive out there they are sitting ducks. I can see as Tziipoor counts four of the winged Hosts above. Their wings are the strength of their attack—helping them close in their target from all sides. They cannot escape to the portal; their only chance is to find a place to hide among the rocks and the salt.

I scream to Sriii and Benoviii on the other side of the thick, rock door. I tell them to find another way out—to find another place where we can let the others in. We need a place that can be well defended, so that we do not risk the Harpies infiltrating the tunnels. We must defend the fort and save our comrades outside. The two on the other side retreat from the closed door following my orders, and I turn to deal with the issue that I face behind it.

Upset and enraged, I aim my anger at the Cat creature that had sat across from me. I wreck its posture by grabbing to its collar and lifting it toward me. I pull its face close to mine and speak disrespectfully into its ear—

"I know that you can hear me, so you better answer my question clearly—no riddles, no puzzles, or mystical answers." I adjust myself, gripping tighter onto its collar. "How many Hosts have to die for this task to be completed?"

I can hear the Voice in Boriisst's head, "Fucking idiot! What does she think she's going to accomplish threatening it! Why the Cat? I warned her about the Cats! *You never fuck with the Cats!* She has no idea what she's doing! They're going to kill us."

I am struck again with rage, and repeat myself, "Answer my question, *Cat*."

"FOUR," it replies plainly.

"What will happen if I leave this room?" I ask next, "Does it affect the completion of the task?"

"LEAVE IF YOU WISH," the Dog says, "BUT YOU MUST RETURN, AND GIVE FRESH BLOOD TO THE ALTAR, OR THE TASK WILL BE ABANDONED, AND YOU WILL NEVER HAVE THE CHANCE TO COMPLETE IT AGAIN."

"Awesome," I say sarcastically, "I'll be right back." I drop the Cat back into its seat and turn back to the closed off doorway.

"How are you planning to get out?" asks Boriisst, "That is solid rock; you'll never break through it in time."

I ignore his question and make a play with my next best option. This is the kind of situation where the advanced abilities of the Yokkaa prove helpful. I close my fist and use the stone's help to smash at the wall—shredding the flesh from my knuckles and exposing the [164]bone. I manage to break through the wall—also breaking my

---

[164] Relic Detail—Yokkaas Advanced Abilities: this is where the 'punch harder' aspect comes into play. By wearing the stone inward, this allows it to help 'boost' the power of its wearers punch—kind of like an invisible rocket blast, intensifying the heat of the hit.

hand, but with a little bit of luck, it will heal back together before I face the oncoming terror up top.

I tell Tziipoor to lead them to the door which I had entered before; I will do my best to shrink everyone to the proper size. And I tell you this next secret with confidence—I hope that you do not see me differently because of this. I must do what needs to be done. I must make the hardest choice. We have to sacrifice four Hosts in order to complete this task. I must choose who will live and who will die. And selfishly, I admit that I have already chosen the four that I am willing to leave behind—it looks like the betrayer is me. They are the three Eiinokrrian guards who are outside with the others, and Benoviii. None of these Hosts are especially crucial in our fight to open the Twelve Gates. They are the only sacrifices that we can afford.

Tziipoor remains silent, as I explain to her what needs to happen. She must guard the Recruits until I get there, and then once inside, we will have to search for Benoviii before we can proceed with completing the task. I can hear the rumble of the clouds outside, as I run through the tunnels back to the entrance. Against her better judgment, Tziipoor does as she is told and protects those who I instructed her to keep safe. One Eiinokrra falls, and just as I pass through the entrance and return myself back to normal size, I am shown the true nature of the Host that is the Harpy.

She holds the Eiinokrra down with her strong feet. Her massive wings resemble a Bats, and she uses the claws on her fingers to pull the beating heart from its chest. She lifts it to her mouth and devours [165]it—drenching herself in black blood and returning again to the sky. Her skin is black, and she has sunken, empty eye sockets like her masters. She wears no clothing; like they have no sense to cover up. She spots us in the corner by the door, and I shrink Tziipoor and the Squeeb, so that they can escape into the safety of the tunnels.

Before I can shrink Reeb, the other three Harpy plunge from a ledge above us. The four who remain up top are: the two remaining Eiinokrrian guards, Reeb, and me. I *must* make sure that Reeb and I are the ones who survive.

---

[165] Host Detail—the Harpy: it is said that the soul of every being is held within its heart. The Harpy eats this organ to obtain the purest form of the Host that it takes it from. The Harpy also has a special magic—uncontrolled and chaotic, just like its appearance. This kills the soul completely.

My hand has still not healed completely, but I am ready to fight. I can manage the pain until the skin rebuilds itself, and if I have to use that hand—making the injury worse—so be it. We are separated; there is one Harpy after each of us. I refrain from helping the other two Eiinokrra, hoping that they will fall, and that Reeb can hold his own against his, as I fight the one that pursues me.

I must be careful not to kill her until the task of sacrificing all four souls is complete. I heard the Squeeb say that if one dies, the others will retreat. We need to be sure that they do what they came here for. The Dog stated clearly that if we fail here, we will not have another chance—it is now or never.

I fight her as best as I can without overpowering her. I have to give them the idea that they still have the upper hand. The two other Eiinokrra fall just as planned, and I push the Harpy that I fight to the side in retreat for the doorway. I move hastily, dodging back and forth between the salt towers and tall rocks. I search for Reeb—this is our time to get away. The Harpy that follows me is closing in, and I am running out of chances to evade it. It is learning my steps quickly.

I turn the corner around a pillar of salt, and the worst possible thing that could happen is already set in motion. The three Harpy that were not chasing me had caught up with Reeb. My heart fills with sorrow, and my head fills with anger. There is a memory, why is this coming to me now? How strange.

When I first met him on the ship, I spent my entire roam-time that day speaking with him. I remember at one point in our conversation I had removed my hoodie and folded it before placing it beside me. Reeb watched in awe and grabbed his wadded hoodie before running to sit on the floor just on the other side of the glass from where I sat.

"Red Blood Tanner Teach Reeb," he says gesturing to my freshly folded hoodie. "Teach. Hmm, teach!" he insists.

I laugh and proceed to show him step-by-step how to do it, "Simpler?" I ask before running through them again. We repeat the steps until finally he is satisfied with his work.

"Reeb fold!" he says. "Huhuh," he laughs, "Reeb must show It!" He prances happily, excited to show the Squeeb his new trick—and for sure excited to be rewarded afterwards.

Back to the Harpy, no longer in need to wait, I pull Reewenniveaar from the scabbard and turn quickly, shanking the Harpy that thought it had the jump on me. I kill the creature, and before the others get the opportunity to flee from the fallen body of Reeb, I manage to grasp the leg of the one that ate his heart.

I am hoisted into the sky, clinging desperately to the creature that ruined my plan. How am I going to tell the Squeeb? What will I say? He trusted me to protect his brother, and I failed him. I cannot use my wings because hers create too heavy of a wind. I place my dagger back into its place, and climb up her body, as we climb higher into the sky. She fights and claws at my skin, struggling to free herself of my grip—I deny her any further freedom. With convenience on my side, I manage to wrestle myself eye-to-eye with her. She takes a bite at my neck, ripping into the skin. I grunt from the pain and draw my weapon in rebuttal. I slice the tendons that control her arms—just where they grow from her body—and we fall, as a mixture of our blood trails behind us.

She tries so hard to fight through the pain, but the wounds are deep; I might as well have just cut them off. She attacks with rage, fighting for her revenge and calling out for her fellow Harpy. But none come to rescue her, and I have gained the upper hand in this fight—for *I* am fighting for revenge too. I position myself closest to the sky and hold to it—she must be the first to hit the ground. As she fights desperately, I am adamant on keeping her distracted while I position her body to land the way I want it to—but I must also make sure that she does not immediately die—I need her to hear what I am going to tell her. I am angry, and I need to speak my fucking mind.

She is a creature of flight, so she is also aware of her surroundings. I have noticed a tilt in our course—her focus is also to land; she is also positioning herself. We crash into the salt flat below at an angle, tumbling and rolling painfully, as the salt skins the flesh, and a bone breaks with every hit to the ground. It finally stops, and I lie still—I need a moment. Her wings are severed, and I was sure to crush her spine on impact. I need to give my ability a little bit of time to begin healing before I do too much. But hey, at least my previous hand injury has healed. I laugh lightly causing pain in my ribs, and the motion sends me over the edge. The agony from my injuries causes me to [166]puke, which only makes the pain even worse. "God," I say to the man who sent me here, "this *fucking sucks*."

I wipe my face, blow my nose, and pick myself up off the ground. I carry myself to the Harpy—retrieving Reewenniveaar on the way, which had fallen from the scabbard when we landed. I sit in the position best suited for facing her, and she struggles with all that she has left, but she has no power. As my body slowly heals, my rage returns, and I begin to cut into the skin of her chest, while I tell her of the problems that she has brought upon me.

"You ruined everything!" I drop the dagger and use my hands to rip open the skin the rest of the way, exposing the broken ribs underneath. "You ruined my chances of ever going home!" I break away the ribs that remain and throw them to the side. "You killed the wrong man!" My voice grows with aggression. "You ruined *our plan*!" I can feel the weak tissue tear away as I dig into her chest with my bare hands. Once I find her heart, I stretch my fingers around, and grip tightly onto it. I lower my head to her ear and speak quietly— "I don't know if you can hear me, but I don't care. I will break your teeth from your jaw and wear them around my neck, as a warning to all of your sisters. I will slay every Harpy that crosses my path, and they will all die because of you."

I lift my head again, and she uses the last of her energy to speak her final words, "The Red Bloods of [167]Earth are the true Devils that we fear them to be." I rip her heart from her chest, and lay next to her, allowing my body to heal. I pass out for a short time, and once I am strong enough, I sit up. I finally drop her heart from my hand. I sit next to her and begin to dig into her stomach. I rip it open to find Reeb's heart still intact, swallowed whole. I hold it close to my chest and stand to turn my back at the dead and gutted creature.

I find Reeb's body and attempt to sew his heart back into his chest. Perhaps the soul is still intact. Perhaps I can save him. In this moment, I no longer care for the task. I stich and I stretch to make

---

[166] Gameplay Detail—Puking: because Tanner does not eat here, there is nothing in the stomach to eject. That means that puking here is like puking on an empty stomach. What comes out is pure stomach bile, burning and painful as ever.

[167] Host Detail—Red Bloods of Earth: it is understood that Humans are not the only red-blooded creatures on Earth. Most Hosts associate the name 'Red Blood' with Humans because they are the most heard of creature with this blood color.

things fit. I cut layers of skin from my leg to use as grafts to patch holes and fill spaces. For hours I perform this botched and desperate surgery in the cleanest way possible, unable to admit that it may not work.

When I finish, I search my pack for any small tools and parts needed to build a [168]device to shock his heart. The chances are low, but I must try. I cannot risk chest compressions because I do not want to tear the newly patched skin. I build a decent contraption and rotate shocks with rescue breaths. But for as much as I want it to work, this fails me, and I am left to live with this.

I sit and stare, in shock from the loss. When I find the power to do so, I shrink him so that I can carry him back to the Squeeb. When I find the others, I relay the sickening news, and head back to the small room to complete the task. They gawk at me, all covered in blood, and bruises, and deep cuts that are not yet fully healed, and the expression of complete defeat.

When I reach the room, Boriisst cusses me, angry that his role was to be here, spending hours convincing the creatures not to leave. We give our blood to the altar, along with the two Puzzlers.

Before I can leave, the Cat stands in front of me and speaks disturbingly slow, "YOU SHOULD LEARN TO HOLD YOUR TONGUE YOUNG WHISPERER. YOUR MOUTH WILL BRING YOU TROUBLE." It tilts its head downward as if to be looking at each of my arms. "YOU SHOULD MASTER HOLDING YOUR HANDS AS WELL." It reaches its hand up, also dreadfully slow, and grasps to the collar of my armor and pulls me close to its empty face.

"YOUR CONFIDENCE COULD KILL YOU." it whispers, "YOU ARE HOLLOW."

It releases its grip and allows me to withdrawal. Then it returns to the place next to the Dog. The two of them disappear. And I struggle to understand weather that was a warning or a piece of advice. Or perhaps both.

---

[168] Gameplay Detail—Tanners Defibrillator: in *some* cases, a device like this is "confiscated" from the user. The Game Runners do not like the idea of fixing things without magic—even though they are created from science. I should also state that there are only a small number of Elites who are permitted to commit scientific debauchery in effort to further understanding of the Players. In *other* cases, a user can keep said device, when curiosity catches the Bugg.

Boriisst stands silently and raises a vain eyebrow. I do not need to hear him think it, he has no need to say it. I can see it in his eyes, they are glazed with the rage of his "I told you so".

We walk silently back to the others and then quietly still we all return to the portal, allowing each other to mourn the fallen. We return to Zephiiitrrax, and as the others are returned to the cell, Sriii takes me to a private room.

"You *bitch*!" she says, punching me in the face. "You left them out there to die! You killed them on purpose!"

"Yes!" I reply to her, matching her anger, "And Benoviii should be dead in Reeb's place!"

"How dare you!" she whispers back to me.

"No!" I interrupt, "How dare *you*! Don't lecture me about deception and murderous deeds when you are guilty of the same things!"

She asks, "What do you mean?"

With which I answer, "You helped them kill Cynniaa. And the whole thing was your plan; you separated him from us so that they could kill him—because of a birthright that he didn't ask for. You are no better than me! And your uncle told me to complete the tasks and take you to Hevaan, they were the only ones that we could afford to lose if we were to complete his request."

She does not reply, for the moment I think there is nothing left to say. She returns me to the shared cell, and just before she leaves me, she speaks one final truth into my ear—

"You're right. I took part in killing him, and I have no right to preach to you about what I have done as well. But Humans are supposed to be better. When I heard that there was a Red Blood here, I expected one like The Red Blood Yeshua. You are not what I thought you would be, and I do not know how to deal with it. And as for my uncle, I am above him, I overrule his order. Everything that you do must go through me, regardless of what he told you."

She leaves and I retreat to my corner. I sink to the ground to sulk. I am sure to die from the stench of the blood on my armor and all over my hands, and face, and in my hair. It is packed under my fingernails and there are small bits of someone's flesh to accompany it, I cannot identify who's.

There is no easy way for me to wash it off. I strip my armor to its most bottom layer, anything I can do to get the smell off me while still avoiding being completely undressed and exposed. The smell is overwhelming, but the feeling is even more disgusting.

I carve a good-sized bowl and collect moisture from the damp walls—I am so desperate to be clean that I would use my spit if I had to. When the bowl is filled, I sit and manically scrub, and pick under my nails, and messuage the clumps out of my hair. I scrub my skin nearly raw, talking myself through the process under my breath with intention to keep myself sane.

I find this hard to do, gagging as the liquid rehydrates the dried blood. I empty and refill the bowl as many times as it takes to feel somewhat cleaner than I was, and I then do the same to my clothing and armor.

The others sit across the cell discussing silently and looking over every now and then, concerned about the muttering and the gagging and the constant scrubbing and rinsing. The Squeeb has noticed the stitching that I had done on the doppelganger body of Reeb, and though I told him what had happened he seems to not understand how to react. Reeb's real body lies in the opposite corner to mine covered in an assortment of garments and blankets. They discuss quietly about what is to be done.

When the cleaning is finished, I crawl into a ball on a cleaner part of the floor and cry, disgusted by my choices, and beaten by my failures. The others refrain from approaching me, too frightened and troubled by my erratic behavior. Even Tziipoor and the Clutch keep some distance, they sit close by but remain silent. They are the only ones who actually saw what had happened. They understand the heavy weight of the blood.

THE NECKLACE
TEETH FROM THE
MOUTH OF A HARPY

THE HARPY
THE DEMONS OF
YHIIN
5'3"

THE PUZZLER
THE CAT
6'11"

THE PUZZLER
THE DOG
7'3"

1,887 Days since the Fall...

Present Day
The Dark City
Zephiiitrrax

That day I lost a lot of my Humanity. I became someone new. I had changed. I made hard choices that were not mine to make, and they did nothing for us in the end. I met new levels of savagery that I had no idea I was capable of. Now, I feel like I am not even worthy of seeing my family or Fools again. They would not know the person that I have become. I am not the girl that they knew before.

I did not truly mean it when I said that I would slay every Harpy I come across. I only said this out of anger, but I did not lie when I said that I would take her teeth. I made a trinket that fits around my neck using the Errok thread. I sewed two chains, and then sewed the top row of teeth to one, and the bottom row to another. Then I connected them, and when I placed it around my neck the Errok chains hardened to stone. I wear it as a warning. I am willing to respect any Harpy, because I understand that not everyone is the same—this also applies to the Eiinokrra. I understand that it is unfair to hold anger for all of them because of the bad deeds of a few.

And I now understand that the ones that I had killed were only doing what had been asked of them. The tasks were created by the Great God, and though I do not see him as my enemy, I really struggle to understand how all of this misery is what is needed to achieve his great plan—whatever that may be. I do not know what to do now that we have lost so much. There is nothing else that I can do. I have failed. I ruined his plan. Because Reeb is dead, the Gates will never be completed.

There are a few other memories that I have recently recovered as well. These are a few more from the time I had spent in the lab. These memories answer some of the questions that I had gathered up to this point. First, I wondered how it is that I can see so clearly. I used to wear glasses, but I remember that I had taken the time to fix my eyesight. I now have 20/20 vision and can see better than I ever could before.

The second memory is about my hair. I had always thought it

odd that the color had not faded, and my roots never changed to my natural light brown color. The blonde is as vibrant as the day I had it dyed. I guess I had spare time because I was able to manipulate the natural growing color of my hair. I guess I figured that if I was going to die, I should at least try to look good doing it.

The third and final memory that I have regained is about the power of convenience. Somehow, someway, I managed to cheat the odds, placing them in my [169]favor—this is a bit of an older memory, as you know, I was aware of this ability in Yhiin.

To finish off catching you up to this point, I must tell you of the final death that I need to be reprimanded for. This is the one that I find the most hurtful. This one was the hardest loss, and the most unexpected one. This one drags away my energy and my will to fight. This one has taken the biggest toll on me and has left me with nothing else. There was no reason for us to continue opening the Gates, but the Eiinokrra refused to accept it.

994 Days after the Fall...

The 11th Hevaanian Gate
The Drowned Castle
[170]Miiqraaux

The task at this Gate is meant for Aneera and me, but she is not the one who is lost here. Before I dive too far into the misery, I understand that *again*, I need to take the time to explain our surroundings, what the task is, and who all has accompanied us. Due to the conditions of our destination, not all of the Recruits are a part of this mission.

First things first, Aneera is a Siren; she is made for land *and* water. She is fully equipped for this kind of environment. The Castle [171]Miiqraaux is a magnificent work of art. Even now, sunken

---

[169] Host Detail—Abilities: the convenience ability helps Tanner in small ways. But it has its limits, and it cannot help her with everything.

[170] [meh-CRAW]

[171] Monument Detail—Castle Miiqraaux: built nearly 980,000 years ago. The word Miiqraaux translates to two different meanings: the first is bright, or brilliant, and the second one is drowned. Hosts were worried that the name would curse

under hundreds of feet of water, its beauty is only intensified by the color. It is carved from a stone similar to black alabaster. The tallest towers can still be seen reaching from the depths up into the sky, and the walls and the halls are [172]open so that the sunlight can shine into every room—making this an absolute underwater marvel.

The reflections of the sun on the water show small rainbows across the castle. My grandmother would call them Trenton's Angels because when my older brother was younger, he thought the lights were Angels. He is another of the Fools, and my final sibling. This is a nice thought; it seems like it has been a long time since I have brought up memories from back home. I smile at the thought of my favorite picture of Trent holding his new-born daughter. I have always admired him and considered him to be the man that I set my standards after. He has a good head on his shoulders and takes good care of himself and his family. He has strong values and good morals. I have always held high regard for my brothers and have hoped to find a person who can love, and care, and understand as they do.

Those who are here are: Sriii, Benoviii, Tziipoor, Aneera, and me. And as for the [173]task, this is just like most of the others. They want a blood sample from Aneera and me, and a sample of whatever stupid-ass thing that they apparently could not—for *some reason*—go get for themselves. It seems simple enough, but as always, there is something standing in our way. How dare it *ever* be easy?

The castle, though abandoned by the Hosts who created it, has found new life. Another species of Siren has infested these waters. These Hosts are mostly water based, but they can come on land if they choose—just not for long periods of time, like Aneera can. They are called [174]Siinaa. They have a darker color skin than [175]her and

---

the castle—built by the sea—and they were right. The water swallowed Castle Miiqraaux 2,000 years later.

[172] Monument Detail—Castle Miiqraaux: when she stood tall on the beach called Sraast [sr-OST], Miiqraaux was decorated with sheets of colorful cloth that took the place of windows, and walls, and doors. This beach was mentioned in one of the books written by Jeexa and found by Tanner in the City of the Lost.

[173] Monument Detail—The Altars: each altar holds its own individual appearance. They were built to match their surroundings.

[174] [see-NAH]

[175] Host Detail—Siren species: Aneera is equally land and water capable. Her species is called Serruumn [seh-RUM].

different patterns. Their skin is sleeker and has more shine than hers. They also have webbed fingers and webbed toes. She says that they are from deeper waters and can travel farther down than she can as well.

In the time leading up to this, I have created a special bond with my Yokkaa—which plays a very important part in this mission. It will allow me to breathe underwater, if the task requires it. It can change my anatomy, and it can feel [176]things that I cannot. It does not speak to me, it never has, but I can understand what it needs.

This mission is easily accomplished with the help of the Siinaa. We reach the room with the altar. The two bowls wait to be filled with blood, as we rush to find a naturally fallen piece of Castle Miiqraaux— they want a piece of the stone, but we cannot harm the castle to get it.

Sriii, Benoviii, and Tziipoor search the beach, and Aneera and I search the sea. We find many shards that are dark in color, but none of them originate from the castle—this is where things take a nasty turn. This is where I find myself defeated. This is the death that stops it all.

On the third day of searching, a Siren named [177]Roorge finds the piece that we need. It fits perfectly inside of the vile. Aneera and I give our blood, but I make a heavy mistake.

I do not wrap my hand before returning to the water—knowing that the skin would heal, I just did not think about it. But it does not heal fast enough. When I enter the water, the scent of my unique blood sends the Sirens into [178]frenzy. They swarm us in the water, and we fight for our lives—or more like everyone is fighting for mine.

We know that we cannot effectively fight them in the water—that is where they have the advantage. They can better track my scent, and they can swim much faster. The leaflet said to be sure that there is no damage when the task is done, so we cannot risk a battle close to Miiqraaux. We have to draw them out onto the shore.

---

[176] Relic Detail—Yokkaa: can sense things in its surroundings. The stone can "see" what dangers lie ahead, and a true wearer can "see" as well if they are bonded well enough.

[177] [ROOR-g]

[178] Gameplay Detail—Bloodlust: though the Game Runners have taken away the Hosts need for food; they have not taken away their primal lust for it.

Tziipoor drags me from the water, just as the Sirens catch up to us. Aneera—being a Siren—understands that we have to leave now, or they *will kill* [179]us. Their bloodlust is stronger than they are. We run up the shore, retreating from the horde that follows. Sriii and Benoviii pull ahead to begin the ritual to open the portal home, and Aneera, Tziipoor, and I turn to hold off the Hosts behind us.

They attack like savages, like we did not just spend a week with them peacefully. We rip and tear at each other, staining the white sand with the different colors of our blood. Sriii finally calls us back, ensuring that our destination is secure. I shove the surrounding Siinaa to the ground and make a break for the doorway. Just as I step into Zephiiitrrax, I feel a hand grab my ankle. I look down, but I do not see what it is that I am feeling. I am flooded with terror, and I look into the battlefield behind me. I can see the look in her eye, as she is stopped, and the Hosts that she cannot block run past her for the door.

"We cannot let them into the city!" I hear an Eiinokrra yell over the chaos, "Close the door!"

"NO!" I scream running back to the portal before I lose her forever. "She's still out there!"

A group of Eiinokrra does their best to stop me, as I hear another yell, "Do not let her go!"

My head is filled with too many emotions that I cannot think clearly, I fight as hard as I can and scream at the top of my lungs, "Let me go!" I punch, and I kick, and I bite; whatever it takes to break free. My anger grows, as I watch the Siinaa tear into her, as everyone else stands back and does nothing. I feel her pain, everything hurts. I can feel them rip into her skin and tear away pieces to eat. I can feel her fear, but the worst emotion that I can pick up from her is acceptance; she is ready to die.

I can feel the strings in my heart rip apart, not ready to let her go. I am pushed even further by the idea that she thinks I will just let her die. There is so much build up inside of me, so much anger and rage, and fear and sadness. I scream again, "NO!" and we lock eyes again,

---

[179] Host Detail—Serruumn: Aneera's species. This species has a lower fueled lust for blood. It is much easier for Aneera to fight her urge to eat.

as she tells me not to come for her. She turns her head away, and fights with all of her strength, challenging the horde head-on, and alone.

The door begins to close, and like slow motion, the world shrinks around me. And for the first time since Sriii gave it to me, the Yokkaa feels the need to step in and help—on a dramatic scale. It can sense my feelings; it knows how desperate I am in this moment. It knows how badly I need its help.

There is a loud noise, I cannot even describe it. And what happens next, I could never have expected. I am finally introduced to the reason why every Host is afraid of the power of its wearer. This is the reason why they are so sought after. I break free from the ones who hold me back, and just before the door closes, the Yokkaa projects its protection toward something other than me. I slam into the wall behind the now closed doorway of the portal, drowning in hysteria. I scream and I cry, begging them to re-open the door. But they refuse.

Then everything stops. The sound around me dies, and I can hear only one Voice. It is her. *"You did it,"* she says weakly. *"Open your eyes and see."* I drop to my knees facing the doorway, and I allow her to show me what she sees. Through her eyes, I can see the power of the Yokkaa. It is the horde of Siinaa. Their skin and their muscles, and all of their meat is torn from their bones and thrown into the sea, leaving their naked skeletons shattered across the sand.

[180]Tziipoor shows me the sea, she distracts me from the bloodstained water and focus' my sight on Miiqraaux. The castle is unharmed, and the task is complete. She speaks very weakly, and my tears fall now for a different reason. I can feel her heartbeat slowing, I can taste her lack of breath, and my lungs suffocate along with hers.

My body is left comatose, and my will disappears with all the hope that had remained. Through her eyes, I see the clouds change color, as the sun sets on the water, and she takes her final breath. Too weak to speak again, her life fades away, and mine goes with her. I am left here, empty. The Voices disappear, and every surrounding heartbeat silences. I cannot hear them anymore. I cannot hear her, or the Clutch, or anything else for that matter. The only Voice I can hear is mine. She is gone, and I am lost in the silence.

I cry again, but no longer are my tears fueled by fire and

---

[180] Relic Detail—Yokkaa: it knows who to protect, and who to kill.

determination. Now they are tears of defeat and sorrow. I hang my head low and sob. I have not the energy to place blame on anyone, only myself. I should have known that she had fallen behind. I should have focused on someone other than myself. I have lost my purpose, and because of my selfishness, I have lost Tziipoor.

Understanding the power of the Yokkaa, Sriii knows that the enemy has been cleared, and she instructs the Eiinokrra to re-open the portal, allowing me to see her one last time. At first, I cannot move. Her body lies in the sand just yards away from me. I crawl out of the portal, and stand upright, walking slowly toward her. I drop to my knees again, and hold tightly to her body, knowing that this will be the last time I get to hug her. This is where I cut myself off from the rest of the group. This is where I decide that they will get nothing else from me.

Sriii persuades the others to stay behind, as she follows me through the portal. She places herself on her knees just behind me and hangs her head after placing one hand on Tziipoor and the other with the palm facing upward in her [181]lap. She mourns the loss with me and then proceeds to help me bury the body—I remember Tziipoor telling me once that her kind buries their dead. We leave the grave unmarked—as not to draw any attention to it. She will be at peace here. I say my final goodbyes and turn to express my anger. I smash the leftover bones of the Siinaa and throw them into the sea, screaming, and cursing, and crying. Why? Why does this keep happening? One after the other, gone.

I eventually return to the portal. Sriii attaches a chain to the ring around my [182]jaw and leads me back to my individual cell. This just goes to show how cruel the Game really is, any chance of hope is taken from you, and even the strongest can die.

---

[181] Host Detail—Eiinokrrian Farewells: they place a hand in their lap, with a palm toward the sky. This represents their release of energy, and the full attention of the Host. They express their means by saying, "I present to you the palm of my hand and the purest form of my soul" or, their heart.

[182] Relic Detail—Jaw Shackle: through the years, Tanner and some of the other Recruits earned Sriiis trust. She will allow them to roam free when there are a low number of other Eiinokrra around—ones that she can easily intimidate into staying quiet. Sriii has never been authorized by her uncle or her father to do this.

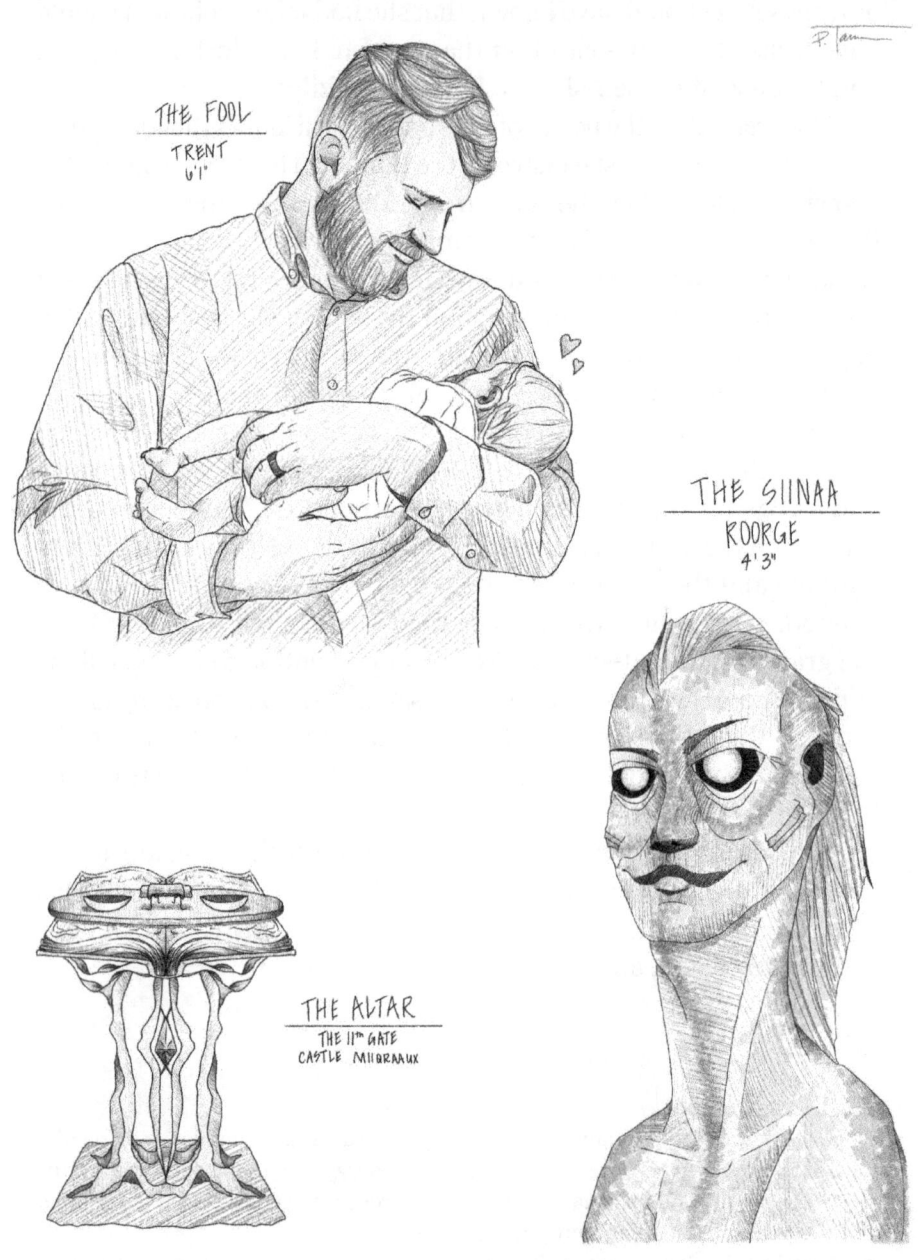

THE FOOL
TRENT
6'1"

THE SIINAA
KOORGE
4'3"

THE ALTAR
THE 11ᵗʰ GATE
CASTLE MIIBRAAUX

1,887 Days since the Fall...

Present day
The Dark City
Zephiiitrrax

That was the last time I saw daylight; it was the last time I left this cell. Almost two and a half years I have sat here, looking through the small window on the ledge. I can see the lower streets of the city and those who live there. All I seem to do is watch them. It is all I *can* do. Some of the others in the cells around mine speak to each other, but I sit silently, just watching. The ones outside have families, and lives, and are allowed to run free. I am trapped here alone and unvisited, and outcasted. Our missions have been halted because the ones that remain are the tasks for Recruits that the Eiinokrra have not been able to locate, or for the ones who are already dead.

Sriii has returned to Anndriiinax—the Hive City in case you have forgotten. And being her personal guard, Benoviii has gone with her. The rest of the original eight Eiinokrra who were assigned to the Recruits have fallen as well—Benoviii and [183]Sriii are the only two who still live.

If my math is correct, and if I have not miscounted days, I have not seen my true family—meaning my mother, my father, my brothers and sisters, or my Fools—for 7,420 days. But this number is just a guess; I have never been good at math. I am also aware that my time spent in my loop does not count for those who were not [184]there, meaning that today could possibly be March 7, 2027. This means that even though I have lived for 44 years, I am still considered to be only 29 years old.

With my age, I feel as if I have become so different. I do not joke anymore or interact with others. I have cut everything off. I

---

[183] Relic Detail—The List of Names: Sriii keeps this scroll hidden. She and Tanner, and the ones who gave it to them—along with the Reader and I—are still the only ones who know of it.

[184] Gameplay Detail—Time Loops: to Tanner, she has not seen Earth in 20 years. Her count includes the 15 years that she had spent in her time loop. My math is not extraordinary either, but by my count, it has been 1,945 days since her abduction. And since the Game itself is in a loop, to her family and Fools, no time has passed at all, meaning that when she returns, Tanner will be reverted back to the age of 24.

have given up. I will never make it home. Without the ability to finish the tasks I am trapped here. My only option is to escape and kill my way to the top. But that is not a fool proof plan. There is no guarantee that it will work. And the guilt, the guilt would make winning unsatisfactory. Even if I see everyone again, there is no way that I could overcome it. I have enough blood on my hands as it is. I will hesitate until the day I die to take any more lives.

With my only option of returning home being a negative one, I cannot carry through with it. I have about four and a half years until a winner is sent home. I do not know how much longer I will be here, and I know that racking up that many points in such a small amount of time is nearly impossible. Especially since I have been out of action for two years, the idea of going home is no longer achievable.

10

THE UNEXPECTED

This suppression of freedom is deafening, and I am depressed—unlike I have ever been before. The others spend their time keeping their bodies ready for a fight by working out and keeping their minds sharp by discussing scenarios for escape—they are broken, but they still have hope. They try to include me again, but I have lost interest, and I choose not to participate. Like I have told you, I just sit and watch the ones on the outside wishing that one day I can be free again. I wonder if Boriisst's separation from Tziipoor was as painful for him as it has been for me.

In all my spare thinking time, I have come up with a rather stupefying question. Barroun said that the winner of the Game gets to go home, but what happens if the winner is a Host that was born here? Then where do they go? Are they given the choice to leave or stay? Or are they just ejected out into the cosmos to find a new place to call home?

My silence finally ends when a familiar face finds me from the other side of my cell door. It is Sriii; she has returned, and she is alone—I do not see Benoviii. She opens the door and drops the bag of things that she carries with her at my feet. When it hits the ground, the contents spill all over the floor—it is my things: Reewenniveaar and my small bag of trinkets (the key and Errok thread, etc.) She also hands me my wings and finally, she gifts me with Cynniaa's belongings and his wings as well. She seems to be flustered and in a hurry.

"Get yourself ready," she whispers, "quickly!"

"Why?" I ask, "Where are we going?"

She replies, "You are getting out of here. Keep your voice down." She removes the magic from my chain and disconnects it from the ring around my jaw. "Boriisst knows the safest way out of the city. Stay out of sight and out of the sky. They will see you if you fly."

I stop her before she gets too ahead of herself, "What is happening? Why do you seem so worried? And what's the rush?"

"I am breaking you out of here," she replies. "This is your only chance. *Do not* fuck this up."

I gather my things, attaching the scabbard to my leg, and the wings to my back. She leaves my cell to open Boriisst's, and removes the magic from his chain, also disconnecting it from the ring around his jaw. After releasing us, she rushes for the door, leaving Barroun, Aneera, and the Squeeb still stuck in their cells. She rushes down the hallway, trying to escape from the situation before getting caught, but I refuse to let it be that easy. I need her to answer some questions; none of this makes any sense.

"Find another Eiinokrra, and threaten him until he releases their magic too," I tell Boriisst. "If we're leaving, then we are *all* leaving. I'll be right back."

I chase Sriii down the hallway, finally catching up with her. I do not care that she is angry with me for following her, I need to know why. What changed? Where has she been? Why help us? I ask her my questions, and though she is reluctant to answer, I finally manage to hear her reasoning.

"My father has instructed me to kill you," she eventually says. "He wants you dead. Without the ability to finish the tasks, you are useless to them. They do not see any reason to keep you alive, and I *refuse* to be the one that kills you."

"That's why you came back?" I ask her, "To save us?"

"To save *you*," she says, almost in a sad tone. "They do not know that I am here, and I will still have to hunt you, so do not make it easy for us to find you. You must hide better now. If you get caught, I will have no choice, but to do as I was told—no matter how much I want to resist."

"I don't mean to be ungrateful," I say, "but why? Why betray your people for my sake? What will you gain? And once they realize that we're gone, you don't think they'll suspect you of letting us go?"

She does not answer, and then she tries to leave me without speaking again. I grab her arm and repeat myself, telling her not to make me ask a third time. I understand that we are pushed for time, and I understand that it is important that she not get caught. But selfishly, I need to fight for an answer, I just need to know. I cannot run free knowing that she is risking her life for me, for a reason that I am unaware of. I need to know what it will take to pay her back for this. What happened? What is the goal? She is the Grand Chief's daughter, the Princess of the Eiinokrrian race. Her father is the most important Chief of their species, so why would she take this risk for me?

She turns angrily and answers my question against her will, "I refuse to watch you die! You disgust me, and I always want to beat the shit out of you. You are a pain in my ass, and there have been times that I *have* wanted to kill you, but now that I have been given the order, I cannot do it."

I laugh, "You know it would be bad on your conscience, huh?" I ask.

"Do not joke about this," she replies bluntly. "It is not funny."

"I didn't mean it as a joke," I say.

I can tell that there is something that she is not telling me. I would not necessarily consider her my friend, but I can tell that she feels uneasy. There is something wrong, something that she is not telling me. She is in a hurry, and I can understand why, but I want to know. I *need* to know what she is keeping to herself. My mind will drive me crazy if I do not find out now. It is not likely that I will see her again, so I have to hear it before I let her go. Was this an order from the Great God? I know because of the scroll that Ehhrn gave me that she is undeniably a Recruit—we completed a task together. I know the names of all 12.

"Are you in some kind of trouble?" I ask her. "Do you need our help?" Or is this another one of her backhanded plans? What is the goal?

She takes a moment again before answering me, and then finally she says—

"I cannot kill you." She pauses, "You are my natural enemy, but I have never felt this protective of anyone before. I cannot watch you die. I have done many things to deceive you, and I have treated you

245

like a pet. But despite that, you have also done well to help me. You carried my friend home when I asked you to, and you did it without me telling you why. You are kinder than you let others see. You act tough and pretend not to care, but I can see the heart that you carry, you can be good for us. Red Blood Tanner," she pauses, "because of you I see fault in my people's beliefs. I can no longer see you as the worst enemy; I think that you have the potential to be good for others even if you cannot do it for yourself. And even more disgusting, I feel as if I see you as a trusted friend."

I am left in shock. Her hidden irises show clear as day; her emotions are pure, and she is telling me the truth. I am immediately filled with guilt, and discomfort. I do not know what to say. What? Why? I do not understand. I feel bad for not giving her a direct reply, but I do not know what to say. I do not communicate well like this; it is not the same for me—it never has been. I do not trust her. I do not believe her. I do not want to hurt her feelings and I do not want to lie, but what am I supposed to tell her—'Thanks, but I don't care about you?' No. She is the last person that I had expected this from.

What should I do? I am so lost, and I am confused. What does she expect from me? She is right, we *are* natural enemies. I have been spiteful of her since they killed Cynniaa, and I never actually forgave her. But I do not have time to explain, and I cannot let myself hurt her—not right now.

She looks me in the eye and says one final thing before disappearing into the darkness, "Be careful not to get caught, and do *not* fucking die." She turns away, leaving me behind. But I guess that it is better this way, I am not sure that I will ever see her again, so perhaps it is best that she does not know how I feel. Knowing her, I doubt that she would want to know. She left in a hurry; she did not want to hear what I have to say back—she does not care if I feel the same way, or not. I guess she had decided that either way she gets hurt—we both agree that it is better that she just not know. I have not seen her show emotion like this since her friend died in Arrtisiiaax.

I struggle to gather myself again, as I return to the rest of the group. We wait for Boriisst to return with another Eiinokrra to open the other cells and free the three remaining members of our group: Barroun, Aneera, and the Squeeb. Sriii obviously only cares that I am the one to escape from here, and she had freed Boriisst only because he could help me, but I cannot leave the others here in good conscience. They are only here because of me, and they have all lost so much on my account. I must take them with me. That is only fair.

Boriisst finally returns, and for once I approve of his savagery. The Eiinokrra has his hands tied behind his back, and a piece of cloth tied around his mouth to gag him. I can tell that Boriisst took the time to beat him before bringing him here too. He has blood dripping from his mouth and nose, and the onset of swelling and bruising around his eyes.

Boriisst holds a knife to the Eiinokrras neck and holds him close to his body to keep control of him. I can see how happy Boriisst is to finally take out his aggression. The Eiinokrra may have raised him, but he is relieved to be freed from their control. He can make his own choices now, and he is tired of being a disappointment to them. Now, he is officially their enemy.

We threaten him until he agrees to remove the magic from the other three members. Once they are free, Boriisst cuts out his tongue so that he cannot speak of how we got to him, and he takes his hands too so that he cannot write about it. Aneera makes the point to also take his toes, just in case—or perhaps just for fun. We all feel a bit of relief being free from our cells. We throw the Eiinokrra in a cell and close him in. Barroun insists that he use his magic to lock the door. This way he will not be able to get out and warn anyone of our escape. Unfortunately for him, this magic cannot be changed or lifted by Eiinokrrian magic—he will be trapped inside forever or until another God can set him free. Since the Eiinokrra are enemies to the Gods *and* the Elites, freedom from this is unlikely. I feel bad that we are condemning him, but my freedom is more important to me than his is right now. I apologize to him before we leave him behind, and I wish him well.

"Good luck my friend," I tell him, "Thanks for your help. I hope everything works out for you."

Boriisst laughs, "You're such a bitch." He reaches through the cell door and uses the stolen knife to cut the Eiinokrra's throat.

"Really?" I say, "You did all of that to keep him silent just so you could kill him?"

"I had to give him some sort of hope," he laughs. "Poor Hiiin, what will his mother think?" he says.

"You're disgusting." I say

"And you're not?" he asks.

"Let's go," says Barroun.

I lower my head and follow the God through the hallway. We step quietly, as Boriisst explains our escape plan. We will have to split up. Barroun and Aneera are going to retrieve their gear, along with the Squeebs. Boriisst needs to make a stop before leaving the city and is going to meet them outside by the back door of the penitentiary; he will lead them through the city to where I am. It is my job to reach the shore and secure us a boat before they get there. Because the Squeeb is so tall—nine foot—I shrink him small enough to fit into my pocket so that we do not risk someone seeing him, and I will move much faster if I am not waiting on someone to keep up with me—the Squeeb especially.

I do not know much about the layout of the city, but Boriisst has given me a path to follow. Before I split from the group, he drew up a half-assed map for me and the Squeeb. We are currently located in the center of the city, so no matter which way we go, it is the same distance to the water. We plan to meet on the northeast side of the island—Boriisst says that the smaller island on that side has the easiest escape route—and the shittiest security team. That is the lazy crew, and we will have better luck escaping past the guard towers and forts. We will have a better map to look at soon—that is what Boriisst is stopping for. He wants to clean out his room before he leaves the city for the last time—that is, if all of his things are still there.

I guess I should try and see the light in this. I am still low on energy, and the depression is a feeling that I will not be able to get rid of easily. I should take this time to see if I can recover. I feel that if I escape the city successfully, I will be able to find purpose again; maybe I can ignite the fight within me. This is the first challenge that I have been given in a long time. My spirit has faded, but I can still sense a small spark. I do not have the faith that I will ever leave this planet, but maybe I can find happiness here somewhere. Maybe, one day, I can return to Vaahiigali. That is the only place that I have found so far that I feel like I could be happy—though, I know that it will not be the same without Cynniaa, and I must first find the courage to face the Fae before I can return.

Sriii told me to stay out of the sky, so I must make it to the shore on foot. I consider the option to shrink myself small enough to be able to fly without being seen, but there are some [185]complications in that. I cannot test this too far; I do not want to put the Squeeb in danger. Enough people have died here because of me. I *must* get out successfully, and I *must* take the remaining Recruits with me. They can separate from me once we leave the city, but for now, they are my responsibility. I cannot let anyone else die here.

The city has a circular shape. At its center are the Chiefs Keep and the penitentiary. There are three main roads that start at the center and reach outward toward the three surrounding islands. The Keep and the penitentiary are at the very top of the hill that the city is built on. Boriisst did say a while back that in order to get out, we will have to go down—but I do not think that "down the hill" is what he meant. I am sure that there is another meaning in that statement. There are also three more major roads that circle around the center, intersecting the three straight roads that lead to the shore—each one is longer than the one before it, as they stretch outward toward the edge of the city.

Boriisst has instructed me to stay off of these six roads as much as possible, as they are commonly used, and I am likely to be recognized. I must take the back roads and alleys until I meet the shore across from the northeastern island called [186]Daiiiuss. The main island is named [187]Aiiiess; the northwestern island is named [188]Oriiiess; and the final island to the south is [189]Riiiuss. Daiiiuss has two guard towers, one guard fort, and a viewpoint. Oriiiess has the same, but the hidden exit is on the far side of the mountains, whereas on Daiiiuss, the exit is on the closer side, and it will be much more easily accessible. Riiiuss, the southern island— and the smallest of the surrounding three—has four guard towers

---

[185] Host Detail—Tanner's Sizing Ability: she can shrink or grow herself with no limit. Because this ability is unique to her, she cannot change the sizes of others too juristically. She can make others larger or smaller, but she has to be careful—other Hosts' bodies can only withstand this change up to a certain point. Tziipoor was able to change to any size along with Tanner because of their bond.

[186] [dee-oo-s]

[187] [aye-us]

[188] [or-us]

[189] [ree-oo-s]

and one guard fort. Each island has a settlement on the shore closest to the main island of Aiiiess.

I finally find my way out of the penitentiary and begin my journey down the hill. Thankfully, I am on the east side of the center square, so I do not have to worry about passing through the Keep. The security here is surprisingly minimal. I guess they figure that there is no possible way that a prisoner can escape—but they are going to learn today. I have to cross two of the three main roads that circle around the center square—there is no other option. Hopefully, I can do so undetected. The nighttime bell has yet to sound, so the city is illuminated. I hope that the sun is down before we pass through the exit so we can easily sneak through the trees on the other side—I assume that we will be let out into the Empty Forest.

I travel to the east, toward White Cove, where I will be able to repel down the cliff and walk along the small, pebbled shore below. This is the safest place for me to travel because it is the quickest way out of the busy city, and the shore has a walkway around the cove, hidden under the overhanging cliff above. Boriisst says that there are usually a few boats that are secured to the end of the small peninsula that reaches around the east side of the cove. We should be able to cross the water safely, as long as we stay clear of the small rock islands that peak out of the water in between Aiiiess and Daiiiuss. I cannot help but think about the possibility that there are no boats there, but that is an issue for when I reach that point. I must get out of the center of the city first.

I cross the first main road successfully and enter back into the crowded buildings between the first and second ringed roads. There is a river that runs through the city, cutting it nearly in half. It begins on the northern side of the island and flows south through the center square before it turns to the south east and splits. One section flows south again and dries out before it reaches the shore, and the other flows east, letting out just south of White Cove. I am lucky not to have to cross it—the bridges that are built over the river throughout the city are large open concept bridges, and I could easily be seen if I crossed one.

I have done much to describe the cities layout, but I have yet to explain its architecture. A lot of places that I have visited here so far have these same similarities—there are tall square buildings, decorated with thin pillars, intricate stone carvings, staircases, and statues. The difference is that the stone in Zephiiitrrax is not the same blissful white color as the stone they used in Vaahiigali. This stone resembles black alabaster like the Castle Miiqraaux on Sraast beach. It is actually quite breathtaking. It stands beautifully in the darkness, but I cannot help but wonder what it would look like under the light of the sun.

The streets are busy, and I struggle to keep in the shadows. There are Eiinokrra everywhere—I am doing my best not to be seen. I sneakily steal a dark-colored shroud from a small [190]burial shop on the corner to cover my head, face, and the wings on my back, but I know that I cannot depend on it to hide my identity—I still need to be careful. I try to stay in the back alleys, using small staircases and narrow passageways in between buildings. There are a few times that I have to stop and wait until a path is clear before I can advance any farther.

I manage to reach the second main road that stretches around the city in a circle. I wait for the opportune moment, then dash across to the other side. There is a large open building in between me and the cove, and I decide to pass through it. There is a large garden in the middle with waist high bushes and a large variety of small flowers. I walk along the wall—not through the center—until I reach the other side.

Just as I am about to exit the building, an Eiinokrra turns the corner, and I must retreat into a hiding place to avoid capture. There is a flight of stairs leading down under the garden that I follow down and around the corner. I wait; standing against the wall until the Eiinokrra passes, and my path is open again. I climb back to the top of the steps and waste no time reaching the cove just outside. There is a bridge reaching over the cove; it is the bridge connecting the two ends of the third main circular road around the city—the longest road.

I check my surroundings, looking for anyone who might see me. When I see that the coast is clear, I lift the shroud up over my

---

[190] City Detail—Eiinokrrian Burial Shops: this shop much resembles a funeral home showroom. It sells many different colors of shrouds and offers custom clothing services for burning the dead. However, this shop is not in charge of services, nor do they dress or burn the bodies. They only provide the clothing.

shoulders and extend my wings outward. I fly down to the hidden passage below and hide my wings again underneath the shroud. I keep the Squeeb in my pocket, in case there is a need to run or hide. I will keep him concealed until we reach the forest—and even then, I will most likely try to convince the others to shrink too. It will be much easier for only one of us to trek across Daiiiuss at actual size. I can carry them out of Zephiiitrrax and repay my debt to them for protecting me.

As Boriisst had said, I find two small boats—similar to the one that Tziipoor and I were brought here in—on the east side of the peninsula. There is no one around that I can see, so I approach the boats and push one halfway into the water, preparing for when the others arrive. I have succeeded in my mission, and now it is just a waiting game. The [191]night bell rings, signaling the setting sun on the outside and the magic creatures dim themselves blanketing the city in darkness. I sit on the rocky shore next to the boat and duck my head low. I discuss with the Squeeb the idea to shrink the others for safer travel, and it agrees that that is our best course of action.

I have gotten somewhat comfortable, and now I am fighting sleep. I know that this may not be the best place to take a nap, but if they do not hurry, it might just happen. I am trying to avoid it, but I am sinking—slumped and tired. I am not free yet; however, the weight of the chain is gone from my jaw, and I feel so free. The ring is still there, but only because I have not the tools needed to remove it yet. It is too strong to remove with just my hands. I am ready to be loose again unrestricted. It would be nice to not have any dependents. Back on Earth, I always felt like I did better when I was alone. I was always very reclusive—of course it is lonely, but I feel like it is safer for my heart that way. Like I said before, I do not deal well with loss. Not often do new Fools get added to my list, the ones who I have now are the ones who I have had forever

---

[191] Planet Detail—Days and Nights: there is no promised number of hours in each day or night. The Game Runners choose when the sun rises and when it sets. A perceptive Host can determine the length of a day by where the sun sits in the sky. The fake sun moves in an orbit around the planet, but the angles and its speed will change sporadically, without pattern. One day can be up to 20 hours of sunlight, and the next can be as low as three—though mostly, the number of hours is about seven to fourteen.

Boriisst, Barroun, and Aneera finally find the Squeeb and me on the shore. Barroun and Aneera were able to find everyone's gear, and Boriisst carries a large bag stuffed full of trinkets, and scrolls, and maps, and utensils. I shrink the bag to make it easier to carry, and then I pitch the idea to shrink them with the Squeeb, so that only one of us is visible—we can be more inconspicuous that way. They agree, and I add them to my chest pocket with the Squeeb—I leave the shroud untucked so they can get some fresh air. I push the boat the rest of the way into the water and climb in. I use the small paddle to move us forward, as we finally head for the island of Daiiiuss.

We depart without a light, so it will be harder for them to see us, but I cannot see well either. I wish Tziipoor were here. With her help I could see through the darkness and safely deliver us to the shore ahead. If we follow the rocks in between the islands, we will meet the settlement on the other side that continues from the city. But since we want to avoid this area, we head for the southern point of the island where it is just open territory—no towers or buildings. The new map that Boriisst had retrieved with his things shows a direct path to the exit. There is a guard tower a way to the left, and a guard fort to the right of the exit, but if we are careful, we can make it through with the cover of darkness.

Sriii broke us out about four hours after the morning bell. It has been close to twelve hours since we began our escape. I have underestimated the actual size of this city, and even more now I underestimated the distance that I will have to row this boat. Boriisst explains that we will be traveling through the night. He says that we have about 30 miles until we meet the shore. That is a long way to go in pitch dark water with no surrounding light to guide us. Luckily, he has a keen sense of direction—something that he had inherited from years of living with the Eiinokrra. He has also perfected the craft of map making. All of the ones that he carries were made by him, and each of them carries his [192]Blood Mark.

A while back, I left a table for you to look at (Fig. 2). This table

---

[192] Relic Detail—Blood Marks: this is a signature. The Host who leaves its Blood Mark on something is leaving a part of themselves. This mark represents the Hosts pure intentions, seriousness, and claim to something. A proper Blood Mark is made with a Blood Stamp—exactly like a wax stamp—and their blood. If a Host does not have the materials to make one, or have one made for them, they can draw their

included: The Names of the Recruits—and the suspected Recruits—their Planet of Origin, Age, Ability, and their Recruitment Date. In the Ability column, I need to add a new row with Sriii's name along with all of her information, and the Ability that is Eiinokrrian Histories + Antiquities + Languages + Leadership.

My arm tires from rowing, but I know that I must push on if we are to meet the shore again. The darkness does not frighten me, but the water below has an eerie silence. Irestiikaar is home to many strange creatures, and I wonder what kinds of Hosts inhabit this massive black lake. With its size, I am sure that there are creatures large enough to swallow us and our boat whole, like Jonah and the Giant Fish. I ponder these thoughts, as **B**oriisst speaks.

He tells us that we are in some kind of underground cavern. Past the three outer isles, the water meets again with a rocky shore. Boriisst traveled there once out of curiosity, but he was met with a dead end. He says that he spent months exploring the shore beyond the city. He had done a full circle, returning to the place that he had pulled his boat ashore and built a small camp to mark his place. It was untouched; nothing had been looted or moved from its place. Through his entire expedition, there was nothing but the shore. The water met the land, and the land quickly met the cave wall that reached upward into depths unknown.

"Upward into depths?" I say interrupting him, "How does that make sense?"

"Think about it," Aneera says. "That can only mean one thing."

Barroun then answers, "The city has to be upside down."

My eyes widen, "We have to go down to get out," I say quietly to myself. He is right, the city is [193]upside down under the ground, so we have to go down to find the surface again. How did I not figure that out before? It makes perfect sense. He had said that there are only three ways in and out of the city and assures that these three places

---

seal, or write their name smearing their blood across the top. This secures the Host to their oath, or their creation by their scent and their soul.

[193] City Detail—Zephiiitrrax: hidden with Eiinokrrian magic. This City is a reflection of the surface above. There is a large lake in the center of the forest, and four islands that match the size and shape of Zephiiitrrax, but they are not hidden in a cavern, and they are not inhabited by anything except for plant life.

are heavily guarded. The easiest way to slip through would be to shrink teeny-tiny, and hope that we can move unnoticed at that size.

As always, I do have questions though. If the content of the cavern is a reflection of the land and water above, and everything is exactly the same, how thick is the land in between? How deep is the water? Could I just dig my way to the other side? Can aquatic Host's travel to Zephiiitrrax by swimming straight down into the waters above? Would they eventually just find the surface of the waters in Zephiiitrrax? Or are there two bodies of water instead of one, separated in the middle by a lakebed? How powerful is the magic that protects it? Did the cavern exist before the Eiinokrra came here, or did their magic create it? I ask him these questions, listening carefully, as he answers them.

First thing, he says that this cavern was created for the city itself. It was their magic that made it, and it is exceptionally powerful. Second, there is only one body of water, but a Host could not swim to the other side—from either side—the magic will redirect the swimmer back to the surface that they dove from. That is why it is called the bottomless lake; no one has actually found the bottom. Third, the land in between is thick, I could dig for the entirety of my Human lifetime, and not even make it halfway. We are deep within the crust of this planet.

This conversation also brings explanation to another problem that I have dealt with during my imprisonment here. Back home—on Earth—I always had problems with high altitude changes and low depths. Because of issues with my ears, I would always get woozy, lightheaded, and there would always be some kind of accompanying pain. Flying in planes (at 42,000 feet) and even traveling to the top of the Arch in St. Louis (630 feet) caused these problems. Under water pressure is even worse. I can handle it—because my mother did not raise a bitch—but it has always been an issue, and I have lost some of my hearing because of it. Even retrieving a ring from the bottom of the pool (13 feet) for lifeguard training was brutal. And the cold, the bitter cold really ignites the pain. I had special earplugs that were molded to fit me perfectly; I was instructed to wear them in water or in loud places, like at concerts, and when mowing the yard.

There has been so much damage done to my ears that every time a doctor would look in one of them—my right side especially—they would react with shock. "Oh wow," or "Oh my God," were common statements. The scar tissue is so bad from years of tubes and blown eardrums, that my eardrums have much less vibration than they should. The reason that I tell you this is to help explain what I was trying to get at. I still have these issues at just the same intensity.

The low depths of places like Zephiiitrrax, and the Castle Miiqraaux, and the high altitudes of Arrtisiiaax gave me these same symptoms. Traveling in between them without time to acclimate was even worse. I always thought the issue had something to do with the portal, and its effect on my body. But now, I fully understand that most of the problem was from the rapid change in environments. I would always be so miserable after returning to the city after a mission. I spent weeks in my cell with deadening migraines and leakage from my ears. My ability to heal could not help in these situations because this was a [194]pre-ability injury.

Back to me and my little rowboat full of morons, we have been on the water for about seven hours or so. Boriisst says that we will reach the shore again in about three and a half, if we keep rowing at this speed. My arms fucking *kill*. I put my worries aside and had brought Boriisst back up to size to make him row. The other three sit on the bench in between us—my pocket had grown too crowded and uncomfortable. I left them at a small size, just as an extra precaution. The three of them sit comfortably: Barroun laying on his back with his hands around the back of his neck to support his head, Aneera with her legs laying straight out in front of her, and her hands out behind her supporting her up-sitting torso with her head hanging back and her eyes to the sky, and the Squeeb—awkwardly—laying on its stomach with its head and arms hanging over the edge of the bench hurling from the constant sway of the water.

I tire of my upright, bent knee position, and I shrink myself down to their size. If anything is to happen, Boriisst can protect us. I find

---

[194] Host Detail—Tanner: pre-ability injuries. Any problems that Tanner had *before* giving her body the ability to heal itself are unaffected by the ability. Her ears for example, if she blows a hole in her eardrum now, it will heal itself, but the scar will always remain, adding to the scar tissue that was already there before. Meaning that even though the hole is healed, the injury is only piling on top of what already existed, causing just the same amount of damage as if she did not have the ability at all. This ability is helpful for quick healing but will cause many problems for her in the future—not just in her ears, but throughout her entire body.

a comfortable place on my own lonely bench, and remove the shroud from my head, wadding it up to make a pillow. I have not been able to take a comfortable nap in years; my cell did not include a bed. I have adapted to sleeping on hard surfaces. I decide, out of boredom, that I am going to snooze until we find the shore. I lay on my side, facing away from the others. I tuck my hands underneath my new pillow and place my knees at a comfortable angle. I close my eyes and block out the low conversation behind me.

The time passes, and before I know it, we slam into the shore. The crash flings my body forward toward the edge of the bench. I manage to pull Reewenniveaar from my hip and catch myself before falling—it is not too far of a distance, but the landing still would have hurt.

"You fucking *dick!*" I hear Barroun yell from the bottom of the boat—he was not fast enough to catch himself.

"*Why* would you do that?" Aneera follows, "You *stupid* motherfucker!" She pulls the large piece of wood from her leg and throws it at him—I laugh at her quietly because compared to his size the piece of wood is nothing short of a splinter.

The Squeeb, who had also been asleep, was flung to the bottom of the boat as well, landing in his pile of vomit. I stand and walk to the edge of my bench to look down at the two below. The Squeeb yells at me with rage.

"Get down here! Make me bigger, right now! Make me bigger!"

I make myself big enough to lift them both from the bottom of the boat and place them back on the bench that they were on before. The Squeeb continues to yell curses, as Boriisst adds to the lively conversation—

"Wake up motherfuckers, we're here." And then he laughs and stands to push the boat the rest of the way onto the shore. Out of curiosity, I make the Squeeb bigger like it had requested, and it lands a blow across Boriisst's face. It hits him so hard that he falls from his feet. I return everyone to their normal size, and we all take a minute to find comfort on land again. I think it would be best for us to travel spread out for the time being. This may prove to be a mistake, but we need a little bit of distance between us.

"Let's get moving," says Barroun. "We have a lot of ground to cover. Stop messing around." He throws rocks at Boriisst and the

Squeeb, who are wrestling around in the water as Boriisst taunts the Squeeb.

"You stink!" he dunks its head, "lets wash it off!" he splashes water across its face laughing and just as I am about to jump in and stop him the Squeeb grabs his arm and reverses their rolls.

"You a biiiitch!" it dunks his head, "Lets wash it ooooff!" it mocks him before splashing water across his face. "Ahaha you're so *fucking* funny!" it says sarcastically.

"Stop," Barroun says. "Get up and be done with it."

"Haha! You're no fun!" Boriisst laughs as him and the Squeeb continue to splash each other like children until they reach the shore.

"The map shows that we have about 23 miles to the exit, I wanted to make it to the forest before daybreak," I add. "That is looking less and less likely the more we fuck around."

"Whatever," Boriisst says, "You're still boring."

"I'm not here to entertain you." I say. I step closer, ready to hit him too.

"*Now* look who's fucking around," he replies. "Let's go, aren't we in a hurry?" He walks past me following Barroun up the hill. Aneera scoffs and follows too, along with the Squeeb. I close my eyes and tell myself to stay calm also not giving him the satisfaction of making me laugh, because I almost did. That is some shit that Jonny would say—I miss that smart-mouthed fucker. I follow the rest of the group and tell them so that they cannot say that they were not warned—

"I'm going to kill him. One day you will hear that he is dead, and I want you all to know that I'm the motherfucker who done it."

1,888 Days since the Fall...

The morning bell rings, and we have a little over an hour left before we reach the exit. The sky illuminates again, and we must be quick not to be seen. We are nearing dangerous territory. We must be even more alert now, as it is daytime the Eiinokrra will be more active. They do not sleep through the night, but most of them will stay indoors until the morning bell rings. The Eiinokrra working in the guard towers and the forts will change shifts after the sound of each morning and nighttime bell.

We are so close to freedom, so close to making the perfect escape. I had expected something to go wrong, nothing ever happens here without some kind of major complication. I knew to expect something, and I am glad that I kept myself ready. However, I was not entirely ready for *this*. I grow distracted from our mission, but I am still focused on the destination ahead—the same place where I can hear it from. I am surprised; I thought that this ability left me when I lost Tziipoor. I have kept up with the practice of leaving a shape in my mind for a Voice to latch to, but this is the first time since her death that I have actually [195]heard anything.

I am filled with rage; I recognize the Voice. I cannot confide in anyone about this issue because Tziipoor is the only one who would truly understand, and she told me to keep our secrets. I *know* this Voice—I know *exactly* who it belongs to. It is the Eiinokrra that killed Cynniaa, the one who hit him, and kicked him, and taunted him the most. His face burns an image into my mind, and I grow angrier the louder his Voice gets. I block out the surrounding conversation, focusing heavily on dick-kicking revenge. This is fate—fate that he is in my path. Giving myself the power of convenience was such a good choice. Though I vowed not to do it again, I am going to kill him. For Cynniaa, I will take his life.

The louder the Voice grows, the more my need to kill its Host aggravates me. We are not moving fast enough; I need to go ahead of the others. If I am quick, I can do the deed and meet them again when they get there. I will move quicker if I go off on my own. I inform the others of my departure, but I do not tell them my true purpose. I say that I am going to scout the road ahead for guards, and now that I know that I can still use the ability to hear others' Voices—and to place mine in *their* minds—I will be able to communicate with them if I need to.

I shrink myself small enough that I can fly without being seen—perhaps they will assume me to be a Bug or other small unthreatening Host. I will move much faster in the air—even at a small size. I will

---

[195] Host Detail—Tanner: hearing ability. She never lost this ability; she had only lost her true focus for it. Because the Eiinokrra are hard to hear, she was unable to catch any of their Voices. The Voice of this particular Eiinokrra has already previously been heard by her, and then was "archived" after—making it easier for the Voice to be found again.

have to find him and lure him away from the others before I can do anything. I must avoid any witnesses, and I must do it in a place that will be easy for me to dispose of the body. Although, I could just shrink it really small and let it rot somewhere in plain sight—just to be spiteful.

I find the Eiinokrra, and as I expected, there are others with him—two others to be specific. I will draw him out with my Voice. If I speak to him in his mind, I can manipulate him into leaving his group and joining me in a place more private. I also ponder how I want to do it. I could tie him to a chair, and beat him, and taunt him, like he did to Cynniaa—but that comes with the issue of finding a chair out here, in the middle of nowhere—or I can castrate him, allowing him to live, but leaving him miserable. I can drag him to the shore by his hair, shrink him real small, tie his feet to a pebble, and throw him in the lake, or I can slit his throat, and let him bleed to death in agony. Whatever I end up doing, it will have to be quick, so that I can rejoin with the others without any suspicion—if only I could manipulate time.

I stalk him from the shadows and follow his small group down a path close to the exit. It is time to make the decision. I am close enough now that I can touch him. It would be smarter to have him leave the group, instead of just shrinking him. That way the two who are with him do not suspect anything. His thoughts are of low intellect, and Boriisst did say that this island has the worst security. It should not be hard to convince him. "Psst," I say to him, so that only he can hear. I lure him saying that it would be safer for his comrades if he came alone, and I press the importance of keeping his reason for leaving to himself. I am not above taking the lives of all three.

He departs to a place more private, and I follow him keeping myself hidden from him until I know that we are truly alone. I bring myself up to size and lead my case with a solid smash of my fist to his face, a broken nose.

"Fuck you!" I say angrily "You hold your head high, and you speak to yourself like you're honorable, but I know what you really are; you murderous piece of shit!"

He grunts in pain, holding his nose and tilting his head back, "What are you talking about?!"

I grab his hair and tuck his head forward, "Why does everyone do that? You are supposed to lean forward to avoid choking. Idiots, I'm surrounded by fucking idiots."

"Ah, fuck you!" he says angrily shoving my hand away. "What is the meaning of this?"

"You killed someone very important to me," I tell him, with my face still covered.

I do not want to give away my identity. It takes all of my strength not to hit him again. I pace back and forth, while he sits on the ground tending to the break in his nose. I am troubled; discomforted. While I was luring him here, I had a flashback—a memory from my past on Earth. It was my grandmother. She did not say anything, I only saw her face, but it changed something in me—it made me stop and think. What have I let myself become? I am so angry, so hell bent on revenge, so drunken on my need to kill. I was never like this before. I strived to be kind, and forgiving, and loving in all situations. I always told myself that killing only made me just as bad as every other killer, no matter the reasoning. I stand now conflicted. This place has truly changed me. What *the fuck* am I doing?

I turn and look at him again. My emotions flood my mind, the depression, and the pressure, and the loss. It all hits at one time. I have not given myself the opportunity to properly deal. I can feel the buildup in my throat—that knot you get just before the tears come. This is it; I am going to unleash it all, right here, right now. And the dumb fuck that I brought here with me is going to witness it. *Why* here, *why* now? *Why* do I have to find my Humanity again like this?

I drop my head into my palms, and my knees to the ground. I sob unapologetically. I allow myself to have the breakdown that I have needed. I have been numb since I lost Tziipoor; I have not given myself any relief. I almost feel sorry for him, he has to witness it—this is a proper breakdown. I rip the shroud from my head and toss it to the ground next to me. I cannot breathe. I gasp for air and work myself up so much that I puke. All of the disgust that I had for him, I now feel it for myself too; I have done the same.

"What the fuck is your problem?" he asks, still holding his nose.

I cannot answer right away, I cannot speak. So, I tell him with my mind. "How do you live with it?"

"With what?" he asks.

"Do you not feel guilt, or hatred, or anger?" I lift my head to reveal my face.

He gasps from surprise and staggers backwards. He says, "You! You're the Red Blood—the...the... the Red Blood Tanner!"

"Yes," I reply, finally able to talk. "I am."

"How are you here? How did you escape? You still have the ring around your jaw, so they did not release you."

"That is none of your concern," I tell him.

I wipe my eyes, clear my throat, and shoot a farmer's rocket from each side to clear the snot from my nostrils. I stand and fix my posture—pulling my shoulders back and holding my head high again. I have released the energy that has been building for years. Until now I was too stubborn to let it out.

"You must keep this secret." I say, "You cannot tell anyone that you saw me. And for that, I will spare your life."

"What loyalty do I have to you?" he asks.

"None," I reply. "But you do owe me a favor."

He replies, "Oh?"

"I had every intention to kill you today. I even fought with myself about how I would do it. I considered cutting your throat and letting you bleed to death. I thought about drowning you in the lake, or shrinking you really small, and leaving your dead body to rot where no one could ever find you. Your life is meaningless to me."

"But you choose to let me live?" he says, "Why?"

"Because I don't want to be what the Game wants me to be. I've taken enough life for now," I answer.

"I think I know why you are angry with me," he says. "You were friends with the Sprite, weren't you?"

I stand quietly, and do not answer. Damn right I am angry. I am livid. Why? Why did he have to die? And why did he have to die the way that he did? I am disgusted, and it is even worse that I promised Tziipoor that I would not tell anyone of what I saw that day. So, I cannot properly scold or reprimand him.

I reach into my small bag to retrieve something. The Eiinokrra watches, hoping to see something that answers his question. I pull my hand back out—and very precisely—flick a small dart in his direction. I aim for an exposed place; I need it to pierce his skin. I had prepared this weapon for times like these—when I am conflicted, torn between right and wrong. This way I can choose to let destiny decide.

The dart is made from the rock walls inside of the penitentiary. I made a total of six. These six darts are injected with Tziipoors venom. We crafted them together, and I have held on to them tightly after she passed.

I carved the rock into the appropriate shape—to make for an effective dart. I used the help of IIIxaanax to apply the amount of pressure needed to hollow out the casing. Then, I used the Errok thread to create a spring-like contraption with a small ball at the end. When I cut the thread from my spool, it hardened. The thread is so thin that the spring portion still bends as needed.

I filled the darts with Tziipoor's venom and I, ever-so-carefully, pieced them together. I attached a frayed feather that I had plucked from the Dragon to the ass-end of each dart; then shrunk them down to the appropriate size.

I feel the need to mention that getting to this point has not been easy. I have had to try and fail many times to achieve this. I have accidentally injected myself a *few* times. I have learned the importance of making sure that it does not happen again. The pain is excruciating I cannot even fucking explain it. It is two days of pulsing agony. Tziipoor says that there is no "antivenin." But I know that even if there was, she would not have given it to me. She would say, "If you are stupid enough to play around with it, you need to be open to its consequences." Basically, if I am going to use it on others, I need to fully understand what it is like, and oh-boy, do I. I feel sorry for every sad loser that I decide to use these on. They may live but the horror of the venom—the fear of it, that shit will last forever.

If I have done this correctly, and if all is still intact, when I flick the dart using the help of IIIxaanax to increase the power behind the flick, the force pulling the ball backwards will be so shockingly reversed when the dart penetrates its victim that the ball will shoot forward inside of the casing breaking the spring in front of it. This will force the venom to eject through the teeny hollowed out needle that I had attached to the front. I have run a few test shots—shooting myself—to be one hundred percent sure that they are effective. This is the first one that I have felt the need to use on the battlefield.

The Eiinokrra falls to his side, and I move him into the bushes to hide him I shrink him to the size of a leaf. If he manages to relay the message of what happened to him, I think that he deserves the glory. I have done enough for now. I pick up my shroud from the ground, and wrap it again, hiding my face. "Yes," I say, "I knew him."

I leave him alone surrounded by trees, and moss, and despair. By the time he is able to walk again, I will be long gone. I will have to be sure to tell the others that we will have to find an appropriate place to settle once we leave the city. We will need a safe house where no one can find us. The Eiinokrra are exceptional trackers. I messed up by letting him see my face; once he can move again, he may find a way to alert the others of my escape.

I find my way back to the others, also checking my surroundings, so that I will have something to report to them when I return. I want to keep them ignorant to my little detour. This decision may prove to be reckless in the future, but I will deal with that problem when the time comes—as I always do. I just want to get away from this wretched city and its erratic inhabitants.

THE SIXTH DREAM

T he Cats. Beware the Cats. Be wary of weathered distractions. For they control the barking Dogs, oh yes, Dogs that bark and bite with the poison of rage; infected by the Virus deemed Rabious. But they must also beware, because they stand in the path of the whisperer of Demons.

The gravity is heavier here. Only the nimble Cats can step lightly against the heavy pull. One must find the right footing. The Cats hide inside a golden fortress, one built under a great river of falling water. They hide high in the cliffs, visited only by those who can fly or skillfully climb. But do not consider it unvisited. A great many creature can fly, or walk, or swim across the sky.

Sex is a pompous distraction, and a valuable distraction at that. This golden tower is none other than a timeworn brothel, however, inside the gravity works at your favor causing great spasms for its lustrous consumers.

But behind the hidden doors, and under the false floors, the Cats disguise their proceedings. They buy and sell beings. But not just any beings, I myself must be cautious here, for I am of the greatest. The Cats do not sell to just any buyer either. And not just any Host can dwell in this canopy of debauchery.

Power and wealth, reputation and greed, luscious appearance, one must have these to enter. Not just one, but the first four, the fifth will require one to cover their face if appearance is not considered worthy. The whisperer treads near. There is something that she wishes to trade. There is a being that she has come to buy. The whisperer comes to bargain, but only cunning and good fortune will see her leave again. She must be cautious as well.

She passes through the mighty door and paces past the purring *and the groaning. She wears a large hood to hide her Human manner. The whisperer watches the floor, she is undistracted and undisturbed by the wide variety of sucking and fiddling and fucking. The farther in she steps, the nastier, and more diluted the consumers play. She continues to watch the floor.*

Deep in hidden spaces she finds a weathered and well grey Cat. He laughs and stands tall in his wealthy suit. He misses an eye and within the socket he carries a milky-yellow Yokkaa.

The Cat has been expecting the whisperer. He leads her through a door and leaves her in a room. There are two creatures that occupy her surrounding space. One is a lavish female Cat with wondering green eyes, and the other is the being that the whisperer has come to buy.

The Cat requests the item promised as payment and the whisperer delivers her dowery. In front of the Cat, she places a small bead—just barely the size of a mustard seed. It shimmers with 9 teal and silver slivers. A small bead indeed, but a bead carved from promise and potential. The Cat laughs and strings the bead around a silver wire. She bends and twirls and cuts the wire before reaching up and piercing it into her ear. The Cat is now the Yokkaas carrier.

The Cat respects all requests, and sells the being to the buyer, the whisperer places a hand on her new dowery speaking gracious thanks to the lavish Cat. But I sense growing hostility, the Cat plans to catch the whisperer, for the Vessel is worth more than the buyers being, and the bead, and beyond.

But before the Cat can pounce, before she can wrestle with her prey, the whisperer closes her eyes and disappears, taking her newly bought being behind her.

Escape was no option, and the Cats do not accept failure. The lavish Cat is collared, and the Yokkaa is torn from her ear, passed to the next worthy carrier. Her reputation is trashed, and her wealth is taken too. She is to be fed to the Dogs. Her orders were to capture the Vessel, but she could not justly explain the strange disappearance of the whimsical whisperer.

11

THE FORGOTTEN ONE

1,902 Days since the Fall...

There is escape from this planet. There is no way in or out that I can find. Only those who control the game know how to escape it—the Game Runners. And they are not "living". There is a countless number of sophisticated AI that collectively generate the entire planet. They are devilishly smart, and they can see everything that happens here through the eyes of what we call the Buggs. They are microorganism cameras created for the Game that infest even the most personal of spaces. We cannot do anything here without [196]being seen.

I have created a secret room: one hidden away. I put it somewhere that they can never find it. This room is much like a workshop, or a laboratory—similar to the one that I had set up in my time loop before I left the ship. I have found a way to make it Bugg free, so that I can let down my [197]guard. I remember spending years in the loop teaching myself about the technology, and the new life that I found before me. I needed to be well informed if I was to survive.

---

[196] Gameplay Detail—The Buggs: these creatures can see everything. They are relentless and will expose every detail of a Hosts life. The Game Runners are very particular. So much happens here, that it would be hard for the Elites to notice everything right away. They have the footage, but not the manpower to watch it all. That is why the Elites created the Game Runners: to monitor what happens and to notify them with important information.

[197] Note from the Prophet—Secrecy: I feel the need to keep certain things secret for our safety. I struggle now to write of this secret room and of Tanner's location.

There were books on every species. I read about their defenses and their weaknesses. I read about their advancements in science and engineering. I tested the limits of my body to strengthen myself. I changed everything about the person that I was—you know this, but I feel the need to explain it again.

I try to lay low and stay clear of my competitors. I tend to work best when I work alone, but I do not really have that option here. Because of my blood, I know that I am being hunted by a few predators that would kill for a taste of my flesh. Some want to study me, and others would like to kill a Red Blood just to say they did it. This makes it hard to trust anyone. I am constantly paranoid and looking over my shoulder.

There are only a few who I would consider an ally; they are the ones that have not died, or left me, or betrayed me. Barroun is the first, but even with him I try and stay at a safe distance. Compared to him, I am nothing to be afraid of. I like to tell myself that I have built a rather threatening reputation, but it is hard for a Human to compare to a God. Along with all the other creatures brought here against their will, even the divine is not safe from the power of the Game—even *he* could not escape coming here. Banished and stripped of his power or not, he is strong. He has not returned.

Another ally that I trust is Ehhrn. We have met up again, and though he never stays around for long, I do see him often—about every two days. He tells me that there is someone I must meet. Ehhrn is the middleman, he brings messages from this suspicious Host, but I have not yet been able to speak with him, nor have I been given a name. I have no idea who he is. We have not traveled to the Gate and done the task meant for us because we have not found the time, and because I have not recovered the desire to finish the tasks.

The Squeeb has separated from us completely. It has been two weeks since we left the city, and I have not seen or heard from it once. I suppose there were things that it did not want us to see—like how I hid my emotions for so long. It is out on its own, dealing with the loss of Reeb—its brother, its best friend. I wish that I could console it, but I know that it blames me for Reeb's death. The two of them had a deep connection and had been in each other's lives for so long. They spent every day together; they slept on the same time, they spoke in the same code, and they fought with the same humility.

Aneera has been back once, she follows her visions. She makes a good number of allies this way. She can see where she needs to go to be of good use. This also improves her score. As willing as she is to help me, she is determined to win the Game too. She has no intention to stay.

Boriisst has left as well. There are a few possibilities I have considered for where he has gone. The first, and the most innocent one, is that he has fled as far from the Dark City as possible. It makes sense that he would want to put distance between him and the Eiinokrra. The second assumption is that he actually went back, and that we were fooled by him. Perhaps this was all a set up, and they are still watching from a distance. Maybe our escape was some elaborate plan with an unknown purpose. The truth is unclear.

The second assumption also brings up the possibility that Sriii had something to do with it. She is smart; it could have been her plan. Did she act the way she did, and say the things she said sincerely, or was it all just to get into my head? I understand that I have a hard time making new friends, but that does not mean that the interaction did not influence me. Was she genuine, or was it all a lie? Am I wrong for accusing her? Or am I safer for not truly trusting her?

Our escape still strikes me as too easy. Other than my meeting with the Eiinokrra that killed Cynniaa, we left the city with no complications. It was *too easy*. This is the main reason for my suspicion. Nothing is ever easy, especially not here—I say it over and over again. And for the one who I had threatened, I wonder if he has kept quiet. I wonder if he even lived. I have been watching for any Eiinokrra in my area—considering how close I am to the Empty Forrest, but I have not seen anything. I also wonder if they found the one that we left behind in the cell, and if so, is the body really stuck there forever?

I have returned to the small shack by the wall—the same one that I hid in before—with Tziipoor, Aneera, Cynniaa, Ehhrn, and the other Fae.

It is the one with the bioluminescent floors, the old workspace, and the fire pit surrounded by seating. Barroun used his magic to place protection on me and the shack; since, he has also put the same hex on Ehhrn and Aneera, and he also managed to get the Squeeb too before it disappeared. My addition was the washer and the dryer, a tiny but handy detail.

I have decided to finally make a [198]journal to track my ventures, one that is full of sketches, and notes documenting my travels and my competition. I have begun to make maps of all of the places that I have been and placing my [199]Blood Mark at the bottom.

My cartography is nothing compared to Boriisst's, I cannot match his attention to detail. But I have done my [200]best. I have also started all the beginning pages over again; I am placing the loose paper drawings from when I was on the ship in binding. I managed to save them.

I am adding a new page to my writings. I hear a knock on the door, and footsteps quickly receding from my front steps. I place the journal aside and stand to answer the door. It has been raining for the last week, and the mud is thick. The sky is dark, and I can see lightning in the distance. There is low light, and I can barely see. I look to my right, and I am surprised to find a body. It is lying on the ground facing away from me, but I can see from its movements that it is still breathing.

As my eyes adjust slowly to the darkness, I can see that the Host is a Humanoid; it is a man. He is covered in mud. I move around him with caution, trying to stay at a safe distance. He grunts in pain. I step closer to get a better look, and to my surprise I can see a river of black, almost purple looking blood pooling under a wound in his stomach. There is only one being that I know of who bleeds that color—Boriisst.

I can see his face now. He looks back at me and smiles, laughing drunkenly—

"Tanner!" he slurs. "I ha—'hiccup'—ha-haven't seen you—'hiccup'—forever!" He sits up and hugs my legs almost pulling me to the ground, covering me in blood, and mud, and booze.

---

[198] Relic Detail—The Journal: this is the one that *you* see—the "final draft" if you will. Tanner used her blood for the color red and made pencils from the soot of the fire.

[199] Relic Detail—Blood Marks: Tanner's Blood Mark is the initials RBT stamped by a personally made Blood Stamp. Boriisst's Blood Mark is a dot to represent him, and a smeared dot underneath to represent his dead mother.

[200] Relic Detail—Tanners Maps: these are the maps that you see at the end of "*The Game of Ten, The Red Blood.*"

I am instantly irritated with the realization that I now have to care for the drunken, wounded, *idiot*, covered in mud, that is dying on my front step. If he were a Host that I did not know, I would have carried him off to die somewhere else. I help him up and take him inside. He giggles and stumbles all over the place before I drop him to the floor again. I strip off most of his clothes to help him wash off the mud and blood, so that I can properly see the damage done, and then care for the wound. I leave him to wash himself the rest of the way and dress himself, as I go to clean up the puddles of rainwater and yuck that had been tracked all throughout the interior.

I wonder if this was meant to be a warning. I step outside again to check for footprints. I find a trail leading up the hill, but it has faded from the rain, and is lost just as I reach the top. Someone has been watching me. They have been planning something for a very long time. They wounded an ally and returned him. I was right to be suspicious of something.

I return to find Boriisst asleep on my bed, still bleeding. I sigh and take the time to wrap the wound. It is a cut just below his rib cage on the left side—a puncture wound. It is not too deep; he should be fine. I return to the seating area in the front by the fire. I try to continue my work on the journal, but I am distracted by this mysterious opponent's first play; what is to come next?

271

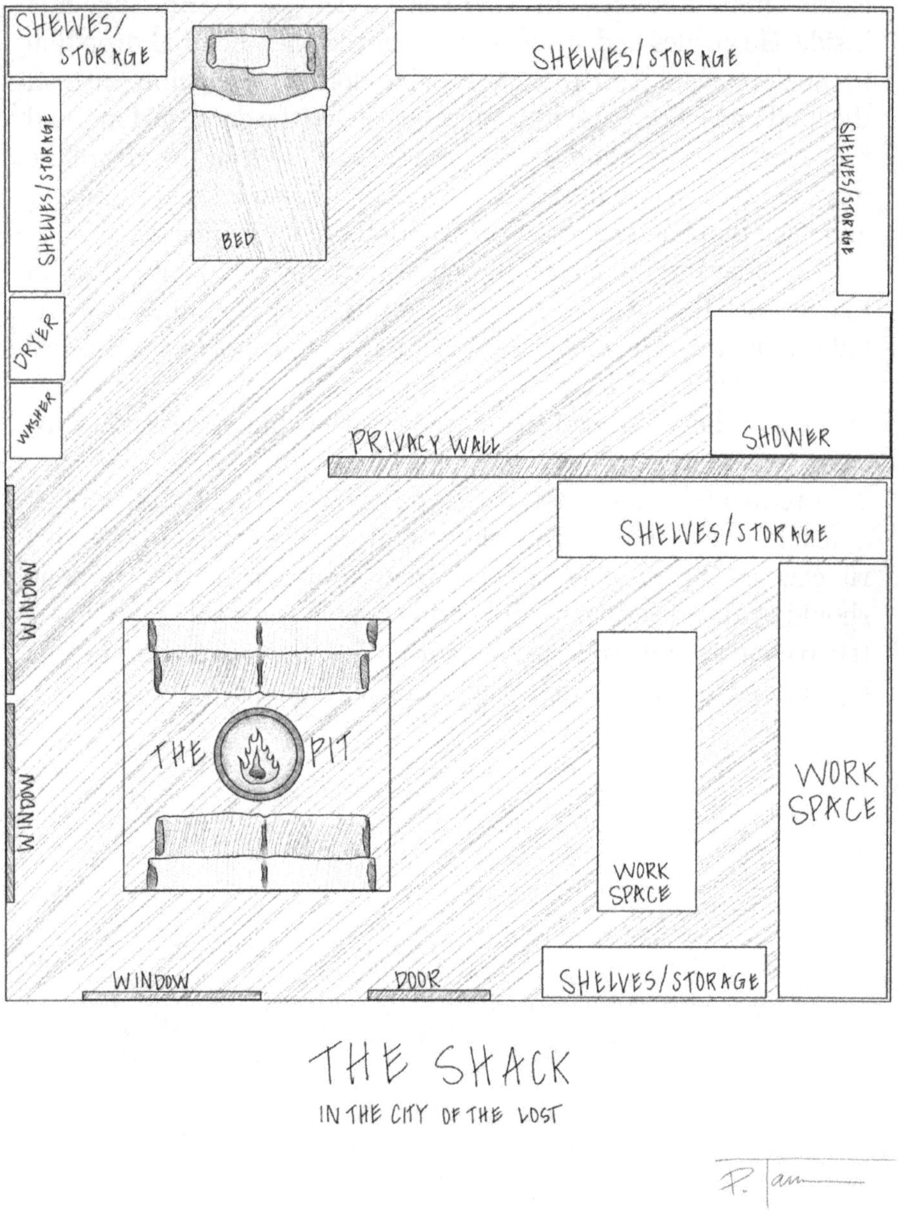

SHELVES/ STORAGE

SHELVES/STORAGE

SHELVES/STORAGE

SHELVES/STORAGE

BED

DRYER

WASHER

PRIVACY WALL

SHOWER

SHELVES/STORAGE

WINDOW

WINDOW

THE PIT

WORK SPACE

WORK SPACE

WINDOW

DOOR

SHELVES/STORAGE

THE SHACK
IN THE CITY OF THE LOST

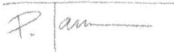

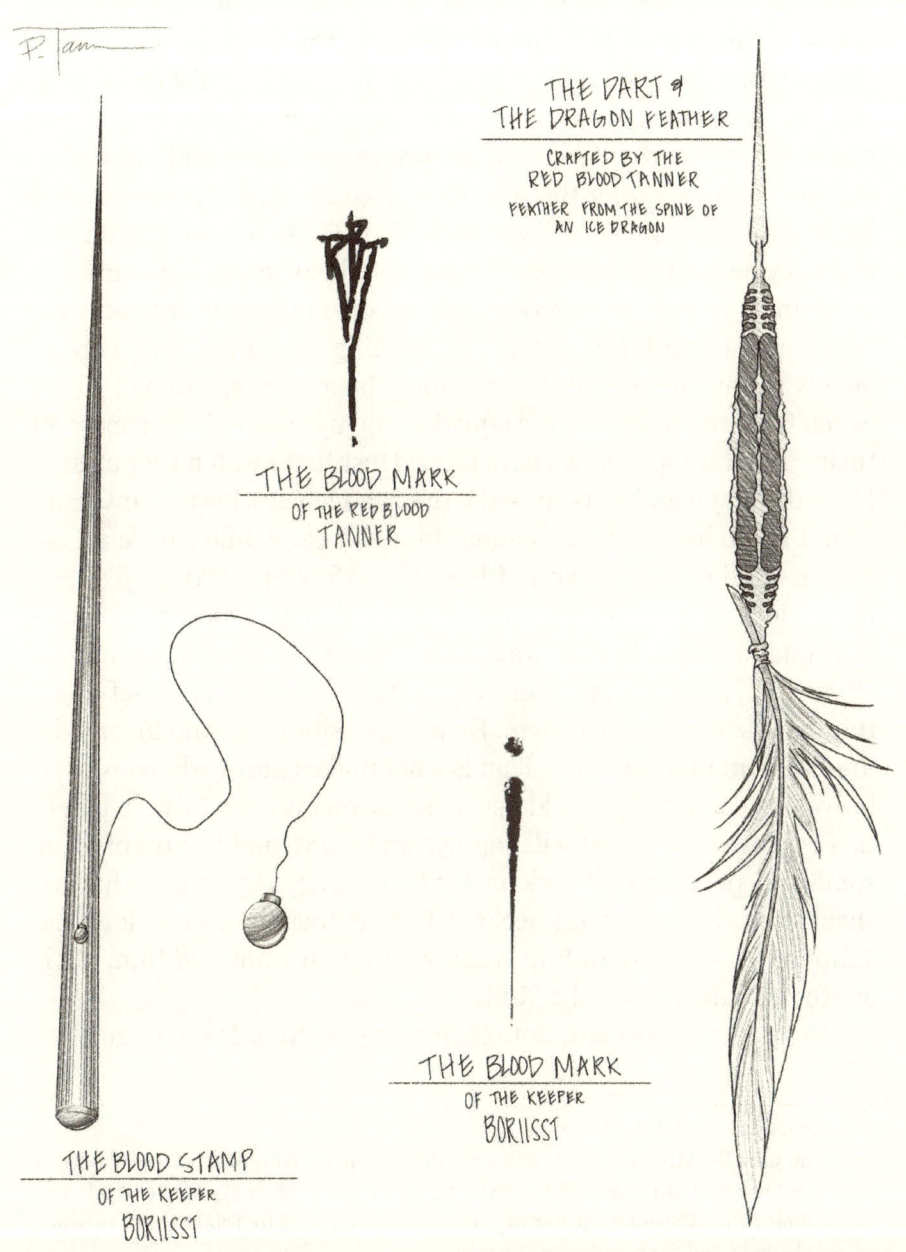

THE DART &
THE DRAGON FEATHER

CRAFTED BY THE
RED BLOOD TANNER

FEATHER FROM THE SPINE OF
AN ICE DRAGON

THE BLOOD MARK
OF THE RED BLOOD
TANNER

THE BLOOD MARK
OF THE KEEPER
BORIISST

THE BLOOD STAMP
OF THE KEEPER
BORIISST

273

1,916 Days since the Fall...

I am in the woods, in a Trial. It is night, somewhere—a long way—to the west of The City of the Lost. The trees here are taller than Redwoods. They reach high into the lifeless and boring false sky. They are thick, and strong, and even the most powerful winds can barely make them sway. Their leaves are heavy and navy blue. It looks fantastic under the sun. This place is called [201]Adnnezzadah Baak, which translates to Trees of the Sky. These trees are so unique that they have their own heartbeats; I can hear them all around me.

I am not here to compete, please do not misunderstand my intentions. I still have no faith in winning this. I am only here to deal with my current situation. I must be as perceptive as I can. I watch from the treetops, as a squad of enemy competitors construct their [202]base camp below. There is one Host that I watch very closely. He is the one who hunts me—the one who left Boriisst on my front step. I try to learn as much about him as I can while I have access to him—and of course while I have the safety of a [203]doppelganger body. He is hard to track on the outside; though I have seen him a few times around that old warehouse where I lost my fingers. He is Humanoid, but there is something about his eyes that is stupefying. I think it is some kind of charm. He is impossible to say no to, or to lie to—he cannot be deceived. That is what makes him so dangerous. If he were to catch me, I would never escape on my own. I live in fear of this because I feel as if it will happen, and I have nightmares of being someone's pet again—it took me six fucking days to remove that jaw shackle. And I am fearful because I remember the discomfort that Tziipoor felt because of him when we first encountered him. He is another creature from the Void.

He is very observant, not much gets past him. He has excellent

---

[201] [add-NEZ-duh BAH-k]

[202] Gameplay Detail—Trials: in each one, there comes a time when all of the weak Hosts are weeded out, and only the strong remain. These parts of the Trials can last a long time. Throughout history, Hosts have battled in Trials that—in some cases—have lasted for hundreds of years.

[203] Gameplay detail—Doppelgangers: Reminder! The Eiinokrra were unable to create one for Tanner, but the Elites/Liiyetrrux have managed to create one for her that bleeds the blood of Gods, because they cannot recreate Humans.

hearing, and a keen sense of smell. It is hard to hide from. Luckily, I still have the protection of IIIxaanax. I have a new connection to it, after recovering my ability to hear and speak to others with our Voices, I am able to now hear the Yokkaa too.

It is strange. It does not actually have a Voice per se. I guess I could say that it uses mine. I hear its thoughts, but I hear them as my thoughts—if that makes any sense? I hear it when I am not listening for Voices. I hear it when I sleep, and when I am distracted with other things. It is always there, even when I am not wearing the stone. Though I have noticed that the longer I go without wearing it, the quieter and less frequently it speaks to me. The connection fades, and I assume that after a while, it dies out completely. But lately, I have been wearing it all the time. I never take it off anymore.

He has caught on to me trailing him before, when I had *not* been wearing IIIxaanax. He cut me, and when he saw that this body bleeds white instead of red, he let me go thinking I was just another Hevaanian God after him. He searches for the Red Blood, so it is better to interact with him in the doppelganger bodies. That way, he thinks that I am unaware that he is after me, and the one that is after him is nothing to be concerned about. I have made a new fight suit that I only wear in Trials. It covers my hair, my ink, and my face. I do not take Reewenniveaar either, the Dagger is a dead giveaway. I carry a different weapon that I had come across rooting through old buildings. It is a small hatchet, and I carry a few throwing knives with me too. But like I said, he is clever. I suspect that he may see through this.

I wake in my real body after leaving the Trial, content with the new information that I have gathered. I return to the shack from the place where I hide my real body while I am in the Trials. For the sake of the story, I will tell you that I return inside of the shack, my hiding place is somewhere there.

I am cautious to move after finding the door wide open. There are few places to hide, but I feel a presence. I fight with myself about whether I should investigate, or just flee and find a new place. I step slowly, deciding to stand my ground. If I am to get caught, I pray that my secrets will stay safe. I do not have IIIxaanax until the hour after my return is up, but even then, I would have to retrieve it from the place where I programmed it to spawn back to. I turn the corner to check my room, and immediately regret my choice to do so. He is here, standing in the corner. He roots through the shelves looking for anything that can give him information. He does not see me yet—I must be quick. But he turns, and then smiles. He is fast than me the chase is over; I know that I cannot run. I have been caught.

1,918 Days since the Fall...

I wake in the warehouse, but now it is clean, and set up as if someone plans on studying me. There are thick plastic walls and floors—I assume to make for easy cleaning. I can see tall tables, and what look like microscopes, and foreign anatomies in jars filled with a vile orange color of liquid placed on top. There is a shelf of books in the far-left corner.

I am hanging by my wrists with a thick black rope that attaches somewhere above me and appears to go nowhere. I am in awe of this meticulous enclosure. My toes miss the ground by a few feet, and I am partially naked—he left my underwear, but took everything else, my torso and chest are exposed. This is not done perversely, but for the purpose of study.

It is unlikely that he found my secret room. I made sure that everything respawns there safely after Trials including: IIIxaanax, Reewenniveaar or the hatchet with my knives, the journal, the darts, my wings, my fight suit, and every other creation, or finding that I have made during my time here—everything that I must hide or keep safe. I also store things that I have from before, such as my phone, and the clothes that I came in.

I notice three small cuts below my ribcage on my left side, and a pool of my red blood in a bucket on the floor. The cuts are fresh. It is as if he were taking samples, but in large amounts—there are many new scars. He must have done some work before I woke up. I hear a clank in the distance, and quickly look to investigate. My head grows very heavy, and I lose the ability to move. I can only see few details through the thick plastic walls. I see a figure appear out of nowhere. It is him.

He is smart; hiding me in an invisible box, so carefully placed, and lost in plain sight. From the outside, it appears that there is nothing here. But he knows where the door is, he knows how to get in. Someone without this knowledge would walk straight through me—completely unaware.

He approaches me. I am silent. I do not speak because I know they will not be my true words. I look to the ground avoiding eye contact. I cannot help but think, what will this encounter be like? He treads slowly in a circle around me. He speaks; his voice is almost comforting, and is very quiet, and gentle. He is very short, maybe five foot. If I met him under different circumstances, I would assume him to be very kind. He has very odd triangle shaped glasses, and well-combed dark hair. He has a nice smile that includes a couple of snaggleteeth that are perfectly placed along the top. His entire demeanor seems comforting, but I know what danger hides behind it.

"I hear many things about you Red Bloods," he says grabbing a small scalpel from his little wheeled surgical tray. He steps closer and places his hand on my sternum. He traces an invisible line down to my navel. He steps the right and cuts a small square in my side. He removes the skin with forceps and steps toward the table to the right. I try to look away, but I am drawn by curiosity. He places it in a small petri dish and turns back toward me. This time I am afraid, so I close my eyes. The only movement ability that I have is my eyelids. I cannot fight back. I can only close my eyes and cry because of the pain.

He cuts a few more pieces, placing them in sample jars, and looking at them under many different sized microscopes, while asking questions that I cannot answer. I have been drugged. I cannot speak, or even flinch, or scream when he cuts.

"You know, you almost had me fooled," he says. "When you bled white in the Trial, I thought you were a God. But I knew that there was red blood left behind the night that you, and that ugly black creature were here. It is strange to see you for so long without it," he continues to say, "It must be dead."

He speaks without emotion, but he does not seem to be speaking with intent to be cruel in nature. He is only stating what he deems possible.

"A friend of mine has recently informed me that a proper doppelganger for you was inconceivable." He holds a test tube up to the light, and swirls my blood around in circles, "I think I could do it. But it is a shame that you had to go and poison yourself before I could get to you. I wish you could answer my questions; this would be *so* much easier."

I remember now, I recreated the memory serum that I used the last time—just with a few tweaks. It is funny how it works, every time I amaze myself. This time I cut off my muscle memory and my body's connection to my brain. My heart still beats, and my lungs still function, but the rest of me is lifeless, and emotionless. I cannot move when he is near me—I can only move my head when he is gone—but I can still feel everything. I can feel the pain of every cut, and the snap of every bone, as he studies how my body heals itself. I took these things away from myself so that no matter how much agony I am in, I cannot break or tell any secrets. And he can test every vein, every blood cell, every neuron, every organ, and every bone, he will find nothing, my secrets are hidden well.

I hang here for months it seems as he returns every day to mutilate and belittle me. My body aches, and I have lost a lot of blood. My healing ability cannot keep up with him, and I am weak. He is testing my limits—moving just slow enough to keep me alive. I expected pain, and discomfort, but I did not expect the extremes that this innocent looking child figure would explore. I fed into this; I let him capture me because I wanted to study him too. I need to know how his brain works in order to defeat him. It is the only option I see, but it is excruciating.

THE HAGING BODY
THE RED BLOOD TANNER

THE LIIYETRRUX
THE SCIENTIST
5'0"

1,997 Days since the Fall...

I am lying on a table. He is here again, standing above me. He reaches for a tool and steps out of my sight. I cannot lift my head to see what he is doing. I feel a deadening pain below my knee on my left side. When he returns to my sight again, he carries something. It is my left leg, severed.

"I have a friend who cannot wait to taste the meat; he has guests coming just for *this*!" he says. I am disgusted. "I wonder if it will grow back like your fingers and your toes do, or if that is too big of a loss to be replaced. I am anxious to see!"

He places my leg on ice and returns to ask more unanswered questions.

"I dug into your gut looking for reproductive organs, I am curious as to how your kind multiplies so quickly. But there was nothing there. However, I did notice that something was there before." He leans to his side to look me in the eye as he cleans the wounds. "Did you remove them? Do Red Bloods try to *prevent* offspring?"

He scrunches his face in thought and turns back to look down at his hands, "Of course, it would make sense that you would do this *here*. Perhaps to prevent unwanted breeding or experiments. You are a smart Host I will give you that."

He is right, I had removed them for that exact fear. And I cannot explain with words the major inconvenience a period cycle would be here. I removed the inconvenience before I had dealt with my regenerative power so that it was gone for good. I have no need to carry children here, this place is untrustworthy.

He cleans his tools and packs up his samples for the day. He finally leaves, and I close my eyes and begin to cry. I know that my leg will not grow back. I know the limits to this ability. To him, I am an experiment, and now a meal. I feel more helpless than I had in Zephiiitrrax. I left one Hell for another. I have not been here for even close to how long I was there, but the pressure is just as sickening. I will be brutalized by this devil until the day I find the will to revive my strength. I do not feel that I have enough information yet; I do not see how I will be able to beat him. He cannot be cut, or poisoned, or burned. I have tried everything that I can think of; I put him through Hell in those Trials. I deserve everything that he is doing to me. I have not tried Tziipoors venom to weaken him because I figure that if a knife cannot cut him, then a dart cannot puncture his skin, and I am not willing to waste a dart just to try it. This plan has failed me. Perhaps I must turn to magic. If all fails, it is okay though; I think that I have been ready to die for a long time. If this is the end, I can accept it.

The next day I am hung again from the ceiling. I know what he has planned. Back to the brutality, he has slowed some, but the lasting pain remains. Am I healing slower because my will has faded? I have been continuously bleeding for days. He shows his concern, but continues his work forwardly, like he is being pushed for time. I wonder, who could he be working for?

"I wish you could answer me!" he says with enthusiasm. "I have *so* many questions! On Earth, how often did you eat? And *what* did you eat, and how?" he asks taking a bite from a fresh carcass. He spits the raw meat from his mouth and wipes the blood from his chin. "Ick! That can't be the way. You must cook it first, right?" He pulls away the hairs that stuck to his tongue and rinses his mouth with water. "At this rate I won't be trying your meat tomorrow." He laughs. "Oh, and I've heard of organ transplants—how do you do that so successfully? Gender changing, brain surgery, body reconstruction, personal modifications, and all without magic!"

He stresses about his unanswered line of questions, as he measures the circumference and the color of each fading bruise from the week prior. "I wish I could test your reflexes," he says poking at deadweight. "I've heard of cookbooks, you wouldn't happen to have one somewhere, would you? Maybe there's one somewhere in one of the old cities. I should find a Host to look into that." He disappears for a moment and returns with expressions of relief.

I am drawn away from his presence when I see a figure approach from the blurred area behind the adversary. My ears ring so loud that I cannot hear, and I cannot keep my eyes open. He is so distracted by his questions that he does not notice the figure approaching him from behind. There is a struggle between the two foggy figures. I cannot make anything out. My eyelids droop closed, and I lose consciousness.

I am shaken awake, and I am too weak to look around, but can see someone is trying to speak to me. He lifts my head from my chest, and stares as I fade in and out of consciousness. I gather the strength to focus on his face, and sigh with relief. "Ehhrn," I am able to say, finding the will to fight again, but just as easily irritated that I cannot continue my research. He jumps to the ground, and the man traveling with him releases me from the hanging ropes, and places me gently on the tall table next to him. He bends to retrieve the abuser's body from the floor and disappears into the night—he must be incredibly strong, I failed to even touch him outside of the Trials. Ehhrn wraps my wounds, and changes to his taller form, so that he can carry me out of this malignant [204]invisible box and deliver me somewhere safe.

---

[204] Relic Detail—The Invisible Boxes: these boxes were created and are used by the Elites. Very few Hosts know of them. This means that the abuser is either working for the Elites or is an Elite himself.

12

THE NEW SAFE HAVEN

I wake in a strange bed in a foreign room. The walls are made of red rock, the same color as the Grand Canyon. I am in a cave. I sit up, and then try to stand quickly remembering the trauma behind my missing limb. Now I can feel the pain even more intense than before. The drug has been cleared from my body, and everything hurts. I am still healing. I need to find the power within myself to become stronger again.

I decide to try and stand again, but the pain remains the same. There is a set of crutches leaning against the wall, so I take them, and struggle to get up. I take a step, and hobble toward the curtain that covers the entrance. I pull it to the side and find myself in awe. There is a big open cavern; I am many levels up, close to the top. There are pathways along the wall that lead to other separate rooms with similar curtains for privacy—a hotel maybe? I look down; the open area of the cavern has been transformed into a living space. There is a pit in the center with seating surrounding it much like the one in my shack, but a great deal bigger. I can see no source of light, but the cavern is not dark.

I make my way down slowly, and as carefully as I can. I have never been a sturdy one on crutches. I slowly investigate. I wander around, and I attempt to find any information that can explain where I am, or who I am now in dept to. It seems odd that I am the only one here. All of those rooms—there are about twenty—and I have not seen or heard another Host. There is a kitchen area with a sink and fresh fruit layed out on the counter—whoever lives here is not afraid to eat here.

There are books layed out along the abundant amount of tables, and there are maps, and charts, and diagrams all along the walls, and a small area set up for experiments, and invention. Most of the [205]maps are of places that I have not yet heard of, but there are a few that have been made known to me. I see, NuuDetruu, Zephiiitrrax, Sraast Beach, and The City of the Lost. There is also a desk with unfinished drawings, and a surprisingly comfortable chair. I look through the many drawers, sifting through papers, and piles of junky trinkets.

I pause when I hear the sound of footsteps behind me and turn cautiously to look. A memory floods through my brain. I am taken back to that first day, the one where I am hidden in the big wall; with Barroun. That day he told me that there were two Gods here: him and his older brother. I never learned his name.

"Are you the other God?" I ask bluntly, unable to look him in the eye. I think that my muscle memory—after seven months of looking away from my torturer—has decided to stick around. I look to the floor. "Are you the one from the Banishment Sphere?"

"Yes," he answers. "Thank you for freeing me."

This confuses me, "What do you mean?"

"You haven't figured it out yet?" he asks. "You never completed the task?"

I shake my head, "No," completely oblivious to what he is saying to me.

He kneels to the ground, and tries to make eye contact, but I cannot help but look away.

"What do you mean?" I ask again.

"Well, if you don't know, I cannot just tell you," he answers. "It is a test for you to figure out. My father is very particular about his tests."

---

[205] Relic Detail—Tanner's Maps: the maps that you see resemble other Human-made maps from the planet Earth as to help the Reader better understand. The maps on the wall, as well as Boriisst's maps resemble the maps made by Host on the Lost Planet. Tanner's maps and drawings were made to share information, not to amuse the imagination.

My eyes widen, and I am dumfounded, "Your father?" I say, "*Your father—Barrouns father* is the Great God?"

"Yes," he says. "You are just figuring this out, as well? Has my brother told you nothing?"

"Your brother is very private," I tell him. "He doesn't ever say much."

"Hmm," he replies, "That's odd, for as long as I have known him, nobody could ever get him to shut up." He laughs to himself.

He continues to tell me of the reason why he and Barroun had been banished. He says they fought over who would take their father's place—or rather, who would not. Neither one wants the responsibilities that come with it. He explains that one day, their father will die, and when he does, one of them will take his place. The other brother will be sent to Earth, to protect it. When the time comes, he will take the place of the leader of the [206]Et'Aangliiel, or the Great Angels. These are also known as the [207]Deead Aangliiel, or [208]Fallen Angels. This job is much easier and does not hold the weight of the crown. Their father decided to send them out into the Universe; he wanted them to learn valuable lessons.

The God tells me that he has recently seen his brother Barroun and was told how long he had been free before he came here. Barrouns sphere landed on Earth, close to Borneo. Their aunt [209]Arrvehht—the current leader of the Great Angels—found him and set him free from his sphere in 1519. Barroun lived on Earth for the next 500 years—boarding the Adreestiaah just four hours before I did.

He says that he does not want the crown because he is not fit to be a King, and Barroun does not want it because he refuses an arranged marriage with the new [210]Et'Aniiaa, or Great Mother. His heart already belongs to another.

"Where are my manners?" he says. "I am [211]Yezzuraa Maandeiim."

"Tanner," I reply.

---

[206] [et ahn-GLEEL]

[207] [dee-ADD ahn-GLEEL]

[208] Host Details—Great/Fallen Angels: Humans have interacted with these Angels before. Fallen Angels are Hevaanian Gods who have passed to the next life as warriors, messengers, protectors, and miracle givers.

[209] [AIR-vet]

[210] [et AHN-yuh]

[211] [ye-ZOO-rah MAH-dee-um], lightly roll the r sound.

"Ehhrn has told me much about you," he says. "He went out for a bit, but he should return soon."

"What is this place?" I ask him.

"This is our bunker, our safe place. Don't worry, nothing can find us here."

That is what I thought about the last place I was hiding. We will see how this place holds out. "What happened to the man with the glasses?" I ask.

"He is no longer a problem"

I sit thinking silently. I am happy to be rid of him, and I am relieved that I was not the one to dispose of him. But my studies had proven very interesting. I will have to find another to investigate and compare to him.

"We are in the Red Mountains, far away from the starter city," the God says, discomforted by the silence.

"Starter city?" I ask.

"IInve Bovaange," he answers. "That is the place where everyone our size starts."

I ask him how it is that he knows all of this, when he had only just recently been released from his sphere. He says that Ehhrn is an excellent informer, and that he has caught him up on everything necessary to know about this place. Ehhrn also found this cavern, and it is protected with more powerful magic than that of the Gods.

A [212]Yokkaa was [213]made here. We are hidden much like my secret room is, and the cavern is also Bugg free.

---

[212] Relic Detail—Yokkaa: It is worth mentioning that wearing a Yokkaa can prove to be more dangerous than helpful—in some cases. A Yokkaa lives with the possibility that it can turn 'Demonic.' In this instance, the color of the stone spoils and its personality possesses the wearer. This is not a commonly known fact, and it is not known why or how this happens. Many Hosts are ignorant to this possibility. It is impossible to know when this is going to happen, unless the wearer has an exceptional relationship with their Yokkaa.

[213] Monument Detail—The Red Mountain Cavern: this cavern was made for Gods Recruits. Ehhrn was led here by the Great God and told of its great protection. A Yokkaa was mined here, and that means that even though the stone is gone, the cavern is still well protected. The stone that was made here has a personality that is compatible with IIIxaanax, making the cavern even safer—now under the protection of *two* mighty stones.

2,048 Days since the Fall...

I have spent a few months here being reclusive from the Game. I have ventured out once, stealing a Siitaa so that I could visit Tziipoor's grave. I sat and told her of my hardships and how much I miss her. I told her about the scientist and his studies and of the rescuers who had found me. I spent a long time there, crying and watching the sun change its place in the sky until the last of its light went out.

I have focused much of my time on new technologies. I have my laboratory here with me—have you figured it out yet? I carry it with me at all times, but I am still reluctant to tell you how or where it is hidden.

My newest invention is a new kind of prosthetic. I want to replace the leg that never grew back. I have tried many different kinds that have failed to work the way I need them to, but this new one is something different from what I had tried before. I crafted it from regenerative tissue. The device is a small circular disk with a mesh-like padding on the inside. I place it on the end of the stump, just below my knee, and grunt, as it latches to the skin. The mesh tissue can detect the memory of the missing limb and creates a replica in its place. A new leg begins to grow, and as it finally reaches the foot, I can move the ankle, and—when they form—I can move the toes too.

The silver color of the band connecting the new limb to the remains of the old one can still be seen, but this does not trump my excitement. I quickly stand and have a hard time with my balance, but the more I limp around, the better I get. I hope to be able to recover quickly. And I hope that this new prosthetic will be the last one. It is not meant for removal, so if it proves defective, I will have to remove it forcefully. I use one crutch for support until I am able to properly walk again.

I leave my lab, hoping that the others are here to see my new attachment. I limp from my room, down the stairs, and into the open area of the cave where everyone spends most of their time. Ehhrn is home, and I rush to him, as quickly as my wobbly ass can manage. I lift my new leg up onto the chair that he sits in—

"Look at my new leg," I say proudly, wiggling my toes.

"How long until this one craps out?" he asks, making fun of the many that failed before this one.

"Hopefully never," I answer him. "Where is the Squeeb?"

Ehhrn was able to track it down and convinced it to come join us again. It has been back for about a month now, but I still do not see it much. It is here to sleep and take small breaks, but then it leaves again for matters that are unknown to me.

Aneera is staying here with us as well, and they are all working together to find the rest of the remaining Recruits. I refuse to leave here, I am working hard on my recovery, and dabbling in new discoveries—some that I should probably stay away from, but curiosity will not let me stop digging. I will keep these things secret for now; I will share them with you when I feel that it is safe to do so.

The three remaining Recruits are: Boriisst, Barroun, and Sriii. I told the others to look for Boriisst near the shack where I had been staying; he had been staying there with me after he had been left injured on my front step. I figured that the best place to start is there, he could not have gone far. Like Yezzuraa said, Barroun has visited here a few times, but he never stays, like the Squeeb, he is on his own personal mission. And for Sriii, I doubt that we will ever find her, and if we do, it would be best not to bring her here. She meant it when she said that she would kill me if she saw me again.

Another shit-show bombshell that I guess I should drop on you now is a conversation that Yezzuraa and I have had recently. I was telling him of my misery, and how I blame myself for every bad thing that has happened—for some reason, I am still unable to look at him, but he is the only one—I blame myself for every life that we have lost. Then he tells me—

"You know Tanner, they are not really dead."

"What?" I say, "How? I literally watched all of them die."

"If my father said that he would keep them safe, then they are safe. I bet they are all with him now, in the Holy City. Except for Reeb, if he was killed by a Harpy, then there is no bringing him back. That's like being killed by a Yokkaa." he says, looking down at the stone.

This news hit me hard. They have been brought back from the dead. All this time, and I never knew—I never would have guessed. I thought that was the end. I was sure that I would never see any of them again. I am still unsure as to how I should handle this. I guess I will not know how to feel until I actually see them. I need proof. If

Tziipoor is alive, then why can I not hear her? And why did Barroun not tell us? The Squeeb was irritated by this revelation as well.

2,062 Days since the Fall...

Barroun has finally returned, and I wake to the noise of the brothers arguing by the front entrance. I dress myself, and descend into the common area, I no longer walk with a limp, and the pain has all subsided—it is like the leg was never lost. I have been training myself for combat again. I have a simulation area in my lab where I can fight with false Hosts to regain my strength. I am almost ready to venture out again.

As I draw closer, I find Aneera seated on the counter in the kitchen area, watching them fight while eating the rare fruit that Yezzuraa had collected yesterday—which is her new favorite thing in existence. I hear the argument that Barroun makes to tell me something, and Yezzuraa argues that I must find out on my own. They go back and forth about my right to know, and I interrupt with the addition that I can make my own decisions.

"You have no room to talk about me finding shit out on my own; you have told me more than he has, so just tell me," I say to Yezzuraa.

"If you say a word," threatens Yezzuraa to Barroun.

Barroun interrupts him saying, "What are you going to do? You have no powers, and you are no stronger than me. If she knew, all of our problems would be solved."

Yezzuraa shakes his head in disapproval, "Father was adamant when he gave us our limits. We cannot just tell her." He turns to me, "And yes, I told you a lot of things, but the things I told you were things that were okay to tell you." He turns back to Barroun, "And no, not all of our problems would be solved."

Barroun scuffs, "Where did this sudden loyalty to Dad come from?" he asks. "You never liked him."

The argument is interrupted by Ehhrn, yelling from his balcony, "For fuck's sake, would you shut the fuck up? I'm trying to sleep. Fuck your God's secrets!" He turns his head toward me and continues. "*You* are the Lost God, you fucking moron! There! Now everyone knows. Now shut up!" He turns, "Fuck!" he yells one more time before retiring to his room. I am left in complete shock. What did he just say?

I contemplate the words that Barroun told me that first day, but I continue to refuse to believe them. That is, until Yezzuraa had told me the same revelation, but this time with much more detail. And now with what Ehhrn has told me, I cannot deny it any longer. He has never given me false information. I was told that I was of high importance, but I never understood how. "You are a very important player in this Game, but so am I." Those are the words that Barroun said to me, and I just now understand why.

I am the Lost God? Where is the sense in that? My blood is red, I do not have their strength, or their knowledge, or their history. I am Human—right? All of this new information is a lot to understand. It is just one bombshell after another. How did I miss this much? I turn away, dismissing them with my hand, instructing them not to follow me. I return to my room, and then back to my lab. What does this mean, and how is this possible? How does one just *become* a God? Is it through some great cosmic selection, or ceremony? Or does the Great God just hand the title out, like fucking Oprah does with big-ass TV's? "*You're* a God, and *you're* a God, and *you're* a God, *everybody's* a God!"

I guess the next best action is to figure out what I should do with this information. Is there really a way that I can still win this, and still return everyone home safely? Is it really possible? I should start with the first clue that I received here. "Find the Lost God." Okay, I found her, what next? I follow my steps from the beginning. Barroun led me to Tziipoor, and after her came the Fae. That takes me to the Hidden Room, and then to the Bhaaktii—and to Sriii. The cavern in the desert—that has to be where I need to go. To the place where I found Yezzuraa in his Banishment Sphere; that is where my name is written on the scroll—Sriii had returned it to me in the bag that she had dropped at my feet when she freed us.

I stand from my chair, after hours of self-discussion, grab my wings and a few other things, and leave my lab and then my room. I see that Ehhrn is sitting around the fire in the common area. He is looking away from me, so I sneak into his room while I have a chance. I quietly root through his things, and finally come across what I came here looking for—his Siitaa.

He interrupts me unexpectedly—

"How do you always do that?" I ask him, sitting on the edge of his bed and inspecting the Siitaa.

"Where were you planning on going?" he asks. "You are the *last* person that we need disappearing right now."

"Hmm," I reply. "I just had a thought. How far do you think this could take me?"

"How far are you planning on going?" he asks again.

"Do you think it could get me off the planet?" I ask him, "Maybe out of the Void?"

"How is it that you're so smart, but also the stupidest one here?" he answers.

I laugh, with intended mockery, "Has anyone ever tried? I bet I could make it work."

He then laughs, mocking my mockery, "I have little faith in that."

"Some is better than none. I'll tell you what," I say, conveying my counteroffer. "There is one place that I can think of that would have the answer to our current issue. If you let me go there, I'll wait to tear this thing apart trying to make it sustainable for off planet travel."

He snatches the Siitaa from my hand and puts it around his wrist, "*You* are not going *anywhere* by yourself," he says. "I am tired of fucking chasing you." He grabs my hand, and raises the Siitaa to his mouth, so that it can hear him clearly, "Where are we going?" he asks me.

"The cave in the abandoned city in the Bhaaktii," I tell him.

"Dessiaa," he says, and we are teleported to the cavern.

He finds a place to sit, as I assess the cave, looking for any type of keyhole or altar.

"You're not going to help me?" I ask.

He replies, "Nope. I'm just here to make sure you make it back." He makes himself comfortable.

Tziipoor told me once that this cavern was a Hidden Room *before* the sphere crashed here. Everything had to be rebuilt. That means that there is a task here still to be completed—and I am the one who is meant to do it. I check over the area by where the sphere had been before I released Yezzuraa. Ehhrn sits on the other side of the abyss, watching from a distance.

My power of convenience must have returned to me, and I find the keyhole that I am searching for. I insert the key and turn it—like always—once to the left and once to the right. A small door appears at the back of the cave, and I enter—ready to complete my task.

There is an altar, but this one only has a single bowl—no vile, or any other requested offering. A golden leaflet folds out from the altar and gives me another clue. To my surprise, this one is written in a language that I can read.

"A bowl for that which gives life and that is all that is needed. But first make the flightless plummet and find the one who's plan must be succeeded."

"'The flightless plummet?'" I look out toward the crevice, the abyss, the hole in the floor. They want me to jump, I wonder. And the one who has a plan, will I finally meet the Great God? Was this the place all along? Ehhrn watches carefully as I remove the wings from my back and place them gently on a large stone to my right. It will be easier without them; I have to trust in the clue.

"What are you doing?" he asks, catching on to where I am headed. "No! Don't!" he yells.

I disregard his order and give him a big smile before leaping from the ledge. He runs to the edge, and watches horrifically, as I fall into the darkness.

I leave him behind, hoping to find the man responsible for bringing us here. I close my eyes and trust the fall. The further I go, the faster my pace increases. I am frightened, but I know that there is nothing that I can do. I have fallen into this pit before, but last time I died before reaching the bottom.

I am stopped with a jolt, and a jerk to the neck. I am just above the floor. I drop my legs and catch the ground with my feet when the air lets go of me; I stand again. The bottom is nothing less than what I expected. There are scattered bones and broken rocks all along the floor. It is dark, and I can barely see.

"YOU FINALLY MADE IT," I hear a mighty voice say.

I turn around, and see a tall man dressed in white, "You're him, aren't you?" I ask. "The Great God, Mr. Maandeiim."

"MR. MAANDEIIM," he laughs. "YES. BUT CALL ME [214]IIPETRRAAH."

---

[214] [yee-PEH-truh], lightly roll the r sound.

IIpetrraah. I have heard that name before. In Vaahiigali. So, this is who they meant.

"Why am I the last to meet you?" I ask bluntly.

He answers, "BECAUSE THIS TEST IS FOR YOU, I WANTED TO SEE IF YOU COULD FIND ME, AND HERE YOU ARE—IT TOOK LONGER THAN I EXPECTED, BUT YOU ARE HERE."

"What is this test for?" I ask again. "What's the purpose?"

"I NEED TO SEE IF YOU ARE WORTHY OF WHAT THE UNIVERSE THINKS YOU DESERVE."

I follow with another question, "What does she think I deserve?"

"HER," he answers, confusing me even more. He sees that I do not understand, so he explains it a little further, "I CANNOT TELL YOU EVERYTHING I AM NOT THE ONE WHO CHOSE YOU. MY JOB IS TO LEAD YOU ON THE RIGHT PATH. *YOU* ARE THE LOST GOD. THAT MEANS THAT YOU DIED AS A HUMAN, AND YOU WERE SAVED BY SOMETHING DIVINE GIVING YOU LIFE AGAIN. THAT DIVINITY WAS THE UNIVERSE HERSELF, THE GREAT MOTHER, MY WIFE—MRS. MAANDEIIM."

"What does that mean? Why isn't *she* the one who's here? Do I have to find her too?" I ask.

"IT MEANS THAT YOU ARE DESTINED FOR GREAT THINGS. I CAN ONLY ASSIST YOU, BUT I KNOW THAT THE HELP THAT I GAVE YOU WILL GET YOU THERE. YOU HAVE MADE IT THIS FAR."

I ask, "If this test is for *me*, why drag all of the rest of them into it too?" My voice grows slightly angered as some questions are left unanswered.

"BECAUSE THEY NEED YOUR HELP," he says, stepping closer to me. "AND YOU NEED THEIRS. I WANT YOU TO HELP THEM SEE WHAT GOOD CAN COME FROM HUMANS. TEACH THEM THE BEAUTY OF LIFE WITHOUT HATE. YOU LIVED LIKE THAT ONCE."

He places two fingers on my forehead, and I am gifted with a terrible migraine. I fall to the floor holding my head, and cry from the sudden pain.

"GOOD LUCK, KID," he says, before disappearing again.

"That's it?" I ask, grunting painfully. "That's all I get?" I yell into the darkness, and squeeze my head tighter, as the pain grows more intense. "What the fuck is happening?" Everything is different than I thought. Everyone thought that they had to protect me, but that was never the case at all. I continue to cry and roll along the floor. The pain spreads from my head to my back, and I feel the sensation of something ripping out of my skin, something is growing. I scream in pain, and drown in my agony, as this transformation lasts forever.

It all finally stops, and I lie on the ground catching my breath, freezing cold from the sweat. I try to sit up, but there is a heavy weight on my back, connected to my shoulder blades. I struggle to stand, and when I finally have the strength to turn and investigate, I find the most beautiful gift that I have ever been given. They are mine; they are a part of me. I have grown wings! The paintings all had them right, the wings of Gods and Angels; they reach out far past the tips of my fingers, so large that I can only imagine their strength. They are white with massive feathers and stunning magnificence.

I could fly before, but these are going to change the game. I can feel the strength in my body increase as well, and I am sure that I could take on anything in my path. I cannot wait to fly; these new wings will have more power than the Fae wings ever did, and I will be able to fly higher, and faster, and with more control. The problem is learning how to use them. I have already tried using my mind, thinking, "up" like I did with the others, but it does not work.

They are grown from my shoulder blades instead of my spine, so maybe—I move the bones that the wings are attached to, and I find that this is how I control them. They are actually a part of my body, so I have to move them like one, I cannot control them with my thoughts. I move them around a bit, learning the angles, and the positions in which I can place them. The weight will take a while to get used to, but I can adjust—

"Fuck yes!" I say to myself, "Here we go!"

I move the wings upward and shoot myself into the sky. The power is overwhelming, and I pass through the cavern, bust through the ceiling, and meet with the sun outside. With just one flap of the wings, I am going higher and higher. The strength is more than I ever imagined. I pass the clouds, and then break through the barrier protecting the planet, ejecting myself out into the Voided Cosmos. I finally come to a stop and float for a moment in peace. I have never known such [215]freedom.

I can breathe and move freely. I could fly home; nothing is stopping me. But I do not know which way to go and my guilt, my guilt would haunt me. I cannot leave the others; they have worked so hard to help me. I am sure that the Void would not be so easily escapable anyway. I make my final decision to return to the surface; if things change, I can abandon the Game later. I need to find a way to help them escape too. Though, apparently killing them might do the trick, If IIpetrraah is just going to bring them back, and gather them all in the Holy City, why not just kill them all, and take my own life, placing us all on the planet of the Gods.

I descend back through the atmosphere and pass again through the clouds. The planet is so much better from up here, more peaceful. I take my time to embrace the beauty. Approaching the place where I had emerged from, I spot Ehhrn inspecting the hole that I had created in the rock.

I move so fast that he cannot see me, and he cannot sense me drawing nearer. I snatch him from the rock and climb into the air again. He screams, terrified by the [216]experience, and once he notices that I am the one who carries him, he cusses me for disappearing— and for reappearing in such a pain-in-the-ass way.

I carry him all the way back to our place in the Red Mountains. I can fly at incredible speeds, and dodge, and turn corners sharper than I could before. As I get my grip, I steady myself in the air, and flip, and coil through the wind, laughing from this newfound freedom. My senses are heightened too. I can sense Barroun and Yezzuraa. Gods must have divine connections to one another I could feel them from above the clouds.

---

[215] Host Detail—Tanners New Abilities: the abilities of the Gods. The wings of Gods and Angels are the most powerful in our Universe. They can fly at speeds faster than light. Their lungs are tough enough to handle the pressure, and their bodies are strong enough to fight triumphantly at these speeds. Gods can also survive in any environment—including the Void, and all of space. Their skin is thicker, and harder to cut, and their reaction time is uncanny.

[216] Host Detail—Abilities of the Gods: when Tanner touches Ehhrn, he is also given the ability to withstand the pressure of the flight. This ability will be lost when she lets go of him or is no longer touching him. This allows Gods to travel with other Hosts safely.

When I land on the ledge that leads to the entrance and drop Ehhrn to the ground, he takes a minute to catch his breath and compose himself. We are met at the doorway by Yezzuraa. He stands and stares with amazement.

"Wow!" he exclaims. "They're stunning!" He runs his hand across the feathers, and I can feel every touch. "So, you met him? You found my father?"

"Yes," I tell him with a smile on my face—still unable to look at him.

Ehhrn interrupts, after finally catching his breath, "How did you do that? What are you talking [217]about? And aren't you forgetting something?"

"Oh shit!" I say, remembering the empty bowl that I had left waiting for me at the altar. "I'll be back!"

I return to the sky and find my way back to the altar; I still cannot believe how fast I can move. It is not close to the hideout by any means, but it takes me no time to find it again. I make my way back down to the altar and slice my hand to fill the bowl completing the task. My blood runs the same color, but now it has a shimmer of white and my injuries heal faster—I am now officially a Human—*and* God.

I retrieve the Fae wings that I had worn before and shrink them small enough to carry safely. I will not use them anymore, but they are of no less importance to me. I take some time to myself and fly gracefully though the sky at a lower speed. I cannot imagine how Barroun and Yezzuraa must feel having lost this freedom. I wonder what it will take for them to get it back.

When I finally return, I find that the others have all gathered and are waiting for me.

"It's about time," Aneera says. "Where have you been?"

"That does not matter," Barroun says. "She is here now."

"What's the big fuss?" I ask.

Barroun stands, and walks toward me, "We have been waiting for this since we got here; it's finally time."

---

[217] Host Detail—The Wings of Gods and Angels: a carrier's wings can be seen by other Gods and Angels—each set is unique to their carriers. Other Hosts cannot see them unless the carrier allows them to. Tanner is unaware of this, so even though she is proud to show them off, Yezzuraa and Barroun are the only ones who can see them until she recognizes the ability to make them appear.

I ask again, "Time for what?"

He replies with excitement, "We're going to leave this wretched Game and return to the Holy City on Hevaan." He turns to his brother and smiles, "We're going home."

"Not so fast," Yezzuraa replies. "You know it will not be that easy. We still need gather the rest of the recruits and complete the remaining tasks."

Aside from all the excitement, this hits hard. It introduces a new chapter. Ehhrn was right, this is only the beginning. There is so much more to accomplish here and the trials to come are to be a level up from this one. I have learned that I am not the main character in this story, just a supporting role and I must be here until the story is over.

Will it ever end? This place is poison, but the kind that chooses not to kill you. It just depletes your strength and immobilizes your happiness. How long? How long must we endure?

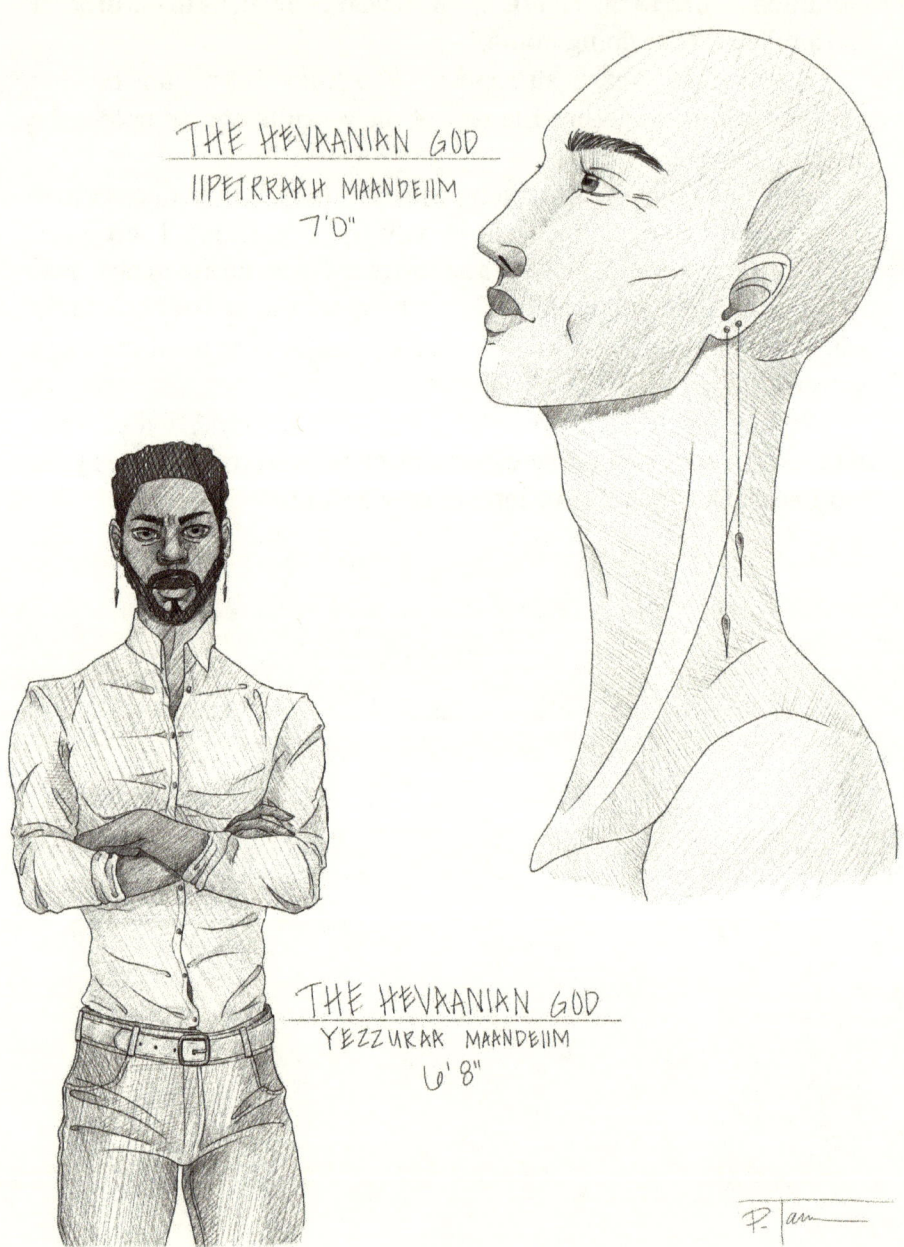

THE HEVRANIAN GOD
IIPETRRAAH MAANDEIIM
7'0"

THE HEVRANIAN GOD
YEZZURAR MAANDEIIM
6'8"

THE SEVENTH DREAM

W e do not gather often. We are not all so happy to do so, though our place of meeting is mystical and grand. I do not much love the company, but I enjoy the many hours gifted to me by the Nymphs. They allow the Universes and the Universes only to swim through the **9** holy caverns that lead to the library.

This is the library that carries life, its contents holds all, even that which is unknown and yet to come. This time, the Red-Blooded one follows me, unknowing of the centuries that I have spent watching her. The Nymphs grant her passage because she was the Vessel of Naaqsaa. She carried the soul of a Universe and will forever keep concealed a piece of her. Naaqsaa chose that body when it was empty, its previous soul had already been passed. She gave new life to the Vessel, she made holy a creature otherwise considered unworthy.

Her intentions were pure, but Naaqsaa, being the twisted tormenter that she is, discarded her previous failed Mother and created a being even more hated than that which calls itself Human. The Vessel is all and nothing; she is God, and Red-Blooded, and Demon, and death, and dead. She carries pieces of any soul that is given to her. For she is a Vessel and nothing more, ferrying souls from one place to another. The Vessel is hated and unnatural, the only one created of her kind. All hate her, and they fear her, and they defy her—until the day comes that they feel the need to use her.

When a Universe is born again, the being that carries her and feeds her life is chosen in the womb. This being is called the Mother. She nurtures the Universe, gives it love and life, until the time comes that the Mother has grown old and withered away and a new Mother is chosen. The Mother teaches the Universe and learns from

299

her as well. They live as one but are entirely different. However, what the Mother is, the Universe will be as well. If she is frail and sad and twisted, if she is dangerous and disgusting and defiled, or if she is love and light and laughter, or perhaps a mix of them all, as the Mother is so too will be the Universe. But a Universe can travel without her Mother, she can stand next to her in a separate body.

The Universe has a job to protect the Mother, oh yes, we will take good care of the soul that feeds us. We too must be sure not to fail, for if we do the Mother will become something untamable and demented.

To be a Mother one must have a strong core, she must be unbreakable, unswayable. She must always stand on the bridge between them, never crossing to either side or soaring into the sky above. She must watch the bridge and protect the river that flows beneath it. And she is never to enter the water. She cannot interfere, even if the bridge is burned, she must hover in its place, holding steady above the river. She must not defend one side over the other. She must not decide what is good or bad. She must feed the river and the ones who drink from it. A Mother must give life; never take it.

Naaqsaa abandoned this rule, she chose a being already freed of the womb, she chose a being who had lost its soul to twisted interactions. And a being cannot Mother without an original soul, thus creating the Vessel.

Naaqsaa's Vessel did not carry her until death, for the Vessel cannot die. Naaqsaa spent years inside the Vessel crafting and growing a new being. She gave it the purest soul. She created her own Mother. She did not seek her out or sit and wait for her. She made a being and left the body of the Vessel inside of the new Mother as she was born into new life.

But this is dangerous. The Vessel now lives forever, carrying and collecting souls, switching them out, and losing them. She can carry souls from any Universe, she can travel freely within all of us. That is why she has been called here, that is why the Nymphs let her pass through the **9** holy tunnels.

The Vessel carries a particular soul, one that we need in order to win this war. She carries a failed Mother, one who did not pass into the land beyond the Void. The creature carries the answer.

And if it was willing to make a deal with the Vessel, it may be the only one that will give deals to its creative beings, however much it may hate us.

The Void may yet snuff out the light. But there are creatures denser than its darkness. There are things scarier than death. And the Vessel could prove to be the deliverer. The others have doubt, but I have been watching. I may be the only to say it, but perhaps Naaqsaa was right.

THE MAPS

River Life

Vaahiigasi

φ Stoneworker's Region
⊖ Blacksmith/Builder's Region
∅ Plant Worker's Region
⊗ Market Region
⊗ Younger Sprites Region

φ The Keep
⊖ Garden of Prophecies
∅ Dance Studio
⊗ Yetziivu's Caves

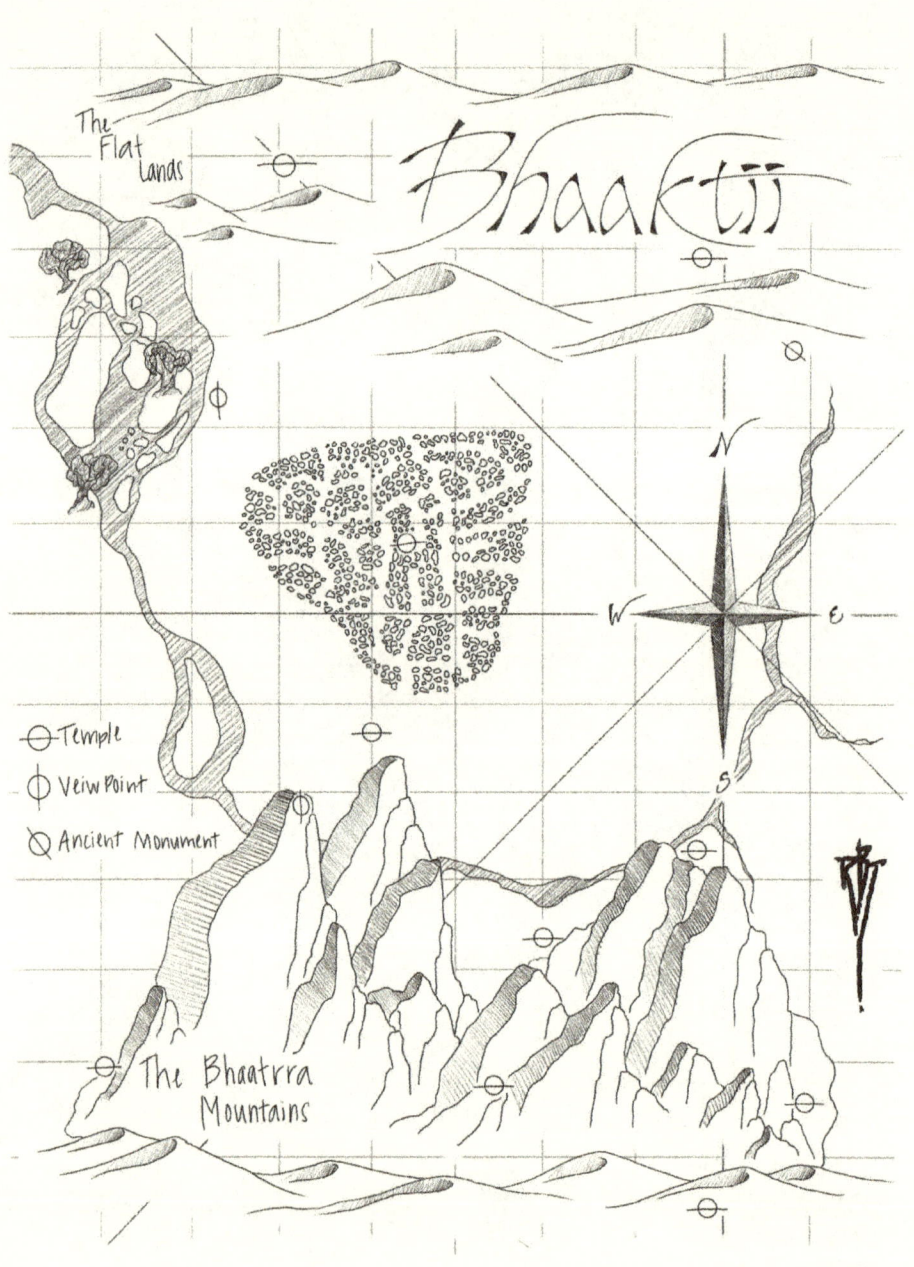

The Flat Lands

Bhaaktii

⊖ Temple
φ Veiw Point
⊘ Ancient Monument

The Bhaatrra Mountains

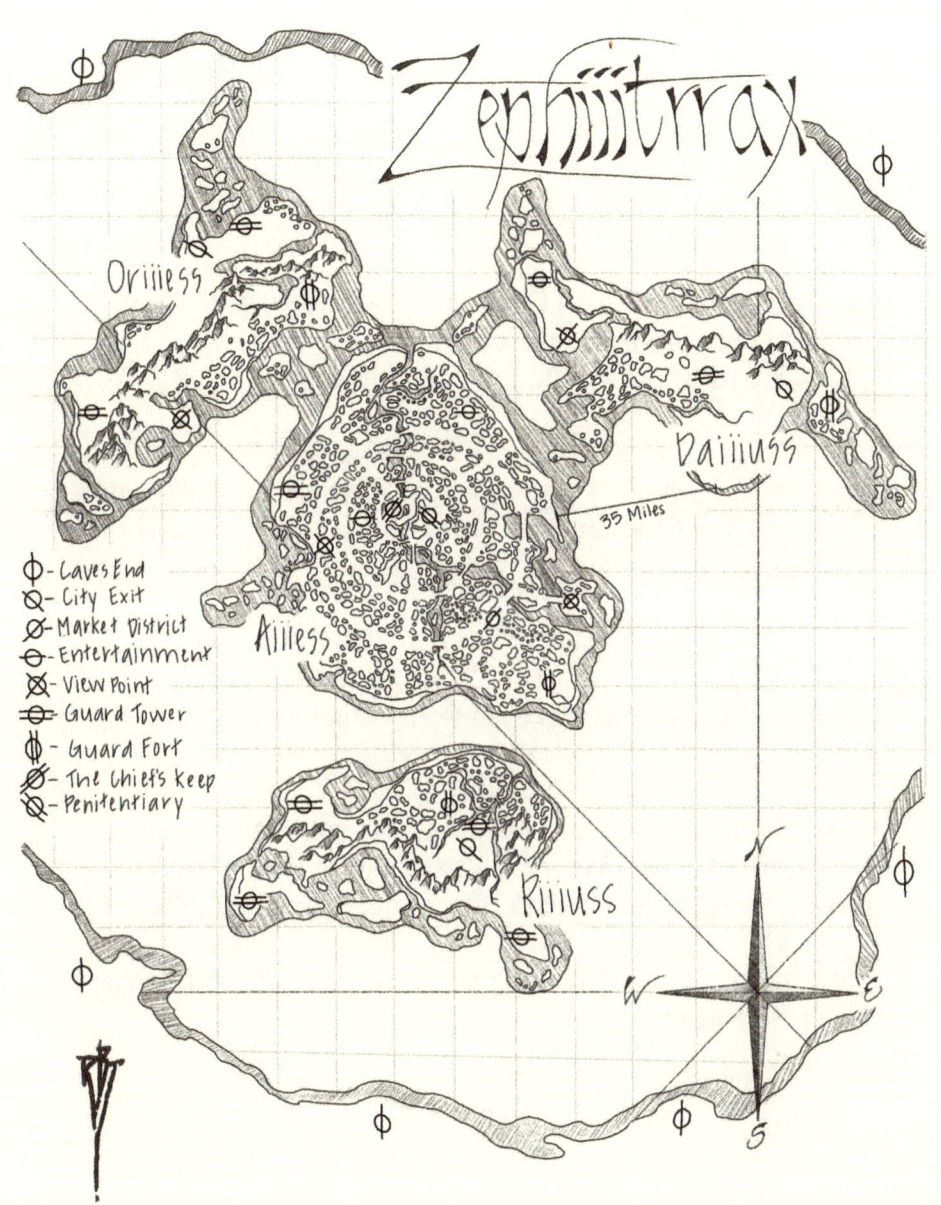

Zephiiiitrrax

Oriiiess

Daiiiuss

35 Miles

Aiiiess

- ⌀ - Caves End
- ⊘ - City Exit
- ⌀ - Market District
- ⊖ - Entertainment
- ⊗ - View Point
- ⊖ - Guard Tower
- ⌀ - Guard Fort
- ⊘ - The Chief's Keep
- ⊗ - Penitentiary

Riiiuss

N
W   E
S

A Note from the Prophet

I have one final thing, a Game of Three just for you.
Within these pages, I have left Hidden Secrets.
Here are three clues to help you find them.

1
Secrets are best found by those who pay close attention. Your guide
will tell you the final name that you thought that I had forgotten.

2
Blood is the issue for this one. Who is who? Or
who is what, should I say? Bold and crooked letters
tell secrets that even Gods do not know.

3
This final secret is about trust. There is not always honor in
what people say. All creatures have secrets, and if you look
closely, some are laid in dark colored numbers within dreams.

Speaking of trust, I trust that you will keep your findings to
yourself. Secrets are meant to be kept.

Readers Guide

A

Aangliiel *[ahn-GLEEL]* Angel, Hevaanian God, warrior of Earth and Hevaan

Aamiineea *[AH-meh-NEE- uh]* see: Et'Aamiineea

Adnnezzadah Baak *[add-NEZ-duh BAH-k]* Trees of the Sky

Adreestiaah *[uh-DREE-sh-TIA]* pretender, Ship created by the Elite Gods; currently under the control of the Hevaanian Gods

Aiiiess *[aye-us]* the main island of the Dark Hidden City, Zephiiitrrax

Aneera *[ah-NEER-ah]* Siren, Serruumn, one of the 12 Recruits

Aniiaa *[AHN-yuh]* see: Et'Aniiaa

Anndriiinax *[an-DREE-nah]* the Hive City, the capitol of the Eiinokrrian empire

Arrtisiiaax *[are-TEE-sia]* the Kingdom of Snow, location of the Second Hevaanian Gate

Arrvehht *[AIR-vet]* Barroun and Yezzuraa's aunt and leader of the Et'Aangliiel, or Deead Aangliiel

B

Baakorraht *[back-oh-RAT]* the Temple in the Trees, and the location of the Third Hevaanian Gate

Barroun *[bah-ROON]* *roll the r sound*, Hevaanian God, Prince of Hevaan, IIpetrraah and Mrs. Maandeiim's youngest son, Yezzuraa's brother, one of the 12 Recruits

Beekrah *[beck-RAH]* Cruxgrriig's Fighting Carrier Ship

Benoviii *[ben-OH-vee]* Eiinokrra, Sriii's personal guard

Bhaaktii *[bah-HAK-dee]* Blue Desert, or Blue Sand Desert, location of the First Hevaanian Gate

Bhaatrra *[bah-HAH-truh]* Blue Crystal City, *deceased*

Boriisst *[BOE-rist]* race unknown, the Keeper, one of the 12 Recruits

Braiiakiah *[brah-EE-ah-kia]* Hevaanian God, one of The Six

C

Castle Miiqraaux *[meh-CRAW]* see: Miiqraaux

Cruxgrriig *[crew-grig]* Captain of the Beekrah

Cynniaa *[sin-YUH]* Sprite, Prince of the Fae, one of the 12 Recruits, Onnemiit

D

Daiiiuss *[dee-oo-s]* the north eastern island of the Dark Hidden City, Zephiiitrrax

Deead Aangliiel *[dee-ADD ahn-GLEEL]* Fallen Angel, Et'Aangliiel, Hevaanian God, warrior of Earth and Hevaan

Dessiaa *[DES-uh]* word used to activate the Siitaa

E

Eiinokrra *[ee-no-KRAH]* Spirit of the ground, Voided creature

Ehhrn *[ha-REN]* Felerrg, Frogface, Fuckface, Angry Toad Prince, one of the 12 Recruits

Emineeptiaa *[em-en-EEP-tia]* Red Blood, Human

Empty Forest the Northern Forest, location of the Dark Hidden City, Zephiiitrrax

Emtepii *[EM-tep-ae]* see: Et'Emtepii'Em

Enookiiv *[eh-NOK-iv]* Trees native to Port Wrritaaz

Entanglement Key made by the Hevaanian Gods, made for the Human called Tanner to unlock the 12 Hevaanian Gates

Errok *[eh-ROCK]* white stone from the Hidden City of Stone, Vaahiigali

Et'Aamiineea *[et AH-meh-NEE-uh]* the Great God, Hevaanian God, King of Hevaan currently IIpetrraah of the House Maandeiim, Mrs. Maandreiim's husband, Barroun and Yezzuraa's father

Et'Aangliiel *[et ahn-GLEEL]* Great Angel, Deead Aangliiel, Hevaanian God, warrior of Earth and Hevaan

Et' Aniiaa *[et AHN-yuh]* the Great Mother, Hevaanian God, Queen of Hevaan, currently Mrs. Maandeiim, IIpetrraah's wife, Barroun and Yezzuraa's mother

Et'Emtepii'Em *[et EM-tep-ae EM]* the Great Game of Ten

F

Felerrg *[FELL-egg]* Frog Person/People, Ehhrn, the Keepers guards

G

Gaaliiniaa Sphere *[gal-en-EE-ah]* Banishment Sphere, created by the Elite Gods, used by both Elite and Hevaanian Gods

Geetra *[guh-AE-druh]* roll the r sound, Humanoid Hosts from the planet Taaviirax

H

Herthhe *[hair-TEH]* Hunters ruled by the Game Runners, Player Stalkers

Hevaan *[hee-VAH-n]* planet, home of the Gods, location of the Holy City

Hffh *[h-ff]* Sprite, Fae, Vaahiigalian wing doctor, Onaaviaa and Hyytrrh's brother

Hnaarax *[NAH-ruh]* The Calm Sea

House Maandeiim *[MAH-dee-um]* see: Maandeiim

Hyytrrh *[heh-truh]* Sprite, Fae, Vaahiigalian council member, Onaaviaa and Hffh's brother

I

IIntiiius *[yee-NEE-tee-us]* Sriii's family name

IIIxaanax *[eek-SAH-nah]* Yokkaa, protection stone,

currently worn by the Red Blood Tanner

IInve Bovaange *[een-VEH boe-VAH-ng]* The City of the Lost, the starter city

IIpetrraah *[yee-PEH-truh]* *roll the r sound*, The Great God, Hevaanian God, The King of Hevaan, Mrs. Maandeiim's husband, Barroun and Yezzuraa's father

Irestiikaar *[ee-REST-i-car]* the Lost Planet, location of the Et'Emtepii'Em, or the Great Game of Ten

J

Jeexa *[yex-AH]* citizen of IInve Bovaange, or the City of the Lost, writer, journalist, *deceased*

L

Liiyetrrux *[lie-YET-truh]* roll the r sound, Elite Gods, Spirits of the sky, Voided Creatures

M

Maandeiim *[MAH-dee-um]* House Maandeiim, rulers of the Kingdom of Hevaan, the royal family, IIpetrraah, Mrs. Maandeiim, Barroun, and Yezzuraa

Meenaa *[meh-NAH]* Hevaanian God, one of the Six, one of the 12 Recruits

Miiqraaux *[meh-CRAW]* Castle Miiqraaux, the Drowned Castle, the Bright/Brilliant Castle, the location of the 11th Hevaanian Gate

Mubaatiis *[moo-BAH-tis]* mountain bandit, Taa, Ziin

N

Naaqsaa *[nah-kah-sah]* Universe of Human origin

NuuDetruu *[new-DET-rue]* Hidden City

NuuGiirti *[new-GEER-tee]* new birth, Eiinokrrian goodbye ceremony/funeral

O

Onaaviaa *[oh-NAH-vee-yuh]* Sprite, King of the Fae, Ovinniaa's husband, Otrrah and Yetziivu's father, Hffh and Hyytrrh's brother

Onnemiit *[oh-NEM-et]* see: Cynniaa

Oriiiess *[or-us]* the north western island of the Dark Hidden City, Zephiiitrrax

Otrrah *[oh-TREH]* Sprite, Princess of the Fae, Onaaviaa and Ovinniaa's daughter, Yetziivu's sister

Ovinniaa *[oh-VIN-yuh]* Sprite, Queen of the Fae, Onaaviaa's wife, Otrrah and Yetziivu's mother

Ovniin *[of-nen]* Sprite, former Queen of the Fae, Ovinniaa's mother, *missing*

Q

Queel *[k-ee-l]* creature from the planet Taaviirax, Tziipoor

R

Reeb *[r-ee-b]* Cyclopes, the Squeebs brother, one of the 12 Recruits

Reewenniveaar *[ree-WEN-eh-veer]* the golden dagger, created by the Hevaanian Gods for the first Human called Yeshua, currently used by the Human called Tanner

Rhhiina *[REE-nah]* Forest of Rhhiina, in the Kingdom of Tooh, location of the Temple Baakorraht, location of the Third Hevaanian Gate

Riiiuss *[ree-oo-s]* the southern island of the Dark Hidden City, Zephiiitrrax

Roorge *[ROOR-g]* see: Siinaa

S

Serruumn *[seh-RUM]* Siren, Aneera

Sevvia *[seh-via]* the royal plant of Vaahiigali

Siinaa *[see-NAH]* Siren, Roorge

Siitaa *[SET-uh]* transportation device

Squeeb *[sk-WEEB]* creature from our Universe, Reeb's brother, one of the 12 Recruits

Sraast *[sr-OST]* beach, location of Castle Miiqraaux and the 11th Hevaanian Gate

Sriii *[s-ree]* Eiinokrra, Spirit of the ground, Princess of Anndriiinax, one of the 12 Recruits

T

Taa *[t-AH]* Mubaatiis, Ziin's brother

Taaviirax *[tah-vee-RAH]* planet, home of Tziipoor, home of the Queel, home of the Geetra, *deceased*

Tanner Red Blood, Human, Hevaanian God, one of the 12 Recruits

Teriinia *[teh-REE-nia]* Hevaanian God, one of the Six

The Six Hevaanian Gods, wardens on the Adreestiaah

Tooh *[t-O]* Kingdom of Tooh, location of the Forest of Rhhiina, location of the Temple Baakorraht, location of the Third Hevaanian Gate

Tziipoor *[t-zip-OOR]* Queel, creature from the planet Taaviirax, one of the 12 Recruits

V

Vaahiigali *[vah-HEE-gah-lee]* the Hidden City of Stone, home to the Fae

Vennnassi *[veh-NAH-see]* Eiinokrra, Boriisst's mother, *deceased*

W

Wrritaaz *[WEE-tah-s]* the Port on Pearl Beach

Y

Yeenokki *[yen-OH-kee]* Hidden City

Yetziivu *[yet-ZEE-voo]* Sprite, Princess of the Fae, Onaaviaa and Ovinniaa's daughter, Otrrah's sister

Yezzuraa *[yeh-ZOO-rah]* *roll the r sound*, Hevaanian God, Prince of Hevaan, IIpetrraah and Mrs. Maandeiim's eldest son,

Barroun's brother, one of the 12 Recruits

Yhiin *[y-IN]* the Island of Salt, location of the Sixth Hevaanian Gate

Yokkaa *[yo-KAH]* protection stone

Z

Zephiiitrrax *[zeh-VEE-truh]* the Dark Hidden City, home of the Eiinokrra

Ziin *[j-IN]* Mubaatiis, Taa's brother

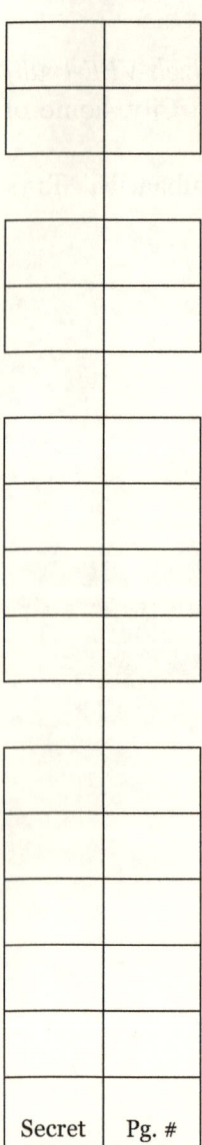

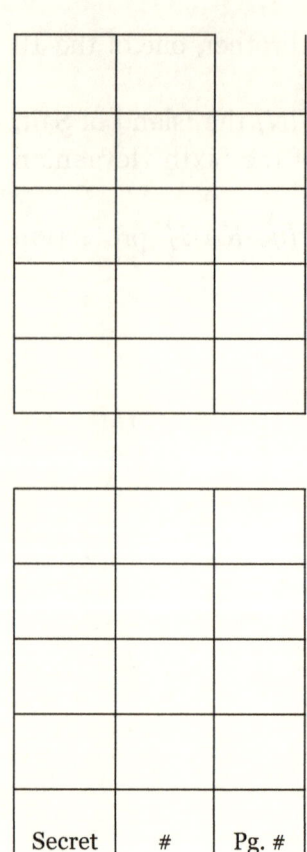

A Note from the Prophet

To Prepare you for the Future

This chapter will settle you in for the next book in this saga. This is the last time that you will read through Tanner's perspective. There are a few last-minute details that I think need to be shared with you, and there is one last secret to foreshadow as well, but this time there is no clue. Happy searching.

13

THE SEA

2,790 Days since the Fall...

Present Day
The Calm Sea
[218]Hnaarax

We begin this chapter on a ship in the middle of the sea. These are the calmest waters on the planet, and they glow a beautiful tint of pink, like the pink lakes on Earth. The Calm Sea is essentially transparent, and I can see the creatures that thrive in the magic rich waters below. It is so clear that I can see hundreds of feet down.

The ship is massive, unlike any that I have seen, and is filled with pirates, and pillagers, and perversions. It is round and is a fighter ship—not built with the intention to fight *other* ships, but to be the battleground for fighting *Hosts*. The crew numbers in the hundreds, and the prisoners outnumber *them* by [219]two thousand. And the Captain—though as incredibly short and fat and goofy as he may seem—is easily the most dangerous Host onboard.

He wears two Yokkaa as necklaces rather than rings. One has three circular beads threaded closer to his neck; these beads are a dark color of transparent green. The other is a long thread with many more beads and these ones are a darker color of red. I do not know

---

[218] [NAH-ruh]
[219] Relic Detail—The Ship: called the Beekrah [beck-RAH], this ship is currently. crewed by 968 Hosts and carries 2, 970 prisoners.

the names of these Yokkaa, nor can I tell you where they were born. But I can tell you this, they have a terribly distressing relationship. His effortless release of power is horrifying.

I am here accompanying Ehhrn and Aneera. We are separated for the time being, but as we had indented, we are free to search for a certain Host. Thanks to Aneera's visions and Ehhrn's ability to convince anyone to do as he pleases, we were granted permission from the captain to roam freely around the ship. We were given temporary rankings just below the Fifth Command Captain and can open any doors or roam into any rooms free to this ranking. Here is a chart to better show you where we stand *(Fig.3)*.

The Beekrah's Crew Rankings

1 Captain [220]Cruxgrriig	*9* Third Warden Captain
2 Second Command Captain	*10* Prisoner Guard
3 Third Command Captain	*11* Door Guard
4 Fourth Command Captain	*12* Ship Entry Guard
5 Fifth Command Captain	*13* Lookout
6 Quartermaster	*14* Mechanic/Engineer
7 First Warden Captain	*15* Higher Crew Member
8 Second Warden Captain	*16* Lower Crew Member

Fig. 3

It is worth mentioning that even though Door Guards are ranked below the Quartermaster, these crew members are to be respected as if they were the Captain himself. If a Door Guard refuses to let a crew member through their door, the Host must see a Captain to gain entry. Violence toward Prisoner Guards, Door Guards, and Ship Entry Guards is not tolerated and can be punishable by imprisonment or immediate death. It was made clear to us upon boarding that Captain Cruxgrriig *does not fuck around*. Though, we have learned that he is rather impressionable if you use the right words.

We are here in search of Sriii. The goal is not to capture her, but

---

[220] [crew-grig]

to kill her. If Barroun's guess is correct, she will be revived and taken to the Holy City to wait for the rest of us—after all, that is what the Chief wanted is it not? I do not plan to fight Benoviii but if he gets in my way, I will have no choice. She will be the hardest Recruit for us to tackle, so I had suggested that we chase her down first. She will not be happy to see me, and I will not feel anything good from our reunion either. We left on strange terms, but the fact that we are now out to kill each other is clear. Now it is all about who finds who first—and of course who can be the fastest to kill.

Barroun, Yezzurra, and the Squeeb search for Boriisst. They began in the Starter City and have moved around quite juristically tracking his scent. He is a smart Host and is also proving to be rather hard for us to find.

I have eight hundred and sixty days until this decades Game is complete and new Hosts are dropped within the Great Walls for the renewal of the Game. If I fail to prove the best by then, I will have to wait another ten years to be [221]truly free. Before, I had said that it wasn't worth fighting for, but now, I feel the need to fight again. I will not lose—I refuse to wait that long.

This is also the length of time that we must wait in order to capture the final member of God's Recruits. I have yet to bring up this Host's name because Tziipoor had told me to keep it a secret when she first saw it written on the scroll. I will speak the name when we have found the other two and she is the only one left to gather. I know of her location, and I know that we have only one opportunity to get her.

I am standing below deck, sifting through the fucked piles of papers meant to keep track of the prisoners. I can clearly tell that the log-keeper does not give a shit about his job and apparently Captain Cruxgrriig does not care either. The piles are scattered and unorganized, though the log-keeper says that every prisoner that the Beekrah has carried is documented here. I have half the nerve to just file the sheets for him. What a *fucking* mess!

---

[221] Gameplay Detail—A Players Freedom: even though some Hosts have the ability to leave the Lost Planet, they are not free of its ownership until they complete the Game—only then will it let the Player be. If a Player escapes the planet without completing the Game, the Game Runners will send advanced Players called Herthhe [hair-TEH], or Hunters to retrieve the retreating Player.

Ehhrn and Aneera are up top watching the fights—sitting next to Captain Cruxgrriig and his Second and Fourth Command Captains. At first, he seemed to be so uptight, but he has really taken a liking to us. I think we may be his favorite Hosts onboard. Of course, the fact that I am the Red Blood Tanner helps that, he is excited for me to pay our debt. In our negotiation to board, I had to agree to a fight. At some point while here, I will have to fight a prisoner of his choosing, and if I lose, I have to stay here as a prisoner until he no longer finds interest.

The sky has gone dark for the night and the ship is lit with many small lanterns illuminated with green flame. I can hear the terrifying buzz of a swarm of Sea Flies approaching and sigh with relief that I am below deck. They sound horrid, like June Bugs— but in the millions. And they grab and hold on like them too, with nasty-sticky-Buggy hands. If you do not know what a June Bug is, look it up. Then, do yourself a favor and find a video for sound and sight. They are completely harmless, but the people where I am from—me included—*dread* them. The *worst* part is their grip, those motherfuckers *do not let go*—especially when they land in your hair.

The Sea Flies give the same feeling, but they buzz louder, they grip tighter, and these ones bite—like Horse Flies! They are basically a mix of the two creatures except where June Bugs are green, brown, or black, and Horse Flies are black with green shimmer, Sea Flies are pink like the water here, and they swarm forever day or night. This family will likely infest the ship until sunup. I can hear the shuffle of many feet above me, as everyone hurries to close the deck canopy to keep them on the outside. The fights are never done for the night, everyone just trades shifts.

While digging, I have come across a few records for rather interesting Hosts. The first strikes a memory, I have seen it only once before, in my nightmares. One night as a child I heard a knock on my window. I got up to see what was lurking just outside. I will never forget its face. His skin is so thin that I can see his bones; his muscles and tendons and everything else is clear and cannot be seen. I woke from the dream terrified and discomforted, it traumatizes me still to this day. I cannot sleep in a place with uncovered windows. I called it "The Window Watcher", but the paperwork has it listed as "The One". Keep memory of this creature, it is to appear again many times. Once you see it, it will stalk you forever if it finds interest. I do not know if it is still here, and I have no intention to seek it out.

The second Host that I find strikes different interest. I wonder if it is still on board, this one I *will* search for. The paper says "Demon." I have always had an interest in the occult. I had never practiced anything other than some light cleansing magic, but my collection back home consists of many books on darker subjects.

I wonder if I can go see it. I know that I am here on a mission, but my curiosity is causing distraction. I make my way toward the Door Guard and ask him if the creature is still here—

"And if so, can I see it? Where can I find it?"

He replies, "Find one of the Prisoner Guards. They will help you."

"Thank you." I say back. I exit the records room and head for another section of the ship down the hall—through here I can access the prison part of the ship and locate the help that I need.

The halls are dark, and I carry a small, green-lit lantern to lead me in the right direction. I walk until I meet another Door Guard who grants me access to the room behind the door that she stands in front of.

I am let into a small room where I am frisked and interrogated before I am set free into the cell block. I am not sure whether this is the [222]one that I need, but I must start somewhere. Knowing my shit luck, both Sriii and the Demon are probably in cell block 4. This is Captain Cruxgrriig's prize block and is only accessible to those who rank above the Fourth Command Captain—who is also not able to access it.

It feels strange to be the one on the outside of the cells for once. I have grown so used to being the prisoner in these types of settings. This is so new to me. I feel so bad for the ones who are trapped inside, I can see the pain in their eyes, the withdrawal that they feel from the outside. When trapped here, you either die in a fight, or win and return to your cell until Captain Cruxgrriig wants to see you fight again. There is no chance at freedom. Maybe someday I can provide that for them, but for now, I must stay loyal to the ships highest Captain.

---

[222] Relic Detail—The Beekrah's Cell Blocks: this ship has 3,000 cells divided out into six cell blocks with 500 cells in each. Tanner has access to five of these cell blocks.

We have been onboard for a week now and I have managed to investigate cell blocks 1 and 2. I am always in awe at the massive diversity between the Hosts on this planet, where does it end? I am constantly finding new and always more curious species of creature. And even more strange, no matter where I go, there is always a creature that looks like a Human but has blood of a different color—some are even colors that I have never seen.

They are fight hungry, they never want to stop, and I understand why. Take Uno for example, if you play in large groups—say, three or more—everyone always tries to win first. But the smartest way to play is to avoid going out too early. Set your sights on being the second to last one to run out of cards. By doing this you technically lose to those who went out before you, but on another scale, you beat everyone entirely. You are in the game until it is completely over, still winning against the final loser—the one who lost to everybody—and then you are able to continuously play rather than sitting on the sidelines watching or shuffling cards until the cards are dealt for a new game. This also gives you the opportunity to manipulate your amount of time spent playing such as, running yourself out of cards before the final one-on-one battle for bathroom breaks, drink refills, beer runs, or using a blank rule card to deal everyone back in basically restarting the game along with pissing off those who had the idea that they had won a moment of freedom from the game. This strategy keeps the player stimulated—playing nonstop, or at their own control.

We were brought here by Aneera's visions. She has foreseen many fights between Sriii and other prisoners here in the past. She continues to see them, but she cannot always tell when her visions will happen. She can see into any timeline of the future—and as I have recently learned, any timeline of the past. She can also focus her sightings on one individual, in particular, if she practices enough concentration.

I have yet to understand how Ehhrn's ability really works yet. When I have asked him in the past he has chosen not to reply. Aneera's visions give us who and where, and Ehhrn's ability gives us when and how. Ehhrn is able to tell us almost everything to be exact. He knows where to go and when to be there. He knows who to speak to and who to avoid. He knows how this seasons Game started and how I will end. He knew secrets that he should not have, and he knows secrets yet to be told. He knows of everyone from my past—he names my mother and father, my two brothers and my three sisters, my Fools, my snake, my eleventh grade English teacher, and some that even *I* had forgotten about. He can speak of the Earth as if he had been born there, and he can speak of Aneera's planet and past as well. Even more curiously so, Aneera cannot see into his past, present, or future, no matter how hard she concentrates. She is blind to his mind.

Even with all this knowledge, we still had a shamefully hard time finding this ship. There is a flaw in his telling's, though incredibly exact as he can be, he cannot *always* answer everything. He knew where we would find it on a certain day but could not tell us where we could find it any time before then. He does not "see" the way that Aneera does—at least I do not think he does. I believe that it is a *considerably* different ability.

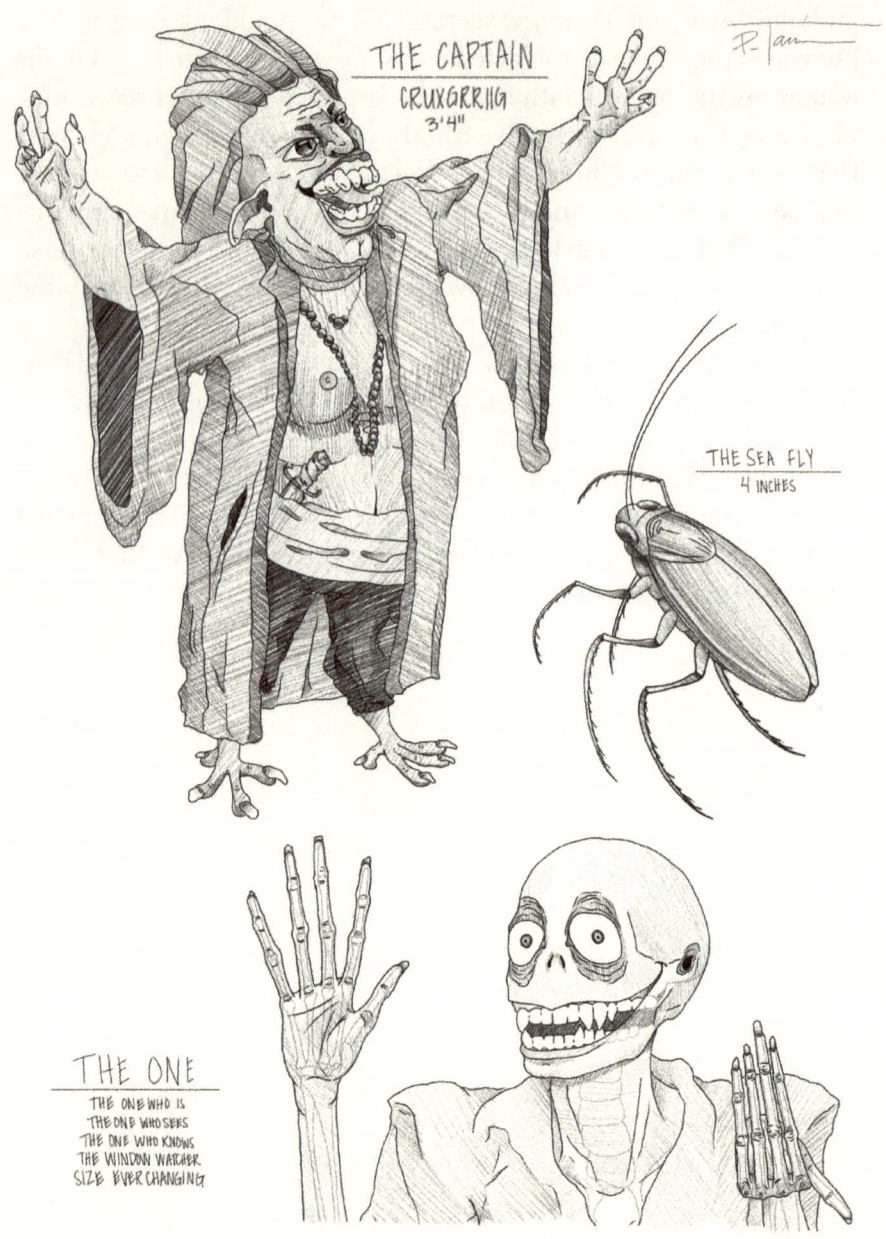

THE CAPTAIN
CRUXGRRHG
3'4"

THE SEA FLY
4 INCHES

THE ONE
THE ONE WHO IS
THE ONE WHO SEES
THE ONE WHO KNOWS
THE WINDOW WASHER
SIZE EVER CHANGING

2,780 Days after the Fall...

The search for the Beekrah
The Port on Pearl Beach
[223]Wrritaaz

This is where Ehhrn says that we will find the ship. We have spent the last two years searching for it. He says that it will make port here tonight, but it will take us three days to board it. We must be delicate with this mission; the ship's Captain can be testy. We must be given permission, this is not a matter of stealth, it is a matter of contract and manipulation. We will need roaming freedom while onboard.

Ehhrn has a plan. He stresses how important it is to follow his direction precisely. Any other movements and we will fail. At daybreak tomorrow, the crew of the Beekrah will engage in battle with a bandit village at the top of the cliff. They are in search of a stone and if we retrieve it first and present it to the crew, Ehhrn says that we will be accepted onto the ship. The problem is that we cannot engage until the crew does. We must wait until they invade the village, sneak in and grab the stone before they do, and retreat to safety. We will fail without the Beekrah's numbers. The bandits are too cleaver. Tonight, we will climb the hill and find our point of entry. Ehhrn takes the lead, Aneera follows behind him, and I travel last watching for any Hosts who may choose to tail us.

The sun is still in the sky. I cannot get over the beauty of this place. The water is clear, shimmering in the sun showing colorful reflections from the pearls that crowd each other along the bottom.

The pearls appear to be many different colors, but one would have to see them during the right time of day because these tints are so light that they need the suns help to show themselves. During other times, the pearls appear mostly white. They come in all sizes too and are incredibly hard to walk on in some areas. The Port by the water—Wrritaaz—has many docks along the bay and stable platforms built with a light-colored wood weaved around the buildings and stables and squares to make for easier foot travel.

The people ride floating Sea Dragons the size of Horses, and craft

---

[223] [WEE-tah-s]

charms and trinkets to hang over them. They have these trinkets along their homes, and their shops, and their docks too.

The buildings are tall and crooked. They are also made from the same light-colored wood. The architecture is very simplistic, missing the criminal amount of detail that some of our other discoveries have given to us. I like it. Some of the buildings sprout out from the water, as the city reaches across the cove and climbs the wall on the other side.

The wood from the crooked trees is a very light-colored green, and the leaves that fall from them are pastel purple. They blanket the ground and the water and the platforms, falling from the tall trees like delicate [224]raindrops. The blooms resemble wisteria, and they hang from above—some vines reaching the length of up to twenty yards.

The colors remind me of the way that I saw the world when I saw through Tziipoor's eyes. Her vision is different from ours. She sees in a sort of negative—to her, the world is seen in blues, and whites, and violets, and many variations of light grey. It is beautiful. I cannot explain how badly I miss her. It feels like I am missing a part of my soul.

The hill seems to grow steeper as we climb. Some spots have exposed rock that make for easier footing, but the rest of the area still holds pearls and is difficult to move across. There is a terribly skinny platform that climbs the side of the cliff to help the bandits who live at the top travel to their own little personal port at the bottom. There is also a path that leads through the forest from Port Wrritaaz up the hill to the bandit's village, but this path is hard to follow, I can tell that it is not heavily traveled. The peoples from the two villages do not communicate often, and when they do, it is not always on good terms. However, sometimes the bandits will come down from their hilltop to offer jewels or small treasures in exchange for other goods.

When we finally reach the top and find a good place to wait for the night, the sun has passed the horizon and the sky has gone dark. Ehhrn and Aneera stay behind to strategize as I fly above to sketch

---

[224] Relic Detail—The Enookiiv Trees: [eh-NOK-iv] these trees continuously grow new leaves, forever causing the old ones to fall. This process happens year around. There is no winter season here.

a small map of the village. It is a decent size, maybe 400 bandits or so. From up here I can see where their leader lives and sleeps, this must be where they keep the stone that we are looking for.

I catch a small conversation in one of the huts off to the side, they speak of a Yokkaa. That must be the stone that we are here for. I move closer and shrink myself small enough to disguise myself as a teeny Bug. I sit on a nail that sticks out from the wooden ceiling and listen attentively to the Host's discussing below.

It turns out that this Yokkaa is not yet here, and it is not the stone that we are searching for. It is in transit up the hill, traded for a considerable sized gem. Perhaps I can loot it before they arrive, quickly and quietly without them even noticing. I have been working on my stealth, my silence. Let us test it, a small lift for practice before the big swipe that is to come later. I promised Ehhrn that I would stay focused and loyal to his plan, but what is one small side-quest? It will be fine.

I leave the hut and move quickly down the hill in search of the traveling bandit. Just before approaching, I notice Ehhrn below retreating from the area without pursuit. If he stole it before I could get there, he did so entirely unnoticed.

"Did you get it?" I ask him, sending my thoughts in his direction. He is cleaver, I assume that he will know what I am talking about. That sneaky bastard, he had not told me this part of his plan.

"Yes," he replies. "Go back to the village and do what you were sent there to do. Stop getting distracted. You can never stay focused!"

"Psshhh," I say to him. He gets distracted too. Look at him running back up the hill after leaving Aneera behind for his own little adventure. "Weren't you supposed to be back at the camp?"

He sends a middle finger pointed to the sky knowing that I am here somewhere but not knowing exactly were. I laugh and return to search for the original stone. I swerve in and out of the cramped huts until I come across the leader's shelter and begin to root through his piles of junk. The idea is that we search through the night for the stone and take it when the time is right. My only goal now is to look and return to Ehhrn and Aneera when I know of its location.

In my few hours of searching I have come across an abundance of interesting things in this little house, the leader is quite the collector. When I come back later, I will have to thieve a few pieces for *my* collection. I must resist my sticky fingers for the time being. I will dwell deeper into undisciplined thievery when I return.

Eureka! A stone! I think this is the one that we search for. It is small enough to place onto a dainty ring, but perhaps so priceless that one would not dare. It resembles a diamond, only slightly more clouded, like IIIxaanax. I found it in a small protective case decorated with turquoise borders. I wonder what importance such a small thing holds.

"Ehhrn," I say, throwing my Voice so that he can hear. "What does it look like? I think I found it."

He replies, "It's clouded, like yours."

"It is in a small silver box lined with turquoise in the bottom drawer of the largest desk." He will need to know for later. I return to camp and settle in for a nap.

When I wake again, Aneera says that I slept through most of the night. The sun should be upon us soon, and the time for us to fight is steadily approaching. The idea is that we go in unnoticed as a third party. We want the bandits to think we are crew members, and we want the crew members to think we are bandits.

The sun begins to peak over the mountains in the distance and I can hear an army of heartbeats climbing the hill. It is time. Ehhrn, Aneera, and I take our places. Ehhrn is to retrieve the stone, and Aneera and I are to watch his back. She will watch from the ground and I will watch from the sky. We will wait until the two rivals engage. Then, we will make our move.

The fight is not the focus of this quest, so I will leave out some of the finer details. Let us focus our attention on the theft. When the clash of weapons and the sound of differing battle cries rings through the trees, our plan is set in motion. Ehhrn speeds through the village, headed directly toward the leader's small house.

But there is a snag, we knew this would happen, but we were not prepared for the degree of it. The house is guarded by more bandits than what we prepared for, but as always, Ehhrn has a plan—

"I got it," he says, "Watch my back."

I can see him stealthily move in between the feet of the bandit guards unnoticed. Another thing about Ehhrn that I have yet to explain is his ability to avoid being seen. It is like a clear camouflage; he releases a scent that distracts the Hosts around him. They do not notice the scent either. He slips and slides through the crowd, like a slithery sneaky Snake. He squeezes through the door—ever so quietly.

"It's not here," he says after a short while. "They've taken it underground!"

"What?" I say aggravated. "You said this was a set plan! What do you mean?"

"There's a door in the floor leading to a tunnel. And don't give me that shit, I told you it would take us three days." He says, "Tanner, come with me. Aneera watch up-top."

"Um no," I say tenaciously. "The last time I crawled into a secret tunnel it was full of rotted corpses; I lost a chunk of my sanity and I was left to die. *Hard* Pass."

"*Last time* you traveled with a moron. I told you before we got here that they are not your friends. Have you learned nothing? Get down here stupid!"

I keep my reply to myself, and Aneera continues to listen in silence to the two Voices who argue inside her head. Reminder, we communicate through telepathy. Aneera has mastered this too, though she does not use it as often as Ehhrn and I.

He is right though, from the beginning there has been something in his judgment that I have trusted more than anyone else's. There is something in his eyes and in his tone when he speaks, there is always anger and disgust, but there is always honesty too. For now, I will choose to follow him.

I said that I would not speak of the fighting around us, but I feel like I must make one thing known to you. The bandits have no chance. They fight fiercely but their efforts will be for nothing. The Beekrah's crew will slaughter them all. When we are done here, there will be no one left to fill this village. The houses will be left empty and the platforms and the pearls that lay underneath will be left tainted with blood. I knew it would happen, Ehhrn told me. But right now, watching from the sky as I approach the leaders house, I feel guilty. I want to help them. I am aiding in this genocide for my own intents and purposes. Am I doing this wrong? A three-day battle, that is what has begun here. I need to remember that I have one mission. Find the stone Tanner, find the stone and get the fuck out.

2,783 Days after the Fall...

It is so dark down here. The tunnels twist and turn and lead to dead ends. We have managed to find the room with the stone, but we are trying not to interfere. We want the crew to kill the leader, and, in that time, we will take the stone. Ehhrn works meticulously, he plans every move, every step. I must follow the path that he lays for us. He is the only one who can see how this will end.

But I will say, I grow tired of listening to the fighting above—the meaningless slaughter. The more screaming and pain that I hear, the harder it is for me to stay secret. My patience is wearing thin. The bandits fight hard to protect their homes and their families. The Voices are overpowering, I still struggle with removing unwanted ones from my mind. It is like they are the Voices that wish to be heard—the ones who have no other way of asking for help.

I sit against the wall with my knees bent to the ceiling and two hands over my eyes. This internal fight is killing me, I do not know what to do, or how to handle this. Do I act for the best interest of the Recruits, or do I follow my heart and protect those who's cries call out to me? What would God do? I do not know IIpetrraah, but the God from my childhood, the one that my mother taught me about, would not want this, *he* would ask me to help them, *he* would want me to defend them.

I pull Reewennivear from its holder and glare through the darkness at the sigils engraved into it. I run my finger over the one that I know—deliver, *he* would want me to help them.

Then, out of nowhere, a small noise—a saddened Voice says, "Help, please help." It is a child's Voice, weak and tired from what must feel like a lifetime of running and hiding. "Please," it says again, "help us. Help us!" I can hear the fear in the shuddering Voice. It overwhelms me. What am I doing?

"Fuck this." I say quietly.

"What?" I her Ehhrn ask.

"I said, 'Fuck this.'" I repeat louder. "You may be able to sit here and do nothing while hundreds if innocent people die up there, but I can't." I stand.

"Innocent? They're bandits, thieves, why do they matter to you?" he asks.

"'Honor among thieves, I guess,'" I reply. "You can stay here but I'm going. I can't listen to the screams of dying children anymore."

He grows big from rage, "You can't! You'll ruin what we've been prepping for!"

"What *you've* been prepping for. I followed you because I thought it was what was right. But it's not—"

"He said you would be hard to keep in line, that you would make your own path no matter how hard I tried to keep you on the right one. He told me you wouldn't listen. He told me that I couldn't stop you."

I stop in my tracks and turn back to him before walking away, "*He*?" I say, "You mean IIpetrraah?" I ask agitated.

"Don't you have children to save?" he says, avoiding my question.

I sigh heavily, "Fine, I trust you can handle things here."

He shrinks to his normal size again and says one final thing before disappearing, "What will you do when they all die anyway? Some things are set in stone and you cannot change them—no matter who you are."

"They won't die." I say, stubborn as the day we met. "They can't *all* die."

"They will, and the guilt will be heavier because you tried to save them. Prepare yourself." —and he leaves me behind to retrieve the stone on his own.

I have to try. I *have to* try. That Voice, it has gone, faded away. I may be too late. What can I do? I am so distraught, I cannot think. I just want to cry. Why did it take me so long?

I find my way to the surface. If I cannot fight the Beekrah's crew perhaps I can lead them astray. How ignorant are they? How impressionable? I need to stop thinking, and just do—do what I know will get their attention, something big and flashy.

I find the surface and what I see throws me into a fit of rage. How disgusting, how vile and grotesque. What once was a beautiful shimmering village, is now one that shimmers with terror. The bloodshed is so thick that I cannot see the true colors of the pearls that cover the ground. The blood is running down the hill, soon to meet the forest, and if this continues, there will be enough to reach Port Wrritaaz.

There are sobbing mothers holding their once healthy babies.

Fathers defending their daughters, daughters defending their brothers, and small children firing arrows toward the Devils who have deadened their friends. They fight with all they have. It is my turn now.

I close my eyes and focus myself—a distraction that they cannot ignore. I hear another Voice from below me—

"It's gone! The stone is gone! They have taken it!"

I smile, "Good job Ehhrn, perfect timing." I think, "Dragon," and match the size. The bandits and the crew stare intimidated by my new size. I reach toward my feet and grab two of the crew members before throwing them over the cliff and into the sea. "I have your stone!" I say loudly. "Come and get it!" As they flood the space under my feet trying to defeat me with numbers. I change sizes again and punch, and kick, and pinch—enough to agitate but not so much to be fatal.

I grow again and throw a few more, then shrink and fly to a new place shifting the crowd away from the villagers and toward the lands edge. With my distraction now heavy in the eyes of those who chase me, I grow again, big enough to throw a few more but remain just small enough to duck and hide behind the tops of the many huts and small buildings. My earlier weight had broken through the platforms below me making it harder for me to run, but this size is much more manageable. Yes, come after me, follow me to the into the sea.

The bandits that remain retreat to safer places, deserting their effort to protect the stone. Now all that matters is their home and their families—their survival. I pace myself through the village, still picking crew members from the platforms and tossing them over the edge. When all is done, and I have made sure that most of them have been removed, the remaining crew members shoot me with their arrows, and throw knives and rocks and spears. They are angered, and I am their only new target.

I begin my retreat, making sure that they still follow. I pick up my pace, running across shattered platforms toward the edge. "Follow me," I think to myself. I reach a point where I can run no more, and I leap from the cliff, returning myself to normal size. I must stay in their sight, "Chase me, come and get me!" I think.

I hit the water and return to the surface. I can see some of them struggling down the tiny path along the cliffside while some others jump from the cliff behind me. The chase is on. I turn away from them and front crawl as fast as I can to the shore on the other side. When I reach the water's edge, I do my best to crawl across the pearls and find a way to stand. I slip and I slide around as I stagger into the trees followed by raging revengers.

"Are they all clear of the village?" I ask Aneera, who has been watching from the trees.

"There are a few who stayed behind, I can take them out. But did you think about how hard it is going to be to board the ship now? They see us as enemies." She replies.

"We can worry about that later," I tell her. "Take them out and protect the villagers who are left."

A sigh is not a thought, but I can understand the discomfort in her Voice. She does not want to, but she follows my command and steps out from her hiding place to extract the remaining crew from the village.

I would like to wrap this up quickly and get to the point behind this. I will not dwell much deeper into the chase, for that is unimportant. It is the chases conclusion that I want you to see.

Our plan fails and the three of us are captured and brought to the ship. When told of our efforts and shown the red blood that flows through me, the Captain threatened to keep us as payment for invading his raid.

Ehhrn, being the wonderful gambler he is, gave a counteroffer, explaining the means of our endearment. Amused and happy with this claim, the captain accepts, and we shake hands with the creature that I would consider the Devil himself. We agree that if I lose the fight, I will go willingly, without argument and I will stay without dispute. He is happy with this, and I am bound to it for we have shared a [225]Gentlemen's Handshake. In return, he agrees that we can search for what we came for, and if I win the fight, we can have the prisoner in exchange for a vile of my blood.

Before the ship sets sail and we leave the port, the Captain makes one last thing clear. Ehhrn tells no lies, and Cruxgrriig leaves

---

[225] Relic Detail—Gentlemen's Handshake: this ability is unique to the Captain. When a Host promises to an agreement with a Gentlemen's Handshake, all vows and rules are complete.

nonalive. He climbs up top his podium and raises his hands to the sky. He focuses his energy and in seconds, the island is gone. Not only the bandits, but the villagers past the forest below, all of them dissolve into the sea.

2,804 Days since the Fall...

Present Day
The Calm Sea
Hnaarax

I have found it, the Demon. It sits in a cramped cave, in the lower intestines of the sixth cell block. We are in the very bowls of the ship. The Demon is nothing to be seen, but more a presence to be felt. It has a low and scratchy Voice that disturbs and disrupts thought. I am ever curious. But I keep my distance.

"HUMAN," it growls, "LEAVE, I HAVE NO INTEREST IN YOUR REQUESTS."

Human? There is that word again, not Red Blood, but Human.

"Why?" I ask it. "You haven't heard them yet."

"WITH YOUR KIND THEY ARE ALL THE SAME. YOU WISH TO MAKE DEALS. TO PUT ONE TO DEATH, TO GAIN POWER, TO ENTRANCE A LOVER, TO HAVE WEALTH, OR STATUS, OR FAME. HUMANS ARE PREDICTABLE." It mocks.

"I have no immediate interest in deals. I just want to try to understand you, what you are."

"THAT CURIOSITY COULD KILL YOU." It replies in an even deeper tone as to give warning; a warning that I have heard before.

"I already hurt, every day—all the time. *This* hurt may make me even stronger," I say, almost cringing at the sentence.

It makes a sound that almost resembles a laugh, very raspy and at a loss of empathetic love, no, it laughs to torment. "IT MAY MAKE YOU STRONGER YOU SAY. YES, I AGREE IT MAY, IF ONE IS STRONG ENOUGH TO ENDURE. BUT YOU ARE WEAK."

You are weak, not Humans, *you*. It said that about me directly, not about my kind, but about myself. "Humor me." I tell it.

"LEAVE HUMAN. I TIRE OF YOU. YOU BORE ME."

"What is a Demon?" I ask, challenging it. "Where do you come from? Are you born or crafted? Or have you simply always just been?"

I listen intently, without interruption. My eyes searching desperately for the source of the Voice. And as I know that it lies within the cell, I can feel its presence growing all around me. I reach for the small stool by the door and sit waiting for an answer.

"CAN YOU NOT UNDERSTAND THAT YOU ARE UNWANTED?" it asks, a whispering Voice in my ear, a breath on my skin, "ARE YOU HOLLOW?" I feel a hand on my shoulder, and I am pushed forward off my stool slamming my face into the hardened bars of the cell door. I turn to see, but there is nothing there. Something grabs my collar and pulls me through the bars and into the darkness of the cell. Hollow, that is what the Cat called me. It said that I am hollow. What does that mean?

"WE ARE BORN OF FAILURE, BUT OF ONLY ONE KIND. I ONCE WAS A SOUL LIKE YOURS. BUT I WAS TRAPPED WITHIN AN IMPOSSIBLE TASK—ONE VERY SIMILAR TO THE ONE GIVEN TO YOU," it pauses for a long moment. "DO YOU WISH TO BECOME LIKE ME? IS THAT WHY YOU DISMISS WARNING? YOU ARE A FOOL, HUMAN, YOU ARE WEAK, AND YOU ARE A FOOL. THE RED-BLOODED TANNER IS A DOOMED FOOL." It throws me back into the hallway, disposing of me like trash. "LEAVE."

I return to my feet and as much as I wish to fight it, I bow to its order. I have no further reasoning to stay today. I will return tomorrow, and the day after that, and the day after that, and every day until the day I leave this ship I will pester it.

2,809 Days since the Fall...

"YOU ARE UNBEARABLY ANNOYING. IT IS A WONDER HOW YOUR KIND HAS NOT YET BEEN SLAUGHTERED, OR YOUR PLANET RAPTURED."

I imagine it sitting with its elbows on its knees, encircling its temples with its fingers in annoyance. "Do you resemble Humans? Can you shapeshift? Do you walk bipedal or—

"WILL YOU *SHUT UP.*" It pleads. "FINE! I WILL SHOW YOU,

BUT ONE LAST WARNING, ONCE YOU HAVE SEEN ME, THERE WILL BE A DEPT YOU MUST PAY."

"What kind of dept?" I ask.

"YOU WILL HAVE TO SACRIFICE SOMETHING TO ME. DEMONS DO NOT SIMPLY GIVE. IT CAN BE A SACRIFICE OF YOUR CHOICE, BUT ONLY IF I CONSIDER IT WORTHY."

I think for a minute before lifting my eyes from the floor accepting its shallow offer, "Show me."

I will not describe what I saw, I will do my best to never relive the memory. Now, for my sacrifice, I give the only thing that I can think would be worthy to gift to such a creature. It accepts and I retreat from the darkened cell of the Demon. I have no more reason to stay. I will not outwardly discuss our conversations further but be sure that I will never return here. My questioning is done, and I am headed back to the top, a different creature from the one I traveled down as.

When I reach the midlevel's, there is an uproar coming from the arena, the crowd is excited for this one. There has been a new fight announced. I must go see. I head to the surface and out onto the Captains viewing area to join Aneera and Ehhrn at his side.

The [226]crowd roars again but I do not see any fighters below. I hear a chuckle and a snort as the Captain grabs the back of my shirt and shoves me over the edge, tossing me down into the pit and closing the lid to prevent escape.

"It is time to fight!" he yells over the cheering. He points at me, "I call on your debt!" —a thing that I seem to be paying a lot today.

I stand and ready myself, not bothering to argue the issue, it seems too early for this, but I have no choice in the matter.

"The fight of the century is upon us!" the Captain claims, as the crowd and the crew hushes to hear. "For two thousand years I have searched the seas and waited. This is not a fight to the death, but a fight for freedom!" the spit flies from his mouth as he roars over the stadium, "One will leave a free Player, and the other will join the rest in the filthy depths of our Beekrah, never to see freedom again!" The crowd and his crew cheers again, now louder than ever. "Prepare yourself for the fight of your lives!"

---

[226] Relic Detail—The Beekrah: Host's frequently board the ship to watch the fights and gamble. Some will bring new prisoners to trade or sell.

I look to Ehhrn and see a look on his face that I have never seen. He is concentrated, and ready for what is to come, like he has been expecting it all along. And Aneera as well, she sits calmly and sends her condolences with a thumbs up and a greedy smile.

"What's going on guys?" I ask them, beginning to panic, "Who am I fighting?"

The Captain shouts, "In this test of fate, we have the Red Blood Tanner!" the crew screams with excitement and a gate opens from the wall across from me. "And her rival, the dark and demented Spirit, the creature of the Void, the death bringer of stealth, the Eiinokrra, [227]IIIntiiius Sriii!"

I knew this was coming, I knew eventually I would have to fight, but I was hoping it would not be her. Aneera never stated who it would be, she just said that she had seen each of us fight, not that we would fight each other. Here, in front of everyone.

This will surely be a challenge; she is exceptionally strong. But if I can win, our mission here can be completed, and I can move on from this drowning crew and its Captain. He made a deal with each of us stating that we would not kill the other, but that was before I knew who I would be fighting. I will have to offer him some of my blood or find other means of escape. Good thing I try to always plan ahead.

It is here that I will leave you. This story must continue on through another's eyes. We need a change in perspective, a new person of interest. The story must be told from all sides. The next Recruit that will guide you further in your understanding of The Great Game of Ten is the Felerrg himself, Ehhrn.

---

[227] Relic Detail—IIIntiiius: [yee-NEE-tee-us], the name of the Eiinokrrian Chief family. Spoken last name first.

CPSIA information can be obtained
at www.ICGtesting.com
Printed in the USA
BVHW042304231122
652631BV00005B/42/J